ASK

Echo of Truth

Also by Connie Monk

Season Of Change
Fortune's Daughter
Jessica
Hannah's Wharf
Rachel's Way
Reach For The Dream
Tomorrow's Memories
A Field Of Bright Laughter
Flame Of Courage
The Apple Orchards
Beyond Downing Wood
The Running Tide
Family Reunions
On The Wings Of The Storm
Water's Edge
Different Lives
The Sands Of Time
Something Old, Something New
From This Day Forward

Echo of Truth

Connie Monk

⌘ **Visit the Piatkus website!** ⌘

Piatkus publishes a wide range of exciting fiction and non-fiction, including books on health, mind body & spirit, sex, self-help, cookery, biography and the paranormal. If you want to:

- read descriptions of our popular titles
- buy our books over the Internet
- take advantage of our special offers
- enter our monthly competition
- learn more about your favourite Piatkus authors

visit our website at:
www.piatkus.co.uk

Copyright © 2001 by Connie Monk

First published in Great Britain in 2001 by
Judy Piatkus (Publishers) Ltd of
5 Windmill Street, London W1T 2JA
email: info@piatkus.co.uk

The moral right of the author has been asserted

A catalogue record for this book is available from the British Library

ISBN 0 7499 0585 9

Set in Times by
Phoenix Photosetting, Chatham, Kent
Printed and bound in Great Britain by
MPG Books Ltd, Bodmin, Cornwall

Chapter One

1922

Veronica spent the morning painting the white lines on the tennis court, one of her favourite jobs and one she did willingly to mark the beginning of the season. But this year was different. Her mind wasn't on the tennis party planned for the afternoon, it wasn't even on the joy of feeling the warmth of the early summer sun. Memories filled her head, she wanted to re-live every precious second of the previous evening. Laurence loved her, just as she'd always dreamed – dreamed and prayed for almost half her life. She'd known that one day that's how it would be; she'd known it and yet she'd been frightened to believe. Now all her doubts were banished as if they'd never been. It hadn't needed words for her to know that he loved her just as much as she did him; his kiss, the way he'd touched her . . . sitting back on her heels she raised her face towards the sun, closed her eyes and tried to re-live the wonder of those minutes.

Laurence Chesterton was home from Oxford for the weekend. From late on Friday evening until Sunday morning may be no more than a few hours, but it filled her mind to the exclusion of everything. On his first night home, his mother always invited Veronica and her parents to Gregory Cottage; ever since she and Laurence had been children their friendship had been encouraged by both their mothers. Two years older than her, Veronica had always struggled to keep up with him, had made a hero of him.

She was twenty years old, already her father referred to her as his 'right hand man' at Blakeney's Bakery, the family business. In a way, she was even more than that. For how many men had a daughter capable of dealing with the ordering of materials, costing

1

of products, invoicing customers, checking orders, paying staff wages and every other side of the business quite as efficiently as he could himself, would also have the special ability that was truly her own? Ever since she'd been a small girl shrouded in a white overall and standing on a box for extra height at the kitchen table, Veronica had loved to bake. At first it had been the usual little cakes children delight in, overseen always by their faithful Bertha. But long before she'd finished at school she'd needed no supervision and – and this was her own special contribution to the success of Blakeney's – she had been fascinated by experimenting, making up her own recipes. Successful experiments had been perfected, the ingredients carefully logged, then tried out in the ovens of the bakery. That's how some of Blakeney's best loved and most unique cakes had come into being. In the compartments of her mind Laurence was apart from all that; he was the only love she'd ever wanted. And now all her dreams were becoming reality.

The white lines were forgotten as her mind raced. Soon he'd come down from Oxford, start to make a career. His mother had confided that Mr Withers, senior partner in Withers, Wright and Lambton, had said there was a place for him in the firm in Deremouth. This weekend, would he talk about his future – *their* future? Or would he wait until after he'd finished at university? She pictured him as a qualified solicitor, Withers, Wright and Lambton one day changed to Withers, Wright, Lambton and Chesterton; she saw herself as a bride walking up the aisle of the Abbey here in Ottercombe. Her father would miss her in the business but, as she knelt on the grass, the sun beating down on her back, it wasn't the family business that filled her thoughts.

'Come on, dreamer,' Monica, her mother, came towards her, stepping carefully over the newly painted lines. 'Really I do believe he gets more handsome with each year – Laurence I mean. That's where your thoughts were, don't tell me they weren't.'

But Veronica's dreams were private, they always had been.

'I was wondering whether we've been stupid inviting two comparative strangers to play tennis. For all we know they'll be useless. Dad, either Mr Wainwright or Stewart, Laurence and me, we know we all play a good game. But what can we hope from a writer and a musician? Probably not much. Then there's Dulcie Wainwright, she'll have to make up the number and she's about as much use with a racquet as I am with an embroidery needle.'

'Never mind, dear,' pretty Monica Blakeney smiled placidly. 'The sun's shining, we are amongst friends. And after this tournament you've arranged is lost or won, we'll have supper and then some music. I'm really looking forward to it.'

'I am, too, Mum. And Mr Holmes may be all right. After all, Dad still plays a good game, so just because he's not young it doesn't mean he hasn't an eye for a ball. That slim, wiry sort often stay lithe.' Hugo Holmes, a well-known crime writer, had recently come to live in the village. 'But I haven't much hope of Longshanks,' she chuckled. 'Little Tommy Bryce told me that's what the boys from the Choir School call him.'

'You shouldn't encourage the children to speak like that about their betters. I'm sure he's charming. A little austere, aloof perhaps . . .'

'Austere . . . aloof . . . I can't think what made you invite him, Mum.'

'It seemed the natural thing to do,' Monica explained. 'I was talking to Mr Holmes when Father Bernard brought him across to introduce him to us. Poor young man, I thought, thrown in amongst so many strangers.'

'Well, we'll have to make the best of it. If he's no use, we needn't ask him again. He doesn't sound as if he'll add much to the fun. Anyway, I must get on with my painting or the court won't be ready. And if they're both useless, well, it doesn't really matter.' Then, chuckling happily, 'It'll just mean Laurence and I will give them a thrashing.'

Monica stepped back carefully over the newly painted line, a look of contentment on her face. Of course they were young, Laurence only twenty-two. But if they felt ready for an official engagement, nothing would make her happier. Wasn't it just what she and Ellen Chesterton had always hoped? She knew Veronica too well to probe, but perhaps that's what they had been talking about last night when they'd disappeared to the old playroom to play the gramophone while she and Herbert had had a hand of bridge with Ellen and Hugo. Personally she'd thought the jazz a raucous noise, but the young ones seemed to enjoy it. It had probably been a smoke screen, something to ensure that they were left alone.

3

Veronica's thoughts took her back to the jazz-filled 'playroom' as it used to be called. They'd danced with the abandon they brought to all their activities. yes, but not all the time ... Again she sat back on her heels, remembering the way he'd kissed her. That had been the beginning. Even remembering it made her heart pound again just like it had as she'd felt the pressure of his mouth on hers, opening it, probing with his tongue while one hand had groped for her breast, snatching at her, hurting her. Yet she'd wanted him to hurt her. Then his hand rucking up her skirt, moving up her leg ... Just thinking about it made her clench her teeth, her body yearning for his touch. He loves me. I've asked for years and years that he'll love me. Thank You, thank You. He didn't say a word, did he, but to kiss me like that, to touch me ... what words could there be? Perhaps this evening – or tomorrow before he goes back to Oxford. Nothing can ever be like it used to before last night.

Following Monica Blakeney through the French doors and into the garden, Nicholas Ellis could hear the foursome on the tennis court, a summer symphony orchestrated by the zing of ball on catgut.

'Forty thirty,' came a girl's clear voice. Again the ball was sent and returned, to and fro, to and fro. 'Deuce.'

'We're sitting over there by the trees,' Monica led the way. 'It really is exceptionally warm for the beginning of May. I don't know how you all find the energy to rush around a tennis court. Let me see now, I believe you know everyone, Mrs Wainwright tells me you have already visited them.'

The last to arrive for the tennis party, Nicholas inclined his head in greeting to the four reclining in deck chairs in what shade the sycamore tree afforded so early in the season. Even in an age of formal courtesy his manner was stiff.

'Indeed, Mrs Blakeney, we are all acquainted,' he assured his hostess. Greetings were exchanged and a deck chair pulled forward for him between Monica and her dearest friend, Ellen Chesterton. She'd described him to Veronica as aloof, but seeing him attired for an afternoon's tennis he presented a very different picture. Tall and slim, yet she was sure he was no weakling. His hands looked strong. His jaw was firm. But all that apart, there was something almost Romany in his handsome face. Dark eyes could be soulful, soft; Nicholas Ellis's were piercing; Monica found herself lowering her own gaze, suddenly realising she'd been staring.

The conversation was lightweight, Nicholas played his part even though his thoughts were on the four on the court. Although he'd only been in Ottercombe a week or two, as the Abbey Organist and Master of the Choir School he was being welcomed into the community. Did he but know it (and perhaps he did) he was looked on with hopeful interest, a man probably of no more than thirty, outstandingly presentable to look at, single, successful in his profession.

'What a pretty sight it is,' Tessa Wainwright leant in front of Monica to draw Nicholas's attention to the game, knowing that her daughter was without doubt the prettiest young girl in the district. 'Just look at my poor Dulcie, she does try so valiantly to hit the ball hard, but tennis is really a game for you men, don't you think?'

'I think the ladies are acquitting themselves very well,' he answered, his expression giving nothing away.

On the court Veronica and Laurence were playing Hugo Holmes who, like himself, had recently been drawn into the local circle, and Dulcie Wainwright. The couples were unevenly matched, so far every game had gone to Veronica and her partner, any moment the call would come 'Set and match'. But for Nicholas it wasn't the score of the game, nor even the ability of the players, that held his attention. It was Veronica, just as she had when he'd looked down from the organ loft and seen her sitting with her parents. He'd not known who the family were, and he hadn't even been sure what had drawn his gaze back time and again to the tall girl. Now, under cover of following the game, he watched her every move. From his chair in the semi-shade of the sycamore not yet arrayed with its glory of summer leaf, he couldn't take his eyes from the sight of her. It wasn't her face he was aware of, it was the way she swooped low to send a backhand return skimming over the net, or the way she leapt high, determined to smash it back into the opponents' court. As graceful as any feline and with as much agility, yet playing the game with purpose and vigour she seemed oblivious to her surroundings. Not oblivious to the young man she partnered though; from the sound of their laughter and from the light-hearted comments that

5

Nicholas could tell they made to each other even though they were too far away for him to hear.

'Well done,' Hugo Holmes congratulated the victors. 'You play a strong game, Veronica.'

'Nothing special,' she laughed, 'I rely a lot on Laurence. He and I have partnered each other so often, we understand each other's game. Ready, the next four? The court's all yours. Hello. You must be Mr Ellis,' casually thrown in Nicholas's direction. 'Toss for partners.'

Standing up, he gave her that same formal bow. There was nothing in his manner to suggest the interest she'd aroused in him, or the impact she made now that he saw her face to face. In terms of beauty, a purist would say she wasn't to be compared with the delectable Dulcie Wainwright. But Nicholas was no purist. Slender, tall above average height, graceful, full of purpose. But beauty? He imprinted a picture of her on his mind: her velvety brown eyes, the clear-cut line of her brows emphasised by her straight fringe. She wore her thick, dark hair cut short, a frame for her face. But beauty? Critics would see her mouth as too generous, her nose too tip-tilted.

Herbert Blakeney, her father, put a penny into her hand and she appointed herself in charge of tossing for partners for the second match.

Nicholas and Herbert were to battle it out against Peter and Stewart Wainwright, father and brother of the petite Dulcie. It was a harder fought contest than the first, but ended in Nicholas and Herbert being the winners.

'Tea and a rest, boys,' Monica told them, 'before the victors' match. I wonder where Veronica and Laurence have disappeared to. What a pair they are!' It was clear that she liked to look on them as just that – a pair. And from the satisfied expression on Ellen's face, her hopes for her son were moving in the same direction. 'They've always been the same, you know, Mr Ellis, hand in glove with each other.'

'So I understand from Mrs Chesterton,' Nicholas answered, his tone no indication of his thoughts on the subject. Childhood sweethearts, and she with no more experience of life than she'd found in Ottercombe or in the family business where, he understood, she worked with her father. Were these two matchmaking women seriously expecting that the blond Adonis could satisfy a girl like Veronica? As if conjured up by the images in his mind, the two appeared through the French window from the drawing room, their hands lightly linked. There was no way of knowing what amused them as they looked towards the party gathered by the tree.

'We told Bertha we'd carry the tea things out. We're just coming,' Veronica's voice was loud and clear (raucous, in Tessa Wainwright's opinion), coming to them down the sloping lawn, over the rose garden and across the tennis court.

'Hush, hush, dear do,' Monica whispered, making apology for her daughter. 'Sometimes she gets excited and quite forgets herself.'

Tessa's mouth smiled, but her eyes seemed unaware of it as she said, 'You mustn't mind, Monica my dear,' then with a mirthless giggle, 'just as long as the neighbours don't think she was extending an invitation to all and sundry! It's surprising how some girls seem to lose their heads when a young man pays them a little attention. And Laurence is such a charming young man.'

She let her gaze rest on her own daughter. There was nothing boisterous or loud about dear Dulcie. And what a picture she was. Dainty, feminine to her finger tips, her rosebud mouth tinted with lip rouge, the hem of her tennis dress at a demure mid-calf – not like Veronica's knee-length pleated skirt that showed her thighs as she leapt round the court in that unladylike manner. It you ask me, Tessa let her thoughts run on, she knows very well the ungentlemanly – worse, the *lewd* – thoughts she provokes, showing her thighs at every opportunity. And if I could see her knickers then you may be sure so could the men! Disgraceful! Playing with fire like she does, one of these days she'll get burnt. Why, even my dear Stewart was watching her in a way I didn't like to see. It's time someone told her: this isn't London with its jazz bands and its 'flappers'. This is Devon. We have standards to uphold. 'No milk, thank you, Monica dear. I have just a slice of lemon. Oh and a piece of your Bertha's sponge, now that's something too good to resist. Thank you, Veronica dear.' Now look at her! Why can't she sit on a chair like anyone else, instead of sprawling there on the ground like the hoodlum she is? A sticky end, I've said so to Peter for a long time. A few more weeks and Laurence will be home from all his studies in Oxford. Then what? If ever a girl throws herself at a young man it's that

7

one. Such nice parents too, one wonders where she gets that wild streak from.

'Tournament time,' Veronica announced when the cake had all been eaten and the tea cups were empty. 'Up you get, Dad, Laurence and I are going to wipe you out,' then as an afterthought, 'you and Mr Ellis too. We're invincible.'

'But not modest,' Nicholas raised his brows, his near-black eyes laughing at her. 'Come on, Mr Blakeney, let's make her eat her words.'

They did. But it was a hard-played match and took all Nicholas's powers of concentration. He'd never known a girl like her. Slender, lithe, she sent the ball across the net with accuracy and speed, exhilarated by the challenge, her mouth opening in a smile of sheer pleasure at each send and return of a long volley. So how was it he was so sure that beneath her façade of vigour and energy, she was no fun-loving adolescent but a sensual woman? His gaze moving to Laurence Chesterton with his fair well-dressed hair perfectly in place even at the end of the match, his white flannels perfectly creased, his tennis pumps perfectly whitened, Nicholas felt a contempt that honesty could have told him was unjust. For weren't his own flannels as well-valeted, his own pumps as brightly whitened?

The guests had been invited to stay for an informal supper at Ipsley House and, after that, they all congregated in the large drawing room. The baby grand stood open.

'Sometimes I try and play duets with Veronica but, oh dear me, she left me behind long ago. Your predecessor, dear Dr Hardy, took such pride in her progress,' Monica said in a confidential undertone to Nicholas. 'Mr Ellis, I wish you'd take my place and share the stool with her.'

'Oh, Mum, they don't want to hear me,' Veronica said gruffly. It wasn't a bit how she'd envisaged the evening. 'There's lots of music there, if you can persuade Mr Ellis, then at least we'll hear something played properly.'

'I'd be honoured if you'd join me,' Nicholas told her.

What a stick of a man he was!

'Get it over,' Laurence whispered to her, 'then we can make some excuse. It's my only evening.'

She sat on the long stool, as far away from the unbending visitor as she could.

'Which shall it be?' he asked.

'Oh, I don't care,' she threw her answer at him casually, 'This'll do as well as anything. It's quite short.'

His brows raised slightly as he looked at her. Sure he was laughing at her, she felt gauche and for one moment envied Dulcie sitting so straight with her ankles neatly together and an expression of gentle anticipation on her lovely face. But it didn't enter her head to wonder whether Laurence might be looking at Dulcie with admiration; Laurence was *hers* just as she was *his*.

'On four,' Nicholas instructed, just as he might to one of the boys from the Choir School, 'one, two, three,' and together they started. She had enjoyed playing duets with dear old Dr Hardy, who'd been her teacher for years. With Nicholas the pleasure of four hands in harmony was as great but she wasn't prepared to admit it. She was thankful when the final chord was played and she knew she hadn't disgraced herself.

She'd been sad to see Dr Hardy leave, he'd been among her favourite people – probably because he had made no secret of his pride in her. Add to that her mother's opinion of his successor as aloof and Veronica's pre-formed opinion was less than friendly. She admitted that he played a good game of tennis, just as she admitted he was extremely good-looking (if you liked the swarthy type, she added silently, at the same time casting an appreciative glance in the direction of Laurence's fair head) but neither of those things interested her. In fact, anxious just to escape with Laurence, nothing about Nicholas interested her. She was unprepared for the sudden warmth in his expression as he turned to her, smiling as he said, 'We must do that again. You used to come to the Abbey I believe?'

'With Dr Hardy, yes. But that was different. Anyway he was my teacher. And I don't want another teacher.'

'Different, perhaps. But need it be less enjoyable? Won't you think about it – please.'

Laurence chose that moment to interrupt. 'Talk to Mr Ellis when I've gone, Ron. I'm only home until tomorrow. Mrs Blakeney, have I your permission to borrow Veronica for an hour? She's promised to run over my words with me. Did she tell you about the play we're putting on after the exams?'

'You have the lead part, I hear. Well done. Yes, of course we'll excuse you. But promise you'll see her safely home afterwards, I don't like her to walk through the village on her own on a Saturday night when they're turning out from the Stag and Hounds.'

With charm enough to ingratiate himself with everyone there – well, almost everyone, for Nicholas's expression remained inscrutable – he said his farewells, being sure to give a final and extra smile in Dulcie's direction. Dull as ditch water, was his first thought, quickly followed by but what a stunner she's turned out to be. In his backward glance the second of his sentiments was clear, while the first was for personal use only. As for Veronica, she wasted no more than a scant farewell on the room at large, already in her mind she was alone with Laurence under the dark canopy of the summer sky.

Lying in bed, alone with her thoughts, there was nowhere to hide from her disappointment. She'd read his cues, checked that he was word perfect and without a single need for prompting. It had taken longer than she'd expected and they'd only just wound the gramophone and chosen a Charleston, when his mother had returned. This evening, except for their linking arms as they'd hurried through the village on their way to Gregory Cottage and the waiting play script, he hadn't touched her. She'd felt his keenness to start rehearsing his words and, just as she had for so long, she'd been glad that he'd wanted her with him and that she could do something to help him. But, remembering with a deeper honesty than she'd let herself acknowledge at the time, she had hoped it wouldn't take too long. The play dealt with, she'd been confident the evening would pick up where the previous one had finished. Then he would say the things she longed to hear. But it hadn't been like that. Walking home he'd talked about the play, he'd even admitted that he was none too sure how his finals would go, something that worried him when he considered the sacrifices his mother must have made to pay for his education. How proud she'd felt that he could talk like that to *her*, for she knew it was something he'd not have said lightly. Even so, not a word had been said about his plans for the future. As they'd talked they'd slowed down until finally they'd not been moving at all. Do hearts really race? she wondered. If they do, then at that moment hers certainly must have. Thinking about it, she again raised her face just as she had then, she'd been so close to him that she could feel the warmth from his skin. But tonight there had been no passion in his kiss. It was as if, his short visit over, he was already removed from her. And with that she knew she must be satisfied. Thus it had been all through his years at boarding school: counting off the weeks until his holidays, but always when the holidays came the bond had been as strong. None of that had changed during his three years at Oxford – at least, nothing had changed until the previous evening. Now it was coming to the end, soon he would be home for good.

The next day she didn't go with her parents to morning service in the Abbey, instead she borrowed her father's motor car and drove Laurence to Deremouth Station. She'd given no thought to Nicholas Ellis's suggestion that she might come to the Abbey to make music with him. So the note her parents brought home came as a surprise.

'He's setting up a local choir – amateurs, nothing to do with the Abbey choir,' she told them as she glanced through it. 'He says,' then in a voice that spoke volumes of her opinion of the Abbey's autocratic Master, she read aloud, ' "I understand that Dr Hardy gave you voice training instruction and that, when he had organised recitals in the Abbey, you enjoyed singing an occasional solo under his direction. It may interest you that I intend to form a group of adult amateurs whom I am prepared to train. I write to suggest you may care to be of their number. A notice will appear shortly in local newspapers, but I write this to extend a personal invitation for you to let me hear you prior to the general testing of applicants." '

'How nice of him to think of you,' Monica beamed her delight. 'We were talking about you after you and Laurence had gone last evening, I did say how you must be missing your weekly visits to the Abbey and how highly dear Dr Hardy had thought of your voice and your playing. And you did enjoy your duet with him, dear, I could see how much you appreciated being with a proper musician. How kind of him to try and fill the gap. Not that you won't be a useful addition to his little group, we know how well Dr Hardy thought of your voice.'

Veronica's glance met her father's. So often it was like that, the two of them sharing a silent, kindly joke at her mother's expense while she chattered on, oblivious that she wasn't carrying them with her.

11

'My lessons with Dr Hardy were always fun. Kind, you call him! More likely puffed up with self-importance. Anyway it doesn't matter, I shall tell him I haven't the time.'

'Of course you have the time, dear. You're not tied to the workplace like some girl at a factory bench. Come home a little early on choir evenings, give yourself some pleasure.'

Herbert put an arm around his pretty wife, her face so full of concern for the daughter she constantly failed to understand.

'She must do as she sees fit, my precious,' he told her and was rewarded by her change of expression. He heard her gentle sigh as one of contentment more than disappointment.

The note Veronica wrote that afternoon was brief.

Dear Mr Ellis,

I believe you have been given the wrong impression of my musical ability – our friend Dr Hardy has known me since I was young and fondness may have influenced his thinking. There are plenty of voices quite as good as mine amongst non-working members of the community who will, I am sure, welcome your plans. For myself, while I appreciate your offer to hear me, the truth is I am fully involved in the business, and am not looking for something to fill idle hours.
Yours truly,
Veronica Blakeney

It was a note as coolly polite as his own and, with a feeling of satisfaction she left it in a prominent place on the organ console that same evening when everyone had gone home from Evensong.

The following weekend a notice appeared in the *Deremouth News*, the local paper with a wide circulation in the district, alerting would-be singers. The Abbey Singers was the name he had chosen for the amateur choir he intended to establish. There was chatter about the project amongst music lovers and local gossips too, for his appointment had aroused a good deal of interest in the region. A Cambridge scholar, and many years younger than his kindly but unexciting predecessor, the Abbey had been full for the recital he had given shortly after taking over. So, when word spread that he intended to establish and train a singing group of local adult voices, there was no shortage of keen amateurs prepared to travel to the Abbey from nearby villages. On foot, on bicycles and on motor cycles they came from Otterton St Giles and Moorleigh, from Deremouth and the fishing village of Chalcombe beyond. Rumour even had it that one or two had shown interest from as far away as Newton Abbot and Exeter.

The grape vine grows strong and fast in country districts, and by the end of May it was common knowledge that no less than eighteen women and seventeen men (the latter including three who sang in the Abbey choir) were meeting on Tuesday evenings. With the exception of the choristers from the Abbey, most had been used to Deremouth Operatic Society's productions of operettas. Soon hardly a soul in Ottercombe didn't know that under Nicholas's direction they were working on Fauré's Requiem and that, while he conducted, the piano accompanist for the practices was Howard Humphreys, organist from nearby Otterton St Giles. If there were times when Veronica wished that her natural antipathy towards their 'too-big-for-his-boots' trainer hadn't prevented her being with them, she wasn't prepared to admit it. She had always suspected that Dr Hardy had pushed her to the forefront far beyond her merits. Add to that the knowledge that her mother had talked with such maternal pride of her prowess, and she wasn't prepared to risk the humiliation of failing the voice test Nicholas had offered. The members of the Abbey Singers may all be amateurs, but they were experienced amateurs. She was just a girl who enjoyed singing and for whom Dr Hardy had had a special fondness.

So the training went ahead without her while she threw herself with even greater energy into the business of Blakeney's Bakery and, at Oxford, Laurence sat his finals.

The bakehouse at Blakeney's was a long workshop-like room, benches on one wall, ovens at the other. The building had been erected when the century was new, transforming the original which had sufficed since the days of Veronica's great-grandfather, a man who'd staked all he had (which hadn't been much at the time) on his own ability and had founded the firm. His trade had been small, but in the beginning he had worked alone and had only two ovens. Gradually, as word spread, orders had come from outside Deremouth. His son had followed him in the business, but it hadn't been until Herbert's time that real progress had been made. Everything the firm produced was still handmade, the fires never went out and for ten hours of each day the beating and whisking never slowed. Despite the unbearable heat during the summer months and the constant pressure of work where timing is always important, the atmosphere amongst the workers was invariably cheerful. This was thanks in no small part to Bert Jenkins who had been in charge of the bakehouse since before the war.

'Have you seen this morning's *Deremouth News*, Miss Veronica?' he looked up from the amounts he was carefully measuring into an oversized mixing bowl as she passed the open doorway.

'No, it never gets delivered until after the dailies, we shall see it tonight.' She came in, wondering what he could have read that was so important. 'Why? Is there something special?'

'I stopped off at Mudds, on the corner of Waterloo Street, you remember, same as I do every morning to pick up my packet of whiffs, and that's when I noticed the placard. So naturally enough I bought a copy. It's sticking out of my jacket pocket over there on the peg. I didn't mention it to the Gov'nor when he looked in like he does for his morning chat. Thought it best you take it up to the office when you go, have a read together of page four. Don't like the sound of it myself. But I'll say no more. You read it for yourselves.' Then, changing the subject, he indicated the list of ingredients he'd been using, their quantities clearly marked. 'That's the lot and, unless I'm much mistaken Blakeney's ought to be on to a winner with this one. It's your almond cake, Miss Ronnie. Come and give the mix a stir for luck, then I'll get it in the tins and start them off baking. I've done enough to make half a dozen, so when you price it out bear that in mind.'

Veronica stirred the rich almond mixture, made from a recipe she'd been perfecting at home.

'Smells gorgeous. I'll cost it out, Bert. I know what I put in mine at home, but that was only one so I want to cost the timing on mixing in bulk. These cakes won't be cheap – but one thing I can vouch for – they can't be bettered.'

'That's it, Miss, Blakeney's has never cut corners. Every one of those almonds hand ground. See I've noted the time I've taken. Don't forget to borrow my newspaper. I tell you, it don't make happy reading.'

14

Puzzled, she carried the newspaper back to the office she shared with her father and together they read: 'New Owners for Clifford Hill Disused Warehouse'. Then a secondary heading: 'Conversion Work to Start Immediately for National Bakery'.

'Clampton's Cakes coming to Deremouth.' Veronica muttered as she read, 'I don't see what Bert was getting worried about. That sort of trade will never threaten ours. Why, Dad, it's cheap rubbish.'

'Don't be too sure, my dear. Clampton's are a national company, they must be backed by resources we can never match.'

'Resources be damned! she scoffed. 'It's not resources that make for high-class products, it's the best ingredients and it's hand mixing. See what they say here about the equipment that's going to be installed – mixers, whisks. What sort of skill can a cook need at a place like that? All they'll need to know is how to turn an electric switch on and off.'

Herbert laughed, putting an affectionate arm round her as they leant over the paper.

'I hope you're right, child. But how many people have the money these days to buy the best? So much has changed these last few years.'

'There you are then! People who want some sawdusty machine-mixed confection are welcome to buy the rubbish Clampton's put out. Honestly, Dad, our trade and theirs can never clash.'

'What about our workers? A smart new factory, probably a higher rate of wage than we can pay. I foresee trouble.'

Moving away he sat down at his desk, his fingers drumming on its leather top, a nervous tic at the corner or his mouth twitching out of control. Head bent, as she made a pretence of re-reading the two bold columns she raised her eyes to look at him. There was something unfamiliar about his manner.

'Dad . . .?' Physically startled, for a second he looked at her as if she were a stranger. 'Are you all right, Dad?'

'What? What? Of course I am. And you're right, we have nothing to fear from Clampton's. Let them do their damnedest, eh?' His smile was over-bright. It gave her no reassurance. But at that same moment they were interrupted by a tap on the office door,

'Come in,' she called, expecting one of their customary suppliers. She even opened her desk drawer to take out her order book.

'I apologise for disturbing you here.' And there, framed in the doorway, was the tall figure of Nicholas Ellis.

Herbert seemed to take the unexpected visitor in his stride, in fact watching the way he stood up, hand outstretched in welcome, Veronica could almost believe she had imagined his previous strange behaviour.

'I have come asking for help.' Having shaken Herbert's hand, Nicholas turned to Veronica. 'Perhaps you heard the ambulance bell late yesterday afternoon, or have heard about what happened? I believe it was very near here that he fell.'

'He?' Veronica prompted.

'Mr Humphreys. He slipped on a banana skin someone had thrown into the gutter. His arm is broken in two places. He has been kept in hospital, I've just come from there. I fear they'll miss his music in Otterton. The thing is, Miss Blakeney, he will be out of operation for some weeks. Are you able to help me? Oh, I know – no idle hours – no need to seek time fillers. This would be doing a service, not just to me, but to the choir.'

'You can't compare my piano playing with Mr Humphreys',' she floundered.

'I'm not comparing anyone with anyone. I am simply saying that if I play myself, I'm not in a position to train the choir as I would want. The performance of the Requiem will have to wait until Mr Humphreys is fit to play the organ, but for practices it's a pianist I need. I know your ability. Of course when we played together I appreciate you were familiar with the piece. How well do you sight read?'

'Extremely well,' she said, chin high. If she refused to help he would think she wasn't capable. The teasing laughter in his brown eyes made her suspect he could read her thoughts and did nothing to endear him to her. 'All right, I'll help you out. But there must be other people who could do it, and I hope you'll soon find someone else to take it off my hands.' Why was it that just talking to him brought out the worst in her? She was angry with herself that she could sound so boorish, and even angrier with him for giving her this feeling of inadequacy.

'I'm grateful, extremely grateful. Now, one more favour. I wonder if you can spare the time to come to the Abbey one evening between now and Tuesday. I'd like to go over the score with you and familiarise you with where the singers stand, how I indicate to you to bring the piano in, and so forth. It would be better to do that by ourselves, I'm sure you agree.'

She most certainly did agree. The last thing she wanted was for him to talk *down* to her in front of a choir she'd been too uncertain to attempt to join. In any case, she meant to practise until she was perfect before Tuesday so the sooner she collected her copy of the score the better.

'As you wish,' she nodded her agreement. 'Suppose I meet you in the Abbey this evening at, say, eight o'clock?'

'I shall look forward to it.' The mockery she'd suspected just now had put her on her mettle, but it had been easier to take than the obvious sincerity. 'Partly because you've got me out of a difficult hole,' he admitted with a smile, 'but mostly because it's something I'd hoped for since we played together at your home.'

After he'd gone, her glance fell on the newspaper still open at page four. His unexpected visit had put Clampton's Cakes out of her head, as far out as her momentary and baffling concern for her father.

She purposely arrived early at the Abbey, walking up the path to the south door soon after half past seven. At the back of her mind was a half-formed idea that she wanted time on her own first, she wanted to sit at the unfamiliar piano, perhaps even look at the score if by chance he'd already put it out. It wasn't that she was nervous, rather that she was determined to impress Nicholas favourably. She felt she owed that much, not just to herself, but to Dr Hardy too. But as she approached the great south door she could hear the sound of music, boys' voices, the organ, silence then the same phrase repeated. A practice was in progress.

Very quietly she opened the heavy door just far enough to slip in, then silently closed it and tiptoed to the back pew. Electric light flooded the chancel where the practice was in progress, but the unlit nave of the ancient building was dim even on a summer evening.

'Take the twelfth to seventeenth bars again,' Nicholas instructed the two rows of boys, then sang the short Latin phrase of the opening (she assumed the twelfth bar) of the anthem they were practising to demonstrate the emphasis he wanted. 'Well done,' he praised after the boys had repeated the phrase. 'Now once more straight through from the beginning and if you remember what you've learnt we'll call it a day.' Her eyes were open and yet it was almost as if she was drifting away from reality, carried by the purity of the young voices in the chancel, the silent emptiness in the high vaulted nave. When the last Amen died away and the boys were again told 'well done', she could sense their pleasure. 'Off you go,' Nicholas told them. 'I'll see you in the practice room at a quarter past eight in the morning.'

They'd sung like angels, but they sounded more like a football team as they bundled out of the choir stalls with their cheery 'Right you are, sir', 'Goodnight sir', their faces beaming with pleasure at an early release. Surely that was her moment to let him know she was here, yet something held her back in her seat. He wasn't expecting her for twenty minutes yet, he'd probably go back to his house. That would give her a chance to sit on the piano stool, get the feel of the instrument before she was thrown in at the deep end to uphold her boast of being 'extremely good' at sight reading.

But with the boys gone, he sat again at the console and started to play. No one here except him, or so he believed, just him and the beautiful, solemn sound of Bach's *St Anne Fugue*. If, a few minutes ago, the boys' voices had lifted Veronica out of reality, it must have been in preparation for the emotion that filled her as she listened. The nave was long, she wanted to be part of the glorious sound. Moving softly she walked up the long aisle, then up the two steps to the chancel. As she sank to sit in a choir stall Nicholas turned and looked down on her from the organ loft, not a smiling welcome and yet his expression telling her he was glad she was there. He didn't stop playing, neither did she want him to. The soulful melody belonged to this time and this place, she knew these moments would stay with her always. Of course the beauty of the music had nothing to do with *him*. She turned slightly away from him and, closing her eyes, let herself drown in the sound. The unfamiliar piano and her plan to study the music were forgotten.

Despite herself, perhaps it was that evening that put their relationship on an easier footing. Had he changed, she wondered after a week or two of rehearsals, or had her opinion that he was autocratic always been unjust? Not that she wasted too much time pondering the question, for on the third Saturday in June Laurence was expected home.

On the morning of that Saturday Ellen Chesterton decked the house with flowers and, almost as excited as her mistress, Alice Gibbs who'd been with the family since 'the poor master' (Laurence's late father) had been alive, prepared his favourite salmon mousse for supper. He was due at Deremouth Station at half past three and by two o'clock Veronica had already changed into her favourite sailor-style skirt and blouse. It had become the custom for her to drive to meet him, something she'd done each time since she'd been entrusted with her father's motor car.

A hammering at the front door sent her rushing down from her bedroom. He must have arrived early! But it was Alice, and one look at her face was enough to tell Veronica there was bad news.

'I ran straight over, Miss Veronica. Afraid you'd be setting off early or something and I'd miss you. He just telephoned to the mistress. At those friends' place in Salisbury he is.'

'So it's a different train – from Salisbury, not Oxford? Did he say what time?'

'Not any time and not from anywhere, that's about the size of it. Staying with his friends. Says not to worry about him. Easy enough for him. His poor Mum, just went down like a busted balloon, she did. She'd set such store on the day. Well, we all had.'

Rather than do nothing, Veronica walked back to Gregory Cottage with Alice, and there she learnt the full story. Laurence was staying with a college friend and his family in Salisbury for a few days. There was a family friend expected and he felt it important to meet him.

'He'd gone out to the Post Office to make his telephone call. They do have an instrument in the house, but he wanted to speak privately. He said this gentleman he's to meet could be very useful in his career. He said to explain to you and say he'd be home soon. So, Veronica dear, we must be patient a few more days. At this stage, his career is so important,' then squeezing Veronica's hand, 'important to you too I like to think.'

And for Veronica that remark was as near as she was likely to get to her dreams coming true on that third Saturday in June.

In fact it was almost two months before he came back to Ottercombe, that sleepy village in South Devon. He wrote saying that his friends owned a house in Tuscany and that, having been invited to join them for their vacation, he would be a fool to refuse. As to his career prospects, things were shaping out well. The person he'd hoped would be useful appeared to be coming up to his expectations. By the time he came home he would have a lot to tell them.

Disappointed, Veronica told herself that of course he would have been stupid to refuse the chance of such a wonderful trip. She was ashamed that the challenge of Blakeney's, even the pleasure she found in accompanying the Abbey Singers' rehearsals, seemed dull by comparison. The early summer sunshine had given way to grey, sultry days, days in keeping with the mood she tried to overcome.

She hated to face the truth, that she felt hurt and rejected that after being away so long he hadn't wanted above all else to rush back to her. Her feelings for him never faltered, but she was tempted by something she saw as a game, one that flattered and amused her.

Chapter Two

Thinking about it, she was never sure when her opinion of Nicholas changed. Perhaps it went right back to that first evening in the Abbey. Had she still been held in the spell of Bach when she'd agreed so readily that they should dispense with surnames? Or, even then, had she suspected a warm and human man sheltering behind what she'd seen as his stiff formality?

Consciously she had thought none of these things, she had found herself simply enjoying being brought into the aura of music that seemed to make up his life. So, if not then – when? Hadn't the Bard said '. . . a rose by any other name . . .'? Yes, but if it were a variety of rose you chose to grow, then you would know the difference; the colour, texture, even the scent would make it especially your own. So perhaps calling him Nicholas when to the members of the choir he was Mr Ellis, or his coolly courteous: 'Once again, Miss Bryant, if you will, *"Pie jesu, Domine, dona eis requiem"*, then the choir straight on with the *Agnus Dei*,' and to *her* with no more than a hint of a smile yet somehow setting her apart from the rest, 'If you'll play the introductory bars, Veronica,' did subtly change their relationship.

Almost without her realising it, she found herself looking forward to the time they spent together. At first she didn't look for a reason, willingly she accepted that her enjoyment came from being part of the music. And when the rehearsals were over and the choir filing out of the Abbey, gladly she found herself lingering. Their meeting ground was the making of music. When he suggested – just as he had the evening they'd played their first duet – that she should come to the practice room like she used to with Dr Hardy, this time she agreed. It seemed the natural thing to do.

21

His manner no longer irritated her. Add to that her enormous admiration for his musicianship and she relaxed into enjoying herself on their first session together in the Choir School practice room. Even then did she recognise something in his manner she'd not suspected before? First of all, it was no more than a chance glimpse at him in an unguarded moment. But once seen, it was something she looked for. She had the power to disturb self-opinionated Nicholas Ellis! The discovery amused her, but it also excited her. No boy or man had interested her except Laurence; still there was only Laurence filling her inexperienced mind. But Nicholas was in a different category: he was older, he was already successful, he couldn't have come to this stage without there having been other women in his life. For, with too little under-standing to know how it was she was so sure, she sensed that behind the cool, unapproachable image he presented there was a man of fire and passion. She knew none of the rules of the game she started to play. A lingering half-smile; a hand lightly resting on his shoulder as he played the opening bars accompanying her in some ballad; a glancing touch of her hand against his.

To her it was a game, an escape from reality. She didn't dig to find what she was running away from. But, if she had, she would have discovered her disappointment had roots in the solitary postcard from Laurence ('Enjoying myself enormously. Sun-shine, indolence and wine. L.'). If the sun shone on Tuscany it certainly didn't on Devon. Add to that, the builders were already transforming the disused warehouse to accommodate Clampton's bakehouse and, something she found worrying above all else, her father's lapses into a troubled world of his own as he sat behind his desk were becoming increasingly frequent. It seemed as if, daily, more of the responsibility of the business fell to her. As the days and weeks of summer went by, gladly she sought escape in the time she spent with Nicholas. By nature there was nothing of a coquette in Veronica; but Nicholas's interest in her was balm to the hurt she wouldn't face. In the few cards he sent his mother, Laurence made no more mention of the person who might be useful in his career. So perhaps he'll soon be home, Veronica told herself in an attempt to ward off some unnamed fear, then he'll start work in Deremouth training to be a solicitor. Holding on to her adolescent dream, not even acknowledging that it was fading, yet she played her game of encouraging Nicholas. If

Tessa Wainwright could have looked in at the Choir School practice room she would have tut-tutted and delighted in her prophecy of 'a sticky end for that girl – and no more than she deserves.'

By mid-August Howard Humphreys had had his plaster removed and was able to take over the accompaniment for the final rehearsals, leading up to the inaugural performance of the Abbey Singers in September.

'I shall miss you at rehearsals,' Nicholas told Veronica as she packed her music back in its case at the end of their practice room session. 'Have you any idea, I wonder, how much your coming here means to me?'

It was as he moved closer that she felt the first warning scorch of the fire she'd been playing with.

'Here? Yes, I suppose if I'm not accompanying the Singers, there's no point in our having these fun evenings either.' She wanted to keep the mood light, suddenly aware that she was losing control of the way the evening was shaping.

'There's no need for us to stop playing together. Veronica, have you honestly no idea what our time together has meant to me?'

'Why, yes, of course it's been fun. I've enjoyed it too.' Then, when she felt the grip of his hands on her shoulders, 'Please, don't say things to spoil my coming here. I've loved it, honestly, I look forward to it all the week. But, any day now I'd probably stop coming anyway. Laurence will be home and—'

'Laurence Chesterton!' One hand didn't loosen its vice-like hold, while the other tipped her chin so that her face was within inches of his. 'He's just a boy. Do you think you could ever be content with the wishy-washy love he could give you?'

'Stop it. You don't know anything about Laurence and me—'

'I know that you're a woman, with a woman's emotions, a woman's passions. And how do I know?' The question hung between them, unanswered. Or was the answer in his next quietly spoken words? 'Have you not known those moments when your spirit and mine have reached out to each other? You have, you have, just as surely as I have.'

'Stop it. It's just emotional twaddle! We've been carried along by the music – it touches a sort of unearthly sense – lifts you out of yourself. I know all that, but that's all it is, Nicholas. You hardly know me.'

23

'I probably know you better than anyone on this earth knows you. There have been women before you – well, of course there have, I must already have been at Cambridge when you were led off to your first day at school. But I swear to you no one has ever haunted me like you do, no one has ever seemed like a part of me. And you've felt it too. If you deny it, then you're lying.'

As he'd spoken he had drawn her closer.

'It's you who's lying,' she breathed. 'I should never have agreed to come here.'

'You couldn't help yourself.'

'Of course I could. I came because it would have been – have been *rude* not to.'

She realised that until that moment she had never seen him laugh. Smile, perhaps, but laugh never. Now he did, a laugh that was at her expense.

'Don't fight it, my blessed Veronica. You haven't the power and neither have I. You and I belong together.' He spoke quietly, hardly above a whisper yet every syllable hammered into her brain.

'I told you,' she panicked. In contrast to his, her voice grew louder. 'Don't you even listen? Laurence and I have belonged together since we were children. Then along you come, arrogant, conceited, pompous—' she could have called him so much more, but the way his mouth twitched in amusement put an end to her unflattering list of adjectives. 'Who do you think you *are*, that you can dictate what I do with my life? Laurence—'

'To hell with Laurence. Are you so besotted with the lad that you can't see how he uses you? When is he coming? Can you tell me?' Nicholas was on safe ground here, for only that morning Ellen Chesterton had said they had no idea of his plans. 'I'd stake my last half crown that you can't. And why? Because he expects to pick you up and put you down to suit his convenience. Perhaps he got away with it when you were children. But *grow up*, woman! That's what you are – not a stupid, moon-struck girl, but a woman.'

She closed her eyes, as if that way she could hide from the truth she couldn't bear to hear. So she didn't see his expression as he drew her close, so close that she felt crushed in his embrace as his mouth found hers.

For a moment she remembered Laurence, the way his tongue had moved in her mouth, while his hands snatched at her breast.

24

Her excitement had been because what he did was surely a sign of his love, his desire for her. Be honest, be truthful, a voice in her brain told her in that second as she was crushed close to Nicholas. You wouldn't acknowledge that his inexperienced fumbling was driven by anything less than passion that wasn't to be denied. He's inexperienced, so am I. We won't always be ... we'll learn together ... If only he'd come home. Thoughts crowded in on her, yet even in those seconds she had no power to save herself, no will to still the clamouring in every nerve of her body. Nicholas's mouth was firm on hers, his hold on her was masterful. When he moved his hands it was only to bring her even closer, if that were possible. Through the thin material of her summer shift she could feel the beating of his heart – or was it hers? Her head was filled with the echo of his words, '... your spirit reached out to mine ...', '... don't fight it, you haven't the power and neither have I'.

She had no power, her own control was gone. What was she doing? Her arms were around him, her fingers caressing the back of his head, instinct drove her to open her mouth and move her tongue on his lips. Her body had a will of its own. Or was the truth, it had no will at all? But even as she heard the sound in her throat of her own stifled longing, she knew the moment couldn't last. She would pull away from him ... he would apologise for his own lack of self-control ... she would pick up her music case and primly tell him she wouldn't be coming back. She knew all that. Of course she did, it's what reason said, while her body knew nothing but an unaccustomed yearning that ached in her limbs.

As his hold slackened she wriggled free, grabbing her straw toque and ramming it on her head without so much as a glance in the mirror that hung on the far wall. She wouldn't look at him.

'Wish we hadn't ...' she mumbled, concentrating on doing up her music case.

'I don't think you do.' He closed the lid of the piano, the action seeming to draw a line under the scene. 'Burying your head in the sand isn't in your nature. Am I not right?'

'I can't come here anymore. You've spoilt it all. Even if you promised—'

A knock on the door and it burst open without waiting for a 'Come in'.

'Surprise! Surprise!' It was Laurence, tanned from the Tuscany sun, his hair bleached even fairer, looking even more debonair than she remembered him.

'There! I said you were coming!' In relief she went to him, hands outstretched. Then, turning to Nicholas, her eyes shining (with excitement or with relief that she'd been saved from a situation she couldn't handle), 'Didn't I tell you Laurence was due home?'

'Good evening,' in that stiff over-polite way of his, Nicholas bowed his head in greeting to his young visitor. 'You took us by surprise, this part of the Abbey is unaccustomed to unannounced callers.'

'I knew where Ron was, when I got home this afternoon Mum told me that Thursday evenings she comes here. I thought it would be a lark to wait till she was here then give her a surprise – a nice one, of course.' Clearly he was delighted at his own cleverness.

'A lovely one,' Veronica laughed, clutching thankfully at the joy and excitement of being with him. She was on familiar ground, once again she was in control of the situation.

'You'll come next Thursday?' Surely the high and mighty Nicholas Ellis couldn't be pleading!

'It depends,' she answered, looking him straight in the eye, her chin raised, her confidence restored. 'If we decide we're doing anything else I'll let you know.'

Nicholas raised his brows, the expression seeming to stir the echo of his warning: '. . . he's just a boy . . .', '. . . pick you up and put you down to suit his own convenience . . .' She glanced away, not wanting to read his message. All he said was, 'After a week of playtime you'll be as ready for music as an alcoholic for wine. Believe me, Veronica, I *know*.'

'About you, you might know. But only I know about me.' Not for the first time, she heard herself speaking to him with childish rudeness. Ashamed that she couldn't have conjured up some succinct and wise comment she tugged at Laurence's hand and led the way out of the room.

Watching as they pushed their bicycles down the path to the Abbey gate Nicholas's thoughts were his own.

'Now Laurence is home, dear, why don't you give up going every single day to the business. I've always said it's no place for a girl.

26

Pass this cup to your father. Wake up, Herbert, and take your cup. Really, I don't know where your thoughts disappear to sometimes.' Monica talked as she busied herself pouring the breakfast coffee. The ritual was important to her, for once the meal was over the other two always rushed off, busy with their lives while she was left with nothing to do that either of them saw as important. If she weren't here to see to their comfort, they'd soon miss her. Other women had companionship from their daughters, but not her! She sometimes thought she was as alone as poor Ellen who'd lost her husband and had no daughter. And lately Herbert had become so strange, as if his thoughts were always somewhere else. Why, think of him only this morning: if she hadn't noticed and spoken sharply to him he would have come down wearing one black shoe and one brown. Whatever could he be thinking about? Not another woman, of that she was sure. When she'd passed him the black shoe and taken away the brown, think how he'd pulled her towards him as he'd sat on the edge of the bed, think how he'd held her and buried his face against her. Then when she'd ruffled his hair and said, 'Come on, now, goose' (for really that wasn't the time of day for the way she believed his thoughts were going), he'd sounded almost frightened as he'd mumbled something about loving her. Well, of course he loved her, just like of course she loved him. But sometimes it did worry her that he seemed to be getting so lazy about making himself concentrate on what he was doing.

'Rubbish,' it was Herbert who answered her suggestion that Veronica should stop going to the business with him so regularly, 'you can't expect the girl to want to hang around all day waiting for young Chesterton to decide whether he wants her company.'

Veronica looked at him in surprise. Wasn't that almost a repetition of what Nicholas had said? But then, Nicholas had said so much that was nonsense. And hadn't it been Fate that had brought Laurence back just at that moment when she'd been struggling to hang on to normality? Since then she'd been determined not to remember that strange, helpless feeling – as if she'd felt herself being sucked into sinking sand – as if her limbs had no power to do her will. Was it really only last night? The rest of the evening had been shared with Laurence, and when at last she was in bed and alone with her thoughts she'd made sure they were all of *him*.

Yet she wasn't prepared to do as her mother suggested.

'There's more than enough work for both of us at the bakery, Mum. We've been through all this before, you know you'll never persuade me to sit on a silk cushion and sew a fine seam.'

'If you think that's all that's involved in keeping the wheels turning smoothly in this household, then you're much mistaken. You're both the same. You think I do *nothing!*' Tears welled in her lovely blue eyes.

'Come now, Monica darling, we think no such thing.' Herbert's face creased in lines of concern. She mustn't cry. Was it his fault? Was he failing her? His fingers started to drum on the table in the way Veronica had come to dread; that nervous tic took control at the corner of his mouth.

'Mum, we never take what you do for granted.' Frightened of tensions she couldn't understand, it was for her father's sake more than her mother's that Veronica tried to pull them back from the emotional scene that threatened. 'If you want the honest truth, I just know I'd be useless at the sort of things I ought to be doing. Learning to run a home, sewing, housekeeping, all that sort of thing. Some girls have a natural talent – you have and I envy you for it. But me? I'm better occupied adding up accounts and ordering the supplies. We don't need talent for that, do we, Dad, just a modicum of common sense and a pride in the business's reputation.'

'Don't know what I'd do without her,' he told Monica, thankful to see that the threat of tears had passed. She shrugged her shoulders, but her smile seemed contented enough to show that she hadn't detected a note of fear in his voice. Only Veronica had heard it.

Breakfast over and Monica mollified, Veronica brought the motor car to the front door and she and Herbert set off for their day. Whatever it was that Monica found to do that was so vital, neither of them was interested enough to question. Their routine never varied: arriving at Blakeney's Bakery in Merchant Street, Veronica stopped so that her father could get out then, while she drove round to the back of the building to park the automobile, he went into the long bakehouse. It had always been his custom to have a friendly word with the staff, his interest in them was genuine and no doubt one of the reasons they were content in a

28

job that, especially during the summer, was far from comfortable. Since Veronica had become what he liked to term his 'right hand man', he left her to go on up to the office and open the mail.

On that particular morning she hardly waited for him to get through the door before she greeted him with, 'You wouldn't credit it, Dad! Clampton's, *Clampton's* of all people have written from their head office. A lot of soft soap about knowing the high reputation of our business, our *small exclusive trade* as they call it – damned cheek! As if we'd want to be associated with the sawdusty trash they flood the market with. Anyway, you'll read it. You'll see what they suggest. Buy us out! *That mob!*' In her fury she had forgotten how protective of him she'd learnt to be. Pulling herself up short she looked at him, expecting to see that expression she'd come to dread. Instead, he was laughing – not at what she was telling him, but at her!

'They've met their match in you, child. And your mother wants to deprive me of you.' It wasn't what she'd said about Clampton's proposal that was frightening him, it was the threat in his own words 'wants to deprive me of you'. 'You won't let her, you'll stay here with me, won't you? . . . come to depend . . .' His voice faded into silence, he couldn't bring himself to say aloud just how much he relied on her.

'Oh you needn't worry about that, Dad. A good job I'm useful, for you've got me here for keeps.' Her voice was over-loud, over-jolly, but clearly it drove away Herbert's devils. As for herself, she wouldn't look beyond the moment and the need to take that frightened look from his face. How could he really mean that he depended on her? When he'd joined his own father in the business it had been no more than could be found in every village. It was he who had built it up so that now they served 'the county', there wasn't a house of note they didn't supply, just as the tip-top hotels looked to them especially for their Christmas fare. Certainly over recent years, their new products had usually been based on her ideas but, before that, the expansion of their trade had been down to him. So why was his confidence deserting him at a time when he should have been at the pinnacle of his career? All these things crowded into her mind, but they couldn't overcome her anger at Clampton's.

'Here Dad, read what they say. I'd like to tell them just—'

29

'And so you shall, child. You write the reply. Blakeney's isn't for sale, eh? Not while you and me are in charge, eh?'

She wasted no time; she wrote before her anger subsided.

Your suggestion was received with puzzlement. We, at Blakeney's, were aware that you are to open a factory in our town, but we had read of it in our local newspaper with little interest. Deremouth is a small but busy town, it has room for many different trades. The fact that Blakeney's is well established need in no way concern you, for there is absolutely no likelihood of our encroaching on any clientele you may build here. Ours falls into a totally different category, one of which we are proud and intend to maintain. If you imagine us to be a small minnow in terror of being swallowed by a whale, then it is because you know nothing of this part of the world. The name Blakeney's is synonymous with quality, mass production is of no interest to us.

No doubt you feel that in adding 'incorporating Blakeney's Bakery' into your name you would be giving the impression of stepping out of the world of the cheap factory-produced goods for which you have gained a wide reputation.

Let me make this perfectly clear: Blakeney's is not for sale. We are a family business with pride in our achievements and confidence in our products. That is how we intend to remain. However, the fact that our businesses have nothing in common does not mean that we do not wish you well in your new venture in the south west.

Yours faithfully,

She carried it to the post box herself, and with a sense of satisfaction listened as the envelope dropped. But, in truth, she was more worried that she would admit, especially to her father. Selling to the gentry of the district, supplying the better hotels, even sending cakes to stock high-class grocers, these outlets had limitations. And, once Clampton's baked locally and probably with daily deliveries, who was to say loyalty to Blakeney's would outweigh a not inconsiderable reduction in price?

That evening she talked about it to Laurence, looking for reassurance. They'd cycled to the beach in the bay at Otterton St Giles

30

and were sitting in the shelter of the cliff. The sun was casting its last long rays across the water before it disappeared from sight behind the headland that projected to their right. This had always been a favourite place, just out of the village the shore was usually deserted.

'In my reply to their letter I sounded much more confident than I am. But don't ever tell anyone that. Dad gets so worried. I don't know why. I just know I have to boost him.'

'I've an idea. While I'm home why don't you ask him to let you drive further afield. The stuff you turn out is thought of highly around here – so it would be in, say, Bath or Bristol, perhaps even into Dorset. We could go in a different direction each day. Put all your charm on, Ron, and no one could refuse you.'

'Blakeney's doesn't rely on anyone's charm – even if I had any.' She was ashamed that she could say it hoping just to hear him tell her what she wanted to hear.

'Have a word with him,' Laurence went on, seemingly unaware of the cue he'd missed. 'Of course you couldn't do it on your own. But I'm not panicking to get tied down to a regular job of work for a bit. It would be a rather pleasant way to round off the season.'

To her it sounded like only one step down from paradise.

That was the last Sunday in August. She was pleasantly surprised at her father's easy acceptance of the suggestion when they put it to him later that evening. He who relied on her more each day; yet seeing they were waiting for his agreement he gave it with apparent willingness.

'We could go in together a bit earlier than usual, Dad. Then once you see there's nothing you want me for I'd drive back and collect Laurence.'

'Yes. Good idea. You could just come in for a while with me, eh?'

'And back again before you were ready to come home, Dad,' she told Herbert. Laurence was about to speak but a slight shake of her head silenced him. Over the last month or two she'd come to read her father's moods, she knew when he needed her support, she knew when he was his old confident self. 'That would be the best idea, wouldn't it?'

'Yes, you do that. If I know you're coming . . .' his voice trailed away.

31

'Coming with my order book full,' she beamed.

So the very next day the two of them set off. To Veronica it was everything she could want: a whole day with Laurence, the challenge of gaining orders for the business, the excitement of driving to places she'd never seen before. That he enjoyed it too was obvious.

'This is great!' he said. 'Let's see your order book. What a team we are.'

She didn't mention that any orders gained had been her own doing, for while she gained interviews with potential buyers he amused himself in town, meeting her back at wherever they'd left the parked motor car. Of course she didn't mention it, she preferred to look on it as a joint project. Monday, Tuesday, Wednesday, Thursday, while the fine weather held they trundled through the late summer countryside. Never once did she lower her standards for the type of outlet for Blakeney's products, the only difference was that they cast their net further afield. They carried a plan of the railway network and were careful only to seek orders from hotels or stockists within an area covered by deliveries by the station wagons.

By Thursday teatime, with four days' canvassing for trade behind them, she dropped Laurence off at Gregory Cottage.

'Tomorrow I ought to stay in the office with Dad,' she told him. 'I've hardly done a thing there all the week.'

'They'll have managed very well without you,' he frowned. 'Has he complained that you've not been there?'

'Of course he hasn't.'

'And has he told you you're to go in tomorrow?'

'Laurence, Dad never tells me what to do. He knows I do what I think best.'

'Well then? You're a free agent. If you don't want to go chasing orders tomorrow, what do you say to our taking a day off? Damn it, Ron, I'm supposed to be on holiday, remember?'

'I thought we'd been having fun – both of us.'

'Of course we have. It's been a great laugh. But I've had to spend a lot of time mooning around on my own.'

'I'm going to work tomorrow, but then we have the weekend. When you start working I won't expect you to drop everything just because I suggest it.' She felt he wasn't taking what she did seriously. But because he was Laurence, his views didn't make her angry. She just wanted him to see things fairly.

'Now that's a red herring, if you like!' he laughed. 'I haven't even finally decided where I'll be – but it's certainly not going to be with Mum's pet solicitor in Deremouth. Get your father home as quickly as you can, Ron. We could go back into town and buy a fish and chip supper down by the quay – the Happy Plaice. I'll expect you a bit before seven. In the motor if you can – but, if not, we'll cycle. A bit of exercise won't kill us, we've been driving all day.' His confident smile showed that he'd completely forgotten that Thursdays she spent with Nicholas. If he'd put his suggestion differently, 'I know you usually go to the Abbey, but you did say you might not be able to,' something like that, then she might have fallen in with his plans. But he hadn't even remembered.

Hurt and angry that he could show so little interest in the parts of her life that didn't involve him, she told him, 'It's my music evening. Nicholas is expecting me.'

'You can't tell me that old Sobersides will shed any tears whether you turn up or not. Come on, Ron, fish and chips won't be half as good without you.'

'Then put them off until tomorrow, I'm free then.' It was remarkable how much pleasure it gave her to stand firm. Yet as she drove on towards Deremouth she wondered why she had done it. She'd told herself that over the seven days since last Thursday she'd wasted no thought on Nicholas. The memory had no power to hurt her – no power, wasn't that what he'd told her? That they had no power to fight whatever it was that drew their spirits together. Oh, but it was nonsense. What a strange, complex character he was: so frigidly formal and yet, held in check behind that aloof veneer, she had no doubt of the sensual, passionate man.

But on that Thursday as she drove away from Ottercombe and Laurence, she was honest enough to admit that much of her satisfaction in how she'd handled his assumption that she would change her arrangements to suit his wishes stemmed from Nicholas's words '. . . pick you up and put you down . . .' Well, she'd proved him wrong. Just as she would prove him wrong about all the other nonsense he'd talked. What she wasn't honest enough to ask herself was why she was so keen to go to the practice room? The evening wouldn't be a repetition of the previous week, of that she was sure. But the prospect of being with him was exciting, dangerously exciting. For weeks purposely she'd subtly led him on. Thinking back, she was reminded of a game she used to play as a child, a game that used to make her pulses race with fear. She would open the huge iron gates leading to the garden of The Mount (the country seat of Sir James Radstock on the edge of the village), then creep up the drive until she knew from the angry bark of the guard dog that her presence had been detected. Then she'd run hot foot back to the gate. The thrill had always been in the danger – supposing the gate wouldn't open, supposing she tripped. If fear had made her pulses race, that was nothing compared to the rush of adrenaline she'd known when, safely on the outside of the gate, she had watched the dog bare his teeth, foaming and snarling in angry frustration. She remembered how sad she'd been when the old dog had had to be put down.

But how could she compare that with the game she'd been playing with Nicholas? The danger was there right enough; last week had been a warning to her. She'd be on her guard. Easier by far to stop going to the practice room. But she'd never been one for looking for the easy way. And in any case . . . She didn't dig deeper.

'I was able to get here,' she greeted him over-cheerfully and quite unnecessarily.

'Your friend had no use for this evening?' She knew he was laughing at her.

'Well actually he did. He wanted to take me for a meal in Deremouth. But—' now what was wiser, to ignore last week or to mention it casually? She decided on the latter. 'I just thought after last week you would think I was offended or something if I didn't show up.'

'So may I take it that you weren't?'

She wished she'd chosen Course Number One and said nothing.

'Offended? It really didn't concern me that much.' She tried to sound as disinterested as her maiden aunt. 'I've heard say that these things are different for men, they can get over-excited. I'm really not blaming you.' She'd kept her head down, concentrating on opening her music case. Curiosity got the better of her though and, as she laid the sheaf on the piano top, she took a very quick peek at him, a peek just long enough to see that he found something funny in her comment.

34

'And there speaks my very own ice maiden,' he said softly.

'I'm not an ice maiden at all. I just don't like – like – casual, cheap, whatever you call it when it isn't love. Let's get on, shall we. Let's not waste time talking about something that's much better forgotten.' She wished she hadn't come. She could have been at the Happy Plaice enjoying a huge plate of cod and chips, laughing and happy with Laurence.

'I couldn't agree with you more – about casual, cheap, gratuitous sex. But that played no part in what happened last week, at least for me it didn't. For you, well perhaps that's all it was, perhaps you were fantasising that I was your young friend. Is that what you want me to believe?'

'Let's do a duet. Let's forget all about it.'

'Choose your music and come and sit down then.' He took her hands and drew her to sit by his side on the long stool. 'This evening we will be content with four hands and one key-board.'

She relaxed. Yet, half an hour later, when his manner had remained as correct as she might have expected from her old friend Dr Hardy, she felt strangely let down. And before she left to go home she had resorted to one or two of her previous ruses. Sitting closer than was necessary she let her hand rest on the stool, conscious, just as he must have been, that it was touching his thigh. Afterwards as together they sang 'You Made Me Love You' – from a song sheet she had bought years ago with her pocket money and used to play and sing feeling like a tragedy queen when Laurence was away at boarding school – she put her hand on his shoulder and leant close in a pretence of reading the words. He appeared not to notice, his behaviour was impeccable. She wasn't prepared to admit to a feeling of disappointment.

'You'll be in the Abbey on Saturday for the Requiem?' It was more a statement than a question, for he had no doubt that she'd be there.

'I'm almost certain I shall come.' She could feel rather than see his quizzical expression. His silence was a reminder of the way he thought Laurence used her. Well, he was wrong! She and Laurence had been together every day this week, and each one had been more fun than the last. All her old antagonism was fighting its way into her mind as she rammed on her hat in silence.

'Veronica,' he started, then hesitated.

'I must go. What were you going to say?' Surely, with her talking so brightly, he must be able to speak whatever was on his mind.

'It was just – please. I shall look for you. Please be there.'

Whatever casual, even flippant, retort she had intended, remained unspoken. With a quick nod she left him, hurrying to get out into the evening air, in solitude to ride home through the dusk.

Saturday was only two days away. As she pedalled home she imagined their group in the Abbey. Probably Nicholas would have kept seats in the front for them. There would be her parents, she'd sit next, then Laurence, then his mother. The image was clear in her mind, she could almost see Nicholas standing in the chancel to conduct, tall and austere in his tailed suit and white tie. And, instead of the sound of her tyres on the gravel lane, she seemed to hear Howard Humphreys playing Fauré's lovely opening bars, the single notes on the organ as mellow as the strings of a cello.

From Thursday to Saturday may be only two days, but a life can change in far less.

Chapter Three

'Have you gone through the wage sheets, Dad? Everything's in the safe, is it?' Veronica asked as Herbert joined her in the office, having had his usual 'good morning' chat in the bakehouse.

'No, no,' he blustered, 'what time have I had to think about wages with you off out every day? And all these extra orders you've been getting – all of it makes more work.' His fingers drummed warningly on his desktop; his eyes refused to meet hers. 'I can't do my job and yours too.'

She didn't want to look at him, dreading the frightened expression that was getting all too familiar. What was happening to him?

'Right you are, Dad. I'll make the wages my first job, shall I? It's good to know I was missed.' She tried to lighten the tone. 'Then, when you've been down to pay the men, we'll go over the order book together, shall we?'

Like a child bribed with a sweet for encouragement, he beamed his pleasure.

'That's the way, my dear. Go over it together. Let's see how much trade you've managed to bring in. I've kept all your orders in a folder for you.'

Her heart sank. Was he telling her that he had done nothing towards processing the orders she'd obtained? And here they were on Friday morning, with a weekend ahead of them. She'd expected that the goods ordered at the beginning of the week would have been despatched to arrive by this time. As she listed the men's wages, checking if any had worked beyond their normal six o'clock end of day, she schooled herself to look composed; he mustn't guess the way her fearful thoughts were turning. What had begun such a short time ago as no more than a warning that all wasn't well with him, was becoming ever more certain. But why? Did he suspect some dreadful illness? Could that be what terrified him? At home, except for the occasional nervous tension she recognised (and even this was something she was conscious of because of what she saw in the office), she believed he was the same as he always had been. Yet here at the bakery, where was the man who used to run the business with such efficient ease?

'You've not got the money from the bank, Dad?' That was something she always did on Thursdays after she'd worked out how much was needed for the wages.

'No, no, child. I didn't interfere.'

'Hey,' she teased, hoping her laugh didn't sound as forced to him as it did to her, 'who's Gov'nor here?'

She shouldn't have said it. As soon as the words were spoken she wished them back.

'Not fit . . . done nothing . . .' his tightly clenched hands pressed against the desktop, while he turned his head away from her.

'I was only joking.' She was at his side in a second. 'Dad, what's worrying you? Can't you tell me? Surely it's not the business; we're doing well. Is it *you*? Are you ill? Please, Dad, if you don't tell me, how can I hope to help?'

'Can't think . . . muddled . . . can't grasp . . . Christ, I'm so frightened . . .'

'Darling Dad, what is there to be frightened of? Does Mum know? I don't understand.'

'Don't understand, you say! It's me who doesn't understand. I try to think, try to get a grasp. Then it goes – don't know the day of the week. Couldn't do the wages, Ron. I wanted to. Got the wage sheets out. Tried . . . couldn't think . . . couldn't work it out . . . How can you understand what it's like? I'm all right now, can think straight with you here. It's like trying to remember a nightmare . . . something that happens to someone else.' With dry eyes filled with fear, he looked at her. 'You see, I'm clear now. I'm outside it all. Give me the papers now and I could work out the men's pay. It's like a black fog comes . . . can't describe . . . can't tell you—'

'You're tired, that's all it is.' She clutched at the first thing to try to take that look from his eyes. 'Why don't you and Mum have a holiday?'

'No. Oh no.' At the suggestion, his grip on her hand tightened. 'I'm better here. She'd see what I get like. She'd worry. I've hidden it from her. And now I've told you, you can help me. We mustn't let her guess. Poor sweet angel, I've always tried to take care of her, protect her. Mustn't fail her. You've got to help me keep this from her.'

'It'll pass, Dad.' Oh, but would it? 'Now that you've told me, things won't worry you like they did. You'll see.' Somehow she had to give him some sort of hope to hang on to. 'Remember what Mum used to say to me when I got wild ideas of something I wanted – my own pony, French lessons in Exeter, roller skates because I'd seen Meredith Bryant skating past the house – remember?' She heard herself gabble the words, saying anything that would steer his mind to a happier track, ' " Just a silly phase, you'll soon grow out of it," she used to say. "Concentrate on all the things you have in your own life and be happy." And she was right, you know. It'll be like that with you, just a silly phase – time will carry all your troubles away, just concentrate on being happy with Mum and me.' It was the nearest she felt she could come to suggesting that while some women made a big thing of something they mysteriously whispered about as 'the change' perhaps, unsung, much the same thing happened to men and it was against that that his mind was rebelling. It was just one of the many, many things she didn't know much about and she had to hang on to the trust that he'd 'soon grow out of it'.

'What would I do without you, Ronnie? But I've no right to cling on to you.' Yet, cling he did, mentally and physically too. His grip never loosened. 'In my nightly prayers I used to ask that you'd find someone worthy to lose your heart to and get rid of young Chesterton. Not good enough for you, never was. But now he's home and I dare say he's talked to you about his plans. His mother tells us he's had the offer of joining Withers, Wright and Lambton in Station Square – Mr Withers has been her solicitor for years, she has great regard for him. Married to Laurence you'd not be taken away from me. See what I've come to?' His eyes were suddenly bloodshot with unshed tears. 'If you agree to marry Laurence Chesterton I shan't lose you. That's how low I've sunk.'

This time there was relief in the smile that lit her face.

'Got to wait for him to ask me first, Dad.' The ring of confidence in her voice matched the sudden smile that lit her face.

'Not good enough for me, indeed!' she laughed. 'Isn't that what all fathers think? Deep down you must always have seen we were right for each other. I know Mum does, and Mrs Chesterton too.'

'I don't want to lose you to any man. There, that's the truth.' The tic in his cheek was working overtime, his hold on her hand loosened, she felt him slipping away.

'Come on, Dad,' she said in a voice aimed at pulling him from the threatening abyss before it engulfed him. 'Wages day and I have to go and draw the money.'

'Going out, child? No, no, wait here with me.'

'Better still, we'll lock the office and go together. how would that be?'

'Together. Yes, yes, that's the way. Pass me my hat and cane. I'll walk with you.'

She was glad to turn to the hat-stand, at least with her back to him he wouldn't see her anxiety. Into her mind flashed the memory of Laurence trying to persuade her to take a day off, not to come into the office at all today. And on the tail of that thought came another: somehow she must persuade him to accept the offer from his mother's 'pet solicitor' in Deremouth, only that way could she continue to support her father. At the thought her optimistic nature took control.

'Here you are, Dad. Bonnets on. Quite a treat, you and me taking a stroll in town together in the middle of the morning – like a couple of people with time on their hands.'

His smile was her reward. The shadow of fear had faded as if it had never been, once again he was father, partner, friend, colleague. She could almost make herself believe she'd let her imagination run away with her. Like a pair of conspirators they locked the office door behind them.

While they collected the wages money from the bank in Waterloo Street, at Ipsley House Monica Blakeney was putting the finishing touches to her appearance. If she knew a moment's guilt, she soon stamped it down. Herbert and Veronica both had full and interesting lives, lives that had no place for her; she was taken for granted. As long as the house was run on oiled wheels, the food promptly on the table, and she there in his bed to be used as his sure way to exhaustion, she saw herself as of no more importance than part of the furnishings. She was entitled to better.

The sunshine streamed in through the bedroom window, catching the cut glass of the tray on her dressing table. The tray served a useful purpose, holding her silver-backed mirror, brush and comb; but this morning it sparkled, sending out shafts of coloured light that held her gaze. Just a glass tray, one she used each day and hardly noticed – ordinary, functional, taken for granted just as she was herself. Yet this morning, its gleam was radiant. Catching her bottom lip between her teeth she took one last look in the mirror, pleased with what she saw and filled with an unfamiliar and almost forgotten excitement.

A minute later she was running lightly down the stairs and out into the bright morning.

Many times during that day, Herbert's words echoed in Veronica's memory giving her a warm glow of certain anticipation. Ahead of her she saw her life with Laurence as cloudless as the last few days had been. But even indulging her imagination, there was one stumbling block her father knew nothing of: Laurence's opinion of Mr Withers as Ellen Chesterton's 'tame solicitor'. Somehow she had to persuade him to accept the offer to join the company in Deremouth. Once they were married she could spend less time at the bakery, just come in each day for a while so that her father knew she was his support. That way he'd regain his lost confidence. Willingly that's what she believed.

That evening when Laurence called for her he fitted perfectly the role she had cast for him.

'I didn't go without you last night,' he greeted her with his confident, cheery smile, picking up from where they'd parted company the previous evening. 'Fish and chips needs company. So I thought if you'd borrow the car we'd have our fish supper this evening. How does that strike you?' Then, with a teasing wink, 'No high-powered musical soirée in your diary?'

'I'll tell Mum I'm out for supper.' And perhaps it was the confidence born of the daydreams that had been the backdrop to her working day that made her take both his hands in hers. 'Friday is the best night of the week at the Happy Plaice, Friday is the right night for fish.'

'Piano night, too. Remember that funny little chap who never takes off his battered bowler plays the "Joanna" on Fridays. Good job you turned me down last night, Ron. This'll be loads better.'

Hardly the words of the amorous suitor of her dreams, but this was the Laurence she loved.

If her refusal to give up her evening at the Abbey or to take a day away from the office had cast a shadow on their previous parting, neither of them thought of it as she drove them back into Deremouth and to the quayside fish café. The Happy Plaice had been one of their favourite haunts since childhood. In those days it used to be part of the summer holiday routine that, after a morning rowing at sea (and perhaps catching a mackerel or two to take home) they would drag his boat up the beach and go for a mammoth meal of cod and chips. Now they were grown up, but to Veronica there could be nowhere with happier memories and nowhere more suited to planning their future.

'I've been doing a lot of thinking, Ron. Particularly today. About the future, I mean.' *This is it*, her heart cried out, *it's really happening, he's really saying it*. 'Mum's been trying to talk me into going to join old Withers and his set-up.'

'And . . .?' she questioned, expectantly, not giving disappointment a chance to surface. This was only leading towards the most important of his thoughts for the future.

He frowned.

'You know how I feel. If anyone knows me and understands, then it's *you*, Ron.' He put his knife and fork down, his jumbo-sized piece of cod temporarily forgotten. 'She says she's waited all these years on her own expecting me to come back when I finished at Oxford. But, Ron, any local fellow with half a brain could fit the bill for old man Withers. That wasn't what I was educated for, that wasn't what I spent three years at Oxford for. What do you say?'

'Would it matter too much being here for a while?' Her knife and fork, too, were laid to rest. 'I mean – where does happiness come from? Real deep down happiness?'

It was unlike Laurence to look so solemn but he was weighing her question carefully.

'I'm not sure that I know. Perhaps it's always one leap ahead of us.' Then, casting off his cloak of seriousness, he reached across the oilcloth-covered table and took her hand in his. 'You and me, Ron, we've always found plenty of it, haven't we?' Her fingers clung to his as she nodded, she could find no words as she nodded in agreement, her eyes bright with adoration and certainty. 'We've

had some good times. Where would I be without you.' A statement, not a question.

'You don't have to be without me, you never have to be without
me.' Only that morning she'd laughingly told her father that they
'had to wait until he asked her'. Now she was giving him her
answer, the words spoken even as she thought them.

'Perhaps not, as long as I stay in this dump. But Ron, life should
be more than that. Leaving Oxford to work in some gimcrack little
office ... Listen, I've got something to tell you.' His voice was
loaded with excitement.

'Yes?' she breathed. It was almost too much to bear as the
words she'd dreamed for so long were about to be spoken. She
picked up her knife and fork and carried an unladylikely-large
piece of vinegar-soaked cod to her mouth.

'Mum's in a state about this. But she can't rule my life, Ron,
you must see that.'

'In a state? But why? Perhaps mothers always get possessive,
but she's never made a secret—'

'I want you to read this,' cutting through her words and seeming
oblivious of their meaning, he took a letter from his pocket and
passed it to her. 'Her age group wouldn't understand, they're too
set in their ways, too hidebound to recognise the challenge of
adventure if it smacked them between the eyes.'

Her cheeks bulging as she chewed, she took the envelope and
noticed it had a London postmark. In that moment the bakery was
forgotten and her father's need of her, too. Adventure, he said ...
London ... he wanted *her* to read it, to share with him. But only
for a moment did she let her own excitement keep pace with his,
then her sense of responsibility awakened the image of her
father's frightened expression, the fear he could neither understand nor overcome. She had to persuade Laurence that their place
was here. Yet how could she? One look at him told her just how
keen he was for whatever adventure this letter promised. Silently
she read, from the headed address of one of the foremost national
magazines to the Editor's signature.

'I thought you wanted law?' She bolted her food so that she
could grasp the red herring that came nearest to hand, 'And who is
Sydney Lansdale? I know he's the Editor, I can see that. But how
does he come to offer you a position like this? Fancy not saying
you were applying for a job there.'

'I did tell you about him – and Mum too. Back when I first came down from Oxford. I met him when I was in Salisbury staying with Harriday, then later when we were in Italy he managed a week with us. I let it be known I would be interested in anything suitable on the magazine. You know I said there was someone I thought would be useful in my career.' Then, with that frank, and self-assured beam she knew so well, he added, 'What a charmer, eh!'

'Charm, be damned,' Veronica folded the letter back into its envelope. 'With your degree, you have no need to rely on charm. False modesty doesn't suit you. Of course you're proud of your-self and so you should be.' That was true; as true as it was that she could imagine him climbing the career ladder on the staff of a London-based magazine far more easily than she could in the dingy offices of Withers, Wright and Lambton. 'What a tempta-tion, Laurence. I've only ever been to London once, it was as if I could feel the pulse of it beating. There's such a bustle, people seem to walk with purpose, everything's awake and vital.'

'There, I knew you'd agree.' Again their fatty supper was cooling on their plates as he gripped both her hands in his. 'Not like sleepy old Devon, eh? Listen, Ron – tomorrow I'm going up on the early train. I'd intended asking you to drive me to Deremouth Station, all decked up for town I don't want to go on my bicycle. But I've got a better plan. Let's both go. I want to find somewhere to live. Say yes, Ron. That wretched bakery can surely exist through a Saturday morning without you. You'd have much more idea than I would about choosing a nest.'

Somewhere for them to live . . .

'Ask me properly,' she whispered, her fingers gripping his and her answer ready. Her heart seemed to be beating right into her throat. The Happy Plaice, with the strange-looking character thumping 'If You Were the Only Girl in the World' on a tinny piano was as romantic as any flower-scented conservatory.

'To take me to the station – or to come and help me choose rooms? You know what you are? You're what old Alice, bless her wrinkled stockings, calls a "funny ossity". But anything to oblige a lady, especially one who gives me more attention than she does her cod and chips. So, here goes. my dear, sweet Veronica, friend of my bosom, will you be so kind as to accompany me to the wicked city tomorrow, to make sure that I find a landlady who will spoil me rotten and be broad-minded about the hours I keep? You will come, Ron? We'll make it a day to remember.'

From the heights she plummeted.

A landlady . . .? But of course a landlady. If he took this position with the magazine he would need to go straight away, not wait until after they were married. A proper home would come later. 'We'll see when we get there. Perhaps I might rise to a small hotel even. You see the salary they're offering? Pretty good, eh? It's better even than I'd let myself hope.'

She had to play for time. The first step must be to make him wait until Monday before going to London.

'We can't go tomorrow. Don't you remember, we're all going to the Abbey tomorrow to hear the Fauré. Everyone has been looking forward to it.'

'You're joking! You can't expect me to believe that's what you'd rather do.'

'I've promised – we both promised. Anyway, yes I would rather. You may not have interested yourself enough to remember, but I played for the rehearsals. It *matters* to me how the performance goes. And I told Nicholas I'd be there in the front row; he'll be looking for me. London will still be there on Monday.' In keeping trust with her promise for the Fauré, somehow she seemed to strengthen herself for her fight ahead. The trouble was, her own heart was racing with the thought of a new life for them together in the bright lights of London. But she mustn't let herself stray down that road, she must hang on to the image of her father, lost and frightened. With a whole weekend to work on him, she must somehow make Laurence see things *her* way.

Laurence shrugged his shoulders. 'Ah well, to each his own. If you'd rather sit in that cheerless Abbey and watch your starchy friend than rattle around the metropolis with me, then that's your decision. But, Ron, the main thing is the station – you will drop me off there, won't you?' He looked at her with exaggeratedly innocent pleading, '*Please.* I've furled my umbrella to perfection and look a treat in my new bowler, don't make me turn up at the station on my jollopy. My train is at half past nine.'

'All right. Dad and I will drop you off on the way in to the office. I'll pick you up at your place at twenty past eight.'

'I needn't be quite that early.'

'If you come with us, you need.'

'Yes ma'am,' he grinned.

They finished their lukewarm fish and chips, something that needed all her fighting spirit. What chance had she of keeping him in Ottercombe? And how could she desert her father when he needed her? Then, surfacing through these thoughts came another she couldn't ignore: was it only in her imagination that she was part of his scheme for the future?

'It's so hard to pull up sticks and walk out on parents when you know they need you,' she went back to where the conversation had started. 'I know it's always possible to train someone – in my case I mean – but that wouldn't be what Dad wants. And I know your mother will be really miserable if she thinks you intend never to come back to work near Ottercombe.'

'She'll get used to the idea. She has friends – there's your people for a start. And you. I know you'll go and see her sometimes.'

'Of course I will, as long as I'm still here. But how long will that be?' With all her willpower she tried to make him tell her: 'No longer than it takes me to get settled and to find somewhere for us to be together.' She daren't look at him as she listened.

'As long as you're here! Ron, you're as much part of Ottercombe as the village green or the Abbey. You've always been there when I've come back. But, once I'm working, once I build a proper life for myself, all that will be different. I doubt if I'll get down to Devon much. But you – give you another year or so and I can see you married to some young man, slipping comfortably into bringing up your family in the village. And very nice too. Don't talk about leaving Ottercombe, I like to think of you always there, the same Ron I've always known still waiting for me when I come on holiday.'

She heard the words, but how could she answer in that same light tone that he'd spoken them? Perhaps it was pride that gave her the courage to try. 'This husband you've conjured up for me may have other ideas.' Only she heard how forced was her laugh. 'Come on, Laurence, we ought to be getting home. I have a few things to do, being out all the week has left me with a backlog.'

'Dear me, what a high-powered business woman she is!' he teased. 'Right you are, let's be off. It's an early start in the morning. I say, though, isn't it great the way things have turned out.'

She must have acted out her charade well; clearly he had no suspicion of her misery.

'We've had poor Ellen here with such a tale of woe,' Monica said when, the motor car shut away in the old coach-house, Veronica joined her. 'Well, I say "we". Nearer the truth, it's me who's been hearing it all. Your father took himself off to his study.'

'Tale of woe? You mean she's upset that Laurence doesn't mean to work in Deremouth? Of course he doesn't. After all, Mum, if that's what she'd wanted for him she ought not to have spent a fortune on having him educated for better things.' Was this how an actress felt as she worked herself into her role?

'You mean you're in favour of all this London nonsense? Oh, Ronnie, have you no care for the rest of us? I suppose the two of you have spent the evening plotting and planning your future. And if it hadn't been for poor Ellen, I should have been here all alone. Children! You bring them up, you give your life to them and all you get is being cast off like some outgrown garment.'

'Oh Mum,' and this time Veronica's laugh was spontaneous, 'I was only at the Happy Plaice! I wasn't gone more than a couple of hours. When did Mrs Chesterton leave? I didn't pass her, she must have been home before I lobbed Laurence off at his gate.'

'You must have had such a jolly evening, young and full of excitement on the brink of adventure. That's what's so sad, but you wouldn't even begin to understand what it's like to know that the good times are gone. For poor Ellen there's nothing to look forward to; all she has is Laurence. And for me, it's not so very different. Oh yes, I have a husband still, but all day and every day I'm here, I merge into the background, given the occasional glance, just like – just like – the grandmother clock in the hall.'

'Just because Dad remembered he had something to do in his study? Oh Mum, what a goose you are.'

'Not a goose! Calling me that makes it easy for you, I suppose.' Monica turned her head away, but from her voice it was clear she was either crying or, at best, on the verge of crying. 'You young ones will shake the dust of Ottercombe off your feet – and I'm not saying that's wrong, you know Ellen and I have always looked forward to the time you and Laurence were ready to marry. She said he'd been on tenterhooks all day, waiting for you to be free

47

from that silly office where you tinker about as if it's the thing for a young lady. She said he couldn't wait to see you, to talk to you about this appointment he's been offered. Couldn't you make him see that his place is near his mother? Or didn't you so much as try? London is hours and hours away . . .'

'He's been away for years. She never made this fuss then.' For Veronica it was second nature to champion Laurence.

'Fuss! That's what it is to you. And of course she knew she had to wait while he was at school and then at Oxford. But always she looked forward to when he came home. You wouldn't understand what it's like – nothing to look forward to.' Veronica suspected that she wasn't the only one playing a part. 'We've watched you as you grew up, eyes for no one but him. And him, always chasing around here after you the first moment he's home. Now if he goes to London, he'll be taking you away.' She let her tears fall unheeded, sinking into the indulgence of misery that Veronica felt was out of all proportion to the situation – even if what she suggested were true. 'And what about *me*?'

'What a romantic goose you are.' Surprisingly, her mother's dramatics were helping Veronica throw herself into the part she must play. 'Of course he rushed straight round here for me, he wasn't exactly spoilt for choice in the village. Mum, Laurence and I are very fond of each other. Brothers and sisters are fond of each other, but it doesn't mean that when one leaves the village the other expects to go too. Being in love must be quite different. We've known each other too long for all that stuff.'

'You mean that wasn't what he was so anxious to see you about? Ellen and I were so sure that when you came home you would tell us he had asked you to marry him.'

Veronica moved to look out of the window towards the unlit village green. 'As much part of Ottercombe as the village green . . .' his words echoed. 'Then you're a pair of romantics,' she answered her mother. 'Of course Laurence wants to spread his wings. He must have made a very favourable impression on that Mr Lansdale he wrote home about. Well, of course he did.'

'Oh dear, just look at me. My eyes must be red and ugly. I was so frightened. But believing you'd be going is only the half of it. He never talks to me like he used to. You've got to tell me, Ronnie: does he stay in the office or does he go off out? Is there some other woman?'

'You mean Dad? Oh Mum, how can you even think such a thing? There could never be another woman and you know it.'

'Don't know it. Don't know anything, anymore. I wish you were older, with a husband so that I could talk to you and expect you to understand.'

'What's being married got to do with it? Mum, promise me you'll never let Dad know you're worried. He'd be so hurt.' Ought she to say more? Ought she to tell her mother the things that worried her? But how could she when she'd promised to keep it from her? And in any case how could she explain what she couldn't understand?

'When we're here on our own, he runs away to hide in that study of his. Is he working? No. I've peeped at him through the keyhold. You see how low I've got! I've spied on him. And he's sitting there, sometimes his head in his hands, sometimes just sitting with his eyes closed. Doesn't want my company, Ronnie. Just running away.'

'Not from you, Mum.' But she might as well not have spoken.

'Different in bed. I shouldn't talk to you about these things. But there's no one else. Poor Ellen is alone, how can I tell her how hungry he is for – well, all that sort of thing. Yet, when he makes love to me it isn't because I'm *me*. I feel like a *thing*. I pretend I don't see any difference. But he doesn't care about me like he used to, I know he doesn't.'

Veronica knelt in front of her mother. 'That's not true. If there's a difference it's that he loves you more, wants you more.'

'I don't mean that sort of *want*. I tell you he used to make me feel like a queen. I don't mean just at bedtime, I mean always. He used to look at me, really see me. Now, if we sit here together, he pretends to be asleep – just *pretends*. It's only in bed he wants me – me? No, more likely something to tire himself out on so that he gets off to sleep. Oh hark at me, how can I talk like it to you, my own daughter? There's nothing in my life—'

'Don't be stupid.' There were limits to how long Veronica could listen to her mother indulging in self-pity. 'You always used to tell me to think of all the good things in my life. You're imagining a lot of nonsense.'

'There's nothing else for me. It's all very well for you, you go off each day full of your own importance. What does home mean to you or to him either? Somewhere to find your creature comforts. But what do either of you put into the home? Nothing. You don't understand. I feel drained. Is it a sin to want more?'

'I don't know what you want, Mum. Perhaps you'd find whatever it is if instead of waiting for him to fawn over you, you let him know you're lonely for his companionship.' She wished she hadn't said it, for it would be interpreted as misunderstanding, lack of care.

But she was wrong. The advice gave Monica's spirit the boost it needed. Sitting straighter, she rubbed her face with her tear-dampened handkerchief before she answered in a voice that had new strength.

'I can't do that. I never quarrel with him, you know I don't. I never refuse him, even though he behaves like a starving man faced with a plate of good food. But the warmth's gone. For both of us, I mean.'

'That's not true, Mum. He needs you more than he's ever needed you. Oh, why can't you see?'

'You and he have always been thick as thieves. I was a fool to try to talk to you. It was just – today just for a moment I glimpsed happiness. It unsettled me. But don't worry, I have myself in hand again. And tonight when I say my prayers, at least there is one thing I must be grateful for: Laurence isn't snatching you away. Fancy, all these years Ellen and I have been so certain – and all the time you say you were like brother and sister. But you'll miss him.'

'Oh, I don't know. I've probably outgrown the sort of fun we always had together. If anyone will miss him it will be his mother. He made me promise I would visit her often.' Her over-bright tone was lost on Monica, who was already standing up and straightening the cushions of her chair.

'I'm going on to bed,' she said. 'A little early, but I don't want your father to see how upset I've been. Tell him I have a bad head and wanted an early night. I'll try and be asleep by the time he comes up.' With the eagerness of an adolescent she climbed the stairs. If she weren't asleep, she meant to close her eyes and pretend. But in the meantime she would close her eyes and dream. The day had given plenty of grist for the mill of her imagination to work on.

Veronica was less keen to face the solitude of her room. With her mother safely despatched, she joined her father in his study knowing that Monica's fears would be nothing compared with his.

Consciously she was holding at bay the moment when she must face what Laurence's cheerful abandonment of her meant; in the meantime she looked for solace in the certainty of what her being with her father meant to him.

'You're happy, child?' He stood up from where he'd been sitting idly behind his uncluttered desk. 'London. That's what Ellen said. Song and dance they were making, the pair of them. I left them to it and came in here. You're happy, Ronnie child?' His over-bright voice didn't fool her.

'I expect I'll miss him, Dad. But he hasn't often been in Ottercombe and what's the difference whether he's in London or Oxford?'

'But *you*? You mean he's going ahead to get used to the new job. And very wise. A bride would be a distraction he can do without in the first months.'

'Dad, I'm not going to London. I'm not going anywhere.'

If she expected him to relax at her words, she was mistaken. That tic in his cheek was working overtime as he sank back into his chair and started beating a rhythmless tattoo on the desktop.

'I can't let you do that. I'd rather sell the business before I run it into the ground. What sort of a man am I that you're not free to make your own life?'

'I do make my own life, you never push me into doing what I don't want. You never have. Come on, Dad,' she forced a laugh, 'you sound as bad as Mum. Only in her case it was the other way round, she meant to persuade me to stay here. But you're both wrong. The idea of my being part of Laurence's schemes didn't come into it. I promised him we'd drop him off at the station when we go in to Deremouth in the morning. That's all right, isn't it? He's going to town to look for somewhere to stay.'

'I don't understand. Ellen said he'd been like a cat on hot bricks all day, waiting to see you, wanting to talk to you about your future. Silly woman, fussing so because he wants to let go of her apron strings. And quite right too. Quite right for the pair of you.'

'Perhaps it might have been, or perhaps it might not. I don't really see me as a stay-at-home wife, living in the shadow of his excitement. He'll do well, I'm sure he will. And of course he wanted to talk to me – we've always shared all our dreams. Yes, I expect I shall miss him. But our lives are busy, yours and mine, we haven't time to sit around and mope.'

51

There! That ought to put him at ease.

'I want you to answer me with the truth, the honest God-fearing truth, Veronica.'

'I don't lie to you, Dad.'

'Over this you might. That's why I want you to promise.'

'All right. You have my word. What's the question?'

'Did Laurence ask you to become engaged to him?'

She shook her head. 'No, Dad. It never entered his head that our parents seemed set on our getting tied up. So you're quite wrong if you think I refused a proposal so that I could stay at the bakery. He'd been away too much to see all those knowing glances between Mum and Mrs Chesterton. Let's forget it now. Promise, we won't talk about it anymore.'

By now the tic was stilled, his drumming fingers at rest on the desktop as he looked lovingly at her.

'What your prayers will be I don't know,' he said. 'But I can tell you what I shall say to my Maker tonight. I shall thank Him for delivering you from a future I'd never wanted for you. Charming, young Chesterton may be – and clever I don't doubt – but his mind will never have room for more than his own affairs. Bear that in mind, my dear. In time you'll learn to be as thankful as I am tonight.'

'You're not fair to him. I know him better than you do.'

'Take off your rose-tinted spectacles, Ron.'

'That's a beastly thing to say. Don't let's quarrel. I don't want to talk about it anyway. By the way, Mum's gone to bed. She'd worked herself into a headache, she said to tell you.' There was so much else she ought to say to him. But how could she? 'I was a bit worried about her, I think she feels out of things because you and I spend so much time together.' There, that ought to give him a push in the right direction. But, if one push wasn't enough, then she'd try another. 'She thinks you don't seem to see her, she was in quite a state. She even thought you'd got some other woman tucked away.'

'How could she think that?' He ran a hand through his hair. 'It's because – because—'

'No, don't talk to me. Talk to her. Make her understand. Dad, don't look like that!' It was as if every nerve in his body was alive, his hands trembled, his gaze went from side to side like a trapped animal looking for a way of escape.

'Can't talk to her. I told you – she mustn't guess. I'll get over it, isn't that what you said? It'll be all right.'

'Of course you will. But why don't you see the doctor, surely you can talk confidentially to him?'

'Old Doctor Morton? You think I should tell him?' She thought for a moment that he'd recovered, he sat quite still as he stared at some spot in the middle distance. But when he spoke it was as if she wasn't there. 'I fail myself, I fail her—'

'Talk to her Dad,' she cut in. She didn't want to hear. 'Whatever the reason, it's not important enough to come between you.' Then dropping a kiss on the top of his head, 'I'm off to bed. It's been quite a day.' He seemed oblivious to her going.

At any other time, her parents' problems would have been an honest worry for her. Shutting her bedroom door, she realised that on this night they had been a merciful barrier between her and the aching void that engulfed her. Sitting on the side of her bed she hugged her arms around her, bending forward as if she were in physical pain, rocking backwards and forwards.

Memories crowded in on her, memories that no longer held pleasure, comfort, excitement. She remembered the evening they'd danced, only a few months ago. She remembered how he'd kissed her, moved his hand up her stockinged leg and beyond, remembered how he touched her, remembered his hands tugging at her breast and how she'd thrilled to his touch, wanting more, wanting *him*. All the time he must have been experimenting, 'finding his way round', so that now when he gets to London and goes out with other girls he'll be like a man of the world. Laurence, her Laurence. Never coming home again for long summer months, never cycling with her through the country lanes, never telling her he loves her. Because he doesn't. He'd never even thought of her as someone to love, but just as a grown-up playmate, someone always there for him. Damn him! Damn, damn, damn him! No, I don't mean that. She sunk to her knees and for a moment she remembered what Herbert had said – that he would give thanks that she'd been saved from a future he'd not wanted for her.

'But I can't say that, not to You, You'd know it wasn't the truth. I wanted him *so much*. For years I've asked You, begged You, to make him love me. But You haven't. I should say "Your will be done". But I can't. Take care of him. Oh, but he'll see to that, him and that charm he brags about. I hate women who cry, I won't cry. But my heart's crying. You must know it is. Please, please – oh, why do I waste time even asking You when, all these years, You haven't listened or haven't wanted to help – but if I don't ask You, there's no one else. You see I don't know what to do, I feel like a ship that's lost its sail. And, if that's what I am, please send something to rescue me. I don't want to fall in love particularly, no I don't want to fall in love at all, it leaves you too vulnerable. And I love the work I do, honestly I do, for the sake of the business as well as helping Dad. Dad – now that's a real worry.' She sat back on her heels. Then, making a further effort, shut her eyes and again lowered her head onto the counterpane. 'I don't know what's wrong with him, if men go through a funny stage. But he needs help, the sort of help *I* can't give. Oh, I'll see he's all right at the bakery, but it's here at home things are worse than I realised. Mum ought to be able to help him, she ought to see that he needs help, but – well, I just don't understand. So please – and surely this shows I *do* still trust You, well I have to, there's no one else – please make them get through this rocky patch and both be happy. And Laurence's mother, help her to find a proper future that doesn't depend just on him. After all, that's just not fair of her. I suppose talking to You does help, it seems to have given me a feeling of hope. Hope? I don't even know what I'm hoping for. It's just I don't feel so sick with miserableness as I did. Perhaps thinking about Mum and Dad and knowing they have problems too has done me good.'

And perhaps it had. But her 'miserableness' was ready to swamp her when she finally lay in the darkened room. Prompted by memory she moved her hand up her leg, to her thigh, to her groin as he had that evening, and as she had so often in what she'd seen as the glorious privacy of her bed. It was a way she'd brought him close in those weeks he'd been away. But tonight her body mocked her. So often, in her imagination, the pillow she'd held close to her had become the warm weight of Laurence. The half-understood movements of her own hands had in some mysterious way been him, awakening desires that made her clench her teeth not knowing what it was that stayed always just beyond her reach. Tonight the spare pillow lay smooth and cool on the unused side of her double bed as she turned onto her front and pulled the covers over her head to muffle the sound of her misery.

The next morning she took extra pains with her appearance, she'd not give him the satisfaction of knowing what his going meant to her.

'If you meet me this evening when I get back, I'll tell you what I've found,' he told her, taking it for granted that she'd be waiting.

'It'll be the station cab for you tonight, I'm afraid. It's the Fauré, remember. And afterwards there's a supper at the Abbey.' If there was satisfaction to be found in anything, it must be in his look of disappointment.

Chapter Four

Pride had to be Veronica's salvation. Better by far to pretend to be amused that their mothers could have read a budding romance into what to Laurence and her had been nothing more than happy-go-lucky companionship. In acting out the part, surely it might ease the pain – and humiliation – of her ended dream.

'I can't understand it,' Ellen said as, ahead of Monica and Herbert, they walked towards the Abbey. She gripped Veronica's hand in a show of sympathy. 'Your mother says there is no thought of an engagement. But Veronica dear, you mustn't let yourself be cast down by the way he's leaving you. Be sure it's only until he is settled and feels he has a secure future to offer you. But why not *here*? Over and over I've asked myself. Did you try and persuade him, or are you keen to be off out there into the big world too?'

'I told him how much you'd looked forward to his being home, Mrs Chesterton. But we mustn't blame him. Of course he wants to test himself against more than he'd find in a small business in Deremouth. You'll see, it won't be long before you'll be buying the magazine and showing off to your friends. "Have you read this week's article by my son?" And as for me,' she gave the hand a friendly squeeze as if to give emphasis to her words, 'you and Mum seem to have been weaving dreams made of nothing more than cobwebs. Honestly, Laurence and I used to be playmates, now we've grown up into whatever you call grown-up play-mates.'

'We wanted it so much, your mother and me. It would have made us one family. There would have been children. But now he'll make a life somewhere else. I'm so alone, I get frightened to look ahead.'

'Friends or family, what's the difference? You've always got us, you know you have.' She heard the warmth in her voice, she listened to it as if it belonged to a stranger. 'We're getting ahead of Mum and Dad, we'd better hang back so that we arrive at the same time.'

'I hope we get seats together,' Ellen made an effort.

'Nicholas promised to keep us our places in the front row.' There would be five seats with cards on them saying they were reserved. Where was Laurence now? Had he found a landlady ready to fall for his charms? Or perhaps a room in a commercial hotel? Would he come tomorrow and tell her all about his day? Yes, of course he would; he'd take it for granted that she would be as pleased to be with him as she always had been. Always there for him ... as certain as Ottercombe Green. Don't think about the things he said, just remember that you and he are like brother and sister ... no brother would kiss a sister like he did me, no brother would touch a sister ... and no sister would almost beg for more like I did. As if to wipe away the haunting memory, she squared her shoulders, then turned and smiled at Monica and Herbert who'd fallen some way behind as they waited for a further figure she recognised as Hugo Holmes to catch up with them. She hadn't seen him since the tennis party at the beginning of summer but even at this distance he was easily recognisable. As was customary, Herbert wore a dark suit, white shirt, black bowler hat and carried grey gloves; for the men in the audience – or, Veronica wondered, as the performance was in the Abbey, were they a congregation? – this would be like a uniform, or so she had supposed. But Hugo Holmes proved her wrong. As the three came closer, she could see that the material of his dark blue suit was velvet, and his wide-brimmed felt hat a pale fawn; closer still, and she had no doubt the powder-blue shirt was fine silk. The colour scheme was thrown by a loosely knotted magenta and white polka-dot neckerchief. Most men might have looked vaguely ridiculous or, at best, self-conscious in such an attire. But Hugo wore his clothes with ease, unaware that his unusual garb was causing nods, smirks and raised eyebrows. Today of all days Veronica envied him his self-assurance and disregard for other people's opinions. For herself, she was determined not to let a chink show in her armour.

'I'm glad you've joined us,' she told him with the sort of grace Monica had tried, not always successfully, to instil in her.

57

'Nicholas promised to keep us five seats, one of them for Laurence who won't be coming.' And, sure enough, there were the five reserved cards just as she'd expected.

Nicholas must have been watching for them. 'I shall look for you – please be there,' she remembered his words. Could it have been only the day before yesterday? It was as if her life had been thrown onto another track ... the day before yesterday had belonged to 'when I believed Laurence loved me'. Then, like a train hurtling over the points, being diverted onto another and unfamiliar line, there was the present without him, a future with no shape, a time when dreams were a mockery.

'I'm glad you came,' Nicholas's voice startled her. 'Is your young friend not with you?'

'He had to go to London.' How bright she sounded, her mouth turning into a smile that matched her tone. 'You should feel flattered: he wanted me to go with him, but I told him I wanted to hear the Fauré.'

'Given the choice, that would have been my decision too. We must see you're not disappointed.' Then he moved along the row, his manner polite, formal, and courteously old-fashioned as he spoke to her parents, then to Ellen and finally Hugo. He was thoroughly part of the 'adult world', something, she realised, that was true of neither Laurence nor her. But that had been during that other part of her life. In the last forty-eight hours she'd come a long way.

'What a striking man he is,' Monica whispered to her. 'Tails look so well on a tall figure like that. I do wish you'd joined the Abbey Singers, dear Ronnie,' still a whisper, but this time it wasn't simply that they were used to being quiet in the Abbey, the hushed tone implied secrecy, 'last night I was very naughty. I'm sad for poor Ellen of course, but all those other things I said – things about myself, I mean – I want you to forget all about them.'

'They're forgotten.' And, for the moment, that was almost the truth. This evening her mother showed no sign of disappointment either in her own life or anyone else's. A walk to the Abbey to hear Fauré's Requiem could hardly count as a wildly exciting social outing, but it was enough to light lamps of pleasure behind her eyes and bring a ready smile to her pretty face. Looking at her, Veronica was conscious of a pang of remorse for her own all-too-often irritation with her mother's tales of woe. Then, leaning forward in her seat, she looked beyond to her father, thankful that there was no sign of tension; his hands rested on his knees, there was no agitated drumming of his fingers. She leant back in the none-too-comfortable wooden pew, waiting for the Singers to assemble on the raised platform that had been built in front of the chancel and for Nicholas to mount the rostrum which was so close to her seat that she could almost reach out and touch him.

Applause for the Singers, for Howard Humphreys the organist, the small string ensemble, the soloists and finally for Nicholas. He stood poised, his baton raised, his glance on the players with their bows ready, their eyes on him. In the Abbey there wasn't a sound. And then the silence was broken, Veronica closed her eyes as they listened to the solemn beauty of the opening bars. How different it was from the accompaniment she had played. Her mind jumped back over the months to the first evening she'd come here. She wanted to hang on to the memory of those practices; somehow, in a way she didn't try to understand, that helped to keep her misery at bay.

The performance of the Requiem was a resounding success. Hearty applause was assured from members of the audience there to support family or friends amongst the Abbey Singers, but many of those who filled the pews weren't local. Nicholas Ellis's appointment had created interest from Exeter to Plymouth – even amongst music lovers as far away as Bath. Add to his own reputation the fact that he'd arranged for the well-known Winterton String Quintet to join the newly formed choir, and Ottercombe was host to a rare amount of visitors on that Saturday evening.

Performers and their close associates were invited to supper in the Abbey refectory afterwards and it was there that Veronica noticed Nicholas in a long and serious conversation with Ellen Chesterton. From there he was waylaid by the music critic from the *Western Evening Star* while, hovering in close proximity and clearly hoping they might manage to get into the background of the photograph that was being set up, were one or two ladies of the choir.

'What an exciting evening it is!' With her bottom lip caught between her teeth, Monica beamed her delight in all she saw. Watching her, Veronica remembered the tearful woman of the previous evening and the conversation she'd been told to forget.

How could such abject misery have given way to joy like this, when in truth nothing of her life had changed? 'What a good thing you helped him with the rehearsals, dear,' she squeezed her daughter's hand. 'That must be why we've been invited amongst all these important people. Oh, look, there's dear Dr Hardy coming to speak to us. Don't you just wish you had an extra hand, what with a plate in one and a glass in the other. Stand-up eating makes it so very difficult to greet ones friends.' But she overcame the problem by offering her cheek to the elderly organist who'd been their friend for so many years.

The large, stone-walled room rang with conversation; as Monica had said, it was an exciting evening, exciting enough that for her there was no longer any underlying unhappiness. Yet for Veronica, no matter how she tried to absorb the atmosphere, constantly her thoughts romped out of hand and were with Laurence. She pictured him, smart and debonair, charming the owner of a guesthouse; she pictured him strolling across Westminster Bridge – the place that had left the clearest memory from her one and only day in the capital.

'I was just telling Mr Ellis how sad we all are,' Ellen Chesterton moved to join them. 'He was surprised to hear that Laurence is going.'

'Yes, I suppose he would be,' Veronica answered, her voice casual. 'Although they hardly know each other. I wonder how his trip's gone – Laurence's trip I mean. I do hope he finds good digs.'

'No one will look after him like he'd be looked after at home. I mustn't talk about it. I mustn't spoil our nice evening.'

'No son stays home for ever,' Veronica defended him. 'No daughter either. We all grow up.'

'Easy for you to say that, you're not a mother yet. Wait until you are and you'll begin to understand. Why couldn't he have been content for the two of you to marry and stay here?'

Despite Veronica's resentment of the implication, mirth got the upper hand.

'What a future to force on us! And even if we'd wanted to, what makes you think he would have cuddled up under your wing if I were his wife? Not likely. You'd never find me marrying a man who didn't stand on his own two feet.'

'No, dear. But you're like a dear daughter to me already. We would have been all one happy family.'

It was a situation that had never occurred to Veronica as she'd dreamed her dreams.

'Veronica,' Nicholas's voice cut across her thoughts, 'how did it compare with our rehearsals?'

'It was beautiful. I don't know enough to give a useful criticism, but there were moments that sent shivers up my spine, they were so – so – spiritual.'

He nodded. 'I'd ask for no more learned opinion. May I have a word?' By which they all knew he meant a word on their own. Tonight she was acting a role, there was a quiet dignity even in her movement as she inclined her head in agreement and led the way to a less crowded part of the room.

'Yes?' she prompted.

'It's nothing very secret. But I didn't want to risk being rejected within hearing of your family. I have to go to Exeter on Tuesday. My business won't take above ten minutes and then I shall be free. I wish you'd come with me. We could have lunch. Will you come? Please.'

Tuesday ... the last day of the month ... the day Laurence would be finally leaving Ottercombe and would take it for granted she would be on hand to take him to the station.

'I'd like that, Nicholas.' Then the cloak of 'grown-up dignity' slipped as she remembered her other commitments.

'What is it? Something to do with young Chesterton?'

'Gracious no. He's starting his new job on the first of the month. Did his mother tell you? That's why he asked me to go to London with him today, to help him choose somewhere to live. I expect he thought I'd be a better judge of landladies than he would.'

'Yes, Mrs Chesterton told me. So, if it's not whether or not he'll have need of your services, what then?'

'It's never been like that with Laurence and me, I've told you that before.'

'So you have.' Was he laughing at her? How was it he could so easily put her at a disadvantage? 'So, if it's not him, what else could be the problem?'

'I can't talk about it here.' Here? But surely she couldn't talk about it at all. 'Dad depends on me in the office each day, we each have our own responsibilities. I'd have liked to come, Nicholas, honestly I would. But – I can't explain – just accept my word, can't you? I don't want to let him down.'

It was always impossible to guess what Nicholas was thinking. She felt he was reading her mind.

'Exeter or Deremouth . . . lunch or dinner . . . you tell me when you could be free. I don't care where we go or even what we eat. I want to take you out – away from the practice room, away from Ottercombe and the shadow of the Abbey.' It wasn't that Nicholas never smiled; often he did, when courtesy demanded. But she realised listening to him and watching his serious expression, it was his lack of a smile that gave weight to what he said.

'Thank you. Day times aren't easy, but if we can find a suitable evening, I'd like to come.' She heard her voice as that of a well-behaved child and his teasing reply did nothing to put her at her ease.

'Ah yes, as I recall you made it quite clear a long time ago that you have a full and busy life.'

'If I sounded rude, I'm sorry. No, that's not true. I wanted to be rude, I thought it was what you deserved. I was angry at the letter you sent me, you sounded so – so – condescending, so bumptious.'

'And now?'

'I expect we've come to know each other better.'

'Indeed we have. So what about Tuesday evening? I'll make a reservation at the Royal Court.'

It was balm to her wounded spirit, let alone her wounded pride, to have her company sought by a man of Nicholas's stature. If her heart was bruised, she didn't mean anyone should be given a chance to suspect it.

Until that Tuesday evening, Veronica had never been to the Royal Court, a hotel in an isolated cliff top position beyond Chalcombe, the coastal village on the far side of Deremouth. With a clientele drawn from an affluent and middle-aged section of society, it was a far cry from the youthful, carefree fun of cod and chips at the Happy Plaice. It wasn't in her nature to be impressed by the trappings of wealth but, knowing where she was being taken, she dressed with natural eager anticipation on the Tuesday evening. Monica added encouragement, deriving pleasure even at second hand from imagining what it must be like to be stepping for the first time into a scene of such adult luxury. She fastened the buttons at the back of Veronica's closely fitting, knee-length dress, revelling in the up-to-the-minute cut of the sea-green satin creation with its matching bandeau.

'Shall I lend you my pearls?' She more than offered, she almost pressed them on her daughter.

'I'm not the sort for necklaces, Mum. I'd love to wear your earrings, the tear-drop ones, if you'd let me borrow them.'

'Yes, of course I will. They need an outing. Pearls should be worn, they aren't happy being shut away in a case. But these days your father and I never seem to go anywhere. Still, never mind that. I'll go and get them – and the brooch to pin in your headband. What fun!' Her pleasure must have been infectious, for by the time Nicholas arrived, handsome in his silk braided dinner jacket, stiff dicky, evening waistcoat, the cuffs of his shirt fastened with ruby links, Veronica felt like Cinderella going to the ball.

The difference between an evening with Nicholas and an evening with Laurence could hardly have been greater. Determined to make the outing a success, not once did she let her mask of enjoyment slip. There was nothing to hint that Laurence was constantly there, a shadow across her mind.

For weeks she'd played a game with Nicholas, encouraging him, getting pleasure from the knowledge that she had the power to attract him. Yet on that evening her smile had nothing to do with kindling the flames she'd found such dangerous fun. Instead, his attentions were somehow comforting, she saw him as an ally. By the time they reached the third course she found herself explaining her feeling of responsibility for helping her father.

'You won't always be there. Wouldn't the kindest thing be to suggest you looked for a manager?'

'Oh, but I couldn't do that! That would be like telling him he couldn't manage. And anyway, I'm not likely not to be there.' The ghost of Laurence was standing at her shoulder. 'I think he's going through a bad patch. He'll get back to being like he always was.'

'Supposing he doesn't? Supposing you want to marry?'

'Supposing nothing of the kind! Most of the time he's not frightened, it's just something that seems to hit him. And me – I'm not thinking of marrying. You sound as bad as our parents, always trying to push Laurence and me into romance.'

'Believe me, that's something I could never do. You know my feelings – about him – about you.'

She was out of her depth. What was she doing here, adorned with her mother's jewellery, aping a sophistication she didn't possess? In that moment she envied the middle-aged and elderly diners round them, all sure of themselves, certain of their place. Nicholas was watching her and, she suspected, recognising her discomfort.

'My earrings are Mum's.' There was no logic in her saying it, yet she couldn't stop herself. It seemed to put a necessary barrier between her youth and inexperience and his tested and tried confidence.

'You look enchanting in them. But, my Veronica, you would look equally enchanting without them. Come, we're becoming too serious. I have something to ask you: Beethoven's *Missa Solemnis* is being sung on Wednesday evening next week in the Cathedral. Perhaps you already know it – but if you don't you've been missing a great experience, one I'd like us to share. I intend to go to Exeter. Can I hope that you'll come with me?' His manner, so formal and yet so personal, only added to her confusion. 'It commences at seven o'clock so we should have to be away from Ottercombe quite by six. Would that be possible?'

'Yes, of course. Dad isn't incapable, you know.' She heard her answer as unmannerly as his had been correct. 'I'm sorry, Nicholas. That sounded rude, I didn't mean it to.' Then with a smile that transformed her into her usual honest self, 'I have heard the *Missa Solemnis* ages ago, when I was quite small, so you see that's one of life's great experiences I haven't been deprived of.'

'Even if I can't have the pleasure of introducing you to it, I still hope you'll share it with me.'

A few months ago she would have thought what a dry stick he was.

'I'd like that. Thank you,' she told him and was rewarded by a smile that somehow made her forget her previous feeling of inadequacy.

That evening drew a final line under Veronica's past, a faint line at first but one that with every passing week became firmer. One or two postcards came to her from Laurence: a picture of the Tower of London with a scrawled message on the back that he was taking the big city by storm. Then, later, one of Trafalgar Square: 'This is the life! Sometimes I wonder how the mag managed before I came!!'

64

Had he still the same power to hurt her? The question presented itself often enough, but rather than answer it she pushed it away. In reply she sent the usual seaside view cards of Deremouth: 'Went to concert in Town Hall with Nicholas. Lovely. Then on to the Royal Court,' she wrote in November intending to impress him. But by the end of the year her mind wasn't on Laurence. Nicholas's courtly attendance, her certainty of the passion waiting to be unleashed, were her first thought in the mornings and her last at night.

'First Laurence couldn't get here for Christmas, and now he's written that he won't be coming for the New Year,' Ellen told Monica. 'What a dreadful year this has been. I shall be glad to see the end of it. Not that the next will be any better.'

'Yes, it will, Ellie. You'd let yourself build too much on having Laurence living in Ottercombe. And not just *you*. She won't admit to it, but so did Veronica, of that I'm quite sure.'

'I can't see any sign of her pining away,' Ellen said, in a voice laden with criticism as if she considered Veronica disloyal in not wearing a broken heart on her sleeve. 'If she were *my* daughter, I'd be concerned at the time she spends alone with Nicholas Ellis. What does she know of the ways of men? Her only tutor has been Laurence – and I'd stake my life there was nothing *like that* in his behaviour.'

'I'm sure there wasn't, they were like brother and sister,' Monica answered tartly, 'and as for Mr Ellis, he's a perfect gentleman.'

'There's no such thing. Your life has been so sheltered, Monica, you and Herbert have always had each other. Didn't you tell me yourself he was your first sweetheart? Well, I think that's lovely. It's what I hoped for for our two young ones, you know that. But I've seen more of men than you have, don't forget I was the wife of a naval officer until I lost him. And I might just as well have lost Laurence too, for all I shall see of him.'

'Nonsense. He'll come back when he has time off. And think of the good time you'll have when you go to see him in London. He's doing so well, it won't be long before he has an apartment of his own so that you can stay with him sometimes.' Monica put her arm around the friend she was so fond of. 'You've got us, you'll never need to feel alone. Why, you and I are like family to each other.'

Ellen nodded, but her cloud of misery didn't lift.

'Like family isn't the same as being proper family. It seems so unfair. You can't know what it's like to feel alone. No friend, even a dear friend like you, is the same as someone truly belonging – even a relative you don't particularly care for.'

'You've just got the blues, Ellie. It's this miserable murky day, it's enough to make anyone see the gloomy side of things.'

'That depends on whether there is a gloomy side. For you there isn't. And I'm happy for you, I pray it'll always last for you. And why shouldn't it? The way things are looking between Veronica and Mr Ellis, either he'll soon speak to Herbert or else he's a lecher if ever I saw one.'

Monica laughed. 'What a thing to say,' she chuckled. 'He's charming and, like I said, never less than a perfect gentleman. Veronica has always been a girl to keep her own counsel, but I do believe she is in love with him. And you think he is with her?'

'I didn't say that. I can't read his mind – and I believe sometimes it's as well we can't.'

'Well, if he *is* in love with her, of course his mind must be running along the sort of lines you suggest – you know what I mean. I do hope he isn't too old for her. I mean, at his age I dare say he's had experiences before. Oh, why couldn't those two silly children of ours have wanted each other. So clean and wholesome, both of them finding out about that sort of love for the first time together.'

'In our days that may have been true. But the young today are different, you can tell from the way they behave. What is it they call those fast young minxes, flappers I think I read in the newspaper.' Then, there in the room by themselves, she leant closer and whispered, 'They know too much, some of them. Have you read the latest in the local paper? Local, mind you, not London or the back streets of some big city, but here in our own Deremouth: they've opened a Family Planning Clinic. The paper says it's somewhere where young women can go to find ways of preventing getting pregnant. Safe birth control, they call it. There! What do you think of that?'

'How different everything was when we were young. It was that dreadful war that put a cloud on everything. But surely, they'd only help married women? I dare say there are plenty whose husbands expect them always to be willing?'

'I expect so. But you may be sure that'll just be the thin end of the wedge.'

'You say it's in the local paper? I didn't notice it.'

'On the back page. Not that it's of any interest to me.' Her eyes filled with sudden tears. 'If only it were.'

'Poor Ellie,' Monica took her friend's hand and rubbed it against her cheek. 'I'm sure your Vincent is watching over you.'

'It's not a ghost I yearn for. Sometimes I lie in bed and hug the bolster in my arms, pretending . . .' She looked at Monica hoping for understanding and finding an expression she couldn't fathom. Perhaps she'd said too much. Sex was a taboo subject in respectable households. 'When Vincent was at sea and Laurence just a little lad, I used to encourage him to creep into my bed. A warm human being, someone who loved me and needed me.'

This time Monica's smile was tender, she was on safe ground. For not to *anyone*, not even her dearest friend, could she bring herself to confide. There had been that night a few months ago when they'd learnt that Laurence was going away and she'd believed that meant they were to lose Veronica. She'd not been sure afterwards quite how much she'd let her tongue run away with her, whether it was only in her mind she'd found relief in admitting how empty her life had become. Herbert was so changed. Passion used to be an outlet for love but now how different he was. Was the fault with her? He must be as he always had been at the bakery or Veronica would show concern. Yet in the bedroom it was as if every nerve in him was taut, ready to snap; he was a mass of nervous energy. Every night was the same, even those times when it probably wasn't healthy and certainly wasn't decent, he was demanding; then, physically exhausted, he'd turn away from her in sleep leaving her frightened and alone. By morning he would be almost his old self, almost but not quite. Remember how this morning, when he'd brushed his hair he had opened his handkerchief drawer not to take a handkerchief but to tidily re-arrange the stack, then carefully place his hairbrush alongside. Where could his mind have been? When she'd chided him, he'd blustered, he'd told her he knew exactly what he was doing and would she please stop watching his every movement.

If she once started to confide in Ellen, Monica knew the flood-gates would be open, there would be no holding back her fears. Fears that the way he was behaving came from something far worse than 'wool-gathering' and, even more pressing, fears that he would make her pregnant. Please God, no. He was always so careful, so caring of me. Now I seem to be no more to him than a female body. But that isn't always true, even now there are happy times. I must just hang on to that, and I must trust that this is just a phase. It might be just that he's frightened of growing older, frightened of losing his manhood and wanting to prove himself. Oh dear, why do people have to be so difficult? If he were really getting funny in the head, then Veronica couldn't be with him each day and not see the signs. If only he'd remember to be careful – and he never gives it a thought unless I remind him – I expect I'd welcome his needing me like he does. Wouldn't it be harder if he just got into bed and went to sleep? As it is I'm like a piece of familiar furniture in the house. Like Ellen says – or more truthfully, what she meant but didn't like to actually *say* was how empty a life is with no one to make love to you. Yes, I'm lucky, I have husband wild for me and a daughter who appears to be going to marry and settle nearby.

She smiled fondly at Ellen. There was nothing to show her thoughts were turning to the back page of the *Deremouth News*, a cloud suddenly lifted from her future.

Since their first evening at the Royal Court, Veronica's treatment of Nicholas had subtly changed. Playing with fire had been a fascinating sport, or so she'd liked to believe in those early days of their acquaintance. Following that evening, he filled a different but increasingly necessary role: if her heart wasn't broken by Laurence's departure, certainly it was badly bruised and Nicholas was her consolation. No longer did he talk to her about her 'young friend', it was as if Laurence had never existed. And that was the way she wanted it as she built an impenetrable wall between the past and the present. First she accepted his invitations as a salve to the hurt Laurence had inflicted, vowing that never again would she be naïve and vulnerable. Certainly her relationship with Nicholas changed as she accepted his invitations willingly, using his wanting her with him as a way to find consolation. If she'd been naïve in the past, she was no less so now as she honestly expected that with Nicholas she could take her own solace, be the one to call the tune and yet not expect the piper to demand payment. But the price she would have to pay became increasingly evident: handsome, confident, talented, authoritative, her half-recognised admiration for him became obsessive. To her it was a new experience.

It was the twenty-eighth of December, a damp, unseasonally muggy evening, when she propped her bicycle against the wall of the Abbey and pushed open the heavy Norman door. The boys from the choir school had gone home immediately after the service on Christmas morning, but would be returning in time for the Watch Night service. They wouldn't be singing an anthem, for that last hour of the old year Nicholas wanted something different. And that's why Veronica was there. Alone except for his organ accompaniment she, who'd lacked the confidence to let him test her for the Abbey Singers, was to sing Mozart's *Ave Maria*. This service had become an important event at the Abbey, the ancient building which had stood through many new years as century followed century.

Closing the door silently she moved as quietly as she could up the side aisle until she reached the stairs to the organ loft where Nicholas was playing. He must have been aware of her approach, for he was already watching the opening at the head of the stairway as she appeared. He didn't stop playing, he didn't even smile a welcome, yet his silent, serious expression drove everything else from her mind. She stood quite still, it was as if she had no power to move. There was nothing but the two of them, drawn together by the closing bars of the Bach fugue; coherent thought seemed beyond her.

Today had been difficult at the bakery, her father had appeared unable to hold his concentration for two minutes at a time and had needed her constant supervision without suspecting that she was watching him. She'd decided to send Nicholas a note telling him she couldn't come, but her mother had persuaded her there was no need to worry.

'Of course you must go,' Monica had assured her. 'Herbert's just tired, Christmas is a busy time. You can't disappoint Nicholas – really he is as keen as ever dear Dr Hardy was that you should sing.' Then with a knowing smile (smile? nearer a smirk), 'And I believe I know why he's so interested. Such an asset to the village. As I said to Ellie only this morning, Nicholas Ellis is a perfect gentleman.'

With a face void of expression, Veronica had ignored the coy innuendo. Monica knew the course her own evening would take:

Herbert would sleep by the fireside, or perhaps he would read aloud pieces of interest from the morning's paper as he often did when Veronica was out. He had no idea that in one short evening he would repeat the same snippet three or four times. This evening even the knowledge of how her hours would be spent didn't depress her. She had other things on her mind, things that made it easy to smile. The bus service to Ottercombe was poor, but once each morning and once each afternoon Mr Jarvis from the old coach-house took what was known as 'his rattletrap' to Deremouth, waited an hour in Station Approach and then brought the shoppers home. This afternoon she had been aboard, the cutting from the back page of the *Deremouth News* in her purse.

Behind Veronica, the dimness of the Abbey was eerie; the shadowy emptiness was filled with sound from the great organ. Then there was nothing but silence as the music ended and Nicholas swung his legs over the long stool and stood up. With his back to the stark electric light that shone on the music, his eyes looked uncannily dark, the face she'd thought handsome was changed by shadows. She couldn't lower her gaze. As he stood still, it was she who moved closer, slowly and deliberately ... closer ... drawn by a power stronger than her own until, when they were only inches apart, she raised her face to his. So often the memory of that evening in the practice room had haunted her, but now when he crushed her against him and his mouth found hers she had no memories nor yet any thoughts of the future. She was like a drowning man going down for the third time, like a person sinking into the quicksand.

'You'll be my wife,' he whispered. 'You must have known it as surely as I have.' Thoughts she might have had of a romantic proposal on bended knee paled to insignificance beside the urgency in his tone.

'Yes. It's what I want.' She was excited by his impatience, it echoed the hunger in her that had nothing to do with a conventional engagement while she collected a 'bottom drawer' and dreamed of the future.

It surprised her that a moment like this he should expect them to practise her performance of *Ave Maria* and yet, as she sang she felt it was an offering of thanksgiving for all that she had. Nicholas loved her; living with him at the Master's Lodge she would always be the support her father increasingly needed; the future stretched ahead, golden and cloudless. Thank You, thank You, her heart sang as their music seemed to her to reach to the heavens.

Walking back to Ipsley House, she tried to put some of her thoughts into words.

'I never knew I could be so – so full of joy – so sure of the future. It's almost frightening,' she said as she clung to his hand. 'Supposing you'd been at one of the other big choir schools, supposing I'd had to choose between *us* and being loyal to Dad? No, don't even think about it.'

'Loyal to your father?' he queried.

'Blakeney's, I mean. Married to you I shall still be here, he'll know he can still depend on me.'

In the darkness Nicholas raised his eyebrows, surprised at what she said. What a child she was. As if working at the bakery would still matter to her once she was his wife.

Perfect gentleman as Monica had said, that same evening he asked Herbert to spare him a few moments alone. Within two or three minutes they were back in the drawing room, Herbert pouring sherry wine to toast their happiness.

'What a joyous day!' he beamed. 'Ronnie to make her home in Ottercombe! The answer to our prayers, eh, Monica my love?' The tic in his cheek was working, his eyes had that strange look that didn't settle on anything long enough to focus.

'A joyous day, indeed, sir, a day I've wanted above all others,' the perfect gentleman assured them.

Veronica straightened an ornament on the mantelpiece. She didn't want to listen to their over-hearty tones, she wanted just to remember those moments in the organ loft.

71

Chapter Five

'I'll come to the gate.' Veronica grabbed a coat from the hall-stand and threw it around her shoulders, sure that her mother would be listening to every word, delighting in the introduction of romance into the dull routine of the home she often saw as a prison.

'Put your arms in the sleeves, it's cold out there,' Nicholas held it for her then, for a second, drew her close, his hands on her shoulders, her back against him. Not a word of the emotion he felt, yet his silent action said it all. Then, collecting his hat and cane, he opened the front door for her.

'All these months,' she said, taking his hand in hers as they walked towards the gate, 'and that evening ages ago, the things you said to me then. Why couldn't I have seen? I knew I wanted to be with you, I believed that was because it made me feel better about Laurence.'

'Never mind about young Chesterton. He has no part in your life, nor ever could have. What is between you and me is bigger than a girl's stupid infatuation, bigger than all we've shared over the last months.' By now he was outside on the cobblestoned pavement, the gate pushed to between them.

'Bigger than your music?' She wanted to hear him say it for, surely, music was the guiding light in his life. She looked up at him, trying to read his thoughts and excited by the intensity of his expression in the clear bright moonlight of the frosty night.

'What I feel for you consumes me. You are my first thought in the morning, my last at night. I see you in every note I play.' Across the closed gate he took both her hands in his. 'I've wanted *you* since the first time I came to this house – to a tennis party, remember?'

'The first day of summer, that's how I thought of that day. You and Dad beat Laurence and me. No one had done that before.'

She wasn't sure whether she read tenderness or triumph in his smile as he answered, 'Then it was an event waiting to happen.' Letting go of her hands he reached across the gate to wrap her unbuttoned coat more tightly round her. 'You must go in, my Veronica. I see your mother watching around the side of the curtain. She's waiting for me to kiss you goodnight, romance battling with decorum.'

'Over the gate?'

He raised her hand and kissed the palm.

'I'm not built for this sort of courtship ... discrete kisses monitored by an anxious parent. I want you, I want to know every inch of your body, every thought in your mind.'

Hardly knowing what she did, she nodded. This evening's discovery had brought into context the strange yearning, the desires that so often led her to follow nature's half-understood way to fulfilment only to leave her lonely and unsatisfied. Soon it wouldn't be like that. Loving would have no mysteries. Her throat felt tight, her heart was racing.

'I want it too, I want to come home with you now, tonight,' she whispered. In the light of her strait-laced upbringing which had been in keeping with the times, she knew that what she said would be heard as shocking. And she was glad. It was just one more thing that made this wonderful evening stand apart from everything that had gone before it. 'That's how I want us to love – all that you are, all that I am.'

'And so we shall. How long does it take to arrange a wedding? A month? You don't want fuss. How do I know that? Because I know you, my Veronica.'

'I just want you and me. And Mum and Dad of course. There in the Abbey.'

'Fix the date with your people – and soon. I'll sort out the licence. What about the end of January? I'll get my brother-in-law to be best man.'

His last remark brought her back to earth.

'You've never said you have a family. You mean you have a sister?'

'I have four,' he told her as if the information was of no importance, 'all of them so much older than me that we might have been two families. The eldest is married and living in South Africa, the next two single and I imagine likely to remain so, one's a teacher in Scotland, the other matron of an orphanage in the north. Then there's Beth, she's near enough to expect to come to the wedding I dare say – Winchester. I never see any of them, haven't for years. We never had much in common. I was a late shock. There's a fifteen-year gap between us. Hardly makes for companionship when you're young. We send Christmas cards, that's about all. But Beth has two girls, they're an age who would like to be brides-maids I suppose. I don't know much about these things. Anyway, fix the date and I'll get in touch with them.'

Out there in the bitterly cold, clear winter night, it seemed so easy. But Veronica had her mother's views to contend with. The joy of a wedding was the planning, the preparing of a trousseau, dealing with caterers, all things she had so looked forward to when she and Ellen had looked ahead with confidence.

'Planning a daughter's wedding should be such joy,' she bemoaned to Herbert. 'And what are people going to think when they want a hole in the corner affair like this? There's no earthly reason for them to give rise to such gossip, they could wait until, say, June. A lovely time of year for a wedding.' She ought not to talk like to Herbert. Lately it had become habit that she protected him from anything bordering on a worry, knowing the state he could get into. But on that occasion she was beyond caring. It wasn't fair: she was to be deprived of a proper wedding for her daughter and she was even deprived of a partner to share her disappointment.

'If they want a winter wedding, Monica my dear, then I think we should be agreeable. In truth we should be on our knees thanking our Maker that we aren't going to lose her. Nicholas Ellis wouldn't have been my choice for her—'

'That's what you always said of dear Laurence. The truth is you're jealous of not being first in her affections.'

Ignoring her comment, he said. 'I think we should go along with what they want. He's not a man to be thwarted. If we make them wait, then who's to say he wouldn't persuade her not to.'

'She's argumentative enough without any help from him.'

'That's not what I had in mind. It could happen, you know. They have time enough on their own – practising music they say. Deny them marriage and you're risking grounds for more gossip. That's my opinion.'

'Oh but she *wouldn't*. How could you even think such a thing? Oh dear, whyever couldn't she and dear Laurence have fallen in love. We shouldn't have had these sort of worries with him.'

'Or Ellis might find another way to spite us. He might look for another post, somewhere away from the area. He was a prize for the Abbey to win. Lose him and we'd lose Ronnie. No, no, we mustn't. No, no, not that . . .' His mouth was working, his fingers were beating a tattoo on his knees and, although he seemed unaware of it, he was making a strange sort of moaning, whimpering sound.

Monica looked away. She couldn't bear the sight of what had happened to him. But it was on that evening that she started drawing up a guest list and wording an invitation to be taken to the printers in Deremouth.

Although it wasn't the wedding Monica had enjoyed looking forward to for her daughter, she took consolation from the fact that it was undoubtedly Ottercombe's wedding of the year – probably Ottercombe's and Deremouth's too. That the daughter of one of Deremouth's best-known businesses was to marry the recently appointed, and locally publicised, Master of the Abbey Choir School gave a fillip of interest in the community. Added to that was the fact that his introduction into the district had raised many a mother's hopeful expectations; undoubtedly he was recognised as 'a good catch'.

'A match made in heaven,' was the opinion of Matilda de Vere, an ageless eccentric who lived in an ancient ivy-clad longhouse on the edge of Picton Heath and presumably made some sort of living from her talent which took her in various directions according to her mood. She painted watercolours which, when she'd collected enough to be worth her while, she pushed in a truck to Deremouth Market. Occasionally she'd write a poem which, for payment of a pittance, would be published in the *Deremouth News*, and a beautifully painted sign nailed to her garden gate announced that she had the gift of prophecy and was available to read palms. Monica had heard it said that when her spirit moved her she would drift off into what the more gullible believed to be a trance and paint a word picture of what the future held in store for them. A palm reading was four pence; a trance came dearer and rumour had it that the deeper look into the future could cost as much as a shilling. If the bread and butter of her existence came from re-trimming hats or re-fashioning last decade's gowns, Matilda would be the last to admit it; she preferred to be looked on as a mystic. It would have taken more than the problems of eking a living to rob her of the romantic streak that was her lodestar. 'I never saw a more handsome couple.' Having waylaid Monica in the village, she appeared to have something pressing to tell her. 'But it's more than that. Handsome or not, a marriage can be made in heaven.' She leant towards Monica confidentially, 'There's nothing they can hide from *me*. And that Mr Ellis, don't you be taken in by his autocratic appearance. Unsmiling he can be, his face as stiff as your washing on a frosty morning, but I can see beyond all that. *Besotted* with her. I came close to them after the service last Sunday, I felt the vibes. Plenty enough young couples have come to me for a reading, but not one of them has ever affected me like he did.'

'You mean they've been to you? Or *he* has?'

'There are plenty who do – usually those who are none too sure of themselves. But those two are full of self-confidence, like to think they plough their own furrow. And how do I know these things? That's what you're thinking. Hardly more than a how-do-you-do to your Miss Blakeney and not even that to him. It comes from *here*,' she rested her hand on her bosom. 'It's a gift, not a thing you can be taught. Believe me, Mrs Blakeney, those two have no secrets from me. I tell you, as I came near where they stood talking I felt quite dizzy, it was all I could do not to go right off. You may have seen, I sat down close by to them, I had to grip the back of the chair I trembled so. This gift of mine, it's a blessing and it's a curse. What I felt took my breath away, made me tingle, made me have to struggle not to be carried right away with the strength of it. Yet, there he stood, tall as a soldier, correct and controlled, not so much as touching her hand. I doubt if even *she* knew what was coursing through his veins. *Besotted* with her. There's only *so much* I can reach with a contact like that. But I came home feeling drained. If only they would come to see me, let me sink into the spirit, see into their future together. But you need have no fear, he is consumed, yes *consumed* by love. Put those thoughts of Laurence Chesterton out of your mind—'

'Laurence Chesterton?' Monica sounded defensive. Matilda and her supernatural powers had always been looked on by the

Blakeneys as a joke. But could the gift be genuine? 'Laurence is in London, he has been for months. Perhaps you didn't know.' Would she fall into the trap, she who professed to know so much?

'Of course I know. Just as I knew he wouldn't stay in Ottercombe. But that was what you wanted for her. You don't need to tell me these things. You ought to have come to see me, I would have told you they weren't right for each other. I knew there was no love,' Matilda raised her hands as if she were trying to pull the right word out of the air, 'no romantic love. Your girl could never have been happy with Laurence Chesterton. Now Mr Ellis – he's a *man*.'

The way she spoke made Monica uncomfortable. A single woman, no longer even young, but there was no doubt what she was implying.

'We're delighted, of course.' It was an attempt to bring the conversation back onto familiar, conventional lines. 'Her father and I are so pleased to find she has fallen in love with someone who won't whisk her away from Ottercombe. There are so few young men in a village like ours.'

'Instead of expecting to have young Laurence Chesterton for a son-in-law, you should have come and talked to me, I knew he'd not settle round here. He was harder to read than Mr Ellis, not a lot of emotion in Laurence Chesterton. They never came to talk to me, but I'm not saying I didn't try my best to look into their future. But there was nothing; I couldn't see his at all. Now your girl, I see her, you won't be losing her from around these parts. But him ... well, now he's pulled up sticks and gone off like Dick Whittington expecting the pavements to be lined with gold, no wonder I couldn't follow a path for them together. But never mind him, he was just a lad. This wedding, now, there's a real romance. Our lives are all mapped out for us, you know. I dare say Mr Ellis thought he took that post at the Abbey because it was his own will to come to Ottercombe. Of course, that's nonsense. He came to Ottercombe because it was his destiny to meet your Veronica. Your life, my life, theirs. I told you, it's mapped out for us. We think we're so clever, deciding to do this or that. Oh no, it's not in our hands. Even I can't always see the road plotted out for a person. But it's not often the fog won't clear. With one like the Chesterton lad, one with no driving emotional force, I could probably only tell him what was on his palm. But Mr Ellis – and

Miss Blakeney too – just remembering now how I trembled, how I had to fight not to go right off, the power was so strong, see how it upsets me talking about it.'

Monica wanted to get away. Matilda had told her nothing to worry her, and yet the conversation had been upsetting. It wasn't for them to tamper with the unknown, she told herself, not giving an inch to her real fear. If Matilda de Vere truthfully had these supernatural powers, what vibes had she been feeling as they'd stood talking? What had she been able to see on the path ahead?

'I must get home, or Veronica and her father will be back before me,' she said by way of escape.

'Come and see me one day, Mrs Blakeney. I'm always there if the road destiny has set seems to be lost in fog.'

What had she meant by that? What could she see? What did she know? Probably nothing, Monica answered herself, it's just her way of earning a living. As if I'd ever go to her ... and why wouldn't I? Because I'm not that much of a gullible fool, or because I'm frightened of what I might hear?

The Abbey was crowded for the wedding. Nicholas had trained the choir then, when the day came, Howard Humphreys played the organ and conducted the unaccompanied anthem. The setting was magnificent, the bride tall and elegant, the groom dignified and handsome, the bride's mother enchantingly lovely, the bride's father nervous – probably upset to be handing his daughter to the care of another man, was the general opinion. The two brides-maids were daughters of Nicholas's elder sister who sat in the front row with husband and an uncle and aunt. Behind them were various cousins, all of them strangers to Veronica. Although he'd only been in the district a year whereas Veronica had lived in Ottercombe all her life, the right-hand side of the aisle was as crowded as the left. The whole of the Abbey Singers considered themselves friends of the groom as did visiting music lovers from around the district.

Three rows from the back, on the bride's side of the aisle, sat two ladies who, fortunately for their peace of mind on this happy day, neither Veronica nor Monica noticed. One was the wife of the Deremouth apothecary and the other a one-time nurse now married and retired; it had been their idea to open and 'man' the Family Planning Clinic. They realised they'd been stretching the self-made rules in persuading the visiting doctor to deal with Veronica before she'd even become a wife. But rules were made to be stretched, before a year was over they were sure she'd come back to them and say she was ready for a family. But in the first months of being wife of the Master of the Choir School it would be much easier for her if she wasn't burdened with a quick pregnancy. The two ladies looked at mother and daughter with satisfaction, it was good to know they'd been able to help them both, one at the beginning of her reproductive life and one dangerously near the end when slips can so easily happen. Watching the three standing at the head of the aisle with the priest, and the fourth – was there ever a more delightfully feminine mother-of-the-bride? – sitting alone in the front pew waiting for the moment when her husband would join her, their thoughts moved along parallel lines, hoping they'd be recognised, perhaps even introduced to the men who must surely be grateful for the understanding help they'd been able to arrange. Had they known mother and daughter better they would have realised that not only had they not confided in their menfolk but, even to each other, they hadn't spoken of their visit to Deremouth's new clinic.

Herbert got through the ceremony well, he passed Veronica's hand to Nicholas at the right moment, then he felt a tug on his jacket as Monica indicated she wanted him to sit next to her. How pretty she looked. So many people, all friends, all bringing good wishes to his darling Ronnie. She wasn't going away, if he lost her … she thought of everything … she carried him … dear God what was happening to him that he had to rely on the child for things he used to be able to do standing on his head? His head … his head … couldn't grasp things … The nerve in his cheek started to jerk out of control. His mouth was dry as sawdust, he felt a trickle of cold sweat run down his chest.

If Veronica had been looking at him she would have recognised the signs, but her thoughts were raised to a higher plane as she made her vows, conscious only that Nicholas's penetrating gaze held her as if in a spell. The words were spoken, they were pronounced man and wife. She didn't even notice how Ellen Chesterton, sitting in the second row with Hugo Holmes, dabbed her eyes with a flimsy handkerchief as the last of her hopes and dreams faded. Laurence had been invited but his full engagement book hadn't allowed him to be there so Ellen had been glad when Hugo joined her.

The reception was held in the great stone-walled refectory of the Abbey, a rare concession having been made to allow caterers to prepare the lavish fare. The only exception was a three-tier wedding cake, made by Blakeneys and large enough that, at Veronica's instigation, pieces were to be boxed not only for each of the staff but despatched to all the firm's regular customers. Theirs was a business built on personal contact, many of their clients had dealt with them since before she was born; others had come onto the books more recently, the outcome of her own salesmanship the previous summer. In her opinion, a piece of wedding cake with the same printed card that would accompany the boxes sent to faraway relatives and friends would be money even better spent than the customary annual calendar.

'Well, my dear,' boomed her new brother-in-law David Holsworthy, 'you've got yourself a dark horse for a husband. Not the best correspondent in the world, well who of us men are?' His laugh was loud and good-natured. 'That's what you ladies are for. Isn't that so? Once a year we hear from him, a box of some sort of sweetmeat for the girls and a card for Beth and me. Not a word that he was contemplating matrimony, not a word about anything for that matter. Just his usual, "Good wishes, Nicholas". And that only those few weeks ago. The next we heard was a request that I'd act as his best man. Not been here long enough to have made any friends, I suppose that's why he fell back on me. A bit sudden wasn't it, my dear? I'm not prying – no, nor criticising. If that's the way things are, then I still say good luck to you both. And why not? Many a good horse has been known to trot behind the cart.'

'And many a good lad has walked behind the horse with his pail and shovel. What he picks up is at least useful around the roses; what you're hoping to pick up is nothing but empty, unfounded speculation.'

'Hey, hey, young lady, steady on.' Not a bit put out by her reply, his eyes twinkled with amusement. 'I spoke in friendship. I merely wanted you to know that if that were the reason for this rushed wedding, then you needn't feel that your new in-laws were holding it against you – either of you.'

'Would it have mattered if you were? You say you neither see nor hear from Nicholas. I'm sure he has plenty of friends who would have been delighted to do the honours today, but perhaps family ties mean more to him than any of us realised. To be honest I didn't know he even had one sister, let alone four, until we started to discuss the wedding plans. Two of the others were invited but declined. They both have careers so we hardly expected them.'

'Spinsters, they haven't the freedom of you married ladies.' Big, tactless, good-hearted and jovial, David knew he had been clumsy in his first acquaintance with his new sister-in-law. Lucky for him she was tough enough to stand up for herself. Lucky indeed for, in his opinion, that was something she'd need to do, tied to Nicholas. Odd sort of chap, that was David's opinion. But, he told himself, perhaps he wasn't being fair. Born when both his parents were middle-aged, that probably accounted for his stiff, stilted manner. Not that his family had spoilt him, rather he'd been left to his own devices. But, remembering him in his teens, he'd always been a loner, not an easy person to be with.

'You know what I think?' he voiced his thoughts aloud.

Veronica shook her head. 'I'm frightened to imagine,' she laughed, 'having discovered the way your mind works.'

Again that irritatingly booming laugh – except that this time it didn't irritate her.

'No naughty thoughts this time,' her burly companion assured her. 'No, I was thinking about this new husband of yours. Never thought he'd marry at all, you know. You must have knocked him off his feet. Not surprising, don't misunderstand me. You know what I always thought?'

'I was waiting for you to tell me.'

'There's no logic in it. As far as I know (and damned if I know much about the chap if I'm honest) he's not a particularly religious man. But all this church music stuff, he sort of wraps himself up in it. Difficult, I find it. Sort of puts a barrier between him and ordinary hedonists like me. But if I'd been asked where I thought he would fit best, I would have said in a place like this. Not with a wife and children (now, now, I got your message, but I dare say they'll soon come along, it's the way things go), no I could see him as one of those monkish chaps. Cut off from the temptations of the world. But then, what's a temptation to one leaves another cold. I dare say those chaps who drift around in their robes, silent, dedicated, keeping a routine that would kill most irks like me, I dare say they're happy enough. You don't miss what you've never had.'

'I'm sure they're happy – and fulfilled. In a way I understand what you say. Nicholas *is* different, different from anyone I've known. Perhaps he is more spiritual. But he couldn't live like they do. Whatever fulfilment they find in their way of life here, he finds his in music.'

'Now there's a problem for you. Other women, and you could pull out all the stops and make sure you didn't give them a chance. But music . . . now there's a mistress you'll find it hard to fight.'

'I shan't be fighting. Anyway, the one thing I shan't be doing is sitting at home jealous of the time he spends with his music. I have a bakery to ru—' she stopped short in time to re-word her sentence, 'to keep me occupied. I've helped Dad there ever since I left school and I certainly don't intend to idle my days away here when there is a perfectly good housekeeper already.'

'Well, jigger me! Go to work, you mean? What does brother Nicholas say to that?'

For a second the question silenced her. David's tone made it clear he found the thought of Nicholas with a wife who maintained her own independence funny. But even in the few moments she'd talked to her new brother-in-law she'd recognised that he saw life as a harmless joke at other people's expense.

'If Nicholas wanted to marry me as I am, what makes you imagine he'd expect to change me?' she replied tartly.

'I'll tell you one thing, Sister Veronica, I reckon that young man has met his match. I'd like to be a fly on your ceiling once in a while, jiggered if I wouldn't. Now come and talk to Beth or I shall get my wrist slapped for monopolising you.'

Veronica's expectations of Nicholas's family had been low so David Holsworthy had come as a refreshingly pleasant surprise. She found the going harder with Beth. Just as Nicholas was reserved, so she was over-gushingly sweet; the effusive manner didn't fit comfortably with a woman who showed so little interest in her younger brother. Of the two, Veronica preferred her husband. But today neither of them more than touched the surface of her concern.

In an era when most wedding ceremonies were followed by the Wedding Breakfast, theirs was unusual. Monica had shown more than her usual perception when she'd suggested that they should provide a stand-up buffet, a chance for guests to mingle; Veronica had agreed, and Nicholas had shown little interest in the details. None of them had spoken the unspeakable, that a formal reception would have put too much strain on Herbert. The party might not have followed a marriage ceremony at all, for it more resembled that new innovation of entertaining – a cocktail party. There were no speeches, the bride and groom moved separately amongst the guests. Then it was over, the enthusiastic bridesmaids whisked Veronica through the cloisters to the Master's Lodge where her 'going away' outfit was hanging under drapes.

She found herself held in Herbert's desperate hug.

'Bless you, my darling child. You'll come back to help me. Promise me, Ronnie.' She could hear the panic in the words he whispered.

'Only a few days, Dad. Don't worry if my things get behind, I'll see to them when I get back.' Then drawing back just far enough to look him in the eyes. 'I promise you, Dad. Nothing will be any different.'

'. . . ashamed,' he bit hard on the corner of his mouth as if that would still the twitching in his cheek.

'No, Dad. Proud. You and me are a great team. Take care of Mum, they say mothers get down in the dumps when the wedding's over.'

'I'll do that, bless her. Not much fun for her these days. How pretty she looks.'

'She always looks pretty.'

He seemed restored and she left him gazing proudly across the starkly bare room to where Monica stood talking happily to Hugo.

Ten minutes later, knowing she looked her best in her new amber-coloured suit and toque created with feathers of varying shades of brown and amber, a red fox fur high around her neck, she waved her last farewells as Nicholas drove them away. By her feet was a rug waiting for her to pull it around her. But for the moment vanity was keeping her warm.

'On the road at last,' he reached for her hand.

Her response was spontaneous. 'The road to the rest of our lives.' She didn't want to think of her father's last words, as she'd hugged him in farewell.

'You won't be away long? Back with me soon. Tomorrow?'

He'd pleaded before for a moment his confusion had lifted, 'Next week? Soon, Ronnie child.'

'Soon, Dad. You've nothing to worry about,' she'd told him, hating seeing that lost, helpless look in his eyes. Remembering it now she felt a shiver of cold fear.

'Cold already? Pull the rug up. I'm too busy driving to be admiring your smart regalia.'

She did as he said. But she wasn't cold; neither was the sudden chill brought on by the memory of her father. She closed her eyes as if that way she'd escape that other memory. Laurence. What if she'd been setting out on that road to the rest of her life with *him* by her side? No, it wasn't Laurence's love she craved; he belonged to yesterday just as surely as all the carefree fun they'd always had together. He'd written a brief note explaining that he regretted not being free to accept the invitation to her wedding, wishing her well – and reminding her of the future he'd seen for her in Ottercombe as if he saw the whole affair as a great joke. All brides must feel like this, she told herself. Marriage was the end of dreams – yes, but it was a time that dreams became reality. She glanced at Nicholas, her mind jumping ahead of her, her un-certainty giving way to excitement, anticipation. The image of herself as mistress of the Master's Lodge had no shape, she didn't even try to bring it into focus. The wild, heady anticipation that gripped her had nothing to do with the unknown future at the Abbey. It was the present, the breathtaking wonder of the way the next few hours would take her. Every time Nicholas had held her he'd stirred some deep primeval need in her. This evening – tonight – she would follow where it led, there would be nothing to hold her back, nothing to hold him back. Even now she could feel the hard beating of her heart. Home, father, Laurence, the bakery, all of them were forgotten.

'Do we have to drive far?' Peering at him in the fast fading dusk she thought he must surely hear and recognise her eagerness to get the journey done. But perhaps he didn't, for he replied in a matter-of-fact voice that made her even more conscious of her own erotic imaginings.

'Just far enough for escape. Then, each day we'll move on. It's time you saw more of the world than one corner of Devon.'

'Tonight – where you'll take me tonight – that's the journey I want.' The words slipped out as she thought them. 'A good thing

84

Mum can't hear me! She'd think that a most unmaidenly remark.'
And, brought up in the strict code of the day, she looked sideways
at him, uncertain of his response.

His left hand moved to grip her right, his thumb caressing her
palm and driving all that she'd left behind even further from her
mind. Fortunately there was almost no other motor traffic on
the road, no one to see, no one to be inconvenienced, as he stopped
the car. At home her mother would be hanging the bridal gown
and veil away, her father would probably be following behind her,
uncertain and not wanting to be alone by the fireside. For a second
Veronica pictured them, then willingly pushed the thought away.
Even if she had no clear image of her future life, as he took her in
his arms she knew wherever her thoughts were travelling, his
were with her.

'Just a few days, that's all she'll be away? She won't be longer?'
It was quite the sixth time Herbert said it as he and Monica sat by
the roaring fire, the winter evening shut out.

'How do I know?' What had started as a tolerant answer was
becoming more impatient each time the question was repeated.
'Dr Hardy is coming back to play at the Abbey for the next two
weeks. I told you, Herbert, not five minutes ago. I wish you'd
concentrate. You don't listen to me, that's the trouble. Too
wrapped up in your own affairs to ever bother about what I say.'

'Not true, not true. I try and think – try and remember –
Monnie, you know I do – can't help – ' He struggled to his feet.
'Work to do. With Ronnie gadding off, it'll all fallen to me.
Everything. Can't waste time here—'

'There's no fire in your study,' she cut off his way of escape.
'Anyway, what work would she be doing if she were here? None.
It's an excuse, you sit in there and pretend to work just so that you
don't have to talk to me. Not that it's any good talking to you, you
never listen.'

'Not true, not true,' he said again.

Picking up her crochet-work she concentrated on that rather
than look at him. It wasn't fair. With Veronica gone, surely they
ought to find companionship. But there was nothing! When did
they last talk, really talk about anything that matters? Always she
had to think before she spoke, being careful not to say anything
that would make him edgy. Today ought to have been wonderful,

wasn't a bride's mother entitled to that much? It ought to be a day they shared. Certainly he'd told her she looked pretty – and he'd meant what he said, she made herself recall the way his eyes had smiled when he'd looked at her. She'd known too that other people there had admired her, she'd enjoyed the special role she'd had to play. Yet all the time she'd had to keep an eye on *him*, making sure he was keeping abreast of what was going on. Things had gone quite well – and she sent up a silent 'thank you' that at least he hadn't disgraced himself with his silly questions in front of all those people. But what sort of a future was there for them now, just the two of them . . . no one else to help share the burden. There! She'd admitted it! It was a burden. And it wasn't fair. A husband should be a companion. Was the business doing badly? Could that be what worried him? But if it were, surely Veronica would have hinted at it. How much use the girl was there, she didn't know. But at least now that she was married she must see that it was time she gave up. Was that what was frightening him, did he feel he wasn't up to running the place on his own like he used to? It was all beyond her understanding.

'You know what I was thinking?' she said as if he'd been following her chain of thought.

'Thinking?' Herbert pulled himself back from wherever his own miserable thoughts had been and repeated the word as if he'd never heard it before.

'Yes, thinking,' she snapped before she could hold herself in check, 'I do think sometimes, you know. I'm not just a vehicle for your end of day entertainment.' She seemed to stand apart, hearing her words and being filled with shame. 'Oh, I didn't mean that. Herbert, I'm sorry.'

'No, it's me. I'm the one to be sorry. I fail you. Every day I fail you. Thinking, you say. What is it, my dear. A holiday perhaps? Is that what you want? Difficult at the moment, but I'll bear it—'

'I've been thinking that you ought to engage a manager. I don't know how much use to you Veronica has been at the bakery, but we have to remember she has a husband now and a home to manage. Although goodness knows what sort of a fist she'll make of that. I suppose she must have been useful in the business in the day to day running of things. And, as you said just now, we could take a holiday sometimes and know there was someone else in charge.'

'You don't think she'll come back to help me? Is that what

you're saying?' He almost shouted the words, his eyes defying her to say yes, that was what she meant.

'Herbert darling, she has a husband. Would you have liked it if I'd gone off to work when my place was making a home for you – and for her. Soon she'll have a child perhaps. You can't look to the future and expect her to be in that office every day. Take a manager, someone with experience, someone who will take some of the burden. Surely we can afford to do that.'

'Not come back. You're mad. Of course she'll come back. She promised. Only today she promised. When she said goodbye it was – I said to her—' then his mind cleared enough to warn him that he was walking into a trap, 'I just mentioned to her about her coming back. She promised. Not long, she said.'

'I was standing there. Not that you noticed where I was, I don't expect.' She knew it was her unhappiness talking, but it was beyond her power to be tactful in what she said. 'Tomorrow – a few days – soon – I heard it all – I heard you begging. Yes, she promised, how else could she have avoided some sort of a scene. Dear God, what's the matter with you, Herbert? Are you a man or what?' Her voice rose, she heard it and gloried in the sound. It was as if the constraint she'd put on herself for months was suddenly gone, she wanted to shout, she wanted to abuse him, accuse him.

But when he buried his face in his hands, shaken by the rasping sobs that tore him, she was more frightened than she'd been in all her cosseted life.

As Nicholas had said, in miles they weren't travelling far on that evening of their wedding day. But that other journey carried her to realms unknown. There was nothing of a shy bride in Veronica, she was a sensuous woman. Just once in the moment that Nicholas reached to touch her, her memory flew of its own accord to Laurence's fumbling exploration; Nicholas's firm caress, her certainty of his suppressed passion, drove everything else from her mind. Willingly she was lost.

The next day they moved on and for a fortnight spent days of discovery and nights of glorious, sensuous love. They went to Evensong in Winchester Cathedral (although being so close to Beth and her family, neither of them gave a thought to visiting them); they went to a concert in the Albert Hall and another Evensong in St Paul's Cathedral. They travelled in her own country, her birthright, so much of it new to her. But looking back afterwards it wasn't the winter countryside she remembered, her honeymoon was made of music and lovemaking, both spiritual in their wonder. They travelled as far to the east as Cambridge where he had spent three years on which his future had been founded and where she felt herself forgotten in his pleasure at being with his one-time mentor. Then turning towards home they drove south of London, heading for the Hampshire coast where they spent a night in Christchurch. As if Fate had arranged the timing specially, they found Fauré's Requiem was being sung in the Priory.

Altogether they were away thirteen days, days that were to form the rock on which they built the time that followed. For Veronica there was the adventure of new sights, the journey into discovery of her own sexuality and always, wherever they went, there was music. Nicholas would probably have placed the importance of these days in a different order; his pleasure in places, whether new to him or already woven into his past, came from seeing her delight. Was it possible that each day he could love her more? She was his, body and soul she was his, her eager, frenzied passion told him so more clearly than any words. And throughout their honeymoon, wherever they went, a visit to a concert hall, a cathedral or a church gave him the music that was the lifeblood of his existence.

'We're back,' she called as she let herself into the front door of her old home. 'Mum! Dad!'

'Hush,' Monica came into the hall, silently closing the drawing room door behind her. 'He's asleep.'

'We called at the bakery. They said he hadn't been in for two days. What's happened, Mum?'

'You've gone away. I suppose that's what's happened. It was yesterday morning, he got dressed as usual – but he's been getting worse and worse, doesn't keep his mind on anything for two seconds at a time – then I heard a thud. I ran upstairs to see what he'd done and he was lying on the floor. Only for a minute or so, and no real harm was done. But he seemed so strange that I sent Bertha to fetch the doctor.'

'And . . .?'

'Dr Saunders said in his opinion he'd had a slight stroke, it had affected his brain, his memory. I told him he'd not been right for some time. Oh, what's the use of pretending? You must know it as surely as I do. The doctor suspected something similar must have happened before without our knowing.'

It was like a bad dream. Only hours ago, Veronica had been bumping happily homeward at Nicholas's side. She'd persuaded him to stop as they came through Deremouth, promising she wouldn't stay more than five minutes at the bakery. She'd kept her word, it had taken her no time at all to learn that all they knew of her father was from a note dropped off when the morning bus had come in from Ottercombe the previous day, saying he wouldn't be coming in for a few days.

'Not unusual for the bride's family to take a break away after all the fuss,' Nicholas had told her.

'Drive back past the house, then I'll stop and see everything's all right.'

'Nonsense. Of course it is.' And instead of taking the second turning off the main road, which led through Ottercombe, he'd continued to the next and climbed the hill to the Abbey beyond the edge of the village. But they wouldn't have gone on holiday, she'd told herself, certain that unsure of himself and frightened of being without her, her father would never have stayed away from the bakery without a very good reason.

'I'll talk to him, Mum,' she said now with more hope than confidence. 'Once he knows I'm home he'll not be frightened.'

'Oh dear, whatever's happened to him? So changed . . . like a stranger . . .' Monica followed a far from silent Veronica back into the drawing room where a fire blazed and the windows were running in condensation.

'Phew! What a fug! No wonder you've dropped off, Dad. What you want in here is some fresh air.' Her unnaturally noisy tone penetrated his slumbers, but not his reason.

'Ah, Ronnie my dear. Been out have you? Take your coat off, child, and come by the fire.'

'Aren't you roasted?' She stooped to kiss his brow.

'Roasted? What's that you've got? Chestnuts? Is that it, you're going to roast some chestnuts.'

Ignoring his rambling, she knelt in front of him.

'We've had a wonderful time, Nicholas and me,' she told him. 'We went as far as Cambridge. Just look at me,' she knelt tall, turning her face into a smile that was supposed to look full of a new pride, 'I'm a much travelled woman now. We went to Oxford, to Winchester, to London, Cambridge, Christchurch. And Dad,' she took his cold hands in hers, 'on the way through Deremouth I went into the bakery. Everything is fine there. You stay home for a few days after your tumble. Now I'm home you can leave things to me, I'll keep your seat warm for you.'

'No, no, no, oh no.' And that expression she dreaded. Perhaps she shouldn't have mentioned the bakery. Helplessly she looked at her mother, but Monica's expression was inscrutable.

'I'll tell you all about where we've been.'

'That's the way. Shopping for your mother, was it?'

She'd learnt her lesson; she didn't correct him. Instead she talked, her voice purposely monotonous, her object to lull him back to sleep. Before she'd covered her journey as far as Oxford where they'd spent their second night, his steady breathing told her she'd succeeded.

'Of course I shall go in tomorrow! And not just tomorrow, Nicholas. What if Dad doesn't get better? I don't mean that – of course he'll get better – but better enough to shoulder the running of the business again?' Even the way she stood, tall and erect, told Nicholas that she meant to do battle. Possess her, body and soul? The preceding days were already fading into a dreamlike mist.

'Go to the bakery tomorrow, if you feel you have a responsibility.'

'*Feel* I have? Of course I have a responsibility,' she snapped. 'Anyway it's more than duty. I don't ask you to give up your music, I don't interfere with how you mean to spend your days,' she blazed. No one had ever told her what she could or couldn't do!

'Now you're talking hysterical nonsense. You are my wife.' Then softening his tone, 'I'm sorry to hear about your father and I trust he will soon be restored to some semblance of health,' he said in the formal tone she'd become so used to that she hardly noticed. 'But for a long time I have realised all wasn't well with him – you've known it too. I agree you go to the bakery tomorrow and perhaps for a few days after. But tomorrow you must do what he should have done months ago: draft an advertisement for a manager. Until you get someone suitable I am prepared to share you with your cakes. Until then – and no longer.'

What a moment for the ghost of Laurence to tap her on the shoulder, Laurence making a laughing adventure of the days they'd gone order seeking in the north of the county, Laurence who had seen Nicholas as a 'dry stick'.

'You expect thanks for graciously allowing me to go in there tomorrow? Well, you can whistle for them. And as for a manager – that I will *never* agree to.'

Without a word Nicholas turned and left her, retreating to the solitude of the Abbey. She saw him as arrogant, she thought his attitude unreasonable. So much between them was left unsaid, and she had no way of knowing how he felt as he climbed the steps to the organ loft. Trying to put the last few minutes from her mind, she went to the bedroom that from this day on they would use. Her trunk had been brought up and was waiting to be unpacked, so she started to work out her anger on putting her clothes in the empty wardrobe that stood ready. But each gown brought a memory alive: the deep gold velvet she'd worn to the Priory, the fur-trimmed coat she'd worn to Westminster Cathedral, each had its own story. Then the nightwear and underclothes she put in the linen basket . . . sitting on the edge of the bed she let her thoughts carry her where they would.

She would walk across the quadrangle to the Abbey, she would make him understand. Yet, when she let herself in through the heavy Norman door, the sound of the organ seemed to hold her away from him. Purposefully she crept up the long aisle but instead of going up the steps to the loft as she'd intended she sat in the choir stalls. Today they had come near to quarrelling, not about something petty but about something that was fundamental to her life. Here in the hallowed atmosphere which had known centuries of prayer, she dropped to her knees.

'I can't do as he says. You must see I can't. Anyway, I don't want to. What's the sense in staying at home to do a job that someone else does better than me, then getting an outsider to do the thing I can do best? It's not going to be an easy nut to crack, I can see that. But, You understand, I know You do. So please, if I stick to my guns and leave it to You, please, please find a way for things to work happily for us. And, while I'm here, I want to say thank You too for these last two weeks. I never knew they could be such – such joy, such glorious – oh I can't say it without it sounding affected, but it was a sort of unity that was beyond

91

words. And You must have made that possible for us. So what I've just asked, please help with that. I can't let Dad down. Poor darling Dad – and Mum, poor Mum too. There's such a lot that's a mess, but if we all do our best You will help, I know You will.'

She felt safe and isolated in the seat that belonged to the Head Chorister. It was evidence of her state of mind that she didn't consider the mirror strategically placed above the organ. Looking in it, seeing her kneeling for so long, Nicholas felt held away from her by something too strong for him to fight. For an instant his playing faltered, stopped; then once again the solemn notes echoed to the glorious vaulted ceiling that had been crafted more than four hundred years before, when the Abbey had been restored. That brief pause had been enough to bring Veronica out of her reverie and to raise her eyes to where he sat, high above with his back to her.

Her anger had evaporated. She was drawn to him with a power beyond her control as she got up from her knees and moved across the chancel to the steps where, by then, he was already waiting for her at the doorway of the organ loft.

But by morning, reality was waiting for her: her father, the business, the men and women in the bakehouse who ought to have been paid the previous day, probably orders that hadn't been passed to them, bills that hadn't been paid. If that had been all, then she would have made an early start to Deremouth and shouldered her own responsibilities and Herbert's too. But one look at Nicholas as he watched her prepare to leave the house on her first morning as its mistress was enough to bring the curtain down on any hope she'd been harbouring that the night had given him a new understanding.

'When you can spare the time,' he said in the voice that had given her her early dislike of him, 'I shall be glad if you will make a note in your diary of my engagements. As my wife, these will involve your time. You remember I told you, in the coming season I shall be playing in Manchester, in Reading, Winchester.' Yes, she remembered, she remembered how they'd planned to travel together; it had all been part of the freedom of their honeymoon. 'That bakery can be run by anyone with a head for business.'

She turned and left him, her head high, her spirit low.

Chapter Six

Her love for Laurence had been simple and unquestioning. She'd refused to accept that he'd taken her for granted and had found pleasure in each carefree pastime they'd shared. An all-day bicycle ride, a morning fishing for mackerel, a silent secret joke, all simple things and yet for her they had been the epitome of happiness. She knew now that much of that happiness had been based on the belief that he loved her, a belief that had been founded on nothing more than hope.

Her relationship with Nicholas was so different. Of course, she told herself, it must be different. Laurence and I were too young to know. Nicholas is a *man*, the sort of things that amused Laurence and me wouldn't appeal to him. I know he loves me – what if he didn't? Imagine if all these weeks he'd been just using me because he enjoys knowing how I want him to make love to me? Him, make love to me? No, it's not like that. It's both of us. It's – it's as if (even in her thoughts she was lost for the right words) as if we're being driven by some power outside ourselves. Could it ever have been like that with Laurence? I don't even want to imagine, I don't want to remember the way his hand fumbled beyond my stocking tops. Yet when he did it, I thought it was wonderful. It must have been what I'd been wanting him to do, or why would I have worn my only pair of wide-legged French knickers? I don't want to think about it. I was just an inexperienced, frustrated child. But not now.

She realised that Nicholas had looked up from the score he was reading and was watching her curiously. Recognising the invitation in his expression she moved across the hearth to him and dropped on her knees, forcing his legs apart so that she could kneel between them, her head against his chest.

'I've been watching you,' he told her, caressing the nape of her neck. 'You've been a long way away. That bakery takes too much of your time, too many of your thoughts. I've been patient long enough. We both know your father won't go back there, it's time you did as I said and took on an experienced business man.'

Purposely she ignored the last part as she answered, teasingly, 'Coming from one who's spent the evening with his nose in a music score, you're a fine one to talk. Anyway,' she added, not wanting the conversation to turn to the subject that, over the months of their marriage had led increasingly to arguments, 'I wasn't thinking of that. I was thinking about us. Are we extra lucky, do you suppose, or is loving the same for everyone?'

'Loving?'

'Lovemaking, that's what I really wonder about. It's like nothing else – such fun and yet sort of deeply, deeply wonderful. Does *everyone* feel like we do? I've nothing to measure against.'

'Nor will you ever have, my darling. You're *mine*.'

'Sometimes I look at other married couples – oh, you can't tell me – they look so *dull*.'

Confidently, he smiled. After nearly four months of marriage, in some ways she was as innocent as a child – yet as natural as an animal in the wilds.

'I'm not trying to tell you anything except that if another man ever touched you, I swear to God I'd kill him. Whether it's normal – whether it's right – to feel like I do about you I don't know.' Then, with a voice that made her raise her head and meet the intensity of emotion in his dark eyes, 'If I lost you I don't think I could live.'

'It's like that for me too,' she whispered. She leant closer, knowing her nearness aroused him and glorying in his need of her. Again the memory of Laurence nudged her mind. If she had willingly let him use her when it suited him, wasn't Nicholas's power over her even greater? Yes, and hers over him. That's how she wanted it to be. Raising her face to his, his mouth found hers, his hold on her was demanding and possessive.

At the back of the house Florrie Beckham, the housekeeper, reigned supreme. With their chairs drawn close to the kitchen range she sat facing the fire, Mary on one side and Dolly on the other. With their day's work done this was the way the final hour of their evenings was usually spent. Dolly, the scullery maid who

94

inherited all the chores neither of the other two wanted, could do little more than write her own name; reading a book would have been beyond her; but listening fuelled her dreams. It fell to Mary, the housemaid who considered herself 'a cut above the other two' to read aloud while Dolly listened in open-mouthed wonder and Florrie Beckham knitted. Between them, each week they bought a woman's magazine, its two serials and one short story enough to provide entertainment (and dreams) for their few hours of end-of-day free time for the whole of the week. So engrossed were they in the last paragraph of that week's romance that none of them heard Nicholas and Veronica climb the stairs.

'I want you to read this,' Ellen passed a letter to Monica. 'It came this morning from Ralph. I wish you'd met him, but Yorkshire is a long way away, what would he ever have come right down here for?'

'Is something wrong?' Monica took the envelope.

'Just read it – then tell me you can see I'm doing the right thing.'

'Ellen,' Herbert nodded his recognition. 'Been away somewhere have you? Yorkshire, did I hear you say? We don't see much of you these days.'

A day seldom passed without Ellen dropping in on them, but it was easier to kiss him in greeting and let him think what he would. Ignoring them, Monica took the two sheets of good quality headed notepaper from the envelope. She knew Ellen heard regularly from Ralph, her elder brother, so what was special about this?

'Read it and tell me.' There was something like excitement in Ellen's prompting.

Monica read while Herbert sat with the newspaper on his knee gazing at her contentedly. Before Veronica's marriage the change in him had been more evident than any of them had admitted. Since his collapse while she'd been away on her honeymoon he had deteriorated rapidly. By this humid, overcast August morning he had slipped sufficiently far from the events of every day that he was far more at peace with himself. No longer did his fingers beat a frustrated tattoo, no longer did his cheek twitch out of control, no longer was he tortured by his unsuccessful attempts to concentrate. So he sat watching his darling Monica, his mind at peace in the certainty that he had her undying love just as she had his.

'But why should he be offering you a home?' He heard her ask the question, but made no attempt to follow the conversation between the two women. Pretty ladies, both of them, he nodded his approval. 'You have a lovely home of your own. And how often do you think Laurence would have a chance to see you if you went to live right up there in Yorkshire? He means kindly, I'm sure. But why now, after all these years you've been widowed?'

'He has just retired. I suppose he thinks this is the time for a new beginning. And it's what I need, Monica – a future that's not just a poor shadow of the past. As for Laurence, we both know he won't want to come to Ottercombe now that Veronica has forsaken him. If only things had turned out like we wanted. Already he's doing well. Why couldn't she have trusted him to come back for her when he'd made a place for himself? School, Oxford, he'd been away so much, but we always knew he'd come back. She ought to have had enough faith in him to be patient.' Disappointment was making Ellen bitter. 'Instead, what did she do but throw herself into the arms of a man too old for her – but she'll regret it, of that I'm sure. Distinguished, oh yes, he's that; and top of the tree in his own profession – I suppose all that impressed her. But what sort of fun will she ever have with *him*? She and Laurence had such good times. Still, it's too late now for regrets. We must look to the future. That's why, on my way this morning, I dropped my letter into the post box accepting Ralph's suggestion.'

'Change your mind, Ellie. Tell him you were too hasty. Please, don't go right up there. You have a place here, you have friends here. You haven't seen this Ralph in years. How do you know you'll be happy amongst a lot of strangers?'

'Ralph is family,' Ellen told her firmly. 'You wouldn't understand. You have Herbert, and you have Veronica nearby. Why, not a day goes by that she doesn't come in on her way to Deremouth. Family. The most important thing in a person's life.'

'Yes. Yes, yes, yes,' Herbert nodded, apparently having understood at least that part of the conversation. He reached to take Monica's hand in his. Looking at him a wave of misery swept over her. Where was her darling Herbert, where in this poor dependent shell was the kernel of the person he'd been? She gave his fingers an answering squeeze and was rewarded by his eyes lighting in a smile that only added to her feeling of shame.

'I shan't be burdened with any more duties than I am here. Ralph is well enough heeled, he keeps staff, I shan't be called on for domestic responsibility. No, it'll be a joy to have a place in society again, not to always be the odd one.'

'As if you've ever been that! Think again, Ellie, don't rush into anything.' But Monica knew it was for her own sake she was asking it.

Ellen's sudden smile spoke even more clearly than her words as she said, 'I've told Alice, given her a month's notice to find somewhere else. Now I'm catching the bus into Deremouth to Mr Morton the estate agent. But I shan't stay beyond the time Alice is working her notice. If he hasn't found a buyer I shall give him the key and leave him to sell it, furniture and all. Memories don't live in sticks and stones, I shall part with all of it. Do you know, I find life suddenly exciting! I never expected to say that again. A new beginning. As I said to Alice this morning – and you'd think the bottom had dropped out of the world the way she wailed and carried on – it's very good for us at our time of life to face the challenge of something new.'

'Good for you perhaps,' Monica spoke sharply. 'If you don't care about leaving *me*, then at least you might have a care for Alice. She's been with you since she was a girl. Where do you think she's going to go now? Yours is the only home she's known for a quarter of a century.'

'You're being unkind. And I was so excited. She'll not leave me without a first-rate reference. She'll soon find somewhere. You're trying to spoil it for me, make me feel guilty when I was letting myself get so excited. Living with a brother, hardly the height of adventure. But who knows what lies ahead . . . a new place . . . new friends . . . new hope.' There was no dissuading Ellen. That was at the end of July. Before the next month was out she had headed north to a new life, Alice had packed her bags and taken a room in Deremouth while she looked for work.

Veronica had heard nothing of Laurence since his brief note explaining that he was far too busy to come to Ottercombe to her wedding. With Ellen gone, her last link with him was broken.

For Alice, faithful to the family since before Laurence was born, the future looked bleak. For the lucky ones, life was good during those years of the 1920s; some lived in the same style they always had. But in every town there were the unemployed, the

97

hopeless. Some of them had come through the war and returned home believing the promises of better times ahead. Others, like Alice, were looking for work at a time when fewer people could afford help in the home; indeed, with newfangled equipment like vacuum cleaners, electric irons, gas cooking stoves and heaters, they needed less domestic help. An attic bed-sitting room with one gas ring was her accommodation as she watched her meagre savings dwindle.

It was towards the end of September that she believed fortune was going to smile on her, for at last she'd found work. A few months ago she would have viewed washing up at the Happy Plaice very differently, but at least it was a way to earn her rent and she walked away from the quay with a new spring in her step.

'Alice!' She heard her name and turned to find Monica hurrying towards her. 'I am so glad to see you. Ever since Mrs Chesterton left I have worried. You've found another place?'

Alice told her, adding with a new note of confidence, 'But it'll just see me through till I find something more to my liking.'

'Oh but you'll be wasted there. Mrs Chesterton would be so upset. What was it she used to call you? A home-maker. Lots of women can cook, she used to say, but you looked after them both – and Captain Chesterton too when he was alive – as if you really cared.'

'Of course I cared. How is she, ma'am? You hear from her regularly? And Master Laurence? Mister I suppose now he's a man about town as you might say.'

'She seems happy with her brother.' Monica's mind wasn't on Ellen. Instead it jumped from one scenario to the next, its spring-board always the faithful Alice. 'You've found yourself a comfortable place to live? Oh, Alice, I know it meant so much to Mrs Chesterton to be with family, but how I wish she hadn't gone. It's upset all of us. Where are you staying?'

On hearing, she was even more troubled. A room above a greengrocery shop was no place for a dear soul like Alice. No greengrocery shop would have been ideal, not even Hunter and Digby's which had the trade from all the better establishments. But Lambton's, on the corner of Wellington Street and Station Square, was a nasty, unwholesome place, smelling of rotting vegetables and with boxes of greens outside on the pavement at just the height for every scavenging mongrel to sniff at before using them as a convenience. It was dreadful to think of kind, caring Alice living above that. Even a job in the bakery would be better than washing greasy plates at the Happy Plaice, and would probably pay her enough to look for somewhere more suitable.

Monica was tempted to offer Alice work at Blakeney's there and then, but a warning voice told her it would be wise to make the suggestion to Veronica rather than take the law into her own hands, it wouldn't do to antagonise her. So after another few words, the two parted company and she walked on to the bus stop. The trouble was, Veronica could be so possessive about what she saw as her own domain. Stuff and nonsense! Blakeney's had got along very nicely before she persuaded her father to let her tinker about there. The sooner they found a good, reliable man to put in charge the better. Who did the silly girl imagine would take her seriously as head of what had always been a good business? All very well for a few weeks, saying her father was ill and she was keeping his seat warm. But the time had come when their customers must see a difference in the way things were done, they must notice there was no one at the helm. This evening Veronica and Nicholas were coming to dinner, it would be an ideal time to make her suggestion about finding a place for poor Alice. With Nicholas there, the silly girl would have more sense than to argue. And if only Herbert dropped off for a while she could bring up the idea of a manager again, with Nicholas adding his support Veronica wouldn't have a leg to stand on. But, of course, this evening Herbert might not want to sleep, company always did him good. Not that he could keep up with what was being said. It was when there were just the two of them he slept.

Standing by herself outside the railway station listening for the sound of the bus, she felt alone and lonely. Poor Herbert, he couldn't help what had happened to him. If he'd broken a leg, if he were permanently crippled and she had to push him in a Bath chair, those things wouldn't make a stranger of him. It was like looking after an obedient child: instinct or habit ensured that he washed and dressed himself – and with the exception of the occasional lapse of odd shoes he managed well. He would sit with her in the garden, he would follow her holding the trug while she cut flowers, he fed himself as neatly as he always had, he even pulled out her chair for her to sit to the table. But those things were part of his nature, they needed no thought. And there was that other change, one that only a few months ago she would have expected to have welcomed but which, in reality, left her feeling unloved. Then, his nightly passion had been out of character and had made a stranger of him; now, passion had died. Sometimes she tried to arouse him, in the vain hope that that way even briefly his mind might clear. But the result was only that her own desire was heightened and, as he slept, she would lay at his side, wide awake, frustrated and empty of hope.

She was relieved when she heard the noisy engine of the Ottercombe bus. At home he'd be waiting for her, sitting just as she'd left him, the unread newspaper on his lap, no idea of how long she'd been out. The other thing she was sure of was the way his face would light with relief and pleasure when she came into the room. Dear Herbert. He'd always been a good man, what sort of God would treat him like this? And not just him – her too.

They drove out of Deremouth, past the turning to the right across Picton Heath to Moorleigh, then across the river bridge and past the left hand turning to Otterton St Giles and the coast. Less than a mile on, the rickety bus left the main road, turning to the right onto the rutted lane to Ottercombe. Long before she climbed down the steep step to the cobbled path of the village her own spirits had taken an unexpected lift. She knew just what she intended to do.

That was on Tuesday morning. Wednesday saw her in Deremouth again.

And so it was that before the week was over, Alice Gibbs arrived back in Ottercombe, tapping on the kitchen door of Ipsley House to be admitted by a smiling Bertha who'd been looking out for her.

'The Missus told me to expect you, bring your clobber in. The kettle's singing, we'll have a cup of tea before I take you to where you'll be sleeping and tell her and the master you've arrived. Be nice to have a bit of company about the place. Shame, it was, Mrs Chesterton selling up like that. Nothing's like it used to be, not for any of us. Funny house this is, since young Veronica got herself married and the poor master was taken so strange. That's why you're here.' She made herself say it casually enough but her sharp eyes watched to make sure Alice understood just where she stood. All very fine – in fact all very pleasant – having another

100

woman about the place, just so long as there was no interfering in her kitchen. 'He needs a lot of attention. Not that he means to be a trouble, bless his heart, but leave him to put his shoes on and bet your last bob he'd come hobbling down with them on the wrong feet. Our young Veronica comes breezing in here every morning, talks to him like as if his brain box was in the same working order it used to be. Seeing her cheers him up I know. But easy enough for her, five minutes and she's gone from the house. The poor missus, she gets it all day long, I wonder her patience doesn't snap. Mine would. I dare say you'll find time to do a hand's turn with the dusting and such but, as I understand it, it's to give him a bit of company you're needed. And take my word, it'll need all the patience you've got. Same old questions over and over, and what conversation he tries to make don't make a ha'porth of sense. Still, it's a roof and a good home. I thought a deal about you when Mrs Chesterton upped sticks like she did. Never a care for anyone but herself—'

'Oh, but of course she cared. But, like she explained, her brother needed her to run his home. Blood is thicker than water.'

By the time Alice had carried her valise up to her new bedroom she felt herself to be part of the household already, images of greasy plates at the Happy Plaice had faded as surely as a nightmare dies on waking.

In May Nicholas had given a recital to a packed hall in Manchester and, with all the appearance of a dutiful wife, Veronica had gone with him. It was what they'd planned in the halcyon days of their honeymoon only weeks previously, but plans and reality had proved to have little in common. With the recital on a Wednesday, they'd travelled north on Tuesday and returned on Thursday. They had never expected to be longer than that, so where had the difference been? Even though he could spare no more time away from the Choir School, throughout the trip Veronica had been aware of his resentment that she, too, had need to be back in Deremouth for her own purposes. A wife's role was as a support for her husband – but not when the wife was Veronica. By common consent, the trip over, they hadn't referred to it; it hadn't given a memory they wanted to probe. Guiltily, she suspected that he would have had more personal satisfaction had he gone north on his own as he would have done not so long ago.

He had been received with enthusiasm by the Music Society who had organised his visit and by his audience while, beyond a polite but disinterested greeting, she had felt herself to be invisible. Certainly his playing had drawn her to him irresistibly, from the softly plaintive to the power and glory of the swelling tones it had carried her just as it never failed to do when she listened in the Abbey. Sitting alone she had watched him, her humble adoration a far cry from the independent young woman who thrived on the challenge of running a business.

The third Friday in October he was to play in Reading Town Hall.

'We'll travel by rail,' he told her, 'there's a good train leaving Deremouth at 8.10 in the morning. That'll give me ample time to familiarise myself with the organ in the afternoon. I'm told the George is very comfortable and not far from the Town Hall, so I'll make reservations for the one night.'

She concentrated on her morning marmalade and toast, avoiding looking at him as she answered.

'I can't be away on a Friday. Manchester was mid-week, but Friday I always check all the week's orders have been dealt with, then I have to pay the men – and women—' she threw in, as if to remind him that his wasn't the only sex!

It became a battle of will. How long could she avoid looking at him when he was silently bending her will to his own? Breaking off a piece of toast, she spread a dab of butter on it and forced it into her mouth as if that would protect her from enlarging on what she'd said. The tick of the clock seemed unusually loud; outside a rook croaked from high in a nearby elm.

'I shall book a double room.' His voice was ice cold. 'I consider it is more than time you remembered you have responsibilities to your marriage.'

'Poppycock!' She swallowed her toast in a half-bitten lump. 'What's marriage got to do with sitting by myself in a hall of strangers. *You* don't need me when you're giving a recital; the locals certainly don't need me – nor I them. Marriage is a two-way thing. Blakeney's isn't just a job of work, Nicholas, it matters to me, really matters. And then there's Dad. He would never have put a manager in just so that he could take more time off. And neither will I. I know the way I want things done.'

'For more than six months we've gone on like this.' His voice was still ice cold. 'It hardly points us towards a companionable future.'

'You're being silly,' she fought her corner. To relax her scowl would be tantamount to his having disarmed her. 'I don't ask you to spend less time with your music.'

'Music was an interest you professed to share.' Now that was hitting below the belt! For a second it silenced her.

Then, in the way her mood could suddenly change, her eyes lit with laughter. 'Of course we do, just like you share the cakes I bring home with me.' Briefly they looked at each other, the ice melting, the barrier whether built by pride, hurt, arrogance or misunderstanding, tumbling. Their hands reached across the table, their fingers met and gripped. Then, breakfast was forgotten, recitals and bakehouses were pushed back to where they belonged as with one accord they got up from the table and moved towards each other.

'I'm sorry, darling Nicholas, honestly I don't want to be a bad wife. But I'm me, I have to be as I am.'

'You're a wonderful wife,' he whispered, his hold on her vice-like. 'If jealousy is a sin, then I'm guilty. I want all your time, all your thoughts, all your love.'

'You have all my love.' And again laughter loosened the stranglehold of emotion, 'But a shadow is just something that follows you around, something you forget even to notice. Surely that's not what you'd like me to turn into?'

'It's time we had a family.' His words fell into the stillness of the room. Was this the moment to tell him the thing she had mentioned to no one? She'd told herself there had been nothing dishonest about her visit to the Family Planning Clinic. She and Nicholas had agreed that they wanted time together before they thought of children, so why had she kept her secret to herself? Why had she not told him he had no need to be the one to be responsible? And, even more important, why did she still say nothing?

His words hung in the air, unanswered. The eager way she nuzzled against his newly shaved chin then raised her mouth to his had less to do with eagerness for motherhood than with anticipation of no protective sheath coming between them as love-making carried them to the never failing climax.

'Wish it was bedtime,' she whispered, her eyes teasing, her voice full of laughter.

So both of them believed they had come out of the argument a victor. He foresaw that soon, like it or not, she would have to hand over the running of Blakeney's to someone else; she was safe in the belief that she controlled her own body, and she realised now why instinct had prompted her to keep her secret.

The *Deremouth News* carried a double-page spread about the opening of Clampton's Cakes' newly refurbished factory. For most of the summer work had been going on there, rows of great ovens had been installed to deal with the end product of the preparations performed by electric gadgetry previously unheard of. Miraculously Blakeney's had lost none of their workers to the new and modern establishment, but Veronica suspected that in some cases this wasn't due entirely to loyalty. The newspaper article described the factory environment, the great vats where the ingredients would be mixed electrically, then automatically as the tins passed along a moving conveyor, a fixed amount released into each one. All day long, non-stop, work would continue. The staff at Blakeney's were used to beating their bowls of ingredients by hand, ladling the mixture into the tins; they felt personal pride in each golden glory that was taken from the ovens. Although the extra penny an hour Clampton's paid was tempting, the general feeling was that to work a machine turned one into a machine. That was what they all said, none of them bringing themselves to admit that they were frightened by the thought of having to keep up with a conveyor belt each working minute of a ten-hour day. Imagine having no time for a friendly word, no time for a joke!

The habit of Veronica calling at Ipsley House each morning arose from her collecting the motor car and driving in to town just as she always had. But long before October the routine had changed at least in part. Monica couldn't drive, in fact she had never approved of Herbert teaching Veronica. In those early weeks of summer she'd clung to the hope that he would get better, she had let the arrangement continue that Veronica rode her bicycle from the Abbey each morning and collected the car. But before summer was over it was obvious that there was no hope of Herbert driving again and it seemed pointless for the car to be housed in their own coach-house when there was plenty of space at the Abbey. Even so, a morning never went by when

Veronica didn't pull up outside the gate and come in even for five minutes.

'Have you seen the *News* this morning?' Monica hardly gave her a chance to get through the door before she asked. 'That beastly Clampton's Cakes has started production.'

'Well, we knew it was all equipped ready. And good luck to them, Mum. Just so long as you don't buy their beastly sawdust rubbish.'

'It's all very well taking that high-hand tone about them. What's it going to do to us, Ronnie? People haven't the same sort of money that they used to have. And anyway – oh well, you're a good girl holding the fort. But we have to face facts.'

'I always face facts, Mum. And the fact is, we don't clash with Clampton's, thank God. At the price they charge the ingredients must be rubbish. Where do they get their flavours? I'll tell you. They get them from bottled essence. People with no idea of quality might carry them home in their shopping baskets, and good luck to them. We don't cater for that sort of trade.'

'Oh dear, Ronnie, you do sound so snobby. A person is none the better because he has more money in the bank.'

Veronica laughed affectionately. 'I know that, Mum. My point is, those people who've been able to afford our sort of produce won't buy Clampton's rubbish. Or, if they do, it won't be more than once. Isn't that so, Dad?' She liked to draw him into the conversation even though she had no hope that he might have been keeping track of it. To see him, who would guess how changed he was? In appearance he was the same as ever, as smart as any man who left the house for a day at business. But how much of it was due to Mum?

'I'd better go. It's getting late.'

Just for a moment he was confused. 'Not ready . . . don't know . . . let me see . . .' one half-finished sentence followed another.

'No need for you to hurry, Dad. You stay and read the paper for an hour, I want to do a few things on the way in. I'll pop home for you later.' She hated lying to him, but her reward was his palpable relief.

'That's it, child. I'll just wait here.'

She hugged him, her eyes stinging with unfamiliar tears, before she hurried out of the room knowing that once she was gone he would have forgotten. It wasn't until she was well on her way to town that it occurred to her that in her concern for him she'd not said goodbye to her mother.

Arriving in her office she found a copy of the *Deremouth News* on her desk, opened at the article about the new cake factory. Knowing that Bert Jenkins must have brought it for her to read, she made herself scan the report. She suspected that, like her mother, the workers in the bakehouse were feeling insecure about their future. She leant back in the swivel chair, asking herself an honest question and seeking an honest answer. Do I really believe those things I said? Can Blakeney's withstand that sort of competition in an area like this? In London, perhaps. But here in Devon? I must be right, I have to be right. It's not just that the family depends on it, it's not even that the people who work in the bakehouse depend on it. No, it goes far, far deeper. This is a family business, right from the day it started with just one oven and people bringing their own mixtures to be cooked when it was free, it has been part of Deremouth; Dad kept it going all the way through the war and the shortages. Now it's up to me. I won't fail, I swear I won't. Why can't Nicholas understand how important it is? As if anyone I could engage, even someone experienced and far cleverer than me, would care as much as I do.

Again she glanced down at the article, her lips set in a tight line. If she heard the light tap on the door it didn't penetrate her thoughts. As she looked up it opened, too late to close the newspaper which lay like incriminating evidence on her desk.

'I apologise for disturbing you. I was told you were here but I didn't hear you answer my knock.' The man who stood in the doorway was quietly spoken, quietly dressed in a well-tailored slate grey business suit, carrying bowler hat and cane.

'That's because I didn't,' she told him, annoyed at the interruption and even more annoyed at herself for the rudeness she heard in her manner. If he were a client this was hardly the way to receive him. 'I'm sorry,' she made an effort, 'I was busy and I didn't hear you. Please come in. You wanted me?'

'You must be Miss Blakeney,' the stranger assumed. 'I received a letter from you some months ago.'

'So it must have been months ago if I was Miss Blakeney, I've been married for more than half a year. But why did I write to you? You have the advantage over me.'

'I see you are reading the article in the local paper.'

She could feel herself bristle, annoyed that anyone should be given the opportunity to imagine she was put out by the new project.

She shrugged her shoulders, as if to dismiss a concern so trivial. 'I wish them well,' she answered, 'I suppose there must always be a market for cheap mass production.' Her tone left no doubt of her assurance that Blakeney's wasn't touched by competition of the kind it could offer.

'Let me introduce myself. I am Merrick Clampton.' Seldom was Veronica lost for words, but now was one of those rare times. 'It's you who have the advantage. If you are no longer Miss Blakeney, then may I know your name?'

'Veronica Ellis. Mr Clampton, I'm sure you have come here in friendship. You can't possibly imagine we're rivals for the same trade, I surely made that clear when I wrote to you.'

'Indeed you did. I have your letter in my pocket.' All too well she remembered the letter from Clampton's head office, and the gist of her reply; but she wished she could recall exactly how she'd couched her none too polite refusal. Even though his face was serious, she had an uncomfortable feeling that he was secretly laughing at her. But perhaps she was wrong, perhaps that twinkle was a permanent resident in his blue eyes. 'This is my first visit to Deremouth since my purchase of the premises.' Now there was no doubt of the smile as he told her, 'I wish I could show you the plant they've put in.'

'I wouldn't be likely to understand such things. Every cake we produce here is made by hand. We have a reputation to uphold.'

'Indeed you have. But Mrs Ellis, there are two sides to every coin. On the one you have those who can afford to indulge in the excellent products of your bakehouse – and I can personally vouch for their excellence.'

'I've no doubt. Every one of our recipes is created here – some haven't changed for years but some I've formulated myself. That's how we do things. At home, by trial and error, I've found the perfect quantities, the perfect temperatures. So if you imagine you can make easy and cheap reproductions to put within the reach of every Tom, Dick and Harry, you'd better think again.' Even as she spoke she knew she was being ungracious to a man who may well have called here in nothing but good faith, perhaps meaning to lay to rest the hostile tone generated by her letter.

107

'I've been in the trade too long to be that kind of a fool, Mrs Ellis. I talked of two sides to every coin – yes, and so it is with people. There is the head side, those who can afford your excellent products. But what of those for whom it has landed tail side up? Those with wages enough for little more than bare necessities, those with even less than that? You brush Clampton's Cakes aside as if what we produce is less than wholesome.' Fair and square he met her gaze and she recognised steel she hadn't anticipated. 'And that I cannot accept. Our ingredients are good, our production hygienic. All right, our profit margin doesn't allow for ground almonds, fresh ginger, newly ground spices, vanilla pods; we use bottled essences, tins of ready-ground spices, I realise the difference. And, yes, instead of butter we use the margarine you would spurn – but it's safe, it's pure. And I'll tell you something else,' in his enthusiasm he hardly realised how long a speech he was making, 'what we produce cheers many a working family's teatable. We put a coating of icing on many of our individual two-a-penny cakes. It takes no more than icing sugar, essence and water, but the object is to turn a diet of bread and butter – or perhaps margarine? – into a treat. And of course to make a profit in doing it,' he added with something approaching a smile.

Veronica looked at her visitor with new eyes. Was he a hard-headed business man? Yes, surely he was, he had factories throughout the country. Was he a philanthropist?

'So we are agreed, our trades don't clash, they pose no threat to each other,' she said warily, still uncertain of the reason for his visit and not knowing whether she ought to be prepared to bury the hatchet or use it.

'They could complement each other.'

'Rubbish!' Immediately she was on her guard.

'Mrs Ellis, I am only in Deremouth until tomorrow. My manager – you may well know him, although you would have been too young to remember his time with Blakeney's before the war – is a very good man by the name of William Gurnsey.'

'No, I don't remember. And if my father had thought highly of him I imagine he would have taken him back when the Army had done with him.' It seemed that being wary was also making her aggressive. Merrick Clampton's visit – his unnecessary visit, she added silently – was casting a shadow on her day.

'His returning here didn't arise. I understand he volunteered in

1914 and served in the Catering Corps. Rapidly promoted, he was given a commission and when hostilities came to an end he didn't return to civilian life. For five years he retained his commission. Chance, good fortune – his and mine too – brought him back to Deremouth at a time the work was being carried out on my premises. He's accustomed to being in charge of men, he is *au fait* with supplies etc.' He looked at her very directly. 'At the back of my mind is a niggling feeling that had you known he was in the market for local employment, he might have been the very man you needed. In fact it was he who told me of your father's illness, so I believe something of the same thought must be niggling his mind too.'

'I see no connection.' But of course it wasn't true. She knew very well that it wasn't expected that she would fill her father's role. 'You should get a manager' – she heard it from her mother, she heard it from Nicholas, she knew the men in the bakehouse were worried about their future. As a 'helper' to her father, they'd accepted her; but whoever heard of a woman in charge? As she'd told Merrick Clampton, for more than half a year she'd been married and through all that time nothing had changed at Blakeney's. To start with the staff had been told Herbert was unwell, nothing more than that; so they'd accepted Veronica, expecting it to be a temporary arrangement. By now she knew they were uneasy, Bert Jenkins had even mentioned that detested word 'manager'.

'I respect your reaction to my earlier letter, but I want you to know that I am still extremely interested. No,' he held up a hand to forestall her as she opened her mouth to shoot him down. 'Blakeney's and the high quality – and high priced – goods turned out here are safe from threat from my new factory. I realise that and it's the way I want it to remain. I give you my word that if you and your father decide—'

'Dad can't,' she blurted out, her confidence almost deserting her. 'Even if I wanted to do as you say – which I don't – it wouldn't be possible. Blakeney's Bakery belongs to him, I'm not even a partner. And he's in no state to talk business, no state even to understand—' She bit hard on her lip, hating her show of emotion, wishing him gone.

'I'm desperately sorry.'

She got up from behind her desk and walked to the window. Even though she had overcome what had so nearly been a moment of weakness, she wasn't prepared to have him watching her face and probably reading into her mind.

'We all are,' she said. 'For *him*, we're all desperately sorry. But I don't need sympathy, neither does Blakeney's.'

'I'm sure that's true of Blakeney's. But you must miss working with him, nothing can be the same here as it was.'

'I'm all right.' She heard her words as hostile. And why not? What right had he to come here, flaunting the wonders of his smart new factory, offering her sympathy, inferring that she couldn't manage without a share of his oh-so-clever manager. Pride came to her rescue. 'I'm afraid I must ask you to forgive me,' she said with aloof politeness, 'I have a busy morning ahead and really must get on.'

'I apologise, I've taken up too much of your time already.' He stood up as she turned away from the window. In her relief that he had accepted her decision as final, she looked at him anew. Had she not been so used to Nicholas's height, she would have seen him as a tall man. His hair was a nondescript dark shade, streaked prematurely grey at the temples, the piercingly light blue of his eyes was accentuated by their fringe of dark lashes; his features were neat rather than handsome, his teeth even, his hands well kept. She realised that she'd been staring and felt the hot colour flood her cheeks.

'I believe I've been less than polite. Forgive me,' she said in an attempt to explain away the confusion of her feelings. Then, honesty prevailing in a way she was so often powerless to prevent, 'You see, the truth is everyone has been saying the same thing to me. Get a manager. Mother says it, my husband says it – I believe the staff are frightened I'll dig myself into a hole and pull them down with me. But it's not true. For months before Dad was finally ill I'd had to be responsible. How can they think I'd sell out and let him down? I won't. I tell you—' She'd heard the pitch of her voice rising, she'd had no power to bring it down any more than she had to stop the outpour that ended on a croak that would let her go no further.

Putting his hat and cane back on the desk he came towards her and took both her hands in his.

'Believe me, I didn't come here to try to persuade you into something you weren't prepared to do. And now you have made your position perfectly clear. But Mrs Ellis, as you said, Blakeney's and Clampton's pose no threat to each other. So surely neither need we? I admit, this is a business I should have been proud to own. Having talked to you I can see it isn't in need of a new owner. But since we aren't rivals, I see no reason why we shouldn't be friends.'

'I thought you were leaving Deremouth tomorrow?' Why was it she couldn't make herself more agreeable?

'I shall be back.' Then with a smile that she knew stemmed from his thoughts more than any newfound friendship for her, 'My daughter has made up her mind on that score. My head office is in London, but as Becky – that's my daughter – as Becky says, how much better to live by the sea. She has lost her heart to Deremouth and is determined we find a house here.' He took no pains to disguise the fact that his pleasure came from pleasing the child. He went down in Veronica's opinion, she would have expected him to have more sense than turn a daughter into a spoilt brat.

'And what about the rest of the family. What about your wife? Has she fallen in love with Deremouth too?'

'If she were here, I think she would have. I lost her nearly two years ago.'

'I'm so sorry.' Not just that he'd lost his wife, but for her all too quick opinion of his indulgence of the unknown Becky.

'Thank you,' he said simply. There was a quiet dignity in his manner, an acknowledgement of grief. Remembering her own bristly reaction when he'd expressed what she now had no doubt had been genuine concern, she was ashamed.

'I'm sorry if I seemed rude – just now I mean – about Dad and Blakeney's – about managing here on my own.'

'If you saw me as Public Enemy Number One, I can't blame you. I've told you I had hoped you would have changed your mind about Blakeney's. But that, Mrs Ellis, was before we met. Now I promise you I respect your decision.'

Her face lit with a smile that banished her hostility.

'I'm glad you came. I suppose at the back of my mind I had been wary – there's nothing worse than an unknown enemy. But now I know you understand my views, then we can run on parallel lines knowing the distance between us is absolute. Like the railway,' she ended with a laugh.

'Indeed we can.' He held out his hand to bid her farewell. 'I

111

shall now leave you in peace.' Then, his features softening into a teasing smile, 'Carrying your simile to its conclusion, we should remember that the lines may not meet but the trains are dependent on one as surely as the other.'

She had a busy morning ahead of her, but the visit had been unsettling. Why should a man like that make a fortune – she had no doubt he did make a fortune – out of producing poor quality cakes? Her description of them was automatic, until she'd thought again of what he'd said and remembered it wasn't so different from her father's opinion when first they'd known Clampton's were coming to the town. Instead of going back to her desk, she stood gazing out of the window. She saw Merrick Clampton walk across the yard to the open gates leading to the street then, through the iron fencing, she saw a child stand up from the low wall opposite where she'd been sitting waiting. That must be Becky, a girl of perhaps nine or ten. It was only as, hand in hand, they started up the road that she noticed the child's awkward walk and saw that one of her thin legs was in an iron.

Going back to her desk she took the letter opener and started to read the mail. But her mind wasn't easy, it harboured too many memories of the friendship between her father and her, memories stirred by the sight of Merrick Clampton and Becky. Nicholas believed it was time they started a family; but was that simply as a way of stopping her running Blakeney's? And why was she so against the idea? Wasn't he entitled to know that so-special bond between father and daughter? Was her stubbornness simply that she didn't want to hand over the reins to a manager or was it because she didn't want anything to alter for Nicholas and her? The idea of being pregnant had no appeal at all. No matter what their days brought, those final hours were a never failing adventure of wonder. She didn't want to feel herself getting clumsier day by day, things would be different for them. And afterwards, would she ever be the same? Still she kept her secret, his disappointment doing nothing to alter her views. One day she would be ready, but not yet; she and Nicholas needed no intrusion from a third person, not even one of their own making.

The mail read, she still felt restless. She'd go down to the bake-house and talk to the men. None of them had ever asked her about Blakeney's future, but it was up to her to talk to them, to look ahead and reassure them. She'd always enjoyed watching them working, discussing any new recipes with Bert Jenkins; a quarter of an hour vanished before she realised it. Then back to her own room and, again to the pull of the window. At that second she recognised Monica hurrying along on the opposite side of the road. It was unusual for her to call at the bakery, could it mean something was wrong? Veronica was about to fling up the bottom window, when something stopped her. Monica didn't so much as glance across the road as she hurried towards the corner where someone waited, her face lit with pleasure, her hand raised in a wave of greeting.

Chapter Seven

'Veronica, you do so worry me. I know there are some women who have to work to help bring home the money. Some in shops, some in the kitchens of restaurants, some even in the bakery. But your situation is quite different. It's a slight to Nicholas to forsake the home like you do.' While Monica gave way to such outspoken criticism she had been stooping to cut the garden's first tulips of the season, it was easier to concentrate on what she was doing than to look Veronica directly in the eyes. Now she straightened her back and turned her full attention on her daughter. 'How can you be such a silly girl? I've a good mind to put my foot down and get rid of the business altogether, put it on the market for sale before it runs itself into the ground with no man at the helm.'

'You don't know anything about the business,' Veronica replied tartly. 'I'm not running it into the ground, it's doing well. If I thought I'd let it fail, then I might even agree with you. Anyway, Blakeney's belongs to Dad so neither of us could sell it – even if we wanted to, which we don't. It's been part of the family in Deremouth for generations. Don't you see, Mum, it's a sort of privilege to build on the past.'

'Privilege indeed, what a romancer you are! But it's *you* I'm talking about, you and your future I worry about. All these months I've stood by and watched you carrying on just as if you had no husband, no home. It's not right, Veronica. You ought to be at home like other women. It's more than a year since your wedding. Most women have a baby in its perambulator by this time, or at least one on the way. What sort of a marriage is it for poor Nicholas with you spending your life in that wretched bakery?'

Veronica refused to take her mother seriously. 'Much the same as yours was, I expect. Dad spent his days there and you didn't complain.'

'Now you're just being stupid! Your father is a man. Or he *was* ...' She turned away, too wretched to speak.

'And so he still is, Mum.' In a rare gesture of affection, Veronica put her arm round her mother. 'He can't remember things, he gets confused – but under all that he's the same man he always was. Look at the way he lights up when you come into the room. All he really wants is to have you close by him.'

'I know,' Monica sniffed, catching an escaped tear on the back of her hand. 'I do my best. But it all just goes on and on, there isn't even a light at the end of the tunnel. He's no age. Neither am I. We probably have years ahead of us like this. My life is empty, you don't know how empty. If you were having a baby, just think how we could sit and sew together—'

There was nothing ladylike about Veronica's guffaw at the idea of her mother and her contentedly stitching.

'It's all very well for you to laugh. But what about me? I used to have Ellie. I suppose that was the mistake we made, Ellie and me. We were like sisters, at least that's what I thought. Every day we were together. We didn't seem to need other friends. Now here I am, day after day, no one even to speak to. No use talking to Herbert. He can't help it, poor darling, but where does that leave *me*?'

'Now that Alice is here you must feel much more free. You can get into town without worrying.'

'Oh yes,' Monica rasped, 'I can take the bus into Deremouth, wander about on my own. And that's all I've got to look forward to. You and he have always filled your own lives, never cared how dull mine was chained to the house—'

'And that's what you're advocating for me?' Veronica teased, trying to lift the conversation from the depths to which it had sunk.

'That's different. Nicholas is a companion – or he would be if you ever gave him the opportunity. He doesn't even go off to business each day. You'd not be left on your own for hours at a time like most women. Yet even when he would have taken you with him to – where was it? – Reading, and then just before Christmas to Winchester to the Cathedral, you put your own silly interests first. The time will come when you regret it.'

115

'Nicholas and I are fine, Mum. Honestly he doesn't need you to worry about him and fight his battles.' Indeed he doesn't! she added silently. 'Now that you can get out more easily, why don't you suggest you and Mrs Wainwright spend more time together?'

'She has a full life. Oh, we have a pleasant enough chat after church, or if we happen to meet in the village. But she has a family of her own. Usually dear Dulcie is with her,' she managed to get in a final dig before she had to bring the subject to a close. 'Oh dear, here comes your father following me. He mustn't see I've been crying. Go and meet him, steer him away while I slip indoors and wash my face.'

Gladly Veronica waved a greeting to her father, going to meet him and linking her arm through his.

'Guess what I've found?' she turned him away from Monica's retreating figure. 'Look, let me show you. I spied some tiny tadpoles in the pond already. Aren't they early!'

'Tadpoles. Frogs. Ah yes.' So far his mind had stayed in line with hers. Then it took a new direction. 'Your mother is frightened when they run up the wall.'

'That's spiders, Dad.'

'Finished your lessons, have you? Good girl.' To him she must have suddenly become the child she'd once been. 'Where's your mother? Off out with Ellen? Yes, yes, that'll be it.'

She kept him out in the spring sunshine long enough for Monica to restore her tear-stained face, then she glanced at the fob watch hanging on her bodice.

'Let's go indoors, Dad. You've not got a coat on. And here comes Alice to carry you off.'

'Ah, Alice my dear. Mrs Chesterton has sent you with a message? You'll want my wife I dare say. What a beautiful morning.' A brief flash, if not of clarity, but at least of his habitually courteous manner. Veronica's hold on his arm tightened as, with a rare show of outward affection, she moved her hand so that her fingers held his.

'I must go, Dad,' she told him.

'Go! Go . . .' Then, time catching up with him, he imagined her driving to Deremouth, the two of them together in his car. Yes, he could see it already parked just outside the gate. Feeling his sudden tension, so she held his hand tighter and said, 'I think Mum would like it if you stayed at home this morning, Dad.

116

There's nothing special happening at the bakery, you can leave it to me. I'll look in on the way home and tell you about everything.'

'That's the way. I shan't be sorry to have a quiet morning. Busy day yesterday.'

'I've put the board with the jigsaw on the table,' Alice told him. 'If you can spare five minutes, I could do with an extra pair of eyes. The sky always defeats me.'

Like an obedient child he went off happily with her. Veronica was forgotten, he didn't even turn at the sound of the engine starting up, so her wave was lost on him. It wasn't so easy for her to put the visit out of her mind, although her thoughts dwelt more on Monica than Herbert. As far back as she could remember, despite having Ellen Chesterton on hand, her mother had always bemoaned what she'd seen as her dull life. Veronica had imagined her attitude had been rooted in jealousy of the affection and companionship between herself and her father. But it was difficult now to brush her unhappiness aside. Poor Mum, she thought, as she jolted along the lane towards the main road. She's right, the outlook is dreadful. And yet she never lowers her standards, never gets careless about her appearance, she always looks a picture. Even when she cried this morning, she managed not to get all blotchy like I would. Those things she said ... Am I a bad wife? No, surely I'm not. I know he would like me to be at home, but if I gave up looking after the bakery, if I spent my days pottering around doing the things Florrie Beckham can do so easily – and much better than I would – I wouldn't be the same *me*. Is that really what she wants? Her parents forgotten, her face relaxed into a smile at the pictures in her mind. She gave the horn two sharp squeezes then put out her right arm to indicate that she was turning off the main road into Deremouth.

The morning followed the Thursday pattern. She dealt with the post, wrote the weekly order for ingredients Bert Jenkins had left on her desk, then worked out the wages from the time sheets. Although Herbert was owner of Blakeney's, long before his trouble had started he had arranged with the bank that she should be authorised to sign cheques. The bank closed at three o'clock, so just after half past two she went out to collect the wage money. Early morning had given a promise that summer wasn't far away, and still there wasn't a cloud in the sky. The town was busy, it seemed full of noise and bustle, the air dusty. Tempted by thoughts of the sea, once the wage money was safely in her purse, Veronica decided to take the longer walk back to Blakeney's. Instead of returning the way she'd come, outside the bank she crossed Waterloo Street and turned off down Fisherman's Walk, a cobblestone lane leading to Vicary Terrace. This was a handsome crescent of Georgian houses fronting a well-tended green sward behind the sandy shore. Another glance at her watch told her it wasn't much after three o'clock. There was hardly any breeze, the warmth of the sun was like a caress as she raised her face towards it. As if she were playing truant she imagined her empty office. Once she'd sorted out the pay packets for the morning, she had nothing pressing waiting to be done. She could leave early. But even as the idea came to her, it was overtaken by the knowledge that there was no reason to hurry home. Nicholas would be in the practice room working on the thing that seemed to fill every available hour of the day, his own Easter Oratorio which was to include his setting for the Eucharist that was sung each morning in the Abbey. If she had time to spare she'd walk up the cliff path, let her thoughts roam where they would in the solitude she knew she would find there in the middle of a Thursday afternoon. So she turned to the left in Vicary Terrace and strode briskly in the direction of the steep track to the cliff top. On a day like this, if she'd had longer to spare, she would have enjoyed walking on along the high track until finally it dropped down to the quayside in Chalcombe, the one-time fishing village eastward along the coast. Memories flooded back, images so clear in her mind that she could almost see herself with Laurence, both of them on their bicycles; she could almost hear their voices, their carefree laughter seemed all round her. She had no idea where he was living and, since her marriage, she'd heard nothing from him. Anyway, she told herself, she hadn't come here to think about Laurence.

On the treeless cliff the fine, poor grass was interspersed with the occasional clump of gorse bushes. Alone, she sat on the ground, taking off her cloche hat and shaking her cropped hair. The freedom of hair not anchored by pins was wonderful, she ran her fingers through it then, just as she had before, held her face towards the sun, her eyes closed.

I've come here to be by myself, to think, she told herself. So I mustn't waste time just lapping up the warmth. What was it Mum said this morning, about if I were to stay at home, then Nicholas would be there too. I mustn't duck the question, I must be honest with myself. I know he wants me to give up the bakery, but not for the sake of my company. It hurts his pride that I have a life away from him. But, have I? If he weren't there, would any of it matter to me? I don't want to think about it, to imagine what it would be like without him is like tempting Fate. I cheat him. Yes, I ought to face the truth. Say it again: 'I cheat him,' this time she said it aloud. Perhaps he imagines I'm barren – or, even worse, perhaps he think there must be something wrong with *him*. But how could there be? I want him to make me pregnant, it would be the supreme miracle to have him put a baby inside me. But if we had children would we turn into just Mother and Father, parents more than two people who need just each other? I'll go back to that clinic place when I'm ready – then I bet I get pregnant the first time we make love. But not yet. If I didn't have the responsibility of Blakeney's, life would be deadly dull. That's the honest truth. Oh, the nights are wonderful, every moment I'm with him is wonderful, but while he's working he doesn't need me. If I ever creep into the Abbey when he's playing wouldn't you think telepathy would tell him I'm there? Unless I sit in the choir stalls where he can see me in that mirror, he has no idea I'm even there. Surely he ought to be aware of the love I radiate? What was it David Holsworthy said after the wedding? Something about music being a difficult mistress. I thought I shared it, but I don't. No one shares it with him. Or if they do it's more likely God, a spirit he finds in the Abbey. Well, that's fine. I know when I can't compete. So I'm glad I have Blakeney's. And I'm certainly not going to give it to someone else to look after just so that I can spend my life looking after babies that would come between us. For they would. They must do.

Lying flat on the ground she rested her hands on her stomach, a stomach that was slim to the point of thinness. Her hip bones stood out sharply when she lay on her back. What would he be doing now? In the Abbey? In the practice room playing, the manuscript book on the music rack in front of him, stopping at the end of each new phrase to fill the empty staves with the neat, perfectly formed notes he could write at such speed. If only he were here. She pressed her hands hard, clenching her teeth, through her closed eyelids the sun seeming to fill her head with

119

orange light. What was the matter with her that she could feel like this? Was it normal? Not many hours ago, just as it always did, their shared passion had left her utterly satisfied, at peace with herself, shaken by love for him. When she'd climbed the track telling herself she'd let her thoughts carry her where they would, this wasn't what she'd expected. There's no one for miles around, a silent voice tempted. Of its own volition her breathing quickened at the thought, excitement was tinged with guilt. Why wasn't he here? Imagine he's—

Voices! Shielded from the track by the clump of gorse bushes, like a Jack-in-the-Box, she sat bolt upright. People! Automatically she straightened her already straight skirt, and reached for her hat and purse as she got to her feet. It was as if, by remaining on the grass, her wayward thoughts would have been evident.

'—between me and my work,' she heard a male voice. 'You're in my thoughts every moment of the day—'

'Do you think it's not like that for me?'

No! There must be a mistake! But she'd known that voice all her life, how could she be mistaken?

Moving a step or two forward she came out of the shelter provided by the gorse, just as the couple passed along the track walking in the direction of Chalcombe.

'Mum!' she called after their retreating figures.

Subconsciously she must have wanted to believe she'd misheard them, or misunderstood their meaning. But one look at Monica's startled – nearer to the truth, guilty – expression banished any hope, even though she was quickly in control.

'Why, Hugo, look who this is!'

'Where did you spring from?' Hugo Holmes laughed in an effort to ease the sudden tension. 'An afternoon playing truant from work – for you and for me too – but I'm afraid I'm the guilty one who has tempted your mother away from her shopping.'

'And who can blame any of us?' Monica backed him up, 'An afternoon like this is heaven sent, it would be a sin to waste it at the shops. When I bumped into Hugo and he told me he was going to walk the cliff, then I decided Bertha's grocery order could wait. I'll drop it in to Mr Burrows on the way back to the bus.'

What could be more innocent, or more believable? And had Veronica not overheard what had gone before, she would have accepted without any doubts. But the echo of their words hung like a shadow between them.

'A pity you didn't get Dad to come with you. He would have enjoyed it.' It wasn't what she said so much as the way she looked at them that warned Monica their story hadn't been believed. 'You and Dad used to walk a lot together, Mum.'

'You're not being fair,' Monica's bottom lip was getting out of control. 'You don't know what it's like. Sometimes I *have* to get away from it, it saps the life out of me. It's all right for him, he doesn't know. Sometimes I need to talk to someone with a mind!'

'Your mother's friendship is very precious to me. She has been kind to me since I moved to Ottercombe. You know that to be true.'

'I thought it was Mrs Chesterton you were hanging around,' Veronica said rudely.

'Oh hush, Ronnie. Don't talk to Hugo like that. It makes you seem so hard, so unladylike.'

'So honest, more likely. And this morning you were grizzling how dull your life was, how friendless you are.'

'And so I am. If Herbert thought I came walking with Hugo – oh, but Herbert wouldn't think it. Herbert doesn't think.' Her face crumpled and she let the tears spill. 'But I still have feelings.'

Hugo put his arm lightly around her shoulders. His manner was gentle, but there was nothing gentle in the look he cast in Veronica's direction.

'This is unfortunate,' he told Monica, 'but it's not worth tears. It's asking too much that anyone as young and untried as Veronica could understand. And it's natural under the circumstances that she wants to protect her father. Indeed, we all do.'

'It isn't protection he needs, it's love.' Veronica rammed her hat back on her head, somehow feeling better for the inelegant action.

'You're unkind,' Monica pleaded. 'Of course I love him, poor darling. I expect I'm a wicked woman that I want more than being a piece of furniture in his home, I expect it's a sin to want someone to see me – really *see* me and not just smile because I'm comfortingly familiar. You're never there for more than a few minutes before you rush off for your full and busy day. You think you know it all.'

'Yes, I do think so. And if you could read my thoughts you wouldn't be feeling very proud.'

121

'That's enough!' Once more Hugo entered the fray. 'Your mother is worn out with the worry of it all. You've no business to try and stop the small pleasure she finds in sometimes walking out with me.'

'I may be as stupid as you seem to believe, Mr Holmes, but I promise you I'm not deaf. You disgust me – the pair of you!' Home, her parents, the never changing acceptance and devotion even as her father's health had failed, these things she had never doubted. Shaken by shock that the foundation stone she'd built on was crumbling, she turned to Monica. 'Mum,' she pleaded, her eyes telling their own story of fear and disbelief, 'can't you just think of Dad? Things have changed for you, of course, they have. But what about Dad? He needs you more now, not less.'

'I'm not a criminal. What harm is there in taking an afternoon walk?'

But Veronica didn't stay and listen. Gripping her purse firmly under her arm she left them, half running and half walking down the slope towards the town. It was almost two years since Nicholas had been aware of her feline grace as he'd watched her on the tennis court. That unconscious grace never deserted her, although it was the last thing on her mind as she put space between herself and her mother. The sun was still as warm, the sky as blue, the waves still broke gently on the shore; yet she saw none of it as she hurried past the elegant houses of Vicary Crescent. Angry and confused, she wanted just to lock the wages safely in the safe and go back to the Abbey; even though it didn't enter her head that she might tell Nicholas what she'd discovered, she needed to be with him.

She drove out of Deremouth, up the incline to turn left to the main road where, almost directly opposite was the lane along the eastern edge of Picton Heath to the hamlet of Moorleigh. Usually at the end of each day she took the next turning off the main road skirting the further side of the heath and leading to Ottercombe. But on that day, for the first time, she carried on to the more direct route to the Abbey, avoiding the village. When there was no sign of Nicholas in either the house or the practice room, she knew where he would be. Often she resented the hours he spent alone in the Abbey. There had been times when she'd followed him, expecting to hear music, only to find the great building silent. There he would be, sometimes in the organ loft, sometimes in the

122

choir stalls. He would remain oblivious of her presence, often sitting perfectly still with his eyes closed, his head held high, as if he were listening. At other times he would be working, no doubt transposing the sounds he had heard in his head onto the sheets of manuscript paper. Either way, she had been outside the orbit of his awareness and had known better than to disturb him.

'I'm home early,' she announced unnecessarily as she went into the kitchen. 'Have you any idea how long my husband has been out?'

'I saw him go across to the Abbey, oh let me see now, it must have been three hours or more ago,' Florrie Beckham told her. 'He'll be a while yet though. Not five minutes back I watched the boys file across. Must be having a practice. Did he know you were expected home before your usual time?'

'No. I didn't know myself.'

'Nothing wrong, my dear?' There was something disconcertingly motherly about the portly housekeeper, especially when she forgot Veronica was her mistress as she did so often.

'No. I didn't have anything else pressingly urgent.' If only she could tell someone, anyone. For one moment Veronica imagined the blessed relief of the Confessional. Not that it was *her* sin. Or was it? She had brought her mother to tears of shame and misery, she had been sarcastic and arrogant. Young and untried, that's what Hugo Holmes had called her. His words had only added to her anger. Yes she was young, yes, her loyalty had never been tried. Was it a sin that her mother yearned to be loved, valued, appreciated? She faced the question squarely and answered it just as she had on the cliff top: yes, it was a sin. Yet she couldn't put the image of her mother out of her mind. Surely that was a new hat she'd been wearing, a frivolous piece of nonsense that would have made most women, including me, look ridiculous, Veronica mused. Had Dad so much as noticed? Probably not. To him she would be everything he wanted even if she were in rags. But for Mum the pleasure of new clothes has always been the knowledge that he is proud of her, that she knows how good she looks, that being beautiful somehow makes her loved. It's all nonsense, but she needs admiration as much as she needs food and drink. Yes, but isn't that a sin too? It's not Mum's wrong doings I'm thinking about, it's my own. Why couldn't I have acted differently, kept calm and tried to make her feel I understood? Wouldn't that have

123

been more of a help to Dad than behaving as if I was ganging up with him against her? And that wimpish fop, Hugo Holmes, with his fancy clothes – he's not fit to lick Dad's boots!

'You look tired, Mrs Ellis, duckie. The kettle's singing, why don't you let me make you a nice pot of tea? Dolly's busy scrubbing the yard and Mary's popped into the village to the paper shop, but it wouldn't take me a tick to get a tray for you.'

'Better than that, Mrs Beckham, I'll stay out here and we'll have it together. There's nothing more miserable than a pot of tea all by yourself.'

Veronica had spent many an hour in the kitchen with Bertha at Ipsley House. That's how she had, by trial and error, found the perfect recipes for some of Blakeney's most popular products. But for Florrie Beckham, having 'the missus' sharing a pot and a chat had been unheard of while Dr Hardy's wife had been mistress of the Master's Lodge.

It was more than half an hour later, the tea already drunk to the accompaniment of a discussion on the success of Veronica's latest creation, a rich coffee and walnut gateau, the outcome of recent experiments watched by Florrie, when Dolly came back from her labours.

'Yard looks fit for the King,' she announced. 'Oh, sorry, mum, I didn't know you was in 'ere. I'd best get on with the veg for tonight, Mrs Beckham, don't you reckon?'

'First things first, my girl. Just you get a scrubbing brush to your hands after being out there doing the yard. You shouldn't need me telling you.' Her plump face relaxed into a smile that took the sting out of her sharp retort. 'Then, yes, you reckon right. Tonight's veg are your next job.'

'We like to get done smartish on a Thursday, mum,' Dolly explained, with little regard for her lowly position in the household. 'That's the day our weekly comes out. Mary's off buying it now. Get the chores out of the way and we have a good read. Ain't that so, Mrs Beckham.'

'Not if you don't get a move on, it won't be.'

There was always something comforting about a visit to the kitchen at the Master's Lodge. It never occurred to Veronica that the atmosphere there might be influenced by anything in herself. By comparison the rest of the house seemed chill, a chill that came from something more than empty rooms. She wandered aimlessly into the uninvitingly tidy drawing room, the plumped cushions positioned so carefully that they defied relaxation. From there she looked into the adjoining dining room with its highly polished walnut table, its gleaming silver. Only on the rare occasions when they had guests were meals served there. Across the wide hall was the breakfast room, and it was here that she retreated now, going to the window and looking out across the quadrangle to the Abbey. In the kitchen she had managed to keep at bay what she'd discovered that afternoon; now it crowded back. Kneeling on the window seat she pressed her forehead to the cool glass as if that was the way to clear her jumbled thoughts. Over the years she and her mother had had many a battle, arguments that had been part of adolescence and happened in most families. But this was different. This had left a stain that nothing could remove. Her thoughts ran riot. Mum, why do you have to put *your* feelings before Dad's? But then, what real harm are you doing with your stupid need to be admired and made a fuss of? Dad will never know. That's what's so awful, that's what I can't bear. If this hadn't happened to him, if you were rushing round with that stupid fop of a man and Dad was able to fight his own battle, then that wouldn't have been so – so – cruel.

Supposing something happened to Nicholas like it has to Dad. Without music he would have no life. What sort of indictment was that on her? Immediately memory stirred, again it was Monica bemoaning her own empty life. Had she always felt that she was less important than Blakeney's? Perhaps all women were expected to merge into the background of their husbands' lives. The idea was academic, for Veronica it had no relevance.

With what an onlooker would have seen as determination, she got off the window seat and stood straight. Her hat and coat were still on the chair where she'd thrown them. Automatically following tradition and habit, she put on her hat then, without bothering with a coat, went out through the wide door onto the quadrangle.

Entering the Abbey by the north door no one saw her come. Nicholas was standing in the chancel, the choir in their stalls as he took them, unaccompanied, through music she'd not heard before. Sitting in the back pew she watched, her mind cleared of everything but this moment, feeling hypnotised by sight and sound. For hours of each day he worked on his Easter Oratorio

125

and, unfamiliar as it was, she knew the music of the *Sanctus* was his own.

Sanctus, Sanctus, Sanctus, Dominus Deus Sabaoth,
Pleni sunt coeli et terra gloria tua.
Hosanna in excelsis.

Watching him, hearing the glorious purity of the boys' voices, she wanted to absorb the spirit of the work, she wanted to feel herself part of it. If the music had been written by someone else, then she would have believed she shared it with him. But it hadn't been; it had been born of the hours he spent in the stillness of this place where for centuries men had worshipped. How often she'd followed him here, wanting to be near him, to find him sitting in silence, listening to what only *he* could hear.

The sound was beautiful, it sent a shiver of – of what? excitement? wonder? awe? – through her. And yet she had never been more aware of the insurmountable barrier that held them apart. As quietly as she'd entered, so she left the Abbey.

An hour later he came home. If the music had affected her, so it had him but in a very different way. She could sense the pent-up emotion in him, and she rejoiced in it. Now he was hers, just hers. The glory of sound had stirred his emotions, emotions that would find release in the glory of passion. She forgot those moments she'd known herself to be outside the orbit of his life. Now he was hers, she was his. Not for the first time – and quite unnecessarily, for no one ever disturbed them – they turned the key in the lock of their bedroom door. Music had carried him to heights beyond this world and far beyond her reach; still held in its power, now he carried her with him. Running a bakery, confused disappointment with her mother, grief for her father, all these things vanished like clouds after a storm. Nicholas was her life and her love.

It was still not quite six o'clock as they gathered up their hastily discarded clothes.

'Perhaps I should come home early more often,' she chuckled contented, nuzzling against his naked shoulder.

He tilted her face so that there was no way she could avoid meeting his gaze.

'You know I want you here all the time.' He sensed that this might be her moment of weakness. Instead, his words brought back to her that feeling of desolation she'd known as she'd sat alone listening to the purity of sound that had been like a glimpse of heaven. Yet it was a heaven that held her away, that drove home to her that it derived from his spirit, from something of him that she could never reach.

'Don't spoil all this,' and he knew that 'all this' encompassed sensuality that went beyond her vocabulary.

'Nothing can spoil it.' Then, with a teasing and un-Nicholaslike smile, 'but my working day is unscheduled, I have many an hour of need.'

'Wouldn't be good for your health,' she responded in the same vein.

The dangerous moment passed, but they both knew it would return and lead to the same arguments, the same bitter jealousy. But that wasn't fair, she told herself. If all he wanted was a chattel, then he should have married someone like prissy Dulcie Wainwright. No wonder she smiled at the image the thought conjured up, secure in the certainty the love they shared was more important than petty jealousy – or masculine arrogance, she added with an inward chuckle.

The boundaries of Herbert's world closed in on him. He was placid, obedient, he gave Alice no trouble. Yet the only two people who could bring a light of real recognition to his eyes were Monica and Veronica.

Throughout the winter Deremouth had become used to its new cake-making establishment. As Veronica had predicted with a confidence not entirely genuine, the coming of Clampton's Cakes had made no immediate difference to Blakeney's local trade. No doubt there were some, among those well-off enough to indulge in their high priced products, who had sampled Clampton's 'sawdust rubbish' as she still referred to them, but they'd soon returned to their old habits. So, by that spring, despite having been pleasantly surprised at the sort of man Merrick Clampton had appeared to be, she had more or less forgotten his existence.

It was the last Thursday in May when, as she came out of the bank with the wages in her handbag, she literally collided with him.

'Mrs Ellis, I am so sorry. I wasn't looking where—'

127

'No, it was me. I was miles away.' Not the exact truth, in fact her imagination had carried her back one week to her unfortunate meeting with her mother and Hugo Holmes on the cliff top. 'Why, it must be six months since we met. I take it you decided against looking for a house down here?'

He laughed. 'Becky isn't given to changing her mind,' he said. 'And in this instance I agree with her entirely. We were fortunate. We heard that one of the houses in Vicary Crescent would be coming onto the market.'

'So you live here now?'

'I'm down here today to finalise the deal.' With a smile – more of a mischievous grin that took years off him – he tapped his trouser pocket. 'I have collected the key. Number Eighteen Vicary Crescent is mine. I wish Becky could have come with me, but poor lass she has been quarantined with measles. It'll be another eight days before I can bring her down.' Realising that he and Veronica were blocking the doorway of the bank, he took her elbow and drew her aside. 'I say, I suppose you're in a tearing rush? You couldn't spare ten minutes to come with me to have a look at the place? But it wouldn't interest you. Why should it?'

'Because I'm a woman, I expect,' she laughed, 'that's why. All women love looking at houses – even hard-bitten business women. And, do you know, although I remember once when I was quite small I sprained my ankle on the rocks and got taken in to see Dr Bingley, apart from that I've never been inside a house on the crescent. So, yes, I'd love to come with you. I'll wait while you have to do whatever you have to in the bank.'

A few minutes later, just as she had the previous week, they cut through Fisherman's Walk to the shore. He was a pleasantly easy companion, he might have been a life-long acquaintance instead of someone she'd only met once before, and had had every intention of disliking.

'Once you move in here, I suppose you'll spend more time in Deremouth. Or is this grand house just for holidays?'

'Becky will live here. I shall come as often as I can.'

So who would live with Becky? Widowed for what by now must be more than two years, did that mean he had married again, or was planning to marry again? There were some questions that couldn't be asked.

'Number Eighteen. Here we are. Empty windows staring out at us like a sightless man.'

'Not for long. It's the best position in Deremouth. You and Becky will be really happy here.' There, that should give him an opportunity to tell her.

'I hope so. It's been a dreadful two years. I can't tell you – and I pray you'll never have to discover from first-hand experience.'

'Losing your wife? Yes, it must have been dreadful, for you and Becky too.' Even though her sympathy was sincere, she felt inadequate.

'Let's go in, shall we?' he changed the subject.

From room to room they inspected the empty Georgian house. In line with buildings of the era its rooms were well proportioned, large with high ceilings and tall windows. Even those on the third floor were airy.

'This will be your main home?' Surely, no matter how wealthy Clampton Cakes had made him, this could hardly be an indulgence to a spoilt child!

'I suppose you could call it that. Although I shall be away a good deal. Becky will be here all the time.'

'Who cares for her? She must miss you when she's left at home.'

For a moment he was silent, his thought far away from Deremouth and the new life he was determined to make for Becky.

'Let's sit on the stairs, shall we?' He said at last. 'Can you spare the time?'

'I'm in no hurry.' Certainly she wasn't anxious to rush away, she preferred not to think of the work waiting for her when she got back to her office. So they sat side by side on the third stair. The staircase was wide, the treads shallow. Even uncarpeted it wasn't uncomfortable, Merrick leaning against the wall, Veronica against the mahogany banister.

'So much has changed.' He spoke quietly, and she wasn't sure whether he was answering her original question or branching off at a tangent. 'It was a rail crash. Esme, my wife, had been staying with her parents. She'd taken Becky, of course. They were on their way home when it happened. I was at the station to meet them. Then the news came through.' What could she say? She said nothing. How easy it would have been to reach out her hand, she

129

had to remind herself that he was virtually a stranger. And, in any case, as he recalled the hours of his agony she knew he wasn't so much talking to her as thinking aloud; she was outside it all, an intruder. 'It was a derailment, there was no other train involved. It was hardly worthy of a report in the national press. Only one life was lost.'

'Your Esme?'

He nodded.

'It was instantaneous, they said. She was thrown and broke her neck as she hit the ground.'

'And Becky?' Somehow she had to lift that expression from his face.

'Her leg was hurt, badly hurt. I dare say all children live on dreams. Hers was to be a dancer. Perhaps, in that, she was no different from most young girls. The crash stripped her even of her dreams.'

'You mean her leg is permanently damaged?' She remembered the iron the child wore. But surely broken legs mended? Wasn't he transferring his grief onto something he could handle more easily than the void in his life without Esme? She'd caught a glimpse of Becky and had seen no sign that anything else was wrong with her.

'Dancing is out of the question. She walks quite well now, at least for short distances. But a dancer has to do more than that. As far as I can, I try to recompense for what she's lost.'

'And that must help *you* too.' Her remark made him look at her anew. 'Knowing you are necessary, knowing she depends on you. It's what we all need, isn't it.' Was that one of the reasons that she was so bound to Blakeney's? Because, in his foggy, lonely world, her father depended on her? Before she could stop herself she was voicing her thoughts aloud.

'I wish I'd known him. Forgive me, speaking of him in the past tense. I just wonder if, had he and I had an opportunity to know and trust each other, the situation at Blakeney's might have been different.'

'Well, you didn't,' she answered with the brusque manner he'd met with on their first acquaintance. 'And as for Blakeney's, we both know the situation so there's no point in going down that track again.'

'Mrs Ellis,' he laughed, 'you don't need to remind me. I know when I've met my match.' Then, the serious expression back in

130

place, 'But never take anything for granted, that's a lesson life has taught me. Don't jeopardise your marriage for the sake of the business.' He held up his hand as if to ward off her answer even before it came. 'It's no business of mine, it may be your husband is proud of your business acumen – as, indeed, he has cause to be. Sometimes Fate deals a hand you can do nothing with but accept; that's what it did when it took Esme away from me. But sometimes we do have control ourselves.'

'That's an underhand way of trying to make me think again.' But it was fear more than anger that gave her words that belligerent tone.

'I'm sorry. I told you just now, I know when I'm beaten. I spoke as a friend.' He held out his hand, not his right one as if for a formal handshake, but his left and into it she automatically slipped her right as they sat side by side. 'And if we are to be friends, then don't you think we might call each other by Christian names?'

'Merrick,' she nodded. 'Yes, I'd like that. And I'm Veronica, or if you think that's too much of a mouthful you can say Ronnie like my parents often do.'

'Ronnie. It suits you. Yes, you shall be my friend, Ronnie. I hope you'll be Becky's friend too.'

'Who is with her now?' The new basis of friendship gave her the right to ask.

'One of the hardest things I've ever had to do was to engage someone to care for her after we lost Esme. It was so important to choose the right one, I didn't want any more upheavals to her life by taking on someone who didn't fit or wouldn't stay.'

'And this time Fate guided you wisely?'

'I suppose you could say that's what it was. It surprised me how many people applied, but I had no hesitation. I engaged Mrs Frewin, Belinda Frewin, a young lady who'd known tragedy in her own life. Only one thing made me hesitate. You see, her husband had been consumptive. I believe losing Esme must have made me neurotic, I saw danger everywhere – not for myself, but for Becky. It was Belinda who made me realise the state I'd let myself get into. She must have read my thoughts, recognised what it was that worried me. She was always fit, she told me, she'd looked after her husband for three years and never had so much as a cough. Ronnie, you've no idea the relief I felt at her reassurance.

131

It was as if I had clear vision for the first time since I lost Esme, as if Belinda had been sent by providence.'

'So she'll be in charge of this house? You'll be able to be away without worrying about Becky.' He didn't answer, and she decided the time had come to put an end to his reminiscences and for her to pick up the broken thread of her afternoon's work. 'I'm sure you'll come to be very happy here. I hope you will.'

His expression lit in a smile that she felt gave her a glimpse of the man he must have been before his life had been shattered by the loss of Esme. Not for the first time it struck her what a good-looking man he was; not distinguished in the way that Nicholas was, nor with the Adonis-like handsome face of Laurence. His features were regular enough, but good looks went beyond features. Standing up, Veronica smiled at him, glad that he was her friend, glad that he and his entourage were coming to Deremouth. And in a generosity of spirit that stemmed from her will to understand how devastated his life must have been, she hoped he would learn to love this Belinda Frewin, the woman he'd spoken so highly of.

I'm so lucky, she mused as she walked briskly back to Blakeney's. And so she still thought as, with the backlog of her day's work dealt with and the wages sorted, she locked the safe and put on her hat ready to go home. It was then that she heard footsteps hurrying towards her door and stood poised ready to answer the visitor's knock.

But there was no knock. The door burst open and there, her expression of – triumph? excitement? – sitting uncomfortably on her appearance of such pretty femininity, stood Monica.

Chapter Eight

Veronica's instinctive reaction was suspicion, followed in an instant by guilt that she could feel uneasy at her mother's unexpected appearance. Since that chance meeting on the cliff top they had been together each morning when she had called at Ipsley House on her way to Deremouth. In front of her father it had been easier to fit into the roles expected of them. This was the first time they had been alone, face to face.

'Another minute and you would have missed me,' she forced a bright greeting. 'What happened? Did you miss the bus?'

Monica nodded.

'Purposely I missed it,' she said, 'I can't talk to you at home. Even though poor darling Herbert wouldn't follow what I was saying, Alice's ears don't miss anything.'

'Of course Dad understands. He can't keep up and answer, but he listens to what we say to each other, he wants to be part of it.'

'Wanting to and being able to are two different things. That's why I came into town this afternoon. Ronnie, this wasn't something I wanted to do. I know you misjudge me, I know you condemn me. But even you must see, there was no alternative to what I've done today.' Veronica dreaded what she was to hear, even though she had no conception of what it might be. It was as if the shadow of Hugo Holmes was between them. Whatever she expected, it wasn't what Monica told her. 'I've never had anything to do with bills and cheques. Running the money affairs is a husband's place. Well, you know I've never interfered. Nothing has changed for you, not like it has for me. I remember his telling me – and how proud he was, too – that he'd given you authority to sign the cheques here in the business. You don't have to coax him

133

into writing his name. That's how it's been for me in the house. And have you ever given it a thought? No. You give all your attention to this wretched place, never a care as to how I cope. Gas, electricity, rates, even the butcher and the grocer, each time a bill comes I have to stand over him, put a pen in his hand and watch him write his name like an obedient child. He doesn't know what he's signing. It breaks my heart. But you never give a thought. Only this place – that's all you care about. How Nicholas stands it I don't know.' There was a warning note of hysteria in her voice but, still mistrustful, Veronica heard it as a defence against criticism.

'Of course I care. If I didn't, do you think I would work here like I do?'

Monica assumed it was meant as a question.

'Yes,' she snapped, 'yes I do think so. I think you enjoy running the show here because it builds your ego. You've always been the same. Even as a child you couldn't behave like other girls. I can't understand why you can't concern yourself with having a family, looking after your husband. But no, you have to carry on as though you were the breadwinner in the family.'

'Was it because you wanted to go over all this again that you purposely missed your bus home?' Veronica retorted, her pretence of welcome forgotten. 'Anyway, you're hardly the one to give a sermon on how to conduct a marriage.'

'You're cruel! If you'd seen me walking with a woman friend you would have been delighted. But since Ellen's been gone, who is there for me? I can't ask anyone to the house. I'd be ashamed to let Tessa Duckworth or any of the other busybodies see how stupid Herbert has become.'

'He's not stupid! He's ill. A broken hip and you would invite people in, you'd enjoy being seen as a loving, loyal wife; you'd be proud that he could suffer so uncomplainingly.'

'If he'd broken his hip I shouldn't be on my own, I'd have companionship, I shouldn't have had to watch him degenerate into this! In you breeze, chatter for five minutes never giving him a chance to make his usual senseless conversation, then you're gone, your duty done. Anyway,' she rushed on before Veronica had a chance to argue, 'I came to Deremouth this afternoon for a very special reason.'

'Oh yes? Not to meet your friend?'

'How can you be so unkind? Well, you're not going to tread all over me. You hear me?'

'What was so important that brought you to town?' She knew from the ominous croak in her mother's voice and the way she was suddenly so short of breath that a tearful scene was hovering, only waiting its opportunity. Despite her anger at what she saw as disloyalty, she felt a sudden stab of pity as she thought of the pretty, over-indulged, unfailingly loved woman Monica had been.

'I talked to Dr Saunders the other day.' Managing to hang on to her composure, Monica went on, 'He arrived when I was trying to persuade your father to sign his name on a cheque for the rates. He could see what a strain I have to live under. It was his idea that I should make an appointment with Withers, Wright and Lambton. I wrote to them there and then saying I intended to come to town this afternoon and would like to talk to Mr Withers. Dear Dr Saunders sent them a letter too, it was there on the desk when I arrived. Oh dear, business affairs do so worry me. But what else can I do? He'll never get any better, each day he gets further away. A young child may not understand what's going on but with a child each day you see its intelligence grow. For him it's the other way round. So I had no choice.'

'So why did you have to talk to Mr Withers?'

Something of that light of triumph Veronica had suspected when her mother had arrived was back.

'You have to ask me that, and you call yourself a business woman! I had to arrange Power of Attorney over your father's affairs of course.'

Veronica slumped down on her chair.

'Oh Mum, that's dreadful,' she said softly. 'His last shred of independence.'

'Yes it's dreadful. I have a husband who can't think for himself, can't direct his own life, can't talk to me, can't put his shoes on the right feet, can't be a partner – not in any way can he be a partner. You've no idea how our lives have changed in this last year, how alone I am.' She pressed her fingers against her jaw as if that way she could hold back her misery. 'You see this hat?' Veronica looked puzzled. What could a hat have to do with her misery? 'I'm wearing it new today. Not that you'd have noticed, you never did care what I looked like. But he used to. I showed it to him today. I said: "Do I look nice in my new hat?" And what did he do? He

135

picked up my grey glove and looked at it obligingly, said "Pretty thing," and stowed it away in his pocket as if it were his handkerchief – or a talisman.' She sat down too, all her spirit gone. 'And you condemn me for being glad to talk sometimes to Hugo, you blame me for not inviting people to the house.'

'Poor Dad. Oh Mum, if there's a God why did He let it happen? Dad's a *good* man, you ask anyone who's worked for him.'

'It isn't he who needs your sympathy. He doesn't know there's anything wrong with him. Sometimes, all alone, he'll sit there talking away, talking to people he used to do business with, laughing, happy as a sandboy. But me? I'm not supposed to want happiness, I'm supposed to give my life to playing make-believe with him.'

Her gloom was infectious.

'Come on, Mum. Let's go home. I was just clearing away my things when you came. Why don't you go and have a word with them in the bakehouse while I lock up, they'd like that.' Of one thing she was sure: talking to Bert Jenkins and the staff Monica would become the adoring wife, patient and caring. There would be no criticism of Herbert, no hint of the strain of looking after him.

During the drive home Monica seemed more cheerful, the visit to the faithful staff seemed to have done her good. However, conversation didn't flow easily. Neither of them wanted to discuss Herbert; neither wanted to mention Monica's isolated life or her need for Hugo's company. Company and flattery, in Veronica's opinion, but she didn't intend to stir the ashes of the subject when within minutes they'd be in Ottercombe.

Five minutes with her father – overshadowed by the echo of Monica's accusations – then she drove on home. From the drawing room came the sound of the piano telling her that the choir school's early evening practice was over and Nicholas was home.

'I'm back,' she announced unnecessarily. 'Did you think I was never coming? I got held up—'

'No doubt,' he answered in that cool tone she was coming to dread, not losing the tempo of what he was playing nor even taking his eyes from the music in front of him.

'It was Mum. She'd been into town and missed the bus. She came to me for a lift – then of course she had to have a word with the staff. You let the boys finish early today?' Her tone made a question of the statement. When he was withdrawn like this she felt helpless. She wanted him to talk, to let her know he was glad she'd come home. But was he glad? Or was she simply a distraction from the music that was the cornerstone of his life? Her comment about the boys' early dismissal was asked as an invitation for him to reply, to pass the conversation back to her, to let her into the magic orbit of his world. It went unanswered.

'I told you Mum came in,' she went on, talking above the unceasing sound of the piano. 'She'd been to Deremouth to keep an appointment with the solicitor. Nicholas, she's been given Power of Attorney. Everything taken away from Dad . . .'

This time he stopped playing mid-phrase and turned to look at her. The piano stool was long, often in the first months they used to sit side by side there to play duets; occasionally they still did. Now, trying to read understanding in his expression, she came to sit at his side resting her head against his shoulder.

'She has no choice,' he said. 'I wonder she waited so long. Or are you suggesting it should have been granted to *you*?'

'Of course not. I've never had anything to do with the household things. If Dad can't deal with the bills there, then of course it has to be Mum. It's just – I can't believe it's happened to him. I know he'd lost confidence, but to have everything taken away from him . . .' Nicholas moved an inch or so away from her and very softly continued to play. 'I ought not to resent it, after all I've had authority at Blakeney's for ages and I've never considered it took anything from him.'

'And now?'

'How do you mean? Now?'

'What are your mother's intentions for the firm? You know my views, and I suspect hers will be much the same.' If only he'd say it kindly, if only he'd tell her how empty his days were while she was away. Instead, in that aloof tone that held her at arm's length, the words 'You know my views' were spoken in the voice of a master ordering his chattel.

'And you know mine.' She stood up, willing him to meet her gaze and holding her chin high. 'I'm your wife, Nicholas, not your possession. And if you'd be half honest you'd have to admit that my hanging around the house all day would make not a jot of difference to you. How long do you spend here? You just want me

137

here waiting and eager when the mood takes you. I'm not a whore earning my bed and board—'

In a second he was on his feet.

'Take that back.'

'Well, what else do you want of me? When do we ever really need each other except in bed?' She was shocked by her own words, yet she gloried in them, hurling them at him like so many arrows aimed to pierce him. 'What fun do we ever have together? Except that sort of fun? You don't want *me*, the real whole *me*. You don't want the *me* that laughs, the *me* that loves to row a boat on the sea, the *me* that thrives on running a business. I'm all of those things. But all you care about is the – the—' She couldn't read his expression. Certainly there was no tenderness in his dark eyes nor in the way he gripped her shoulders, his hands like a vice through the thin fabric of her blouse. She'd wanted just to pierce his cold complacency. Now she was horrified at what she'd done, what she'd said. Not that his anger would ever have frightened her, she could stand up to him or any other man. But no matter how they'd argued, always they'd come together in love, love so glorious that it erased every angry word. But what she'd just said was different, it stained the memory of those perfect hours, it threatened to echo into the future, to be there to cast a shadow.

'I didn't mean that. I was being hateful,' she blurted. 'Nicholas, darling Nicholas, don't look at me like that. I wanted to hurt you. I suppose I'm jealous, I hate always coming second to you to music. I know it's wrong. I didn't mean it.' Somehow her arms were around him, she was holding her face up to his.

'Jealous?' he whispered, crushing her against him. 'How can you be jealous when you're the only woman I want. But I want all that you are – every thought, every act. I'm only half your life – half? Not even that.'

'But I try to talk about what I do—' She might as well not have spoken, even if he heard her words he wasn't listening with his heart.

'You know those things you said aren't true.'

She nodded. 'I believe I wasn't really alive until you taught me how to love. Like the sleeping princess.'

The mood had changed, they were close again.

'Remember our weekly music evenings?' She heard him with a sudden lift in her spirit. In that moment he was hers again, the piano, the Requiem, the choir, the Abbey, none of them had the power to hurt her. 'I may have woken my princess, but if ever a princess was troubled by dreams and cried out to be woken then it was you. What a child you were, my Veronica, with your clumsy invitations,' he laughed. 'Lucky for you I was an honourable man.'

She'd been married to him for sixteen months, she believed herself his equal in every way. And yet the way he spoke of her blatant and innocent flirtation filled her with embarrassment that her wiles had been so transparent. Dropping a light kiss on her forehead, he drew her into his arms. They seemed to draw strength one from the other. For almost a minute they stood like that, not speaking, her face buried against his neck.

'I must go.' He put her away from him.

'Go?'

'Surely you've not forgotten. This evening the Abbey Singers start practising. I did tell Florrie I'd not be in for a meal, but remind her to leave a plate of sandwiches or something. I'll probably be quite late. The first practice is always long – testing new people, deciding on soloists.'

'I wish you needed a pianist,' she said, a gentle reminder of the early days of their finding each other.

'Mr Humphreys has two good wrists. Two years since you played for our rehearsals; it seems far more.'

'Have you chosen what they'll sing?'

'Mendelssohn's *Elijah*. I must go, I like to be there before anyone arrives. Don't forget to remind Florrie I'm out until late. She needn't fill a flask; by the time I get through this evening I shall need something stronger than stewed coffee.'

'I love *Elijah*. I'll come with you. I could join the choir.' Then, her chuckle surely a sign that the recent stain she'd made on their memories had already been wiped away, 'Mum wanted me to join when you first started it. Remember the pompous letter you sent me saying you would be prepared to test my voice. Didn't I just take you down a whole row of pegs, and didn't I enjoy doing it too!' Her eyes alight with mischief she looked at him, 'But Mr Ellis, please sir, my life isn't so full that I can't spare Thursday evenings for rehearsal – and you know now that I sing in tune.'

'No use, my dear. Two years ago you were a comparative stranger, albeit one who interested me more than I was prepared to admit. Now you're my wife.'

139

'So? Marriage might have destroyed my virginity, but it hasn't wrecked my voice.'

'It would make a difficult situation. I prefer my choir members to be no more than voices to me, that's as far as my interest in them goes. To have you there – in tune or out – would be jarring.'

Her amazement must have shown in her expression. 'I've never heard such twaddle! Anyway I've got more than enough to keep myself busy. And tell Humphreys to be careful how he goes, another fall and another broken wrist and – and – well, you can whistle for a pianist as far as I'm concerned.'

By now he was laughing at her. 'Do you honestly think I couldn't have conducted the rehearsals from the piano?' he teased. 'But how else could I get you to fit me into a life that was already so full of activity?'

'It's like looking down the wrong end of a telescope, all so long ago and far away. We were different people.' She wanted him to argue, to tell her that he still felt as he had then. But he was already collecting together the conductor's score, the pianist's score for Humphreys and a list he had written of the solo parts, his mind on what he was doing. 'But we're not different,' she pressed him. 'Not deep down different?'

'I like to think you've grown up,' was all he said as he closed his music case. She felt spurned, she knew that already she'd lost him to that part of his life he shared with no one.

Although, remembering what Nicholas had prophesied, Veronica was wary of her mother interfering at Blakeney's, over the weeks of summer it became apparent that her fears were groundless. Except for that one visit on her way home from Withers, Wright and Lambton, Monica didn't come to the bakery. It seemed her reason for gaining Power of Attorney had been just as she'd said, the ability to pay the bills for Ipsley House.

Veronica's routine didn't alter. She spent a few minutes with her father each morning on her way to Deremouth, then all day she immersed herself in overseeing the running of the business. There had been a time she and her father had both been kept busy; now she worked alone, her hours full and her mind absorbed in what she did to the exclusion of all else. If she'd been honest with herself, she would have realised that Blakeney's was more than the challenge of carrying on the family business, it was salve to her loneliness of spirit. At the end of her day she unfailingly paid another short and purposely cheerful visit to Ipsley House on the way home and then, more often than not, was faced with an evening of her own company. Although Nicholas's first choir training session of the day was before the boys of the school had breakfast, the men spent their days in other occupations. Tuesdays and Fridays were Choral Evensong at half past six, followed by practice for men and trebles combined. Thursday evenings Nicholas was occupied with the Abbey Singers, Sundays with Evensong, leaving just three evenings in a week for him to plan as he chose. And, invariably, his choice was to shut himself away in solitude. The music of the Abbey never suffered for his absorption in his oratorio or for the hours he spent alone at the organ console. More and more often she thought of his jovial brother-in-law's warning, that music was a harder mistress to contend with than another woman. In her innocence she'd laughed at the sentiment, never imagining anything could come between Nicholas and her, not a woman, not music, not Blakeney's. What a blind idiot she'd been to have imagined that those jolly songs and duets they'd shared could ever have been enough for him. Sometimes she'd stand outside the drawing room door listening, imagining him at the piano as she heard his softly played phrases, noting the silences when he must have been writing the notes in his quick, unerring hand, then repeating the same phrase this time accompanied by the Latin words. A closed door was between them, but her isolation was far deeper than that.

She doubted whether he even missed her when she was out during the day, his resentment that she chose not to be at home stemmed from his arrogant assumption that being his wife should be role enough. When did they ever discuss anything that mattered? Perhaps they never had, came the silent reply. Occasionally he told her he was expecting guests, an organist friend from Christchurch passing through the district, members of a visiting quartet, a one-time student friend who was giving a piano recital in Exeter and coming to them for the night. She knew he was proud to introduce her as his wife, she was determined never to fail in her duties as a hostess; but they were *his* friends, not hers. She wasn't expected to take part in their conversation. Indeed, it was mostly over her head. Veronica had always loved music, her spirit could never be touched by anything visual as it was by sound. But she was no musicologist and listening to Nicholas and his friends only shut her further away from the very thing that gave his life its purpose.

As Nicholas was driven by his need for the work he loved, so Veronica immersed herself ever deeper in the business. But there was one big difference. His brought him peace, fed his spirit; hers brought her increasing worry. The account books showed that sales were decreasing, the thing she had vowed wouldn't happen. She'd expected that Clampton's Cakes would make a short-term difference locally, but she'd been confident it would be no more than a hiccup. But what if it wasn't? What if the county trade she'd been so sure of was lost? There was no one she could talk to. Better to say nothing than to invite Nicholas's all too familiar criticism of her doing what he saw as a man's job. As for her mother, even to hint at a drop in sales to her would be to invite trouble.

Her greatest temptation was to talk to Merrick Clampton. Their friendship was undemanding, it could have been all too easy to tell him her worries. Two things stopped her: the first was obvious, how could she discuss Blakeney's falling trade with the owner of Clampton's? The second was something she wasn't prepared to acknowledge – even though an honest streak in her wouldn't let her ignore it: it was her inborn pride in what she did and the fear of throwing her methods open to criticism.

It was about a month after he'd shown her around his house in Vicary Crescent that he arrived unexpectedly at her office.

'Throw me out if you haven't time for me,' he greeted her, 'I just wanted to tell you we are installed and to hope you'll drop in on Becky and me from time to time.'

'Of course I'm not too busy.' With something like relief she closed the ledger trying to banish the gloomy truth it presented. 'And is everything as good as you hoped? Is Becky thrilled to be by the shore?'

'The move has put new life into her. New hope. We moved in nearly a fortnight ago, but except for one weekend I'm afraid I've been in London until yesterday. Yesterday I didn't tell her to expect me, so I was able to walk in unannounced.' He smiled, remembering. 'She has a sitting room of her own on the first floor. That's where I found her, sitting at her easel by the window, trying to capture the view looking across the estuary to Otterton St Giles

142

– that's what she told me the village across there is called – and the high headland.'

'The most painted view in the district,' she laughed. 'So Becky is an artist, you hadn't told me that.'

'To be honest, she never showed any interest until after Esme was killed. Esme painted beautiful watercolours. It was as if Becky felt painting was a way of holding on to her. I hope you'll soon meet her. I would so like you two to be friends. It's what she needs.'

'And her companion, has she settled?'

'Belinda Frewin, oh yes, she seems to have a firm hold on the reins. I need have no worries there. I was wondering whether you might find the time to come and meet Becky? Perhaps when you go to the bank you could make a detour like we did when we met that day.'

'This afternoon? It's on Thursdays that I collect the wages, that's what I'd been doing when we crashed into each other.'

'Tea, cake and conversation. I wish we had time to indulge ourselves more often. But this afternoon at, shall we say, three o'clock?'

'It'll only be a flying visit. But I know you'll understand.'

'I realise you haven't time for leisurely afternoon tea,' he smiled.

'How awful that sounds! As if I want you to see me as some sort of business dynamo here in my tiny bakery, or tiny by Clampton's standards.'

'Business is all relative,' he laughed. 'A large concern demands a large staff. Therefore I probably have more flexibility than you do.'

'I'm really a one-man band here, now that Dad can't come anymore. But, even a one-man band plays better with refreshment. When Dad was here too, about this time of morning I used to boil the kettle and brew some coffee. On my own I often don't bother, coffee needs company. If I make us some, can you stay to share it?'

'That sounds like a good suggestion. I see the gas ring and the kettle, but where do you fill it? Can I do it for us?'

She directed him along the corridor to what was grandly known as the kitchen while she took the small jug, part of the matching china crockery she had brought from home when she'd first joined her father, and went to the bakehouse for milk.

Listening to her retreating along the stone passage to the bake-house, Merrick took stock of the room that called itself a kitchen. A small room with a high, uncurtained window, the only suggestion of its function was a stone sink with a never-polished brass tap. The single item of furniture was a small table covered with oilcloth on which was an enamel bowl; so it must have looked through each generation. It was a far cry from his own newly built and well-equipped factory where the staff facilities were probably better than most of them knew at home. He had never understood why his advertisements in the *Deremouth News* had tempted no workers away from here. Standing by the open doorway, not for the first time, he wondered what gave the workers their loyalty to this place. It was then that he heard a sudden burst of laughter from the bakehouse where he knew Ronnie was filling her cream jug; and he believed he had his answer. Practical business man that he was, and aware that not only the local trade but also the orders Clampton's had received from the village outlets in the county must have affected Blakeney's, he felt uncomfortable about the very success of his new venture. After all, he told himself, was Devon any different from any other region where he had opened up his factories? High-class trade, catering for the well-heeled, could be found nationwide. Yes, he was giving them a jolt, making them realise automation was changing the scene in their industry as in so many more. Until now it had never worried him.

He rinsed out the kettle thoroughly, then filled it and carried it back, taking a box of vestas and lighting the gas ring.

'I know it's a bit primitive,' Veronica laughed as she re-joined him, 'but the end result's good, I promise you. While you were getting the water I've fetched some cream from the bakehouse. I brought us an almond slice, not even cold yet.'

'A Blakeney's speciality,' he smiled. 'Their fame has spread before you.'

She made herself smile, but his words had brought her face to face with something she'd managed to put out of her mind for the last few minutes. Clampton's were probably making their cheap copies; people, even people able to afford the best, were trying them and deciding it wasn't worth paying more than twice the price for the genuine article. She ought to hate this man, he was rocking the very foundations of all she'd known. But in truth it was herself she was angry with: she'd been so sure that Blakeney's moved on a higher plane, safe and untouchable.

She watched him as he bit into the almond slice, defying him not to taste the difference between that and what came out of his gleaming factory. She even tried to whip up the dislike of him she felt he deserved. Yet when their eyes met, she read teasing appreciation in his and found it was impossible not to respond in the same vein. Neither of them commented; there was no need.

Just as she'd promised, the strong Colombian coffee was good. Conversation flowed easily as he talked of buying a rowing boat and she told him of the fishing expeditions she and Laurence used to have. One thing led to the next, the minutes disappeared unnoticed. It was only when the clock on the mantelpiece struck twelve that they looked at each other in amazement.

'I do apologise. I only meant to look in to ask you to come and meet Becky. And do you know, the word "cake" hasn't been spoken.'

She laughed. 'And why should it? There's more to life than cakes – whether they're your variety or mine.' Purposely she said it as if to remind herself that for Blakeney's, Clampton's spelt danger.

It was only after he'd gone that again she let her mind become swamped by the problem there was no escaping. Somehow she had to draw trade from further afield. She'd seen delivery lorries in the town with the words 'Clampton's Cakes' painted on the sides. That was how they had been able to gain county orders: cakes fresh from the factory to the village stores. For Blakeney's there was the daily collection by the station van, boxes would be off-loaded at Exeter, Taunton, Bristol, Bath, or in the other direction at Newton Abbot, Totnes and Plymouth. But outside the towns she had no access, and already shopkeepers – even the high-class grocers she had been so proud to have on their books – were cutting their orders, preferring factory to door delivery.

Pushing the weekly time sheets away from her she sat with her eyes closed, letting her imagination run riot. Excitement was stirring in her. She'd been confident she wouldn't be beaten by Clampton's – in fact, she'd been confident she wouldn't be affected by their smart new factory, but she subtly changed the word to 'beaten'. And neither would she.

This afternoon she was going to meet Becky and her carer. Probably Merrick wouldn't be at home, but if he were she would tell him what she had decided. She looked forward to seeing the admiration she knew her decision would merit.

Then this evening she'd tell Nicholas. That is, she added, the smile replaced by something less fathomable, if he's in the mood to listen by the time he comes home from *Elijah*.

Almost as she touched the bell-pull she heard footsteps.

'It's all right, Dora, I'll open the door. We'd like tea brought in in ten minutes.' A clear voice, a voice of gentle authority, doubtless Becky's carer. Veronica reminded herself not to make any pre-judgement about the daughter Merrick's life revolved around, or the woman sent so providentially to look after her. 'Becky and I were watching from the drawing room window. Do come in, Mrs Ellis. I do appreciate you sparing time in your busy life to come and see us, to be welcomed means a lot when one is a stranger.'

Veronica stood tall, glad of her superior height. So this must be Belinda Frewin, Becky's carer, dainty, fair and fragile, her appearance femininely pretty.

'Of course I want to meet Becky.' As soon as the words were out, Veronica was ashamed. 'And you too, of course, Mrs Frewin. Mr Clampton has told me how relieved he is to know you are here with her.'

'Merrick leaves everything to me. And that's the way it should be. Poor Becky has had disruptions enough – her mother killed, her father seldom at home. I represent continuity. So important to a child.'

'I'm sure.' Despite her good intentions Veronica found it hard to hold the smile on her face.

'Do come upstairs. We have our own drawing room on the first floor. I insisted we should, and Merrick saw the wisdom of it. Often Becky walks quite well – short distances, of course. But there are times when she would find coming up and down stairs a trial. Poor little darling. If she has a good day and takes liberties with it, then the next two or three she has to pay the penalty.'

'Merrick tells me she paints.' It wasn't so much that she wanted to discuss Becky's prowess with the paintbrush as a sudden need to call Merrick by his Christian name to this 'too-cocky-by-half' woman. 'Too-cocky-by-half' was one of Bertha's expressions, it was what she used to accuse Veronica of being in her early days of

146

experimental cooking under the housekeeper's watchful and kindly eye. Remembering, Veronica felt her own mood change, she felt 'the creases ironed out' – Bertha again.

'Hello, Mrs Ellis,' an eager voice called as they came to the door of the large front room on the first floor. 'Daddy said you were coming. You're our very first visitor.'

'You'll soon get to know people. And by the sea there is always lots to do.'

'We do have to be careful,' Belinda put in a reminder.

Feeling mean and ungracious, Veronica ignored her and told Becky, 'I was talking to your father this morning. He tells me he's thinking of buying a rowing boat. That used to be one of my favourite things when I still had the time.'

'Why don't you have the time now?'

'Hush, Becky dear. You mustn't pry into people's affairs,' Belinda rested a gentle hand on the child's shoulder. 'Do forgive her, Mrs Ellis.'

'For showing an interest? I'm flattered that she does. What do I do with my time, Becky? Try and stretch it to get more hours out of the day. That's the worst thing about being grown-up. I run a bakehouse.'

'Like Daddy?'

'Oh no, nothing like his. Mine is quite small, everything we make is done by hand. And,' she added laughing, 'everything we sell is extremely expensive.'

'Are your things as nice as Daddy's?'

'Really, Becky!' Belinda tried again.

'I'll let you into a secret,' Veronica laughed as she answered Becky, 'I think ours are the best in the world. Well, I would wouldn't I? May I sit down, I don't like looking down at you while we talk.'

'Oh Mrs Ellis, do forgive me,' Belinda dragged a chair nearer to where Becky was sitting by the window, 'all her silly talk confused me. I do apologise.'

Drawing it closer to the window, Veronica looked out, peering to see across the estuary to Otterton St Giles. Appearing to give the view her full attention, at the same time she noticed that today the child's right leg was in a supporting iron.

'I saw you out with your father one day,' she said. It was impossible to ignore the iron on her leg and instinct telling her the little girl would rather have honesty than tact, 'You were walking really well, not a bit of a limp.'

'You mean because of Clamper?' she raised her skinny leg, quite a feat considering the weight of the iron support. 'That's what we call it, Daddy and me.'

'Poor little soul,' Belinda still kept her hand on the slight shoulder, 'I could weep to think that a child has to put up with it. If I could bear it for her she knows I would. But so often she has to wear it.'

Veronica wasn't going to leave the subject at a point like that. Poor little soul Becky may be, but no child could want to be treated like some frail old lady! 'Some days you can escape without him, is that it?'

Becky chuckled, wriggling in her chair. Having had no experience of children – at least not since she was one herself – there were no known rules for Veronica to follow, but she felt an instinctive liking for this freckle-faced girl with her unruly mop of gingery-brown hair held back by a wide velvet Alice band.

'Sometimes he stays in my cupboard for days and days,' Becky explained the leg support, proud of the times she could manage without 'him' and not elaborating on those, like today, when she needed 'his' help.

'And I bet you manage more often all the time as your leg gets stronger.' From Becky's enthusiastic nod it was clear Veronica had said just the right thing.

'We don't encourage her to overtax herself,' Belinda said possessively. 'Merrick trusts her thoroughly to my care, I dare say he's told you. It isn't everyone who is cut out for the care of others but, for myself, it was something Fate decided. I lost my husband, having nursed him nearly all our married life.'

'Yes, Merrick told me. I'm sorry.' Sorry or not, the irritation she felt with Belinda didn't lessen. 'An illness like his must have been so sad for you. But of course it's so different with Becky. I understand she's making great strides, getting better all the time.'

'The kindest thing we can do for her is to keep her within her limits. She's a good girl, she understands I can't have her trying to climb over those slippery rocks.'

'I promise you, Becky,' Veronica's answer was directed at the worried-looking child, 'climbing over slimey rocks isn't the adventure it probably appears when you look at it from this distance. But there's lots of other fun to be had on the shore. With summer coming I expect you'll spend a lot of time out there. Then there's the boat your father was talking of getting. You persuade him to take you fishing. There's nothing, absolutely nothing, more satisfying that bringing home your own tea. When it was too choppy for the rowing boat, Laurence and I – Laurence was my friend – used to take our rods to the beach just across the road opposite here. People turn their noses up at pout whiting, but sweet and fresh from the sea they are gorgeous. A bit bony, but that doesn't matter. With sharp eyes you can always pick out the bones.'

'With your eyes? Pick out the bones with your eyes? That's what you said,' Becky giggled, delighted at her own cleverness and at her visitor's spontaneous laugh. Neither of them had noticed Merrick come through the door behind hem.

'You may have damaged your leg, but your brain's bright as a button,' Veronica said, choosing to ignore Belinda's embarrassed tut-tutting.

'Ronnie! I see you three are getting to know each other,' Merrick's voice surprised the two of them even though Belinda had seen him come in.

'I've been telling Becky you're going to buy a boat. Merrick, it would be lovely for her.'

'You mean you think she could manage getting in and out of a rowing boat? What do you say, Belinda?'

'I'd be cautious, I'd not raise her hopes. There are so many interesting things she can do to amuse herself without putting a strain on her poor weak leg.'

Veronica shrugged her shoulders. Perhaps she shouldn't even have mentioned it. Clearly Merrick put complete store in Belinda's views and, equally clearly, Belinda believed in cotton wool treatment.

'Oh well,' she said, 'it's none of my business. But if you ask me, nothing gets strong if you rest it. Why don't you have a word with Dr Bingley? You must have seen the plate outside his gate, he's only about four houses along the crescent. You'll like them, him and his wife Jane too.' Then with a note in her voice that Merrick couldn't be sure was humour or defiance, 'She used to be my hero when I was persuading Dad that I ought to be at Blakeney's; she runs her family brewery, Bradley's Beers.'

'The doctor's wife?' Belinda couldn't believe what she was

hearing. 'The doctor's wife running a brewery. We'd all think it strange if the menfolk were the homemakers and cared for the children, but where would be the difference?'

Veronica recognised her comment as a way of throwing down the gauntlet, even though there was no logic in why she should stir such resentment in the feminine bosom of Becky's carer.

'Jane manages to combine both roles. She has two children. But they're both boys and both away at school in Rugby. A shame; they would have been company for Becky.'

Merrick agreed to go and have a talk to Matthew Bingley.

'I don't want her pushed to do more than she's ready for,' he said as he drew a table forward for the tea tray.

'Of course not. But I'm sure there are so many things here at the sea she could do. Your boat for one – and I told her about it, so there's no back sliding or changing your mind. You'll both have tremendous fun.'

'We will, Daddy.' Supported by Clampers, Becky's stick of a leg looked pale and weak, but her eager expression more than made up for it. 'And you too, Mrs Frewin,' she remembered to add.

For a second Veronica caught a glimpse of the naked love in Merrick's expression as he looked at the child but she immediately looked away, she felt she had been looking at something no stranger should see. Belinda took control of the tea tray, making it apparent she was only one short step down from being mistress of the house.

'May I cut you a slice of cake? It looks as though it might be ginger. Or perhaps you'd prefer one of these petit fours?'

'Ginger please,' Veronica answered. Then, turning to Merrick, 'How do you do it? The same colour, the same shine to the top . . . and the petit fours. In appearance even I couldn't tell the difference, the same small decoration, the same—'

He was laughing. 'The same stable, Ronnie, is the answer.'

'I don't understand?'

'I invited you to tea. Do you honestly think I would have given you less than the best?' His blue eyes teased her. 'I wasn't here when you arrived because I walked to Tidbury's, the best grocery in town, and as far as I'm aware the only one to stock your products.'

She was laughing too. They both knew that the joke they shared wasn't appreciated by Becky or Belinda, they both knew it wasn't even funny. But they laughed anyway.

'You're making me altogether too welcome,' she said. 'Back in the office I have a mass of things waiting for me. As soon as I've drunk my tea I really must fly. But I'll come again if I may – or better still, why don't you drive Becky, and Mrs Frewin of course, over to the Abbey? The boys from the choir school are free on Saturday afternoons, there is usually plenty going on.'

So a visit was arranged for the coming Saturday and farewells were said. She supposed what she wanted to tell Merrick would have to wait until then for she had no intention of discussing business in front of Belinda Frewin who was already standing by the drawing room door ready to escort her downstairs.

'I'll see you out,' Merrick told her.

'Good. I wanted to talk to you about something.'

Outside, he took her elbow and guided her across the road to the iron seat on the grass opposite. That's when she turned to wave at Becky and saw that it wasn't only the little girl who was watching them.

Belinda was uneasy. Until today she'd never even heard of this young woman. And what business was it of hers, a stranger, to come here interfering with what was best for Becky? The child needed care, she needed watchful attention. All this talk of playing like other children, even going out to sea. What if she fell in? What if she was seasick? Life had been hard enough on her already without a boisterous, hearty creature like that trying to winkle her out of the rut they all tried to make smooth.

'I wonder what she's saying,' Becky voiced what they were both thinking.

'Nothing that would concern us you may be certain, dear. Mrs Ellis is a business woman, it must be something to do with that. See how seriously they're talking.'

'Yes. But it's a happy sort of serious. I did like her, Mrs Frewin, didn't you? Perhaps she's talking some more to Daddy about a boat.'

But she wasn't. She had trusted Merrick Clampton from their first meeting – with exception perhaps of the initial few moments of suspicion – and now she felt that their conversation, watched so intently from the house, confirmed that trust.

At that stage she decided to say nothing to her mother of her plans. Enough for one day to tell her plan to Nicholas. But, as so often on

Thursday nights, he was late home. The Singers' rehearsal was long and unsatisfactory, it taxed his professional skill and his patience too. Somehow out of this group of keen but not-as-talented-as-they-imagined amateurs he was determined to wrestle the sort of performance that would meet his exacting standard. The result of three hours sent the singers to their homes exhilarated by the heights to which he'd raised them. It left him drained. And as he did so often, he lost himself in music of his own making, filling the solitude of the Abbey with the sound of the organ.

Chapter Nine

When at last the singers had gone on their chattering way and Howard Humphreys had closed the lid of the piano and followed them, Nicholas had been thankful for silence and solitude. Even in what seemed like pitch darkness he knew his way to the organ loft and that's where instinctively he'd turned, switching on the single lamp on the console and resting his hands like a caress on the familiar keys. Even in that act, the comfort he'd found distanced him from the imperfections he'd battled with through the evening. Unlike organs in many churches, that in the Abbey no longer needed someone on hand to pump the bellows. Like an alcoholic reaching for the bottle, he had switched on the power, and then had started his journey to tranquillity and beyond. Time had lost its meaning. From the solemn, sacred simplicity of Stainer he'd moved on to Bach's *St Anne Fugue*, and on again to the Gloria of his own Easter Oratorio, in his mind hearing the accompanying voices of men and boys, then to Fauré. As the minutes had passed, he had found the calm he'd sought, his spirit had been carried onward and upward. All around him had been darkness, the lamp on the console isolated him from everything but the swelling notes that had been his universe, filling his head and clearing the irritations of the evening. Neither past nor future had held any meaning, there had been only the present.

Veronica had heard the singers leaving, some walking together and talking in loud excited voices as they spilled out into the soft, summer darkness. No doubt others would have cycled and there must have been two with motor cycles, for she'd heard the engines. Moving to the window she'd looked expectantly towards the colours of the stained glass windows of the Abbey. Any minute the lights would go out, she'd thought; then Nicholas would come home. How ought she to tell him what she had decided? A bald statement? Cajole him into a gentle and malleable mood first? The lights had gone out, the stained glass windows had become one with the darkness. But he hadn't come. She'd waited impatiently, returning every now and again to the window. Should she go and find him? Even as the thought was born so it had died. She'd known what was keeping him in the Abbey. She might have crept in to sit in the darkness and listen, but she'd known that to disturb him wouldn't be to 'find' him. Finally she'd gone to bed, leaving him still out.

Lying staring at the ceiling she waited for him to come home. Like waiting for a man to return from an evening with his mistress? Oh no. Music was like a drug he couldn't live without; in it he seemed to find that 'peace which surpasses understanding'. But it always sent him back to her. She didn't even attempt to understand but she knew how often he'd been drawn to it after one of their increasingly frequent battles of will. And she knew, too, the effect of its healing power. His anger would be gone, replaced by a need that brought him back to her, a need that was carnal and emotional, a need that brought them together and threw every niggling problem into insignificance.

This evening she hadn't seen him, Florrie Beckham had said he hadn't been home between the boys' practice and the Singers' rehearsal. Lying waiting for him, the excitement that kept tiredness at bay had no clear direction. All the evening she'd had her own plans at the forefront of her mind, her eagerness to tell him and to make him understand. That's where she tried to keep her thoughts as she waited, but mind and body pulled in different directions.

She tried to concentrate on her visit to Becky, hoping that her invitation had been a good idea. But thoughts of Becky were soon overshadowed by her conversation with Merrick. How strange it was that the owner of the company she had so despised should be her confidante. More than her confidante, he was the one person she could talk to about the business and know that his interest was as genuine as his understanding. Re-living their animated yet serious discussion, it was brought home to her just how much she missed her father. If only he were still well, how they would have enjoyed the challenge of what she meant to do.

154

At last she heard Nicholas's step in the cloisters. What made her so sure he wouldn't stop to eat the plate of sandwiches Mary had covered with a second plate and put ready for him on a tray with the whisky decanter? Marriage to Nicholas had trained her hearing, she could tell by the sound of his step that it wasn't ham sandwiches he had in his mind, possibly not even a quick nightcap of whisky. If the bad rehearsal had left him tense, his nerves ragged, there was no evidence of it now. Two at a time she heard him mount the stairs and by the time he opened the bedroom door she was sitting, her eyes shining. Not surprisingly he misunderstood the reason for what he saw as eager excitement that matched his own.

'I thought I'd wait for you here,' she said unnecessarily. 'Was it a good rehearsal?'

'Rehearsal? Abominable. God save me from the tremolo of the female voice. In fact God save me from the female voice.' But after more than two hours of the organ's therapeutic healing he could say it without a venom.

'What a good thing I didn't join their ranks. I've been waiting for you,' she changed the subject, ready to launch into her plans for Blakeney's.

His answer was to pull the covers from her and sit on the edge of the bed. 'You don't want that nightgown,' he whispered, his mouth against her short, tousled hair.

She laughed, wriggling as she started to pull it off. 'For one who's kept me waiting for hours, you sound remarkably sure of your welcome. Your ladies went home more than two hours ago, I heard them.'

'I wasn't fit company, not then.' He'd started to pull off his clothes, hanging his jacket on the back of a chair, folding the creases in his trousers. Watching him, she knew that Blakeney's would have to wait. If he looked then at the excitement in her expression, he would have been right in his assumption of what put it there. Kicking the covers out of the way, she held her arms out to him. Their lovemaking was a new adventure each time. It drove them, it consumed them, there was nothing else but *this*, this moment, this wonder. Neither the quivering tones of the local ladies nor the healing balm of Bach existed for Nicholas; and for Veronica there was nothing, no failing order book, no plans and new hopes, nothing but erotic craving and, ultimately, the miracle of fulfilment.

155

'Are you still awake?' she whispered much later, to be answered by an affirming grunt. 'Nicholas, I've been waiting all the evening to tell you.'

'Tell me?' Suddenly he was wide awake. 'Tell me? What?' Was she pregnant? Had she realised at last that she had a role to play as his wife?

'I'm casting my net further for orders. If we just cater for the West Country, we shall be ground down into being just a small local business. It's not what I want. We are too *good* for that. We need outlets in the high-class London shops.'

'Go to sleep,' he laughed, she suspected not taking her seriously. 'Why is it sex always wakes you up?'

'Noting to do with sex,' she wriggled to sit up. 'I've decided to have a few days in London. I want to talk to the buyers. I know just where I shall call.' The emporiums she listed were no more than names to her, but that wouldn't deter her. 'Then this afternoon I went to see Becky Clampton.'

Since Nicholas had made his way to the organ loft in the pitch darkness, the moon had risen. Now it cast its pale silvery light on Veronica. Disappointed that he'd been so wrong in his expectation of what it was she'd been waiting all the evening to tell him, he too sat up, turning to face her. Sleep had lost its battle, the aura of joy in each other had vanished.

'You'll do no such thing,' he told her. She heard it as the voice of arrogance, the voice of a self-appointed dictator.

'I have responsibilities.' Unmoved by the anger she knew she was provoking, she kept her voice steady. 'You cannot, you *will not*, rule my life as if I were here to be your plaything. If Dad were well, then it would be up to him to make the decisions – yes and keep the appointments to widen our trade. But he isn't – and I'm not going to let Blakeney's down.'

'If you have responsibilities, they are first to your husband.'

'Poppycock! You're not some half-wit or an invalid—'

'Hardly the way to refer to your father.'

'To Dad? But I wasn't! He isn't a half-wit! That's hateful of you.'

Could these be the two who not five minutes earlier had been united in such perfect and erotic harmony?

'So be it,' he answered, lying down and turning his back on her. 'Hateful or not, I am as I am. I refuse to have a wife who puts a business before her marriage. Any other woman would have had a child by this time. That would put paid to all your nonsense.'

'I'll have a child when I'm ready.'

'What are you saying?' Again he was sitting up, this time his hands on her naked shoulders as he pulled her round to face him. 'When you're ready? It's months since I stopped—'

'Oh, that! You imagine because you're Big Chief Mr Man everything has to be up to you,' she taunted, childishly. 'I went to that clinic in Deremouth. The doctor fitted me with—'

'Dear God! You're telling me you've had a doctor mess about with you!' Was it only in her imagination that he drew away from her? 'And what makes you think it's your sole decision when – or if – we have a family?'

'It could just be because it's *my* body we're talking about. Of course one day I want to have children. But not yet. Why won't you ever try and understand? Blakeney's is important to me. I can't let it fail.' Then more to herself than to him and hardly above a whisper, 'I *won't* let it fail.'

She'd accused him of never trying to understand, but there was something in the way she said those last few words, that told him even more than she could have brought herself to confess.

'So that's the reason behind this sudden whim to dash about scratching up orders: business is declining. Of course it is, what did you expect? *I* warned you, *your mother* warned you. Once word spread that your father was out of the business, did you honestly expect anyone to take you seriously? If you'd done the sensible thing you would have put a manager in right from the start.' No longer did he touch her; his voice alone was sufficient evidence of the distance he had put between them. 'I've stood more than enough of it,' he might have been speaking to some errant domestic, 'and as for your gallivanting off to London and God knows where, you can forget it right from the start.'

If he were honest with himself he would have admitted that her silence surprised him. They'd covered much the same ground so many times and silent acceptance wasn't part of Veronica's nature.

She wriggled down the bed to lie flat beside him, gazing at the dark ceiling. She'd handled the situation badly, surely she ought to have been able to steer him into seeing things from her viewpoint. She used to be angry at his assumption that he was her master, but as time had gone on she had learnt to discount his opinion. Tonight she couldn't do that. Tonight she had moved the goalposts by telling him of her visit to the clinic.

'I ought to have talked to you about it – about the clinic I mean. But it was before we were married. It seems silly now but, well, things were different then.'

'By Christ they were.' He never blasphemed, it was just one more thing that made the barrier insurmountable.

'Or I should have told you just afterwards, then you needn't have had to be the one to take care. Only I couldn't, because even then it would have seemed as though I'd been deceitful.'

'Would have seemed . . .?'

If he wanted her to feel low, he succeeded. But not for long. Everything she'd told him was true: it was *her* body, it was for *her* to decide when she was ready to have a child, it was *her* responsibility – yes, and her ambition – to build on the foundation previous Blakeneys had laid. Her spirit bounced back as quickly.

'Yes, "would have seemed deceitful",' she repeated. 'Are you trying to tell me that we make love just for the making of babies? Now, where's the deceit? Anyway,' she turned her back on him, hunching her shoulders and burrowing into the pillow, 'you know now, so that's that.' Metaphorically she thumbed her nose at him.

The silence was unbearable, both of them wide awake, both hurt and resentful.

'By the way,' she said at last, conversationally, as if she were taking tea with the vicar, 'on Saturday I've invited Becky Clampton to tea. I don't expect you remember, but I told you Merrick Clampton and his daughter are living in Deremouth.'

'Neither do I expect you to remember, but I shan't be here on Saturday. I am giving a recital in Truro.'

Immediately she forgot the atmosphere of hostility.

'Heavens, so you are. I forgot. They're making arrangements for both of us for the night, aren't they? I'll pop in to see Becky tomorrow, I'll tell her to make it the following week.'

If he'd answered immediately, agreed that that was the best thing to do, that might have lightened the shadow that hung between them. But her words hung in the silence of the room.

'Nicholas . . .?' she prompted when she could stand it no longer.

By now he was lying with his back to her, making pretence of drifting towards sleep.

'Let the arrangement stand, there's no reason for you to come with me.' And how could she tell whether he was disappointed, hurt or relieved when he seemed so devoid of emotion? 'You'd know no one—'

'Neither will you.'

'Hardly the same thing. Much better for you to stay here and entertain your friends.'

'You say that, but – Nicholas, if you want me to come – just tell me the truth – willingly—'

'Go to sleep.'

As if she could! As if consciousness could be switched off like the electric power that had recently been installed in the Abbey buildings. Purposely she recalled the events of the day. Wide awake, she remembered her own inspired decision, and from there it was easy and comforting to recall Merrick's interest and his suggestions. Then she imagined Becky's eagerness for Saturday and Belinda Frewin's over-protectiveness of her – and hard on the heels of that the idea that Merrick might be seeing Belinda as a partner for his lonely future. Well, that would be nice for him, after such a happy marriage his life must seem intolerably empty. A happy marriage . . . and here her thoughts rushed headlong down the path she'd been trying to avoid.

Often they'd argued, often they'd lashed out to hurt each other. But they'd never ended the day in isolated silence. She couldn't bear it. Lying back to back her foot moved across the separating gap, her instep nestling against his leg.

'Are you still awake?' she whispered, imperceptibly moving nearer to him.

When he didn't answer she turned round and raising herself on her elbow leant across him. Was he really asleep? How could he have put the last dreadful moments behind him so easily? For her it was impossible. She rested her naked body against his, warm and familiar. Surely if he were really asleep he would have made some sort of movement, but he lay on his side, as still as a statue. She'd never felt so alone, so shut out. Following instinct she moved her leg across him. Surely as she straddled him he would roll onto his back, surely he would hold her. Yes, he was turning . . . he couldn't pretend he didn't want her . . . her hand moved down his warm body to guide him . . . her mouth covered his.

'No!'

She wasn't prepared for the way he pushed her away, breath-lessly she lay at his side.

'Yes, Nicholas, yes. We can't end a day like this.'

Without a word he changed positions, mounting her. In her thankfulness she longed for them to rush together to a climax that would blot out all the bitterness and hurt. It was all that mattered to her, it filled her being as she cried out – and then from the heights she plummeted to the depths.

Usually they stayed close in each other's arms. But not tonight. Moving off her he said in that voice she dreaded, 'Now perhaps you'll go to sleep.'

'But you wanted—'

He didn't answer. Within seconds she knew his steady deep breathing was genuine. Physically exhausted, Nicholas slept; haunted by misery, Veronica lay awake until the first pinky hint of dawn told her that the long night would soon be just another memory. Whichever direction her thoughts took they hurtled her towards disasters magnified in the loneliness of the long night. She imagined the business failing, the loyal workers being made unemployed, the premises boarded up; she imagined her marriage failing, she and Nicholas living like strangers; she imagined her father becoming ever more dependent, and her mother – here she pulled her thoughts up short. Nearer the truth, she tried to pull them up short, a streak of superstition in her frightened to acknowledge there was a repressed joy in her mother's manner these days, a lightness in her step. Tears and self-pity she could understand, but what reason could there be for the change? There was no way she could prevent the question pushing itself to the forefront of her mind; but she could turn away from it before she looked for the answer. Deep in her heart she was angry and hurt for her father, furious that her mother couldn't find loving him and caring for him enough. So her thoughts chased each other; nowhere could she find peace. Yet at last nature must have taken control, for just as the first light broke in the east she lost herself in sleep.

When she woke she automatically turned towards Nicholas, just as she did each morning. Or, as he did to her, if he were the first. His side of the bed was empty. Sitting up she peered across the room to the clock on his tallboy: ten minutes to six. A man of rigid habit, he always started his day at half past six, ensuring that by the time the boys of the choir school clattered into the practice room an hour later they found him freshly shaved and immaculately groomed. Occasionally a boy might give the appearance of having got straight from bed, managing only to throw his clothes on; if he did it once, it was certain it wouldn't be repeated. In all things Nicholas set high standards.

Getting out of bed, Veronica put on a dressing gown and quietly opened the bedroom door. Was he in the bathroom? She tiptoed along the corridor and turned the handle, half expecting the door to be locked. Instead, it opened onto the empty room, the only sign of recent occupation a damp towel on the towel-horse. There was only one place he would be. Always it was his retreat. She stood irresolutely in the empty bathroom, her bare feet on the damp mat. How often she'd had to come second to the hours he spent at the organ. What hope had she to come near to him when he never talked to her, *really* talked. Oh, he loved her, she was sure he loved her – but he didn't depend on her. In moments of stress, in moments of joy, where would he turn? To her?

She heard Mary coming down the back staircase from her attic bedroom and knew her first job of the day was to rake the kitchen range so that the water would be hot by the time he bathed at half past six. From the dampness of the towel it was evident that this morning his ablutions must have been anything but pleasant. Serves him right, she told herself silently. How could he have wanted to go out without even waking me? He was miserable, I know he was. But so was I – and he must have known it. So why couldn't he have woken me? That's all it would have taken and we could have put everything else behind us. It's all so silly, so petty. Yet, is it? It can't be petty to him, or he wouldn't have preferred a luke-warm bath rather than risk having me wake up before he'd gone. He's behaving like a sulky child, rushing off to that – even in the silence of her thoughts she needed the relief of damning the 'musical mistress' that had such influence on him – to that wretched, damned, bloody, beastly organ. It's not even his fault, it's as if the wretched instrument has an evil hold on him.

Letting her thoughts run away with her had replaced some of her loneliness with anger. But, even so, she knew she wasn't being honest. She couldn't hate him, no matter how hard she tried. Closing her eyes she conjured up an image of him: tall, elegant, arrogant, that was as the world saw him; only *she* knew that other side of his nature, the tenderness, the passion. And above all only *she* shared with him a love beyond anything she'd imagined.

Even as she thought it, she seemed to hear his voice, cold, unemotional, 'Now perhaps you'll go to sleep.' He couldn't have meant it, she told herself. By this morning he'll be feeling just like I do, he'll want just to forget last night, to push it from us as though it hadn't happened. I'll dress quickly, then I'll go and find him.

Like an off-stage cue, the grandfather clock in the hall struck six. The sound spoke to her as clearly as any words: no one will be awake for ages . . . don't waste time getting dressed . . . go now . . . creep so that Mary doesn't hear you on the stairs, then go out through the side door and across the grass. Even as the thought was born, she was halfway down the stairs. Once outside, the stone of the cloisters was cold to her bare feet, but in seconds she was on the grass. Except for the dawn clamour of birds in the trees beyond the Abbey there wasn't a sound. Too early for sun, but in any case it would be hidden by the canopy of grey. Hurrying towards the north door, she felt part of nature. She rejoiced in the low cloud and the gust of wind that carried the first hint of rain, she rejoiced in the primitive feeling of grass under her feet.

It was only as she pushed the heavy door open that she was assailed by doubt. How often she'd come here wanting to be part of what he did, only to find herself sitting alone in a pew, unseen and isolated, excluded. But not today; it wouldn't be like that today. There was but small hint of morning in the cold, dim Abbey. The flagstones were unwelcoming, colder even than those in the cloisters, the pale shadows cast by the dreary morning light through the stained glass windows lent a macabre atmosphere to the ancient building. Often, even sitting alone, she'd been aware of centuries of prayer, centuries of worshippers seeking comfort. This morning she cared for none of that, as she hurried soundlessly along the side aisle and up the stairs to the organ loft. In the soft, solemn notes he played she heard his heart calling to hers. In seconds she'd be with him, all the beastly things they'd said would be banished.

'Nicholas,' she breathed, breathless from excitement as much as from hurrying.

Turning on the long organ stool he looked at her.

162

'I had to come,' she came towards him. 'You couldn't sleep either—'

'What in the world are you doing here dressed like that?'

'I didn't waste time with clothes. I just put on my dressing gown.' Surely he'd make some move, give her some sign that he understood and was thankful. 'Why didn't you wake me? You must have crept purposely.'

'There was no sense in our both being up early. I expect you've a busy day before you – and I know I have.' His voice was devoid of emotion, as polite as if she were a mere stranger. 'I came for an hour's peace to work before morning practice.'

'You mean I'm disturbing you? Oh Nicholas, never mind an hour's work. Aren't *we* more important than your wretched – whatever it is you're playing? Anyone would think you were a backward pupil, needing to practise for hours each day. It's just an excuse to get away.'

'Think what you like,' he answered with a slight shrug of the shoulders.

'It's what I think, but it's not what I *like* to think.'

In his sigh she heard resignation. 'Veronica, go back to the house. You're behaving like an emotional child. Another few minutes and the domestic staff will be about, do you want them to see you wandering the grounds in your night clothes?'

If he called her an emotional child, then that's what she would be! Her dressing gown was held around her by a sash, one pull and it was open, held wide as she faced him.

'What night clothes? Since when have we used night clothes?'

'Behave yourself.' Turning, he swung his long legs over the stool and stood up. 'It seems I'm to have no peace.'

'Oh, you can have peace. Don't know why I was such a fool as to come. I thought we could talk, I thought if we were together, if we were honest ... we've argued before, lots of times we've argued ... but we've never gone to sleep miserable like last night.'

Sitting again on the stool, this time with his back to the organ, he looked at her with her short hair dishevelled and unbrushed from the night, her dressing gown hanging loosely open.

'So we'll talk,' he conceded. 'You say last night was different. Perhaps it was my fault, perhaps I shouldn't have criticised you for assuming that your body is your own affair. I apologise. Perhaps I should have accepted it in the same vein when you merrily told me that all those months you'd deceived me into using that damned sheath you'd known it hadn't been necessary. Do you know what I'd supposed when I'd realised my bride wasn't a virgin? I believed that your friend Chesterton had been—'

'That's a horrid thing to say. It was never like that for Laurence and me.'

'I admit, it did surprise me,' he said mockingly, 'but every lad has to sow his first wild oat somewhere and you were always ready to do his bidding.'

'Don't pretend you were jealous of Laurence,' she sneered. 'You were much too sure of your own superiority to be jealous of anyone.'

'Of that boy? That's hardly likely. Strangely, it didn't bother me.' There was no mirth in his smile. 'I knew a bumbling boy could never satisfy you.'

'So, if you thought Laurence and I had been lovers and you say you didn't even care, why did you get in such a stew about what I told you last night?'

Again he shrugged, half turning so that he sat astride the stool, letting his right hand rest on the keys. 'I hate deceit.' So he might have reprimanded one of the choir school. 'A childish infatuation I could ignore. But a visit to the clinic, letting some doctor touch you, talking to him about things that concerned no one except you and me, those are the things I couldn't accept.'

'What if I go back to him – it's Dr Bingley, he's not even young, he's a kind, understanding man – if I go back to him and tell him I'm ready to have a family—'

'Indeed? You must watch your emotions, Veronica my dear. You are no more ready to start a family today than you were yesterday. As for me, I'm even less so. A child needs parents who trust each other: clearly you didn't trust me, and after this I find it hard to trust you. Even now, how do I know that you didn't go to see this kind, understanding doctor so that you could enjoy the freedom you wanted with Chesterton?'

'If that's what you want to think, then think it! I'm sorry I disturbed you.'

'Yes. Go home, Veronica. In twenty-four hours we shall have immersed ourselves sufficiently in other things to be able to carry on. Don't they say marriages are built on shared difficulties?' As she turned away down the shadowy staircase, he called after her, 'And before you go outside, just make sure you fasten that dressing gown.'

From the Abbey he went straight to the morning practice, one that was longer than normal and if it gave little satisfaction to him, it gave even less to the boys. By the time he came back to the house for breakfast Veronica had already left. They would get immersed in their work, he'd said; and that was just what she intended. She drafted pamphlets advertising Blakeney's products, stressing the West Country theme, even including a highly illustrative account of how, four generations back, the first bakehouse had been run by her great-grandfather. She painted a word picture of the rich pastures of Devonshire, the locally ground flour, the families who had come into the business in its early days of development and whose ancestors were still employed. Her efforts were rich in poetic description – and used more than a little poetic licence as she warmed to her theme. At the end of the morning, reading her written pages she was well pleased. Then she dug in the drawer of the bureau that had stood in the office as long as she could remember and for many years before, knowing exactly where to find what she wanted. As a child she'd often come here with her father and looking at the treasured memorabilia of yesteryear had been one of her favourite pastimes. Now she found the sepia photographs she wanted, one of her grandfather with *his* father, the originator of the business and, by the time the picture was taken, a very old man glad of the support of two walking sticks. His double breasted knee-length frock coat, his tight-legged trousers and stove pipe hat showed him belonging to a different era. She knew he had married late and certainly he might have been taken as grandfather rather than father to the young man with him. Such early photographs were a rarity for, from the youthfulness of her own grandfather, she assumed it must have dated back to the 1850s. What better to illustrate the booklet she meant to have printed? Then another of her grandfather, and with him her own father who was holding the hand of a small girl – her, at the age of about four. To those she added more recent pictures, illustrations of their more elaborate creations used to market them as they'd been added to the list of products.

Arriving in her office that morning it had taken all her strength of will to concentrate on what she meant to do. Yet, once started, she had become so engrossed that time melted as her enthusiasm for the job carried her along. Usually she went into town around mid-day to have a light lunch at either the Copper Kettle or, defying raised eyebrows that she should enter such an establishment without the company of a male escort, at the Harbour Lights Inn. Why not the Happy Plaice? It was a question she wasn't prepared to answer. On that particular Friday, apart from taking the wage packets down and giving them to Bert Jenkins to pay the staff, she stayed behind the closed door of her room, oblivious to the passing of the hours.

By the time she stacked her sheath of papers, well satisfied – in truth, exceedingly pleased with herself! – it was nearly three o'clock. Suddenly ravenously hungry she remembered the single piece of breakfast toast, like dry sawdust in her mouth. But there was no time for food. Before she took her order to Watts and Morley, the printers in Townley Street, she meant to make a detour.

Halfway along Wellington Street she turned to her left and started to climb the steep incline of Clifford Hill to the one-time warehouse at the top, now the smart, modern production house of Clampton's Cakes. Unlike at Blakeney's, here the glass double door at the entrance led into a reception area where a toothy – and 'too pleased with herself by half' in Veronica's opinion – young woman greeted her.

'Why, surely it's Miss Blakeney?'

'Mrs Ellis,' Veronica corrected her in an uncharacteristically unsmiling voice. The woman's manner had implied surprise at her visit, it had even invited a smiling confidence, probably some snippet of knowledge to pass on to the rest of the staff. All too well Veronica knew there were those who thought it only a matter of time before Blakeney's let themselves be swallowed up.

'Will you tell Mr Clampton I'd like a word with him.'

'Is he expecting you?'

'No and if he can't spare the time, tell him I understand.'

'You'd better wait here.' Mistress Doorkeeper scurried across the foyer to a narrow flight of stairs and disappeared upwards. How different from the first time Merrick Clampton had called at Blakeney's; she had no such protector.

'Veronica!' he greeted her, hurrying down the stairs, 'what a nice surprise. Come along up to my room. May I offer you tea?'

166

'If you can spare the time, that would be lovely. To be honest, I'm starved, I was so wrapped up in what we were talking about yesterday that I forgot to get any lunch.'

'Today you shall feast on Clampton's fare and, I promise you, you will be pleasantly surprised.'

She laughed. Suddenly her troubles seemed lighter, the future brighter.

'I tell you, I'm hungry as a hunter. Merrick, I've done what we talked about. I was on my way to Watts and Morley to get it printed, when I thought I'd like you to see it first. Tell me what you think.'

'I'm flattered. I'm glad you've called, I've been thinking too. Miss Dobson,' to the protector of his privacy, 'I'd like you to bring us tea and a selection of cakes if you will please. Up we go,' he indicated for Veronica to precede him up the stairs, 'the first door on the right.'

With a new lightness in heart and step, Veronica climbed the stairs. In Merrick she found someone with interests akin to her own, talking to him almost filled the void left by her father's illness. Heads together they poured over her written pages, his smile of appreciation a sign of approval as he read.

'Splendid,' he said when he came to the end. 'And so much the better if they are able to make facsimiles of these photographs. A splendid introduction to the complete catalogue of your products.'

'Watts and Morley always print our catalogue, they update it as necessary, so that's no problem. I thought the cover ought to be one of the pictures—'

'Why not see if they aren't able to do something in stages from the material you give them? Your great grandfather – and the date he opened his first bakehouse, then your grandfather – your father with you as a small child – and finally, that small girl grown up. The largest and most prominent would be the present-day owner—'

'But I'm not, the owner is still Dad. Only even that's not the whole truth anymore, not since Mum was given Power of Attorney.'

'You mean the future of the business depends on what your mother decides?'

Veronica nodded. Then, remembering what in getting to know him she had almost forgotten, 'But don't start getting ideas. She

167

leaves the business side to me.' There was something of her former aggression in her manner.

'And so she should,' he said. 'So to all intents and purposes, you are the face of Blakeney's in this generation. Well, I think you've done a very good job, Ronnie. Now, here comes tea.'

Hearing Miss Dobson's step on the stairs he opened the door ready to take the tea tray.

'Shall I pour for you?' she asked, hopeful of the opportunity to glean something of the nature of Veronica's visit.

'Mrs Ellis will do that. Thank you, Miss Dobson.' His courteous manner set a firm line beyond which this toothy stenographer-cum-receptionist knew she couldn't pass. Disappointed, she plodded back to her desk in the foyer. The best she could hope for was another visitor and the chance to show her authority in barring the way to the master's den.

'Well?' Merrick asked, a twinkle in his blue eyes, as he watched Veronica take a large and hungry bite of Madeira cake.

'Not sawdusty at all,' she conceded, her smile taking any sting from the remark. 'There *must* be a difference between this and what comes out of our bakehouse, a difference in the cost and a difference in the flavour. But this is really very acceptable.' Then, her smile broadening as it was answered by his own, 'So acceptable that I shall probably ask for another slice when this is gone. You won't influence me into changing our ways but, although I hate to say it, I can see why it is our local sales are falling. No wonder I am having to find a way to spread our wings.'

He nodded. 'You know what I believe?'

'I'm frightened to imagine.' And so she was, more frightened than her laugh implied. She had come to know him as an astute business man, it was impossible not to be on her guard as to where Blakeney's fitted into his scheme.

'I believe you will approach the high-class outlets in London and will find good trade with them. And so you should. There is always a rich market for good quality produce. I said when you arrived that I had been thinking. You may not agree with my suggestions. Outlets in London may be sufficient for you. But, Veronica, the world is changing, world trade is changing. If your great-grandfather could look at today's chain of supply he wouldn't believe how things have changed.'

As he spoke he cut her a second slice of Madeira and, as she ate it and re-filled their tea cups, she listened and let her imagination take wing. It carried her on the journey made by Blakeney's over the years, from the local area that had given her great-grandfather his first customers, to areas within the region of the railway as far away as Bristol and Bath (and how proud she had been when she and Laurence had brought home the new orders). All that was familiar, but it was the future that beckoned. It was impossible to talk to Merrick Clampton without being infected by his enthusiasm. So in her mind she conjured up images not only of the great shops in London, Blakeney's produce proudly displayed, but further, much further. The New World was a blank page to her but, as she listened to what he was suggesting, perhaps as much as anything it was that challenge of the unknown that called to her.

'Don't say anything now,' he told her, 'just take these pamphlets home with you. This is a good firm, I use them myself. Their tins are excellent airtight containers, but more than that they will manufacture them to your own specification. The front could carry that picture of the four generations – or why not an eye-catching Devonshire scene? For Christmas cakes a thatched cottage or a village church, perhaps carol singers, something very English, very Devon? There is nothing the Americans look for more than history, they yearn for the roots of the old countries of Europe. Think about it, Veronica. What is there to lose?'

'The way things are going at the moment, I know I must do *something*. You don't know how much I wish I could talk to Dad.'

'I believe I do understand. I'm no substitute, but I've had experience in the business and I'll always be interested. I know it's not the same. Take these pamphlets home with you, talk about it to your husband.'

She didn't answer. She kept her head turned away from him as she thrust the leaflets and price lists into her bag. But there was very little he missed and, susceptible to atmosphere, he suspected that rather than being a shared interest, Blakeney's was a subject of discord between her and the husband he'd never met.

'Don't forget you're all coming to the Abbey tomorrow,' she changed the subject. 'I'm afraid Nicholas will be away, he's giving a recital in Truro and staying overnight. But I'm looking forward to seeing you all.'

'I fear I shan't be with them,' Merrick told her. 'I forgot when we talked of it yesterday, I have a prior engagement.'

169

He heard himself say it. But why? During the morning he'd looked forward to the following afternoon and Veronica's visit had done nothing but cement their friendship. Just for an instant they looked directly at each other. Did she knew he lied? Did she care whether or not he came with Becky and Belinda?

'Never mind,' she told him brightly. 'Another time. I'll look forward to seeing the others. I hope it's fine so that Becky can play with the boys. Now I must fly. I want to get this to the printers. Thank you for my tea and that very acceptable Madeira.' To her own ears the friendly words sounded brittle, they lacked the ring of sincerity. Was that how he heard them too? She was glad to be out in the street again, hurrying down Clifford Hill, her mind firmly on the work she wanted from the printers.

It was only later, back in the solitude of her own office that there was nowhere to escape her thoughts. When she'd invited Merrick, Becky and Belinda to visit her home and imagined Merrick and Nicholas together, the idea had pleased her. For herself, she was prepared to give the afternoon to being hospitable to Becky and her carer even though, on first acquaintance, she hadn't felt drawn to the so perfect – and so protective! – woman. As is second nature between women, she had recognised Belinda's unspoken message that it was only a matter of time before her relationship with Merrick took on a permanent nature. And that's good, Veronica believed; both of them are lonely, both of them care for Becky, both of them have known happy marriages. She had looked forward to their visit, and she realised now that, partly, it was because she was eager for Nicholas and her to be seen as a symbol of married unity.

After last night, and even more after those early morning minutes in the Abbey, she was thankful that he wouldn't be at home. Equally, she was thankful Merrick wasn't to be there either. Perhaps it was simply that it would be easier to give herself solely to playing hostess to Belinda and the little girl than watching a budding romance that could only make her ever more aware of the confusion of her own emotions.

170

Chapter Ten

'I do so worry about her. I ought not to have let her go.' Belinda Frewin bit her bottom lip, every conceivable fear in her expression as the two women watched the exodus of children. For the boys of the choir school, a walk to the village with their weekly penny 'sweet money' was routine; for Becky it was high adventure.

'It'll do her good,' Veronica answered, making an effort to hide her irritation. 'I don't expect she has much opportunity to be with other children.' Polite words, but what she meant was an accusation, and that's how Belinda heard it.

'I try to protect her. I don't mean just from danger, but from feeling she is different from others.'

'She always will be different if she doesn't learn to mix. There are always some who can climb higher than others, or run faster, or play better tennis. Coming to terms with competition is part of growing up.' Conscience prodded Veronica, reminding her that when she'd been Becky's age she had been a picture of health, she'd usually been the one to run fastest and she would never have let any other child climb higher. As for tennis, how proud she'd been when her father had taught her to play and, later on, even prouder in her claim that as a team she and Laurence had been invincible. Now, hearing her firmly believed views expressed in such positive terms she sounded more priggish than she intended. To make amends, she rushed on, 'Put her side by side with – well, with the sort of child I remember being – then even if she can't win at those sort of things, she would leave the others standing if they had to paint a picture. We all have our own strengths and weaknesses. Anyway, Mrs Frewin, you needn't worry about her today. The boys will be delighted to have her in their care. I promise you they won't let her feel left out.'

'I do hope you're right. Poor little darling. She's come to mean such a lot to me.'

Veronica's first impression of Becky's carer hadn't been promising. A fussy woman, she had thought, over-protective; over-assertive too, going out of her way to make it clear how established she was in the family. Now she looked more closely at her visitor, tried to see deeper.

Petite in build, her features were even and delicate. Only her hair seemed out of character, mousy-fair, plaited and pinned to the crown of her head, yet somehow managing to convey a flyaway appearance. Sleek hair in that style could give a woman an air of sophistication; but Belinda's was wiry, not wavy and yet giving the impression of the sort of frizzy mop that defies hairpins. As for her clothes, the dark grey skirt and off-white blouse owed nothing to the newer, liberated fashions. They took Veronica's mind back to the days of the war that had ended more than five years ago, a time when cloth makers hadn't been able to buy attractive dyes. Hard on the heels of the thought came the image of her mother, re-styling her pre-war clothes rather than 'look as though I belong in the workhouse', as she'd discounted the gloomy colours of any available material. The image changed, but still her thoughts were on Monica and her excitement when the dressmaker delivered her first post-war silk dress, her delight in replenishing her wardrobe and, with each new garment, looking to Herbert for the adoring admiration she craved.

Avoiding where that line of thought would take her, Veronica turned a warm smile on drab, pretty Belinda.

'How long have you looked after her?' She brought her mind back to Becky.

'More than two years. To start with after that dreadful accident she was very ill, her leg – oh, I hate to think of what happened to her – it was so crushed. Merrick must have been distraught, well I know he was. I understand just how he has suffered. I'm sure he and Becky's mother were a devoted couple. He engaged a full-time trained nurse to care for Becky when she first came home from the hospital. She was there for months. Even after I was engaged she only gradually gave over the care to me. She could have gone sooner, I was quite capable. Merrick knew he could entrust Becky to me, as soon as we met he knew. Isn't it strange how that can happen? He'd interviewed people with more experience of children that I'd had. Yet as soon as we met, well, we just felt right. Has that ever happened to you, I wonder? Perhaps it did when you met your husband?' Fortunately she didn't wait for an answer. 'All my life I've tried to care. My grandmother lived with us when I was a child. Poor darling, I loved her dearly. She was blind, she used to say I was her sight.'

'And you nursed your husband, too?' There were a dozen things Veronica would rather have done with her afternoon, but having invited the paragon of kindness there was nothing for it but to muster up some interest. She gave herself up to leading the conversation away from Becky (and hopefully taking Belinda's mind off how long the children were out) and on to a subject that would keep going of its own volition.

'I was so miserable when Grandma died. Such a sad time, you've no idea what a void her going left in my life. Then I met Roderick. It was as if Fate brought us to each other. He was in poor health, just couldn't shake off his cough, you know. Poor darling, he lived in a beastly bed-sitting room, he had no one to cook him good food. After only a few months we married. We both thought that once I was caring for him he would pick up. But he didn't. You should have seen the milk and eggs I used to make him have. Even when we knew he was consumptive, I made myself believe we could conquer it. But whoever heard of anyone conquering advanced consumption? We had just three years. There were times when we thought we might be winning. Or even if we didn't think it with our hearts, we made a pretence and we hung on to hope. It had been months since he'd been able to work. I lied to him. I don't know why I'm telling you this. I've never told anyone, not even Merrick. But I think, in my circumstances, you would have done the same as I did. I told Roderick I had been given two hours work each evening reading to a blind old lady. Knowing about Grandma he believed me, never doubted. But the truth was, I spent the two hours each day cleaning at Craven Manor, an asylum quite near where we lived.' Remembering, she suppressed a shudder. 'The jobs I had to do ... if I hadn't been almost demented with worry myself I could never have gone through with it. But it brought in a few shillings, it paid our rent and let me buy enough food to put on Roderick's tray. I used to

173

pretend I was eating mine downstairs. He was in bed by that time, too weak even to get downstairs.'

'But how did you survive?' This delicate woman must have a will of iron. Veronica's opinion of her was improving by the minute.

Although she was telling her story to Veronica, in her own mind Belinda was re-living the horrors she'd endured each evening. 'The patients weren't just feeble-minded, at Craven Manor they were more like animals than humans. Sometimes it's hard to hold on to your faith, people like that go on living and Roderick was taken. How did I eat, you say? The people in the kitchen were kind, they used to give me a plate of food before I went home. To say I didn't fancy it sounds so ungrateful, but when you've spent two hours cleaning up after – oh well, let's not think about it. They were as they were, poor souls, they could none of them help it. Then when Roderick lost his battle, I was left with nothing.'

'Where were your family?'

'In Sussex. They never liked Roderick, they were stubborn, wouldn't even try. So I couldn't go cap in hand to them. Remembering it is like looking back at some sort of hell, hurrying home each evening to Roderick yet frightened at what I'd find when I got there in case he was worse, in case he'd had another bleed when he'd been alone. Watching as each day he got weaker, more dependent, further away from me – and that dreadful asylum. After he died I could have gone back to my parents, it's what they wanted. I think they saw his death as some sort of evidence that they'd been right and I'd been wrong. But I couldn't forgive them. I gave up going to the asylum. From the day he died I never went back there.'

'And that's when you heard Merrick wanted someone to look after Becky?'

Belinda nodded. 'The very day after Roderick's funeral I went to a domestic agency. I expected I'd be offered a cleaning job, hopefully one where I lived-in. I wanted to be free of our rented rooms, the ghosts. Instead, the man who ran the agency talked to me for a while, asked my background and my circumstances, and said I might like to meet someone he called Mr Clampton. He didn't sound at all hopeful, he stressed that he had already sent two people, both with more suitable qualifications than mine. So I kept the appointment expecting it to be a waste of time. But,' then she smiled and the worried expression vanished, 'as I told you, we both knew right from that first moment.'

Veronica smiled too, a smile that had to be held in check so that it wasn't taken over by the laugh that it was hard to repress. To bury a husband on one day and have that 'we both knew from the first moment' experience on the next, must surely be a record! The time had come to change the subject, she had no wish to hear of the developing relationship between Belinda and Merrick. Guiding the conversation she talked of Deremouth and the surrounding area, describing where the shore was safest for non-swimmers beneath the cliff to the east and away from the entrance to the Dere estuary. With one ear listening for the clamour of returning children, she recommended picnic places that could be reached by bus from Deremouth's Station Square. Memories crowded back of herself and Laurence in Downing Wood on the outskirts of Otterton St Giles on the other side of the river or Picton Heath north of the main road and 'where the blackberries grow twice the size of any-where else'.

'Here they come,' Belinda was on her feet and across the room to take up position at the window. 'She really must come indoors now, she mustn't get overtired. That's the trouble, you see, she won't want to admit to being less able than the others.'

All Veronica's recent sympathy vanished as irritation regained the upper hand.

'Rubbish!' she said, good intentions forgotten.

'You say that, but you haven't seen the state she gets in some-times. Cross with herself, cross with everyone else, as if it's our fault she can't keep up. And you wonder I try to hold her back to a pace she can manage.'

'I'll ring for tea,' Veronica gave up her struggle on Becky's behalf. 'Open the window and call her in if you like.'

Becky came, but with ill-disguised resentment.

'What did you buy?' Veronica asked, before the child had a chance to open the cone of paper containing her pennyworth of purchases. 'No, don't tell me. Let me guess. I bet you got at least a ha'pennyworth of Rainbow Marbles. That would be ten unless they've got dearer.'

Becky giggled, her ill-humour vanishing. 'I got sixteen. That was my whole penny, so they must have got dearer since you used

175

to buy them. Johnny Downs, he's the one I got to know best, he told me they were the best value.'

'That's what we used to think, Laurence and me. As you suck them they change colour; if they start off pink a few sucks and take them out to look and see, they'll be white or mauve or even green.'

'I know. We sucked on the way home, then compared. Do they go to the shop every Saturday?'

'Yes. That's the only time they're allowed out – right away "out" I mean. Mostly in their free time they play ball games on the grass just beyond the Abbey grounds. You must come again on a Saturday.'

'You mustn't push yourself on them, dear,' Belinda said, her voice dripping with kindness.

'Small chance of that,' Veronica guffawed in a way quite unsuitable for the wife of the Master of the Choir School. 'Young lads aren't given to over-politeness. If you enjoyed being with them today, Becky, you can be sure they enjoyed having you there.'

Becky didn't say anything, but Veronica's words seemed to have pleased her. Undoing the cone of twisted paper, she popped a Rainbow Marble into her mouth.

'Not before tea, dear,' Belinda admonished. 'You really should ask before you eat sweets.'

'If you haven't finished sucking it by the time the tea tray arrives, take it out and put it on the side of your plate for afterwards,' Veronica suggested. She knew it broke the rules of good manners. That's why she said it, laughing inwardly at the tut-tutting of Becky's 'oh-so-caring' carer.

So the afternoon passed. After tea Belinda produced a piece of easy piano music and insisted her charge should show off her ability. From the mechanical pounding of the keys and the sulky expression on the child's face, it was hard to believe anything would ever turn her into a musician. More out of sympathy for her forced performance than for appreciation of her skill, Veronica praised her. She even suggested a repeat of the same tedious little offering, and sitting next to Becky improvised harmonies that turned it into a duet. Her reward certainly wasn't the 'music' they made, it was the spontaneous smile that replaced the little girl's sulky pout.

176

Then it was time to drive them home, for the bus's last run to Deremouth had already gone. Only then did Veronica have nowhere to hide from her own thoughts. An evening at home on her own did nothing to tempt her back to Ottercombe, so she drove to Merchant Street and left the car in the bakehouse yard, then walked back to the shore. Without a glance in the direction of Number Eighteen, she strode past Vicary Terrace and on towards the cliff path.

Where would Nicholas be now? The recital didn't start until half past seven so she imagined him in his hotel bedroom. Was he missing her? Was he as miserable as she was? And it was all so silly, so unnecessary. It wasn't fair of him to blame her for not talking to him before she persuaded Dr Bingley to help her. All right, she argued silently as she climbed the hill, I can see that if it had been *now* that I'd wanted him to do it for me I would have talked to Nicholas. But *now* and *then* are quite different. And he can't pretend that when we married he wanted us to have children straight away; if he had he wouldn't have used that beastly sheath. Then when he stopped using it, did he honestly think I was so dense that I didn't know why he wanted me to be pregnant? Not for the sake of having a child, oh no, what he wanted was to make sure that I did as he said and gave up Blakeney's. Why, with Dad the way he is, won't he see that I can't do that? If I wanted to, I wouldn't. And I don't want to. If I didn't have Blakeney's to organise what in the world does he think I'd fill my mind with? He ought to have married someone like Mum, dependent and pretty. Well, I'm neither, I'm *me,* the same now as when he first knew me. Is that true? Am I the same? No, I'll never be the same, there's no going back to being that virginal young girl . . . virginal? She seemed to hear his voice, 'I knew my bride wasn't a virgin.' He'd thought Laurence had been her lover. Supposing he had been, would her whole life be different now? Often enough Veronica was stubborn and wilful, but always she believed she was honest and it was that honesty that told her nothing would have changed for Laurence and her if he had been her lover. That same honesty told her, too, that in the new awareness of adolescence her one aim had been to lead him into making love to her. Wanting no one and nothing except him, how often she had let her imagination (imagination tinged with ignorance, she knew now) carry her forward to what she had

177

never doubted, a moment when she would know she was wholly his and he was hers.

Automatically, as she came to the grassy cliff top, she sat down in the shelter of the familiar gorse bushes. Sometimes in her dreams this had been the spot where Laurence had lost his last shred of willpower. What a child she had been! But she wished that was really what had happened, she wished she'd lost her virginity in what she had believed was love. It should have been a great moment in her life and she believed that even Nicholas would have accepted it more readily than knowing about her appointment to see Dr Bingley at the clinic.

'I saw you pass the house,' a voice startled her. 'Am I intruding?'

'Merrick! I thought you were out of town.'

'I don't think that's what I actually said,' he answered with a half-smile. 'The truth was, I preferred not to visit you *en famille*, so to speak.'

'So you fibbed?' she laughed.

'A prior engagement, I think I told you. An engagement with outstanding correspondence. Becky seems very full of the marvellous time she had, she even pressed something she called a Rainbow Marble on me.'

'A sure sign of great affection. They're a childish delicacy to be sucked slowly and with relish. Believe me, I know.'

All hint of a smile had gone as he sank to sit by her side, turning to face her.

'I wanted to thank you. That's why I followed you. She leads such a restricted life. Don't think I'm criticising, Belinda is wonderful to her in every way. But, sometimes a child needs to try to do a little more than she is comfortably able. Don't you agree?'

Veronica nodded.

'Child or adult, I entirely agree. What was it someone once said about the road to success? It's always under construction.'

'To success ... to happiness ... and like all roads, there are rough patches, deep ruts on the way.'

She felt a sudden sting of tears and turned her head away from him, pretending an interest in a sailing boat further round the coast towards Chalcombe. She mustn't let him guess her aching misery. If only she could talk to him, really talk to him.

'Trade is changing,' she heard him say, 'yours, my own, it's the same the country over. Perishable goods used to have a much smaller area to supply.' Relief flooded through her as she realised that he'd believed her troubles to be merely with Blakeney's.

'I know,' she heard the break in her voice but it was too late to hold back. Instead she snatched at problems that had been over-shadowed in the last hours. '... lost customers ... people don't want to pay our prices ... that's why I want to find custom in the London outlets ... don't know why I'm telling *you*, *you* of all people—'

'Because you know I'm your friend,' he took her hand in his.

She gripped his fingers as if they were a rope thrown to a drowning man and, not caring now that in those few seconds her eyes were already bloodshot and her face had lost the battle and was distorted by her tears, she turned towards him. Her control gone, she found relief in pouring out to him the tug-of-war of her life, her belief that under her care Blakeney's would prosper and her sense of failure that she was losing trade. Ought she to acknowledge that Nicholas and her mother had been right and she hadn't the ability?

Merrick listened, saying nothing. Then she came to that last frightened suggestion, a widening crack in the confidence he had admired from the first. Holding her chin so that she couldn't look away from him, he slowly shook his head.

'We both know the answer to that, Ronnie my friend. You have been the driving force behind the business for longer than the time your father has been too sick to be there with you. An illness like his doesn't develop overnight. Don't forget, I have the letter you sent in reply to my interest in the business,' and the warmth in his smile as he said it was lost to her as her eyes filled again, 'the letter of one who can travel the road however rough it may get. Just keep the wheels turning, if you get bogged down and need a sack under the wheels, then let me bring you one.'

'Why should you?' She gulped, ashamed and yet thankful that at last her pent-up emotions had found release, 'It would be better for you if Blakeney's caved in.'

'If you'd said that to me a year ago I would have been the first to agree—'

'You mean you wouldn't want it now? While it was on a steady uphill climb you wanted it but now—'

'I mean I didn't know you then. This may be no way to talk to a married lady, friend or no friend, but in the time I've come to know you I've learnt to admire you probably more than any other business acquaintance. You're tough, Ronnie, you're clear-headed and wise. Blakeney's will prosper again. Its tomorrows will be brighter than its yesterdays.'

'The road to success is always under construction,' she went back to where the conversation had started then, making a supreme effort at control and forcing something that was almost a laugh, 'I wish this Mr McAdam we read about in the newspapers would repair my immediate muddy patch.'

'Good girl.' His words were intended to put a line under the show of weakness he knew she was already coming to regret. 'Here, mop up,' he said, passing her the silk handkerchief he wore in his breast pocket, a pale grey and white spotted affair that matched his bow tie, 'then let's walk on for a while. If you can spare the time, that is? I recall that your husband is away giving a recital.'

'He's in Truro. Time's my own, I'd like a walk.'

He was an easy companion. As they walked he drew her to talk. She painted a word picture of the home she'd grown up in, of the security that had stemmed from the affection of her parents for each other and for her. She said things she'd never spoken to another soul, admitting how her father seemed to accept his present life without question as if he'd known nothing different. Even in this evening of soul-baring, though, she couldn't bring herself to tell him of her mother's need for admiration and flattery, and certainly not of her 'friendship' with Hugo. For herself, none of that mattered. Her anger was on her father's account.

'In the beginning he was worried, frightened; that was dreadful. You could almost feel him trying to remember, trying to get back in step. But now it's as if the past had never been. How can it happen to a person? I wish you'd known him . . .'

'I wish it too. He is highly thought of in the town. And your husband, I've heard him play, you know. Not here. We were staying in Canterbury. One of the last times Esme and I went out was to hear him give a recital in the Cathedral. One of those occasions that stay with me.'

Time slipped by unchecked, they walked until they were within sight of Chalcombe, nestling in the dip still some two miles

180

distant. Then, realising how far they'd come they turned back towards Deremouth. When, coming down the final slope from the cliff top, he suggested they might find somewhere to eat supper together, she accepted willingly. Harbour Lights had always been a favourite lunchtime venue for Herbert and her, the upstairs room was away from the bar, the service friendly and the food wholesome. Occasionally she and Nicholas dined at the more stylish Royal Court, the sort of establishment where ladies were elegant and gentlemen wore evening suits; many, many times she and Laurence had devoured huge helpings of cod and chips at the Happy Plaice. To suggest Harbour Lights for supper with Merrick seemed natural.

After a miserable start to her day, followed by an afternoon of making an effort to be hospitable to a woman for whom she had no instinctive liking, the evening had done wonders for restoring her spirit. It was only when they got back to Merchant Street where she had left her car in the bakery yard that trouble decided it was time to put an end to her enjoyment. Merrick swung the starting handle . . . he swung it again . . . and again . . .

'You're sure you have petrol?'

'Yes, I had it filled yesterday. It's never not started before.' She felt helpless, she knew nothing about cars except how to drive them.

'When it comes to motor cars, I'm afraid I'm ignorant,' he admitted. 'I'll undo the bonnet and see if anything looks obvious, but beyond that if I tinker about I shall only make things worse.'

She got out of the driver's seat and came to his side so that, in the fading light they peered at the engine. Then she started to laugh.

'We're the blind leading the blind if ever a couple were,' she giggled. 'Well, I'll just have to leave it and ask Mr Wilton from the garage to come and have a go at it on Monday. It won't be the first time I've come in on my bicycle.'

'I expect your husband will bring you.'

'Yes, of course,' she agreed brightly. 'Not to look at it though – Nicholas would have about as much idea as we have. You know what I think? In this modern age, it would behove us all to learn about the mechanics of these monsters.'

'You're probably right. But, there again, we probably won't. Ah well, Friend Ronnie, I must ask you to walk back to Vicary Terrace and let's hope mine behaves better than this.'

'You're going to drive me home? You don't have to. There will be a cab in Station Square.'

'What nonsense the girl talks.'

She laughed, not because anything was funny but because she had enjoyed the evening, she felt comfortable and relaxed. Even a stubbornly silent motor car couldn't knock her spirits down to where they had been twelve hours earlier. The original owners of the houses in Vicary Terrace had used horse-drawn carriages, in fact one or two still did. However, Number Eighteen's stable was empty, and the carriage-house was home to Merrick's Renault. Instead of walking along the front of the terrace facing the shore, he took her straight to the back, to Vicary Mews. And she was glad. Waiting indoors would be the oh-so-caring Belinda Frewin, probably wanting to fuss over him just as profusely as she did over Becky.

'I'll drop you off here,' he said when they reached the gate of the Abbey grounds. 'Thank you for this evening, Ronnie,' he said as he came round to open her door. 'Don't know when I've enjoyed myself so much.'

'Hearing all my troubles? It's me who should say thank you. And I do. Not just for supper and bringing me home – although that too – but for – for – well, believing in me, I suppose.'

'Oh, I believe in you all right. Blakeney's need have no fear while you're at the helm. You're going through an uphill patch, my dear, but when you reach the top the view will be marvellous.'

She nodded, then, her smile suddenly driving her cares away, 'Like it was from the cliff this evening. Wonderful. I won't forget it either, Merrick.'

'I have to go to London first thing Monday morning,' he said. Then with a smile that even in the soft summer darkness she knew was there, 'And this time I have a genuine appointment. In fact I shan't be back in Deremouth for a week or two, I'm going on to look at a site in Yorkshire. But I'll be thinking of you with your new ventures.'

She watched him drive away, conscious of how much good her evening had done her. She knew the direction she meant to go, she was looking forward to Monday so that she could talk to Bert Jenkins about a recipe that would be expensive even by Blakeney's standards. But it would be of such high quality that no American Christmas would be complete without it! Her mind raced, there

182

was no stopping the heights of success she could foresee. A cake almost black with fruit, rich with brandy, a choice of decoration to its snowy white icing, packed in a tin bearing a picture of – of what? A snow scene? No, there was more snow in North America than in England. A village scene, timbered houses, crinolined ladies? Possibly. Or a church with a steeple, choir boys outside singing carols by the light of lanterns? Thoughts tumbled through her mind, one chasing another. She concentrated on the seed Merrick had planted, nurtured it with his encouragement and his faith in her, all these thoughts crowding in on her as Merrick turned the car and she listened as the sound of it was lost in the distance. Only then did she turn to go into the grounds of the Abbey.

'I saw you come.'

She was startled at the unexpected sound of a voice she didn't immediately recognise.

'Who is it?' Yet she believed she ought to know.

'Who else but me would be walking under the stars? People are so silly, they rush out when the sun shines, they even put up their brollies and pretend they like the rain but, except for the courting couples, how many look up and watch the stars appear as the sky darkens?'

'It's Miss de Vere. I ought to have recognised you.'

'We've not spoken since the days you were Miss Blakeney. I've seen you, of course I have. You go driving past my gate every morning. I talk to your mother sometimes. Poor soul, if ever I saw a spirit in anguish then it's hers.'

'What nonsense!'

'You may disregard me, write me off as a silly woman full of fanciful nonsense as you call it. But you, you with your busy life and your successful husband, how can you even start to understand what she must be suffering.'

'I don't know what sort of story she's been telling you but—'

'As if I need to be told. I have eyes to see. Yes, I watched when your father lost his grip on his own thoughts, I saw what it was doing to her. And I've watched as she's fought to find herself again. She's a young woman still. And if she's happy she'll always be a young woman. Years aren't everything, you know. Now you,' she peered closely, her eyes seeming to pierce what light there was on a moonless, starry night and defying Veronica to look away, 'you're made of harder stuff. If you weren't, you couldn't run the

183

show at that bakery. But I've known it since you were a child. If tragedy befell that husband of yours, you'd still have a life.'

'You live in a dream world, you don't know anything about us.' Matilda de Vere had always made Veronica uncomfortable, now fear gave her voice an edge of aggression.

'From being told, certainly I know nothing. But there's a truth deeper than words Miss Blaken – Mrs Ellis. I worried about your mother, I've always had a fondness for her. But now I see she is finding her own way. Convention might not approve, but she's a happier person for it.'

'*She! She!* What about *him?*'

'Your father? Don't you think he's more content to see her smiling than sad? And you like to think you understand! I tell you, you know nothing. You fill your head with that bakery, you take your life and your husband as your due. Not *me*, not *you*, *nobody* should take anything for granted. Listen to me, Veronica – oh, I've known you all your life, I can't be doing with all this Mrs Ellis talk. I used to watch you with Laurence Chesterton but I told your mother then that nothing would come of it.'

'Were you waiting out here for me to get home?'

'How would I have known you were out? I would have expected you to be snug indoors with that husband of yours.'

'I beg your pardon, I imagined you were so clever you would have known that Nicholas is away.' Veronica's answer was heavy with sarcasm.

'I know the things that matter. I know that he will never be a man to be trifled with – and you'll forget that at your peril. Or perhaps peril is the wrong word, perhaps you don't value your marriage as much as most young women. Why should you when you consider yourself such a business woman? I watch, I listen – oh, not to gossip, I've no time for gossip. No, what I listen to is something that only a few are blessed with the power to hear. Hear? No. Not hear with my ears, but hear with my spirit. Perhaps it's because I've watched you and your family all your life that I care. And it's because I care that I can pick up the – the resonance. You say did I come here to wait for you to get home? How could I when I expected you'd be safely indoors already. So what brought me here, what made me tarry? Was it just that here at the top of the hill first stars are clearer? Was it that Fate brought me here to see you driven home by some stranger while your husband is away?'

'What I do is my own business. You may mean kindly, Miss de Vere, whether you do or not I've no idea. And I don't much care. I had business to discuss. Not that it matters to you what I was doing.'

'You're offended. Well, that doesn't worry me. I have this sense of trouble, something waiting to engulf you. All I can do is warn you so that you can head it off.'

There was mockery in Veronica's mirthless laugh, just as there was in her voice as she turned to open the heavy gate in the stone wall of the Abbey grounds.

'No use keeping my eyes open if you know it's coming. That's a contradiction in terms if ever I heard one.'

'Silly girl. You'll put your head in a noose and then realise you could have walked round it if you hadn't been so blind.'

Matilda de Vere walked away, not towards the village, Picton Heath and home, but on along the higher lane beyond the Abbey. Like a bat, Veronica told herself, more at home in the night. Stupid woman. But, once indoors, there was no way of escaping her troubled thoughts and, woven into those thoughts, was the recurring warning.

Even without the meeting with Matilda she would have found it hard to escape her worries in sleep. Matilda de Vere was a joke, she always had been. No one with an atom of sense would have taken her seriously. And yet ... and yet ... how much did she know about Monica? How much had she known about Laurence and the future Veronica herself had been so sure of? So, if there was a black hole ahead where would it be? The business, with it's thinning order book? Nicholas and his cool aloofness since that dreadful – no, she wouldn't even let the memory of it into her imagination, it would blot out everything else. That must be the black hole waiting for her to tumble into it. Well, she wouldn't let it trap her. When he came home she'd talk to him, she'd even be honest with him and tell him about falling trade, tell him what Merrick had advised, make him listen, make him understand.

But still she couldn't sleep.

The days went by, Nicholas treated her with cool politeness that made talking to him impossible. But worse even than that was the subtle change in his lovemaking. Lovemaking? However tense he had been, however heightened his emotions whether exalted by

185

glorious sound or irritated by notes that jarred, she had rejoiced in his need of her. Lovemaking had been a joyous and glorious adventure, surely for him as well as for her. So what was different? she asked herself, the answer past comprehension. As if she were indeed the 'chattel' she'd so often accused him of wanting to make her, intercourse would be a regular end to their days, brief, demanding, devoid of tenderness. Whilst he reached the climax that would lead him to oblivion, she plunged to new depths of loneliness and frustration. Each night she resolved 'This time will be different' as with every movement of her body she strained to bring them back to the miracle their love used to be. But 'this time' was never different, always she was left like a starving man with a plate of food snatched away, or like someone hanging on the edge of a cliff with no one to drag her to safety.

She'd imagined herself setting out her business plans to him, she'd even been fool enough to imagine him taking an interest.

'London? It seems to me utterly unnecessary. If you can't sell your goods down here, why should people in London want them? They've baking houses of their own I'm quite sure. And as for thinking you can get orders from the other side of the Atlantic, for heaven's sake wake up. Your business is failing – just as I predicted if you remember. *I* know the reason, *you* know the reason. However, like your body, these things are your own affair not mine.'

'Nicholas, you're not being fair!' She heard the croak in her voice and dreaded that he might think it was put there by anything but the anger that filled her. 'But, you're right. Blakeney's is no more your business than what the choir sing is mine. Anyway, Merrick Clampton thinks the catalogue I'm having printed is good and even *you* can't accuse him of not knowing what he's talking about.'

'Far be it from me to criticise your friends. All I say is, be careful you're not throwing good money after bad. If he's so interested I wonder he doesn't offer a price for the business. Why don't you suggest it? You appear to be on such good terms with this producer of what I seem to remember you call "cheap sawdusty rubbish" that—'

'Clampton's goods aren't rubbish,' she snapped.

'Your words, my dear, not mine. What I was trying to say was, since you and he are on such intimate terms I'm sure you could persuade him to let you continue to go in there and play about just the same even if it came under his umbrella.'

'I am not on intimate terms as you put it. But I'm grateful for his friendship, he looks on me as a proper worthwhile person. He doesn't talk down to me like you do. Talk down to me or roll on top of me, that's about all—'

'Dear God preserve me. You're behaving like an hysterical child.'

'I'm behaving like you treat me.'

Hysterical child or not, she was ashamed of how she was behaving, ashamed that this was happening to them. She felt they were hurtling towards some disaster and neither of them had the power to draw back. Across the room they glared at each other, seeing the anger in each other's eyes but not the hurt.

'Let's leave it.' She heard his voice as weary, something that only added to her sense of failure.

'I have to go to London,' she told him. What pride didn't let her tell him was that she'd imagined them going together. There would have been plenty for him to do while she was visiting the buyers she had in mind. Surely if they spent an evening dining and perhaps dancing, then a night in the hotel Merrick had recommended, they would find the ingredient that had vanished from their relationship. 'This is where I intend to stay—'

'How did you get this?' He held up the piece of paper on which Merrick had written the address and telephone number of a London hotel.

'My intimate friend Merrick recommended it to me,' she told him, sarcasm in every word. 'If I go up on the eight ten on Monday morning I'll stay one night and come home on Tuesday.'

'Indeed. How kind of you to condescend to tell me your plans.'

At that she reached breaking point. 'You're just not fair. How can I give my mind to what I have to do, when all I have from you are taunts and sneers?'

Picking up a pile of music from the top of the piano he walked out of the room. If, a minute later he had turned back, what he would have seen might have helped him pull on the brake and stop them hurtling so fast towards pain they couldn't prevent. This time her tears had nothing to do with anger; she had never felt so unloved, so desolate and alone.

They had had plenty of quarrels, usually stemming from her dedication to Blakeney's, but never one that put such a barrier between them. Never had they ended a day as they did that one, lying silently and as far from each other as a four-foot six bed would allow. Both were very still, both breathed deeply and evenly. Neither slept.

By mid-morning she was in a taxi-cab being driven to the hotel Merrick had recommended in Kensington. She'd left home while Nicholas was still at early choir practice, driving to Deremouth and leaving the car (restored to good health by Jim Wilton on the Monday following her outing with Merrick) in the bakehouse yard. It was the first time she'd driven straight past Ipsley House, but she'd told her mother not to expect her. She tried to push the conversation to the back of her mind. Her mother's opinions had been very like Nicholas's and, in her view, the idea of chasing off to London trying to find orders was nothing but stupid, girlish nonsense, not the act of a woman who claimed to have her feet firmly on the ground when it came to business.

'You just wait and see, Mum,' Veronica had told her with far more confidence than she'd felt. 'But tomorrow I shan't be coming to see Dad on my way to town. Keep him occupied so that he doesn't miss me.'

'He's all you care about. You don't even pretend that it might be *me* you come to see.'

All that had been a preliminary to the scene with Nicholas. But as the train had puffed out its clouds of smoke and she'd listened to the steady rhythm of the wheels on the track it had been impossible not to feel her spirits rising. London! Even Dick Whittington couldn't have felt more excited than she had as she'd been carried further and further from Deremouth. As her excitement had grown so had her confidence.

'This day will be a turning point in my life,' she vowed silently, her eyes shining with eager anticipation as she sat forward on her seat in the cab, wanting to take in the passing scene, wanting to feel herself part of it. 'Let it be a day that changes our fortunes.'

They were turning into Kensington High Street when she saw him.

188

'Stop! Driver, can you stop. Don't go away. Wait for me.' And leaving taxi-cab and luggage, she chased the tall fast-walking figure.

'Laurence!' she yelled sounding exactly like the companion of his adolescence and not a bit like a successful business woman. But one glimpse of him was all it had taken for the years to roll away, taking her worries and disappointments with them.

Chapter Eleven

''struth!' His handsome face lit with pleasure, 'Ron, here in "the smoke"! Can't believe it!'

The years melted. In the wonder of seeing him so unexpectedly, she felt the same thrill as she had each time he'd come home. Suddenly the cares of the day vanished. Being with Laurence had lost none of its power.

'Nor me. Seeing you like that, I mean.' Where was the sophisticated young business woman now? Her face beamed her pleasure, her eyes shone. Was he conscious of the transformation? Probably not, for hadn't this always been the way she'd greeted the start of his holidays?

'Why didn't you write and tell me you were coming to town? I suppose you are with that husband of yours?'

'I didn't write and tell you because – because—' in her confused emotions of the last days and weeks the thought hadn't entered her head, but a more tactful reason saved the moment, 'I didn't know where you lived. As simple as that. Your mother and Mum keep in touch, so I knew you had moved to a smart new apartment, no longer a bed-sitting room. But London's a big place, searching would have been worse than the proverbial needle in a haystack.'

'So this is Fate. And your husband? That sounds too silly for words, Ron, my friend Ron being dragged along as someone's wife.'

'Silly or no, it's not true. I'm on my own. I have appointments for Blakeney's. I'm on my way to take my things to the hotel first. Are you in a hurry? Why don't you ride with me to the hotel, we can talk in the taxi-cab.'

'Great,' he agreed. 'Where are you staying?' Then, when she told him, 'We're as good as there. Get rid of the cab and I'll carry your case. How would that be?'

They seemed to have slipped comfortably back pretty well three years. The initials 'VRE' on the shiny leather case he carried for her were the only evidence of the world she'd left behind at the Abbey. She booked in, signed the guest book, then they ate lunch together in the hotel restaurant.

'Bit different from our Happy Plaice. Here we are, me well on my way up the ladder – I've got lots to tell you. When I think I might have been dying of boredom in a solicitor's dingy office in Deremouth! But then, I wouldn't have let myself be talked into it. I get a regular weekly page on the mag. Did you know? Do you read it? I bet you do. I know Mum is as proud as a peacock to show off about me.' Veronica laughed. Darling Laurence, he hadn't altered one bit! 'And, add to that, I often interview well-known stage people. Life's never dull. Poor old Ron, still stuck in Ottercombe. Ah, here comes our soup.'

'Ottercombe isn't dull,' she defended as she smiled her thanks to the waiter. 'You have to have a dull wit to find things dull.'

Her pursed his lips and sent a mock kiss across the width of the small table. 'She doesn't change,' he teased. 'It always was fun, getting you rattled.'

'I'm not rattled. I'm just telling you that there is nothing dull about running Blakeney's.'

'Running? Ah yes, of course, I'd forgotten. Mum hears all the news of course and she told me about your father in one of her letters. Rotten luck for them both, your parents I mean. Particularly for her. From what Mum says, he probably doesn't know the difference, but her wings are really clipped being so tied.'

'Huh!' Not a word, hardly a sound. 'Anyway, I was saying, I have come to talk to buyers, I intend to get our goods into the two or three really top class shops in London.'

'Tell you what,' he said, in the voice she had heard a thousand times when he had suggested some outing or other through the years, 'I could get something in the magazine. You're quite a looker, you know, I suppose I always took that for granted and never really thought of you as someone who would make a good picture. First of all, collect orders for your cakes or puddings or whatever it is you're up to, then I could do a write-up as if we'd had an official interview. We'd see we got a flattering picture too, and I could say I'd talked to the daughter of this Devon business etc. etc.'

'That would be marvellous. Not about me, but about the firm. Remember what fun we had when we went selling in Bath and Bristol?'

'That'll be nothing to *this*.'

'Take a look at this,' she pulled one of her catalogues from her large handbag and passed it to him. 'Or perhaps you could use something from it. Emphasise Devon, it's a county that always makes people think of lushness.'

'This isn't half bad,' he said scanning through it. 'First you've got to land your buyers, then never mind telling me how to do it, you can leave the article to me.'

'I didn't mean it like that.'

He grinned, well pleased. Their positions were established: the fact that she ran her own business didn't put her on a par with him, he was the one whose pen had the power of influence.

'How long are you here for? I want to take you out on the town. There's no place in the world like London, Ron. I say, this is great. My little country bumpkin's come to the big city.'

'What cheek!' But she laughed, caring nothing that he called her a country bumpkin, simply hanging on to that one word – 'my'.

She'd thought nothing had changed between them, but experience through the intervening years must have left a mark on them both. As a boy he'd been away to school; as a youth he'd been to Oxford, he'd even travelled to Italy with his friends. And through all that time she had lived in Ottercombe, mentally crossing off the days on the calendar as she'd waited for him to come back. Hero-worship can be a fleeting thing, but that could never be said of hers for him. He'd taken her adoration for granted. Now though she had a new assurance, whether gained by successfully running the business or by marriage he didn't question. Her stay in London would be short, she talked of one night, or two at the most. He was determined that he would give her such a good time that he would ensure his erstwhile exalted place in her affections had lost none of its importance.

'When you've finished charming the buyer of whichever of

these emporia you are gracing this afternoon, let me take you out this evening. We could have dinner, we could dance.'

Her mind raced. She had nothing suitable to wear to the sort of place he meant to take her. Excitement was a physical thing, she felt it in the beat of her heart and in a strange kind of ache in her arms as if the blood was racing too fast. If she scooped a good order from the buyer she would take that as an omen and she would go to the fashion department, she would spend money she could ill afford.

Travelling up on the train she had known moments of uncertainty as she'd anticipated the task she'd given herself. But lunch with Laurence and, more than that, the thought of an evening with him and the certain knowledge that he was as pleased to be with her as she was to be with him, took away all her fears. She seemed to be walking on air as she entered the great store which, until that afternoon, had been no more to her than a name. Always honest and outspoken, she never knowingly went out of her way to charm. But talking to the buyer, confident of the quality of the products she was offering, her charm was natural.

How different her trip would have been had she not seen Laurence, she thought as she dressed in her ridiculously expensive outfit. Imagine eating a solitary meal in the hotel restaurant, nothing to come between her and her thoughts of how things had been at home. For a second there was no escaping the memory of Nicholas's farewell, as cold and formal as if she were a visiting, and none too popular, maiden aunt. It was that that hurt. Anger she could accept, but cool disinterest was intolerable. And that autocratic manner of his was worse even than coolness, it was as if she were no more than an irritating intrusion on the things he found important. Well, she wouldn't think about him, not this evening. She wouldn't let him spoil these lovely, lovely few hours. With a conscious effort, she concentrated on fastening her new dress, admiring the glittering bandeau she fastened round her forehead and, above all, picturing how at the same moment Laurence would be preening himself with satisfaction. She chuckled as she imagined him, knowing just how pleased with himself he would be. Conceited? Yes, of course he was, he always had been. He was Laurence, he knew how to squeeze the last drop of adventure out of life. In front of the long mirror she twirled, her bottom lip caught in her teeth as if to hold back her excitement at where Fate had brought her. Surely this was how Cinderella must have felt as she dressed for the ball. She didn't question her sudden happiness, her thankfulness that something had come between her and the misery she'd not been able to escape. Laurence had shared all the carefree pleasures of her adolescence. It was still there for her, and thankfully she grasped it.

He took her to the West End where they dined and danced just as he'd promised. As if by common consent they didn't talk about Ottercombe. He preferred to forget that she had a life apart from him; she preferred to forget that she had a life beyond the evening's oasis of pleasure.

Neither had life at Ottercombe stood still. Monica's disapproval of Veronica's trip to London may have been tinged with jealousy, although she had disguised it with her argument that for a small family business to aspire to the sort of market 'the silly girl' had dreamed up would prove a waste of time and money.

'Do stop looking out of that window, Herbert!' She couldn't hide her irritation as for quite the tenth time in half an hour he had got up from his chair and gone to peer as far as he could see, visibly listening for the sound of the motor car.

'Late this morning,' he answered, not seeming to notice the sharpness of her tone.

'I've told you and told you. I wish you've just try and concentrate. Veronica has gone to London.'

'London. Gone to London. Fancy.' Seeming satisfied, back he went to his chair. But less than five minutes later, he was back at the window.

'What do you think can be keeping her?'

Monica turned away. How much more was she supposed to take? Usually Alice came to take him off her hands as soon as breakfast was over. As good as gold, he would let her lead him away to 'help' with the endless supply of jigsaw puzzles – or was it the same puzzle that, once it was completed Alice would take it apart ready to start again? Herbert wouldn't know, and Monica didn't care. She had always thought jigsaws a complete waste of time. This morning, just when he seemed more fidgety than usual, Alice had had to catch the morning bus into Deremouth. With a scarf wrapped round her swollen face she was going to ask Mr Frith, the dentist, to pull out a tooth. She had promised to be back by late morning, Monica had given her the money to come in the station taxi-cab for, today of all days, it was important that she got into town herself. She'd seen Mr Withers more than a week ago and he'd promised to deal with the accountant for her, get everything in order. In Monica's opinion women had no place in the business world. She had felt disloyal in talking things over with Hugo, but who else was there? She believed Nicholas would be in agreement with what she intended, but how could she be sure he wouldn't betray her confidence and talk to Veronica. Silly girl, with her wild ideas!

'Perhaps something's wrong,' Herbert was saying, making yet another trip to the window. 'Can't think where she can be.'

'Oh for goodness sake, sit down and be quiet about her. I've told you over and over. The stupid girl has gone to London on some hare-brained scheme. Any other morning and you hardly notice her coming, yet today you have to behave like this.'

He sat down, his shoulders hunched, his demeanour one of utter defeat.

In a second she was at his side, sitting on the arm of his chair and cradling his head to her. 'I'm sorry. Darling Herbert, I'm sorry. Don't look like that, darling.'

'I'm no use, no good to anyone.' Just for a moment his mind was clear, he saw himself as he was.

'That's not true. Look at me, darling Herbert.'

He looked at her, his eyes bloodshot with unshed tears. Then, as he rested his head against her, the mists closed in on him again. In her embrace his contentment was restored; he was safe with his beloved Monica. A few minutes more and he'd forgotten even to be anxious about Veronica's non-appearance as he drifted into sleep. Very gently Monica disentangled herself and rested him against the chair-back grateful for the opportunity she'd wanted. Creeping out of the room she went upstairs to get ready to go to town as soon as Alice returned.

So it was that as the taxi-cab drew up at the gate and Alice climbed out, Monica took her place. She was free, Alice's tooth trouble hadn't been able to throw her carefully laid plans into disarray. Going by cab she would be in good time for lunch at the Harbour Lights, then she would stroll through town to the offices of Withers, Wright and Lambton. Believing Herbert to be asleep, she hadn't looked back into the drawing room before she'd left the house.

195

Perhaps his sleep had been no more than a cat-nap, or perhaps it was the sound of the taxi-cab drawing up that disturbed him. In an instant he was on his feet and hurrying to his post at the window. Ronnie! That must be Ronnie! No, it was a taxi-cab and there was Monica talking to the driver. Alice was coming in holding a large blood-stained handkerchief to her face. Now Monica was getting in the cab. Something must be wrong. Into the chaos that was his mind there were images of Veronica lying hurt – Alice with a blood-stained handkerchief and Veronica being injured seemed to him to make perfect sense.

'What's happened. Ronnie! What's wrong with Ronnie?' he shouted as he blundered into the hall and came face to face with Alice.

'Nothing's happened,' the kindly woman assured him, trying not to let it show how thankful she'd been when Monica had said he was asleep. The taste of blood made her feel quite sick, what with that and being dumped and jolted in that cab, no wonder she hurried by him and straight down the passage to the kitchen and the downstairs cloakroom. They were hiding something from him, he knew they were. How dare they try and keep it from him if Ronnie was in trouble. And why else hadn't he seen her this morning? She *always* came at breakfast time, seeing her was as much part of his day as the bowl of porridge Monica put in front of him.

He'd let himself drop off to sleep, that was the trouble. A messenger must have come. Ronnie must be ill, that's where Monica had gone, she'd gone to see Ronnie. But why hadn't he gone with her? Why was he here all by himself when somewhere something must have happened to Ronnie? But which way was the Abbey? With all the stealth of a thief he had crept out of the house and down the garden path where he looked up and down the lane. The Abbey? But surely that was to the left. The taxi-cab had taken Monica the other way. Perhaps he was wrong, perhaps he was muddled which way the Abbey was. He had to follow the taxi-cab, that was the way to find out what all the fuss was. By that time he'd forgotten Alice arriving home, yet impressed on his mind was the picture of a white handkerchief stained with blood.

In the kitchen Bertha poured a cup of strong, sweet tea.

'Now you just try and get that down you, that'll set you up.' She spoke with more confidence than she felt. For the past two days

Alice had eaten nothing, her poor face had got more and more swollen. Now just look at her, white as a sheet. Nothing inside her but the blood she must have swallowed. 'Come on now, Alice m'dear, just you sit quietly and sip this. I can hear your insides rumbling from here, you can't have a crumb inside you. Open up and let's have a look at what he's done to you. Gor'struth, he's not half torn at your poor swollen gum. Turns your stomach to think what you must be swallowing.'

It turned Alice's. Retching emptily she bolted back to the lavatory. When she finally emerged, trembling with weakness, despite the day being unseasonably sultry, she was glad to sink into the fireside chair.

'Not a sound from him, he must be asleep again,' she breathed, 'Thank God for it, I don't think I could stand over that ruddy jigsaw this morning to save my life.'

'You shut your eyes for half an hour, Alice m'dear. Up you go and lie on your bed. I'll keep an ear open for when he wakes. Usually if he's left quiet he dozes, poor soul.' Only silently did she add the rider: 'I suppose the Missus has gone gadding off after that writer chap. Ought to be ashamed of herself, a woman of her age behaving like some stupid lovesick girl. Make a laughing stock of herself – and serve her right.'

Alice needed no persuasion. Left alone Bertha made a pie ready for supper, then cut cold beef to take in for Herbert's lunch. Such a lonely life for him, she thought affectionately as she fried cold sliced potatoes and made him a salad. Fancy, in there all by himself to eat it. Pure gold, he always was. Now, just because he couldn't piece his thoughts together, he was left alone as if he counted for nothing. What could she do to make his food look more appetising? An extra spoonful of her nice home-made chutney, yes, that might cheer it up, he'd always liked her chutney.

To Veronica the evening had a feeling of unreality. Never before had she been anywhere like the hotel where they dined, or danced to the music of such a splendid jazz band. Never before had she walked on a pavement where even at nearly midnight people were still abroad, or known street lights that turned the summer sky into nothing more than a dark canopy. Was it starry? Was it cloudy? Laurence said that someone on the magazine had come up from Dorset that afternoon and had said the West Country had had thunderstorms. The difference between that and the dry warm night in the city made home and all she had left behind seem even further.

Laurence hailed a cab and opened the door for her while he told the driver the name of her hotel. Perhaps he read her mind and knew how she dreaded the evening being over; or perhaps he had intended to see her back to the hotel in any case. Either way he climbed in beside her, taking her hand in his.

'You said one night or two. Ron, you're not going tomorrow? Promise me you'll be here for tomorrow evening.'

She nodded. 'Yes, I'll stay until Wednesday. I still have two more interviews.'

'And mine, that makes three.' But she knew from the way he said it that whatever he wrote would come from long-standing knowledge garnished with poetic licence. 'I've had a word with our photographer, Matthew Reynolds, and he can do the picture tomorrow afternoon. What if I suggest he brings his camera to my apartment to take it tomorrow afternoon? That would leave us a free evening. Tonight was fun, wasn't it.'

'It was – was as if we were still the people we used to be.'

'Perhaps. Or perhaps we've learnt a few lessons. Anyway, tomorrow afternoon?'

'Perfect. I have two appointments, both for the morning. So by the afternoon I shall know whether I've done as well as I did with my first order.'

'You will. No one could refuse you.'

'They won't buy my wares because of *me*, they'll buy them because I tell them about the top grade ingredients, I tell them our standards—'

He held up a hand, laughing. 'All right, all right, you don't have to give me the sales talk. Think what you like, Ron, it *is* because of you that they are prepared to listen. Once they taste the excellence of your incomparable delights, then they'll see they've made a wise move and come back for more. But in the first instance, never under-estimate the value of physical looks and charm – of which you have more than a fair share.'

No wonder there was a feeling of unreality about her evening. How often in the past she had lain awake imagining a scene such as this. Listening to him she chuckled softly; it was like being eighteen again. So it had been as they had danced, carefree and abandoned. Time had had no meaning, whether in hours or years. She liked to think they had picked up their relationship where they had left it.

And later, alone in her hotel bedroom, her smart new dress carefully hung up, she kept her thoughts firmly on the crowded hours of her day – starting from the moment she stepped onto the platform at Paddington Station. How different the night was here. From outside, she could hear the sound of a city that seemed never to sleep. It must have been more than one o'clock but there were still people in the street; she listened to the sound of footsteps on the pavement, to taxi-cabs, the occasional motor horn, people shouting or laughing . . . city sounds. How different it was from the stillness that surrounded the Abbey where only the hoot of an owl or the distant bark of a dog broke the night silence. But she wouldn't go down that road, she wouldn't imagine her room at home, she wouldn't think of Nicholas. Yet how could she keep her thoughts away from him. Easier by far to whip up anger at the way he was behaving: he was arrogant, he wouldn't even try to understand. Why should he resent her having something in her life apart from being his shadow? Not that he wanted her all the time even as a shadow. How different it used to be when she went to the practice room for her weekly 'fun music' evenings with him. But now if he ever chanced on her playing the piano she felt he listened ready to criticise. She knew something now that she'd never suspected in those days when she had played her game of temptation with him: to him music could never be fun. It was the very reason for his existence, but it was never fun. Now Laurence . . . yes that's it, think about Laurence. What was the reason for *his* existence? And the answer sprang straight into her mind: *fun*. Turning to lie on her back she gazed up at the ceiling, struck by how much light came into the room through the long window. Had it been Fate that had thrown him into her path that afternoon, she wondered. Fate, God, what was the difference? Either way she sent a silent 'Thank You'.

The next day she bore in mind what he'd told her about appearance and charm and, not surprisingly, approached her other two selling ventures with a new confidence. Well pleased with the look of her order book and the obvious interest she had aroused, she ate lunch in the hotel restaurant with as hearty an appetite as she'd always shown at the Happy Plaice then spent time titivating ready

199

for her photographs. It did occur to her to wonder whether Merrick was in London, she would have been so proud to tell him how well she'd done. And more than that, he of all people would have been genuinely interested. And again came thoughts of home, of Nicholas hearing of her success in polite silence, of her mother tut-tutting and saying that rushing around the country chasing orders was no way for a woman – especially a married woman – to behave. And her father? If only she could talk to him, if only they could share their plans ... But she wouldn't let anything spoil this, her last evening.

Laurence collected her and took her to his apartment on the first floor of a solid Georgian house where they found Matthew Reynolds waiting for them, a white sheet hung against the wall and lights set up. He was an enthusiastic worker, in fact he appeared excited at what they were doing. Some of that inevitably rubbed off on her and, as for Laurence, he was quite cock-a-hoop at the respect he knew Matthew felt for him that he could casually produce a friend both good-looking and with a story to tell worthy of publication. The photographs taken and the plates put safely in the case, she realised they had been nearly two hours. It was coming towards six o'clock and Laurence was busy at the cabinet making cocktails. To her it was the height of sophistication, never before had she seen anyone shake cocktails. The act was so in keeping with him, a dash of one thing, a splash of another, whether he followed set rules she had no idea but she liked to think he didn't. She seldom touched alcohol, but she didn't intend to say so. It wasn't that she was teetotal, merely that it didn't fit into her normal lifestyle. Often if he came in late Nicholas would have a nightcap of whisky, occasionally after Sunday morning service he would pour sherry or Madeira for her and her parents, but cocktails at a quarter to six in the evening made her feel gloriously depraved.

The scene was set for their last evening. Matthew packed away his camera and, each of them carrying something, they stowed his screen-like sheet and lights in his motor car.

'Now the evening's our own,' Laurence said, taking her hand. If any other man had done that she would instinctively have pulled away, but Laurence wasn't any other man and it was a natural act. Side by side they went back up the wide stairs.

'Where can I take you to eat?' he mused. 'Last night we got dressed up and hit the high spots, we mustn't try and repeat it.

What about a little restaurant I go to sometimes in Soho? Do you like Eastern food?' They both knew, of course, that she had never tasted it so her nod of agreement meant that she was willing to follow his lead, just as she always had.

Different flavours, different textures, the illusion of the Orient, all lifted her further from her normal life. Laurence's dexterity with chopsticks was just one more thing that secured his place on the pinnacle she'd built in their childhood.

'Last night we danced,' he said, the caress in his eyes again setting her emotions spinning out of control, 'I could touch you, hold you. Ron, I was such a bloody fool. Why couldn't I see then,' and she knew 'then' didn't mean last night nor yet last year, but when they'd both been young and free, 'what I've learnt since.'

She had to stop him, she mustn't listen. But what he said was so true, so right. If only he'd loved her three years ago, what a different course their lives would have taken. Logic wanted to whisper that even then she knew how dependent her father had been becoming; logic reminded her that even if Laurence had whispered those magic words she'd longed for, he would have taken her adoring loyalty for granted. But this evening she didn't want to listen to the voice of logic, for where else could it lead her but to Nicholas and the barrier of ice that held them apart. Purposely she tried to draw back from the memory of his scornful voice, his cold 'Now perhaps you'll go to sleep', the altered way he took her in lovemaking lately as though he resented his own need and cared nothing for hers. The evening belonged to Laurence and her, there must be no clouds, no recriminations. And if Laurence told her he regretted their parting, then she would be glad. Until he spoke those words she had never realised just how much his easy desertion had clouded her memories of all the happiness they'd shared.

'We were just children,' she tried to sound more practical than she felt. 'It's always easy to imagine that everything would have been perfect, if only . . .'

He was watching her closely and, knowing her so well, she was sure he could read thoughts that she didn't want shared.

'I suppose like a fool I thought that what I felt for you couldn't be grown-up love. You didn't fall in love with the girl you'd taught to climb trees or to put a worm on a hook. I'd been away from you often enough, school, university but always you'd been there, the most important thing in my life and I was too blind to see. Why couldn't you have trusted me, Ron? You must have known that you and I were right together.'

'Don't, Laurence. I don't want to think about it. And anyway what's the use?'

'Just tell me I wasn't wrong,' his hand crept across the small table with its brilliant white cloth, his fingers found hers and clung to them, 'tell me that when I went away you were as devastated as I was when I heard you were marrying Nicholas Ellis. Why couldn't you have believed in me, Ron, you must have known that I always came back to you. You didn't love him, not like you did me. Do you laugh at the same jokes? Do you share the same interests? From what I hear,' and he sounded so confident that it didn't occur to her to suspect there was no way he could have heard any such thing, 'his world is music, a wife can never be more than a convenient bedmate or a social asset.'

'My marriage isn't your business,' she clutched at the nearest weapon of words.

'You're right. But Ron, the girl you were wasn't a sober married woman. Have you changed so much?'

'I've not changed at all,' she lied. 'And yes, if I'm honest, I used to believe I was in love with you. But we were too young to know.'

'*I* was too young to know,' he corrected. 'It wasn't until I left Ottercombe, left it for good I mean not just a few weeks before the next holiday, that I saw how empty my life was going to be without you. Have you eaten enough?' he changed the subject, 'if you have let's go back home. We can't talk here with waiters hovering.'

In fact she'd eaten very little, carrying the toothsome morsels from plate to mouth with the aid of a pair of chopsticks had proved far more difficult than Laurence made it appear. He had suggested she might like to ask for a fork, but pride had made her decline. If he could manage, then so could she!

'It was lovely, but I've had plenty,' she said. 'Let's not get a cab straight back, let's walk, shall we.'

The idea pleased him, to stride along side by side just as they always had put them on to the old footing – the same and yet not the same. Not for the first time he put his arm around her as they finally came off the busy street and into the park, it was an automatic movement, reminiscent of the times they'd walked together from one house to the other through the village at home. And again she thought – the same and yet not the same.

'I don't want you to go back,' he said. 'Now that I've found you again I can't push you back to be kept in Memory Lane. You can never belong just to yesterday, Ron. You're part of my today and all my tomorrows.'

'We're always friends, Laurence. It was so horrible when we didn't hear from each other. We mustn't let that happen, not ever again.'

He stopped walking and turned her to face him. At first neither of them spoke, he because what he meant to say could so easily damage all those tomorrows he talked of, and she because she was aware they'd brought themselves to a moment that was important. It was like tottering on the edge of a precipice, uncertain whether it was possible to regain her balance and having no idea of what she might plunge into far below.

'Time for that cab,' he whispered. 'I want you to myself, I want ...' Whatever he wanted hung in the silence of dusk. It wasn't until they were almost out of the park that he said what was in his mind. Ought she to have been surprised? Or shocked? Or angry? Ought she to have felt this sudden eager joy?

They drove to her hotel and while she went to her room, hurriedly to re-pack, he settled her bill. Outside the cab waited.

She had no feeling of guilt. One night with Laurence, one night that would take away the hurt of their parting, one night that would put a blessing on the innocent, adolescent love they'd known.

'Remember that evening years ago when we made the excuse of dancing to the gramophone just to get away from our parents. The first time I touched you. I didn't know what to expect – but I know now that you were wanting more than my ignorant fumbling.'

'I did,' she whispered. If she spoke too loudly she might wake to find all these precious hours had been a dream. 'I wanted us to make love. I didn't know much about it but I loved you and I believed you loved me.'

'I did. I do. Let me look at you. Ron in her nightie. Here with me. I'm not taking what's *his*, you know that, don't you? You were mine before you were his. In every way but this.'

She wished he hadn't said it, at least she wished he hadn't phrased it like that, turning her thoughts to Nicholas and the miracle of love that he'd taught her.

'I'm no one's, I'm *me*. And I want this, too. We've shared everything else, we've understood each other, we've – yes, it's true, we've loved each other always. So this can't be wrong.' It was really happening ... Laurence had become just the sort of man she knew he would ... still her hero, always her hero ... and tonight the business woman had gone as surely as the organist's wife. Wearing just a sleeveless, silk nightgown she stood in front of him. They would make love because he loved her, that was what she yearned for. How long since it had been like that with Nicholas? No, don't think of him, don't think of the Abbey, don't hear the echo of his music, don't remember the wonderful abandonment of giving herself wholly to the love they'd shared. Think just of *this*. Dear Laurence, the soul-mate of all my years. His hands rested on her shoulders then moved down her body; she closed her eyes giving herself to what her body craved. It was right, it must be right. By tomorrow she'd be gone, but this time there would be no pain and misunderstanding. In this next hour they would wipe away the hurt she knew now she'd never been able to forget. She didn't take seriously what he had said about all their tomorrows; this would surely draw a line under an adolescent love that had been carefree and innocent.

Guiding her to the bed he was already fumbling excitedly with the cord that held up his pyjama trousers. Then he climbed above her. Just as she did, he must have felt a need to wipe away the bad times, to come together in a final and perfect union, sealing the bond that had held them close since childhood.

Another voice echoed unexpectedly in her memory: hers, telling Nicholas her body was her own. Forget Nicholas, close your mind to everything except a need you can't deny, this clamouring in every nerve. And as, all too soon, Laurence's triumphant cry told her it was over, still her body clamoured for what was out of reach. But now there was no hiding from reality.

'Sorry, Ron. I wanted it to take ages,' he panted. 'Oh boy,' he half whistled, 'but that was good. Give me a while,' and another gasp or two, 'we'll do it again.' When she didn't answer he began to take heart. Probably she hadn't expected anything better than knowing it had been good for him. Talking to the chaps on the magazine, hearing the tales they told of their exploits, he knew some women had a good time too. But poor old Ron, stuck with that starchy organ grinder, not likely he'd exactly transport her to realms of glory. He drew her hand towards him, giving her a hint that with a bit of work on her part he could soon manage again.

'Ron, where are you going? Oh, the bathroom's through that door. Don't be long, I shall miss you.' The smile in his voice only made her despise herself more.

'I'm going, Laurence. Don't say anything. Don't try and stop me. Don't know what happened to me, how I could have let you . . .'

'Oh come on, Ron. We talked about it, we both knew it was what we wanted. You're not going to turn round and accuse me of raping you for God's sake.'

She shook her head.

'I just want to go. Want to forget what I've done.'

He too got out of bed. And that was a mistake, for to see him standing there with his hair tousled, his legs looking white and thin and his pyjama jacket falling open to display his spent passion, made a stranger of him. Picking up her bundle of clothes she went into the bathroom and locked the door.

Ten minutes later, dressed and with her hair and face ready for the outside world, she emerged. But, although he wore only pyjamas and dressing gown, of the two he was the more restored.

'You can't go off at this time of night. Anyway, what time is your train?'

'There's an early one, just after five o'clock. Newspapers or mail I suppose. I remember when I checked the timetable. I shan't come to any harm at Paddington. I can handle people, you don't have to worry.'

'Tell me you're glad we met again. Don't go away like this.'

'Yes of course I am. I've had two wonderful days – and it's you who've done so much to make them good. But I shouldn't have come back here tonight. I thought it would sort of round things off.'

'Nothing is finished between you and me. I'm sorry I let you down just now. The first time together—'

'First and only.'

He knew better than to argue. Instead he turned to her with that look she had never had the power to resist. 'But you'll come to

London again, you'll not want to rely on shops like that sending orders if you don't chase them. We'll go to the theatre next time, and we'll dance again, I'll even take you to dinner somewhere where you can eat with a knife and fork. How's that?' Despite herself, she laughed. Nothing ever changed him, nothing ever would. 'And Ron, that ought to be in the magazine probably the week after next. Can you buy it down there in the wild west?'

She nodded. 'Yes, of course we can. I always read your articles,' she added just for the pleasure of seeing him smile.

'Wait while I get my bags on, then I'll come outside with you and see you into a cab.'

It was nearly eight o'clock by the time her train shuddered to a smoky stop at Deremouth Station. Already London, Laurence, even last night's escapade had taken on the semblance of a dream. If she hurried she would be home before Nicholas finished early morning choir practice and, on that morning, getting home was more important even than spending a few minutes first in the bakehouse. The chimneys were smoking, she knew the men – and one or two women – would already be working at their mixing bowls. After she'd seen Nicholas she would drive back to town, she wanted to tell them about the success of her trip. Success? Mocked a silent voice. From a business point of view it had been a wonderful success – and hadn't that been the reason for her going?

In London the early morning had held the promise of another summerlike day; on the Devon coast there seemed no air, the sky looked threatening and the roads were running with water from storms that had done nothing to clear the air.

At the Abbey she parked her car next to Nicholas's in the yard then purposely walked past the window of the practice room on her way to the Master's Lodge. At that moment Nicholas looked her way, although he gave no sign of having noticed her. Now that he knew she was home he'd finish the practice quickly, she thought confidently. But it was more than half an hour before she saw him crossing the grass. How silly to feel nervous, as if guilt was written in large red letters on her forehead. How could she be guilty? Last night had belonged to her past, to the time before she'd even known Nicholas. Wasn't that what Laurence had said?

'I must have misunderstood you,' he greeted her. 'I understood you to say you'd only be away one night.'

She smiled at him, coming near and holding her face towards his, thankful that he'd missed her. A few hours apart was all it had taken to bring them back to each other. Thank You, thank You, she sent up her silent message.

'You missed me?' she teased.

'I made excuses for you, for Celia Humphreys's sake not for yours. No chance, I imagine, that you remembered it was the evening of her supper party?'

Covering her mouth with her hand she looked at him in horror. 'I'm truly sorry. Why didn't you remind me before I went? I was so excited at what I was doing I didn't even look at the diary. What lies did you tell for me?'

'For you, none. To save her embarrassment I told her you had been sent for to see a sick friend.'

'That was almost a half truth. Not that he was sick. You'll never guess who I met, actually saw him in the street before I even reached my hotel? Laurence!' So she rushed into a report on the chance meeting, their lunch together and his willingness to do an article about her and about Blakeney's. 'Before I could have pictures taken or let him interview me, I had to be sure I'd scooped good orders. And I did, Nicholas.' Silently her eyes begged him for praise as she hung on to the hours of her visit she wanted to remember and pushed those she preferred to forget to the back of her mind.

'You must have left the hotel very early to get a train home so soon?' How politely he spoke, so politely she found she couldn't look at him as she answered.

'Yes. There is an all-night porter, I asked for an early call and arranged for him to have a cab there to meet me,' she lied, hating herself for doing it, hating Laurence for his part and, in that moment, hating Nicholas who stood before her like an inquisitor.

'Indeed.' Yet in her ears it sounded more like a question.

'I wanted to be home before you and the boys finished practising.' Her voice trailed into silence, one that with each second she found harder to break. Why couldn't he say something, *anything*? 'You might at least pretend some sort of interest,' she blurted out when she could stand it no longer. 'You expect me to follow your career – and I do, well usually I do. But you don't even pretend to care about what I do. You think yourself too high and mighty for business. Well, let me tell you, it's people like me

207

– like me and Merrick Clampton, yes, even Laurence and what he does for the magazine, that make money and give employment, keep the country going. You escape to the Abbey and cushion yourself with music – well, God help the economy if it relied on people who did no more than that.'

Another silence. This time she couldn't look away from his dark eyes, she felt hypnotised. What have I done, she cried inwardly?

'So is that where you were?' If only he'd show some sort of emotion, even anger would be better than the expressionless tone of his question.

'Where I was? You know where I was.'

'Indeed? But then, why should I? What you chose to do is your own affair, you've made that abundantly clear.' Mystified, she was at a loss to find an answer. 'I expected you to be home by the end of yesterday aftenoon. When you weren't, like a fool, I drove to Deremouth to meet the train that I found arrived at six-fifteen. I stupidly thought we ought to have some time before we rushed off into company at Humphreys's place. Like an even bigger fool I waited for the next, forty minutes later. Yes, I was angry that you could treat my friends with such little courtesy. When I arrived back from their supper, I put a call through to the hotel where I'd been gullible enough to believe you'd stayed.'

'But I did—'

'I was told you had stayed one night and had checked out during the evening. A talkative man, the night porter. He remembered clearly what time you'd left because he'd just come on duty. You'd seemed in a hurry, while you'd fetched your things your friend had settled your account and a cab had been waiting. What a pretty scene. *My wife* having her hotel bill paid for by – by whom? Clampton I dare say, for I can't imagine young Chesterton spending a penny except on himself. Or did he get his money's worth?'

'Stop it!' Somehow she was standing close to him, her clenched fists pounding his shoulders. 'You don't even try to understand. Yes, I was with Laurence, just like I'd been with him for all the happy years of my life. But *you*, all you can do is make hateful, beastly jibes.'

Holding her firmly by the shoulders he drew back from her.

'I want the truth. Did you let that callow youth touch you?'

'What callow youth? I don't know one.' Then, just like a party balloon that floats too near a candle flame, she lost all her fight. Unashamedly she cried. 'Yes, I went to bed with Laurence. I had to. He loves me, I wanted love to be everything. That's how it should be, how it used to be for us. Forgive me, Nicholas. Don't look at me like that.'

'Out of interest, tell me, did you enjoy your illicit romp?'

She shook her head. 'No,' she croaked. She moved closer, her arms around him. 'It was always so wonderful – you and me.'

'Indeed.'

'You and your bloody "indeed"!' Somehow the balloon had taken flight again. 'Why can't you ever treat me like a proper woman, an equal? All right, I was wrong to go to bed with Laurence, I suppose that's why I ran away before it was even light and spent most of the night on Paddington Station. Don't look at me like that, Nicholas. Can't we go back to how things used to be?'

'And how far back would you suggest? Before you and your body prepared yourselves with the help of Dr Whatever he's called. To a time when I thought you intended to be a wife, not a business woman who enjoyed sharing my bed? Leave it, Veronica. The more we say, the deeper in trouble we get. The truth is we have nothing in common, nothing but sex.'

'Not like it used to be, nothing's like it used to be. I'm not a *thing*, I'm a person, I have a brain in my head. I won't let you turn me into a cabbage.'

'I said leave it. We are married, we have to make a future together. That you could have been persuaded into bed by that selfish young pansy, then you can hardly be surprised at my disgust.'

'I said I was sorry,' again she couldn't look at him.

'I suggest we try to behave in a civilised manner and perhaps over a space of time we'll learn to accept each other. Now, if you'll excuse me, I have work to do.'

Left standing alone, she watched him go out through the side door into the quadrangle, then cross the grass to the Abbey. There he would find solace, but what was there for her?

Her face washed and given a more than usual helping hand from her make-up jars, she took the car and drove to Ipsley House trying to suppress the ghosts of the last hour with thoughts of the success her time in London had brought to Blakeney's. If only her father could understand what she was going to tell him. Even her mother must retract the scorn she'd poured on the trip.

Usually as she got out of the car she would see Herbert's face at the window, for even if he'd been cat-napping the familiar note of the engine would wake him. The windows stared emptily as she came up the path and let herself in with her own key.

'Hello, I'm back!' she called into the silence.

The last person she expected to see was Hugo, but as she burst into the drawing room he stood up to greet her, his arm around Monica's shoulders. Ignoring him, in fact ignoring them both as far as a greeting went, she looked towards the empty chair where Herbert always sat.

Chapter Twelve

In London, Laurence had casually mentioned what he'd heard about the violent thunderstorms in the south west. Storms had never bothered Veronica, in fact she had always been exhilarated by them, loving the clear air that followed and, if she'd been honest enough to admit it, using her own thrill at every crack of thunder as contempt for her mother's cringing fear. So, surrounded by the excitement of her successful day in London, thunder and flooding in the West Country were of no importance.

Even before the rain started, the first flashes of lightning followed by distant rumbles of thunder heralded what was to follow.

'Oh dear, hark at that!' Monica looked helplessly at the clerk who was seeing her out, her appointment over.

'You don't like storms either, Mrs Blakeney? Truth to tell, neither do I.' Over the top of his half-moon spectacles, the elderly man smiled appreciatively at the sweet-looking client. 'But it may well go round, no sign of rain yet.'

As if to prove him wrong, as he closed the door behind her the first heavy splashes hit the pavement. For a moment she panicked, she even found herself asking silently and fervently that she would be safe and not frightened. Then, making a supreme effort for bravery, she hurried along Waterloo Street towards the turning to the bakery. With the rain threatening her hat she put up her umbrella, only to put it down immediately as the thunder rolled nearer. Supposing she got struck by lightning! An umbrella was dangerous, like not covering the mirrors and knives in the house, or sheltering under a tree! Walking faster, almost running, she

211

turned into Merchant Street and thankfully reached the warmth and safety of the bakehouse.

'Come along in out of the wet, Mrs Blakeney ma'am, best you wait in here till it passes. Perhaps it won't come to much,' Bert Jenkins welcomed her, sensing her fright. 'Miss Veronica's off up country today, but you know that of course. How about someone makes you a cup of tea or coffee or something, we'll bring it along to her room for you if you like.'

'I'd rather drink it in here with all of you.' Then, visibly jumping as the heavens sounded to be torn apart, 'Oh dear, I know I'm silly, but a storm does so upset me. I don't want to sit in poor Herbert's room all alone. Always it's Herbert's room for me, I can't get used to it being Veronica's.'

'It's a sad thing, Mrs Blakeney ma'am, but you must be proud of the way she's carrying on. I just wish he could see it for himself and really understand how she's shouldering the responsibility.'

Monica didn't answer, but the tea and cake that was brought to her on a tray seemed hard to swallow.

For more than an hour she sat on a wooden chair in the bakehouse watching, listening, thinking. Had she made the right decision? Yes, of course she had. But it wasn't fair, it wasn't right that she had had this burden of responsibility pushed on her. If there was a God (oh, no, don't say *if*, she told herself, that was like tempting Fate to repay her with some even worse trouble), why, why had He let it happen to Herbert? He'd always been a good man, ask any of them working here. No, don't ask *them*, that would only make me feel worse. But why? What good is it doing anyone for him to be like he is? Each day he gets worse. When did I last say anything to him and feel he could understand, let alone answer sensibly? It's not fair. I've always tried to be a good wife. And I've loved him, honestly I've loved him even though there have been plenty of times when I've thought he gave more thought to this place than he did to me and to our home. But I've done my best. And I still do my best. So am I wicked to want . . . want what? What is it I really want of Hugo? I used to say it was companionship. And is it just because poor Herbert is like he is that I feel like this about Hugo? I never thought making love, sex, all those sort of private things, meant so much to me. Remember how Herbert was two years or so back; I can see now, that must have been when he was frightened at what he thought was happening to him. Every night he wanted me. It was never in character for him to be like that – I used to think he used me like the animals in the field. He didn't make love to me because I was *me*, it was as if he was proving himself He got careless too, no wonder it worried me: that was why I went to that clinic. As things are now, I needn't have humiliated myself, talking to that Dr Bingley about our private lives. For Herbert, all that sort of thing is over, I sometimes think he doesn't even remember any of it. He lets me help him into bed as if he were a child. So is it so very wicked of me to think of how it could be with Hugo? Yesterday when he took me back to his house, he was thinking of it too, I know he was. He loves me. He's told me so – and, yes, yes, I can't pretend, I am in love with him, he makes me feel like a girl again. Just being with him makes me glad to be alive, makes me want to touch him. And if I didn't know it would be a sin, a sin against poor Herbert, how would I feel if I were to let him love me like he wants to? How would I feel if I were lying in his bed? What rapture it would be! Yes, it would. There! Now I've said it, I've said it aloud in my mind. I want to be so close to him that we become one. When did I last feel like that? When darling Herbert and I were first married, I suppose I must have. Then after I'd had such a difficult time having Veronica, I knew I couldn't face all that again. In those days there was no chance of going to a Family Planning Clinic, it had to be up to Herbert to be careful. If he'd not been so altered, so – so – yes like an animal, how else can I think of it? – in the way he used to take me night after night, I would never have found the courage to go there when I did. But now all those fears are lifted. I almost feel that I went through all that humiliating business with Dr Bingley fitting that beastly thing, whatever it's like, so that I would be free to fall in love with Hugo. I can't help it if it makes me sound like a scarlet woman, I'm *not*. How can it be wicked to want love? Life has become so dreary, or it would be if he weren't there for me. And what harm could it do poor Herbert? He's gone from me. That's the truth. All that's left of my darling Herbert is a shell, a sham. What is a person except a spirit, a soul, with the trappings of a body to make it live? Well, he still has the trappings, but his spirit and soul have been taken. Yet they can't be in Paradise, not as long as his body is here on earth. What sort of a God could do that – to him? To me? Even to Veronica, for silly girl though she is with all her nonsense about

213

running this place as if she were a man, she must miss her father's companionship. Often enough, I've thought she's had more of it than I have.

'Storm seems to have moved away,' she heard one of the men say, and another answer, 'Good thing too, it's time for us to make tracks home for a bite to eat.'

'I must go too,' Monica carried her tray and put it on the workbench. 'Thank you for sheltering me and feeding me,' she smiled. To a man – and woman – they liked her, she was always gentle, never threw her weight about because she was the boss's wife. The hour she'd spent there had restored her courage, it had even given her that bit of silent thinking time she'd needed. She decided that instead of getting a taxi-cab home, she'd have a look at the shops, perhaps indulge in a new blouse from Sherwin's, the ladies' outfitters; then she'd have a light lunch at the Copper Kettle and go back to Ottercombe on the afternoon bus. Knowing that Alice was looking after Herbert gave her a feeling of freedom; the only thing to cloud it was the thought of Veronica's day, the busy London thoroughfares, the wonderful shops all so different from those in Deremouth. Still, the thunderclouds had rolled away and she owed it to herself to snatch at what pleasure she could. Perhaps on the way home she'd get off the bus at the corner of Picton Lane and go along to see Hugo for five minutes instead of carrying on to her usual stop by the Green.

But the afternoon had other plans for her. As the bus splashed though the muddy ruts of the lane across Picton Heath, she gathered together her parcels ready to get off. That's when she saw Bertha.

'Wait!' she called to the driver, 'Can you put me down here. Whatever's Bertha doing out here on her own?' In a village like Ottercombe everyone knew everyone, by sight even if no more than that. The two shoppers left on the bus wished they'd been able to get off too and find the answer to pretty Mrs Blakeney's surprised exclamation.

'Oh, thank the Lord you're home, mum. The Master, we can't find him anywhere. I even went up to Miss Veronica's place at the Abbey, but they'd not seen hide nor hair of him. Mr Ellis was off at Exeter, and Miss Veronica, well you know she's away—'

'What do you mean, you can't find him? I didn't go out till Alice was back. And the storm, he can't have been out in all that rain.'

214

Bertha nodded. 'Alice is out looking, same as I am. Perhaps when we get home he'll be there waiting. When she came home from the dentist, oh mum, I never seen her look so bad. Sick as a dog she was, with all that blood she'd been taking down. So I sent her to lie on her bed for an hour. Well, so would you if you'd been there. I said I'd keep an eye on him. But when I looked, he was gone. Just can't think where he's got to. I been to the shops in the village, but he'd not been in. Would he have gone to see that friend, Mr Holmes, doesn't he live somewhere hereabouts? Or would he have tried to walk down to the bakehouse?'

'I would have seen him from the bus.' Was it her punishment for the things she'd been thinking? Was this God's way of making her feel guilty? Why couldn't he have slept through the morning? Often enough that was what he did when she was there, yet the moment she tried to have an hour to herself he did this to her! No, no, I didn't mean that, she petitioned silently. Let us find him and I promise I'll not – well, You know what I mean – I won't do *that* with Hugo. Even to her Maker she was reticent about spelling out in black and white what her intentions had been.

'I wonder, mum, do you think we ought to have a word with the constable? If the police take up the hunt, we'll get him home that much sooner. The air might be warm, but it's wet underfoot and he could only have his indoor pumps on his feet, no good stout boots.'

'I'll go and see if he's with Mr Holmes,' Monica remembered the pact she'd just made, but to have Hugo with her would lift this feeling of helplessness. 'Even if he's not there, Mr Holmes will know what we should do. I can't bear to send the police out looking for him, as if he's some sort of criminal.' Tears of fright welled in her eyes, she let them fall unheeded.

'Now, mum, don't you take on like that. Another hour and it'll all be but a memory. He'll be home and dried out, you'll be eating your tea same as any other day. Now then, I'll nip on back to the house and you have a word with Mr Holmes. A bit of male company will cheer the Master up when he gets home.'

Walking down the muddy lane to Hugo's house Monica let herself be comforted by Bertha's faith. She knew Herbert wouldn't be there, as far as she was aware he'd never visited Hugo. It was *she* who needed him. Who else was there for her to turn to? If a silent voice suggested she could have sent another message to Nicholas, she ignored it. The honest truth was, she never felt entirely comfortable with him, as though he considered her responsible for the fact that Veronica fell so far short of what a wife should be. How unjust life was. As if it was her fault that Veronica's head was full of nothing but that bakery, if it were anyone's then the one to blame was Herbert. Herbert ... please help us to find him ...

'Where's Dad?' There had been plenty of other times Veronica had arrived to find him out of the room, perhaps upstairs resting, perhaps in her old playroom bent over the everlasting jigsaw puzzle with Alice. So why did she rasp the question, as if instinct warned her?

'*You* can ask! What made him so unsettled on Monday morning? You did. You with your stupid hare-brained ideas. If you'd called to see him – but no, nothing must upset your plans.'

'Mum, what are you talking about? Where is he?' Fear was a physical thing, it pinched her entrails, it ached in her arms and legs.

It was Hugo who took up the story, his voice calm and kindly in his attempt to support Monica. But Veronica wanted no kindness from him.

'It seems he was very unsettled, kept looking for you, couldn't take in that you weren't coming.'

'But that was Monday. Today's Wednesday. Where is he *now*?'

'In Deremouth Hospital,' Monica croaked, 'where he's been since he was found. Oh, I can't talk about it. You breeze in here when you find five minutes to fit us into your busy life – and now see what it's done to him!'

'Never mind about that, tell me what happened.'

'I'm so tired,' Monica wept, feeling the comfort of Hugo's arm and leaning against him unashamedly, caring nothing for Veronica's look of angry scorn – probably not even seeing it.

'I'll go to the hospital, perhaps I'll get some sense out of a doctor there.'

'No, wait,' Hugo interrupted. 'This shouldn't be the cause for you two to quarrel, not now, not when he's so ill. And he is, Veronica, he is extremely ill. He needs the support of both of you, you mustn't let him sense that you are blaming each other.' A one-sided assessment of the accusations of blame, but none of

216

them stopped to consider it. 'Monica had a very important appointment in Deremouth on Monday morning, she was worried about leaving him in such an agitated state but she had no choice.'

'I suppose you never gave a thought to Alice,' Monica wasn't ready to grasp the olive branch, 'oh no, after seeing her poor face so swollen with toothache at the weekend it wouldn't have entered your self-centred head to consider the sort of night the poor dear had. It couldn't have been a worse day as far as I was concerned, this appointment – and I'm coming to that in a minute – was important. So I sent her off to Deremouth to have her tooth pulled and gave her the money to come home in a taxi-cab. You know how, without her here, I'm tied to the house every second of the day. When she arrived, I went back in the same cab. What I didn't know was that she was so poorly that between the pair of them she and Bertha decided she wasn't fit to be doing her job so she went off to her bed. Bertha crept up to the door once or twice but it was closed and he was quiet so she believed he was dozing and didn't go in to disturb him. But I know how he is, the first sound of a motor and he's at the window looking for you even if he'd seemed fast asleep a moment before.'

'Never mind all that. Why is he ill?'

Again Hugo took up the tale, while Monica gave up the battle and let her tears overflow as she dabbed her cheeks with a wispy handkerchief

'He must have gone out looking for you. He must have been following the road to Deremouth, perhaps meaning to come to the bakery. Then – and we don't know why – he changed course and started across Picton Heath.'

'Along the track where he and I used to walk, that's where he'll have gone. Up the path to the high point – the cathedral, we used to call it—' Veronica was talking more to herself than to them. Then, 'Is that where he went?'

'How was I to know where you and he used to go? I was always left at home,' Monica choked, overlooking the fact that if they'd gone without her it had been because she disliked country walks and the obligatory stout, flat shoes. 'During the morning there was a storm, oh such a storm. You know how I fear them. I was sick with fright, there on my own in Deremouth. I went to the bakery – listened to all the silly rubbish that man Jenkins was talking about the wonderful thing you were doing going off on your silly jaunt. I felt like a limp rag by the time the storm abated, you know how they do so upset me. So I went to the Copper Kettle for some food then came home in the afternoon bus.'

Hugo again took up the tale.

'By that time the search was on. Bertha had been to the Abbey.'

'But why didn't Nicholas get a message to me? I told him where I was staying.'

'I doubt if he knew anything about it. Your maid said he was in Exeter and you were away, so Bertha didn't say why she'd come.'

'Of course she didn't,' Monica gulped, 'she has more loyalty to poor Herbert than to let gossip get about that he was being searched for like some runaway mongrel.'

So, bit by bit, Veronica heard how, long after the storm had passed, the still-warm and airless evening had tempted a courting couple to the high peak on the heath. There, by the clump of trees that formed Herbert and Veronica's 'cathedral', they had found him, unconscious and as wet as the ground around him. Whether he had collapsed and broken his hip in the fall, or whether he had tripped over something and, unable to move, had lain there until unconsciousness had overtaken him, no one knew. By the time the courting couple had got back to the village, knocked up Miss Radley at the Post Office and asked her to telephone the hospital, and at last a team of stretcher bearers had carried him back across the heath to the waiting ambulance, night had taken over. By evening, in desperation, Monica had had to tell Simon Tigwell, Ottercombe's local policeman, that Herbert was missing. So it was that at nearly two in the morning there had been a loud rapping at the front door of Ipsley House. Bertha had been first down the stairs to answer the summons, and there had stood PC Tigwell (his uniform pulled on over his pyjamas, but no one except he and his wife knew that), to break the news.

'Can they mend his hip? They can't splint it, how do they do it? When is he coming home?'

Monica sniffed into her hanky; Hugo shook his head.

'He is very ill. The hip is only part of the problem—'

'I know all about that!' She snapped, immediately suspicious that Hugo saw this as an excuse for her mother to be relieved of the 'duty' of caring for her own husband.

Hugo carried on as if she hadn't interrupted.

'He was out there through the whole of the storm, probably on the ground unconscious for most of it. Now he is lying flat on his back. They say it's pneumonia, from the damp perhaps or from the fact that fluid is on his lungs. For a man in his condition . . .' His voice petered to silence.

'And *you're here*,' Veronica turned accusingly on Monica. 'Dad's ill and you hang around the house with *him*.' The nearest she came to indicating that it was Hugo she was talking about was to nod her head in his direction.

'I've been there all night,' Monica wept. 'While you – where were you? Did you give a thought to him, even though you supposed he was safely here at home? No, I'll wager you didn't. There in the bright lights. Probably at the theatre, or swanning round the shops.'

Veronica preferred not to remember last night.

'I'm going to the hospital,' she turned to leave. 'Shall I tell Dad you'll be in later?'

'What's the use of telling him anything?' Monica sniffed. 'You glower at me as though I'm some sort of a sinner because he's ill. If it's anyone's fault, it's your own. You don't care about me, all you think of is that damned bakehouse. How Nicholas puts up with it I don't know. Well, before you go, I've something to tell you—'

'Let it wait. I want to see Dad.'

As the front door slammed behind Veronica, Monica turned to Hugo.

'You see what she's like. It's always been the same: I'm nothing in this house.' Relief flooded through her as he drew her into his arms.

'You're tired, my darling. And she was shocked at what she heard. Try and be brave.'

'I was ready to tell her, I had myself strung up ready. With you here, I feel brave.'

'Plenty of time to tell her later,' his quiet voice comforted her. 'It can't be long, sweetheart. No just God would let him linger as he is.'

'I pray you're right.' She drew back from him, far enough so that she could look him squarely in the eyes. 'That sounds wicked, but it isn't. My Herbert has been gone for a long time. He has become nothing but an empty shell. Now, if God is compassionate, He will take him.'

Hugo fondled the back of her head as again she rested against his shoulder. 'So, be glad you didn't tell Veronica. It's only a matter of time, darling, we both know that. Hours, days, perhaps weeks, but from the Matron's words I imagine not. So tell her nothing until after that. Then she will have no leg to stand on.' An unfortunate metaphor, he realised too late to withdraw his words. But Monica was in no state to look for veiled meanings, all she asked was the comfort of his nearness.

Veronica had known there was no logic in her wanting to rush to tell her father the outcome of her trip to London yet, even knowing that he wouldn't understand what it could mean to the business, she had hurried to Ipsley House. He always listened to every word she said, he took his mood from hers. So she'd looked forward to the way his eyes would smile with pleasure as she recounted her trip.

Now, London, prized orders, even this morning's scene with Nicholas, were as nothing as she pushed her foot hard on the accelerator and hurried towards Deremouth.

But she was too late. Stunned, she listened to the brisk Sister telling her that he had died less than five minutes earlier. All by himself in a strange bed . . . an unfamiliar room . . . no one who loved him with him.

'I want to see him,' she pleaded. 'Please, before he gets moved.'

For a second the Sister looked uncertain. Then, leaving Veronica, she went into the ward where curtains were pulled round Herbert's bed and two young nurses were about to prepare him for the mortuary.

Veronica was taken through, her own footsteps the only sound as she followed the Sister through the ward between the rows of beds. What a moment for her thoughts to turn to rubber soled shoes and the reason nurses wore them.

'I can't let you have long,' Sister Bryant told her as she opened the curtain that divided Herbert from the rest. 'I'll come back in five minutes.'

Veronica nodded, then closed the curtain behind her.

'Dad,' she mouthed silently. 'Dad, it's me. But you know, don't you. You know now, and you understand. I don't want to cry, Dad. No I mustn't, I must be glad for you that it's all over. Now you can remember again, can't you. Did you remember when you went to the cathedral? You must have. You must have been thinking of – oh, of all of it. Dad, I don't want to be without you. Isn't that awful? I'm grown-up, I'm a married woman. But it's not awful, it's true. I want to cry, I want to howl. But, I'm ashamed. You see, for you I'm thankful, honestly I am. Howling would be because I can't bear for you not to be there for me. Even when you didn't follow what I was telling you, deep down inside you I knew you cared. Remember how we used to go off together each morning, you taught me to be what I am. All right, Dad, I'll not let you down. I'll pull myself together, for you, for both of us. Just keep on watching over me, please do that. But you will, I know you will.' Dropping to her knees she rested her face next to his on the pillow, half-frightened to touch him in case he felt different. But life had left him only minutes before, his cheek was soft and cool to her touch. Then, without waiting for the Sister, and without a backward glance at the still figure, she left.

Nicholas made all the necessary arrangements; the funeral was to be in the Abbey on the following Monday. He treated Veronica with unusual consideration yet, even more than that, what she was aware of was his lack of emotion. Perhaps it was because losing her father had thrown her own life off balance that she couldn't accept that to him it was no more than 'a happy release'. He meant to be kind, she told herself. Whether or not that were true, how much did she care?

Stunned by her father's death she believed she could sink no further. But she found she was wrong. So often she had been out of sympathy with her mother, but this time she was resolved to make an effort. To act differently would seem like failing her father – added to which it would give that horrid Hugo Holmes even more opportunity to get his foot in the door! So, the following morning she forced herself to stop on her way to Deremouth just as she always had. She dreaded going into the breakfast room, seeing Herbert's empty place at the table, so she was unprepared for the sympathy that surged through her when she saw her mother sitting alone.

'You're an early caller,' Monica smiled wanly. 'I ought to be thankful for him. But I'm such a coward.'

'Of course you're not a coward, Mum. It's hard for you, it's hard for all of us. But we have to carry on like he would want.'

Veronica purposely sat in the chair that had been her father's, whether to help herself or her mother she didn't question. 'Anyway, I'm not early, Mum. This is the time I always come.' 'What do you mean? You can't mean you're going into that wretched office this morning? My poor darling Herbert hardly drawn his last breath and you carry on as if nothing is changed!' 'Of course I'm going in. How do you think Bert Jenkins and all of them would feel if we ignored their existence? Monday we shall be closed all day, I'd be surprised if to a man they didn't find their way out here to the Abbey for his service.'

Monica sighed. 'Of course they were fond of him. They never saw how far he'd sunk since he had to give up running the place, I dare say they always hoped that one day he would be back.' Then she made a visible effort for bravery, sitting very straight and looking straight at Veronica. 'It's the end of an era for all of us. There's something I was going to tell you when you got back from that senseless trip to London—'

'It wasn't senseless, Mum. With so much else, I haven't told you about how well it went. I brought back some good orders. Blakeney's goods are to be on the shelves in the finest stores in the country. Do you believe Dad knows? He must do, mustn't he?'

'If he does, then he knows what I'm going to tell you, too. And, Ronnie, he knows that I made the decision because even before that dreadful day when he was so worried that you didn't come to see him, I was positive it was the right one. I did it in his name. But now, of course, all that is changed. There is nothing you can say will make me alter my mind, absolutely *nothing*.' In defiance, there was a ring of drama in her voice, even in the way she held up her hand to ward off anything Veronica might say, and in the way she tossed her head. 'The deed is done; the die is cast.'

'What deed?' Immediately Veronica was suspicious. As soon as she was out of the way in London, her mother must have advertised for a manager. Perhaps she'd heard that the paragon at Clampton's would rather have come back to Blakeney's if there had been a place for him. How dare she do this! Power of Attorney had been given to her so that she could run the household affairs, not so that she could interfere in things she didn't understand!

'I told you we don't need some outsider. Dad and I ran things together, until I had to manage on my own. And that's what I shall go on doing.'

'Manage on your own, you say. And a fine mess you were getting it into. You forget I've talked to the accountant, I know the profits are down. Just like I said they would be without a man at the helm. Stupid, pig-headed nonsense. Well, it's too late now.'

'It's me who'll have to interview the man, you don't know anything about the—'

'Will you just be quiet and listen!' Another pause, perhaps to add to the drama, perhaps to grasp at the courage Veronica's angry glare threatened. 'I told you I had an appointment last Monday morning. That was why I had to go to Deremouth as soon as Alice was home from the dentist. I went to see Mr Pyle from Morton and Pyle the estate agents and surveyors.'

'But why? You can't have wanted to move Dad away from here? What did it matter if it was too big for you, he was secure—'

'How dense the girl is! Mr Pyle deals with the commercial properties. You know I was given Power of Attorney over your father's affairs, so I had every right to decide as I did. It seems there was no other way to make you come to your senses!'

'What the devil are you telling me?' Unable to stop herself Veronica was on her feet, leaning across the table at her mother. She was panting as if the air had been physically knocked out of her. 'Power of Attorney surely didn't give you the right to close a business started by my great-grandfather. Not *your* family, but *mine*.'

'It's no use taking that tone to me, Ronnie. I said earlier, this is the end of an era. It isn't fair that you blame me for everything. For once, just for once, can't you try and see things from my angle? Of course I would never have done anything to unsettle poor Herbert, fancy even imagining that I would have sold the house where he felt safe, bless his dear heart. But we didn't lose him yesterday, he's been gone from us for so long that to remember him when he was whole and well is like picturing a stranger. You can't begin to know what it's been like, hour after hour, day after day, month after month, watching him lose his grasp of things. How long ago is it that we could speak to him and know that he understood? And I've lived with that! I've looked after him like caring for a child. My husband!' Tears rolled unchecked down her cheeks.

'Oh Mum, I do know. How can you think I haven't cared?'

'Oh, you've cared about him. By what about *me*? I've had more consideration from Bertha and Alice.'

'To say nothing of Hugo Holmes,' Veronica retorted even before she considered what she was saying. The words hung in the silence between them, she wished she hadn't said them. Monica caught her bottom lip between her teeth, wiping her tears with the palms of her well-kept hands.

'Yes, and Hugo,' she said quietly. 'I told you you didn't start to understand. Who else have I had to turn to? I never thought it could happen to me again. I'm not young anymore, but Ronnie, I've learnt that romance isn't just for the young.'

'I don't believe what I'm hearing,' Veronica's words were hardly more than a whisper, as if to speak aloud would be to prove the reality. 'How can you talk about that fop, Mum, when you were Dad's whole world?'

'Perhaps I was, once, a long time ago. When was he last a companion?' Then with a sly look at Veronica's frank condemnation, 'When was he last a true husband, a lover?'

'You make me sick! Yes, you do. Just talking to you destroys all the happy memories, all the things that used to be good when I was a child and I thought we were a perfect family.'

'We were. Always we were.'

'Looking at you now I think you are more changed than Dad ever was. If you'd been ill do you think he would have been casting around to find some other woman to pander to him or take to his bed?'

'Oh, hush, Ronnie, don't say such things.'

'Oh, so you haven't been to bed with this wonderful lover of yours? But I suppose you will now, after all you're a free woman. Or will you try and wait until after Monday, is Dad's service when you draw a line under this era you say is at an end?'

'Please don't. I've always loved my darling Herbert, it's just that over these last years it's been so hard – you don't know how hard – even to see the man he used to be. I held him on a pinnacle, he was like a god to me when we were young. That's what I want to remember, not a helpless shell, someone who had to be dressed and bathed, not a person, not a person, just a – a – I told you, a shell.' Control gone out of the window she blubbered like a child. 'And you think I'm wicked to want to be loved, to feel human again and know that when I look pretty someone sees me and is proud. To know that I'm still desirable, still a woman—'

Veronica turned away. The last few days had been worse than a

224

nightmare; one woke in a cold sweat from a nightmare, but from this there was no escape. Dad gone ... Nicholas, even as her thoughts turned to him she pulled them away ... Blakeney's on the market for sale ... her mother talking of romance with another man ... nothing but hopelessness whichever way she looked. Perhaps she ought to have lied to Nicholas, told him that she'd spent the evening with Laurence, just missed the last train home and spent the night on Paddington Station. So why hadn't she? Was it to hurt him that she'd admitted being unfaithful to him with Laurence? Her own body ... the words taunted her. She realised that between gulps and sobs Monica was speaking.

'. . . thank me for making the decision,' she was saying. 'At last you'll begin to live the sort of life expected of a wife. If you don't, Ronnie, you'll build a life that has no room in it for love. Nicholas is a good man, he deserves to have a properly run home, yes and children too. I don't know why he hasn't put his foot down long ago.'

'He married me as I am, why should he expect to change me?'

'Don't be such a child! Tessa Wainwright called to bring her condolences yesterday evening. I must say it was nice to have another woman to speak to.'

'I should have thought Mr Holmes was effeminate enough,' Veronica sneered, but Monica ignored the interruption.

'She tells me that Dulcie has fallen for a baby already. She married Ernest Biggs, you remember, he works at the bank where his father is manager. That was just ten weeks ago and already she and Tessa are busy with their knitting. You would tell me if you thought there was anything wrong with you, wouldn't you?'

'Probably not. But I can tell you that I'm perfectly normal if that's what you and Mrs Wainwright are worrying about.'

'They have such a close relationship, Tessa and Dulcie. You and your father were thick as thieves, it was always me who got left out. Now I've been blessed with love again. Don't look at me like that. If you want the truth, I doubt if you know what love is, proper love between a man and a woman. I always thought you married Nicholas on the rebound after your infatuation for Laurence.' In their unhappiness they needed to hurt each other.

'I almost forgot to tell you – I met Laurence in London. He's doing an article about Blakeney's, he brought a photographer to take pictures of me and I gave him our catalogue to use.'

'Bless his heart. Why you two couldn't have settled together I can't think. Then Ellen wouldn't have rushed off.'

'But then you might have missed out on this glorious romance,' Veronica jibed.

'You'd better write and tell him not to waste his time with the article. The sooner I get a good offer, the sooner I shall close the deal. What we must all look for is a new beginning.'

It seemed to Veronica that their conversation was going round in circles and getting nowhere. She wanted to be gone.

'I shall say nothing to Bert or the men in the bakehouse. Even wallowing in this new syrupy love, I can't believe you'll bring yourself to sign away all Dad did. Especially now that we have the sort of high-class outlets I've found in London. That won't even be just London sales, firms like that fill orders from all regions.'

'I've told you, my mind is made up. While my poor Herbert had even a little understanding, then I wouldn't have done it. But I *will not* play a part in seeing the ruination of your marriage. So grow up and learn to be a wife.'

In Deremouth Veronica spent half an hour or so in the bakehouse, talking to the staff, hearing their ill-expressed but genuine sadness for Herbert's death. She went to her own office, but it was impossible to settle so, paying attention to neatness, she wrote – in clear block capitals – the reason that the bakery would be closed all day Monday and the time and place of the funeral. It was still not much after mid-day when she pinned the notice to the gate. Monica's voice echoed in her memory, warning her that this was no way to run a marriage. If Nicholas were at home waiting for her, wanting to be with her and share her misery, listen to her wretchedness about what her mother intended for the business, then she would have rushed back to him. But she was too unhappy to face the cool aloofness she knew he felt. Was it because he was unhappy too? If she could believe that were the reason, then she would sink her pride, she would beg him to love her like surely he used to. But he wasn't unhappy, oh no, not he. As long as he could find sanctuary in the Abbey, surround himself with his bloody music – yes, bloody, bloody, bloody music, with her lips set in a tight line she repeated the thought ever more loudly – then nothing could touch him.

She'd go down to the beach. Surely, there by the sea, she would see her problems in perspective. I can't get near to anyone, she thought. If I try and think of Dad, if I try and 'find' him and 'talk' to him, I can't because my mind is in such a tangled mess with thoughts of Nicholas – yes and Laurence too, although he doesn't count, he's there to make things worse. And if I try to think of Nicholas, to remember the wonderful part of being with him, to try and cling on to how it used to be, then I can't do that either. All the time there's this empty misery because for the rest of my life there will be no Dad. Mum says I should grow up. Perhaps she's right, perhaps proper grown-up people don't feel like I do.

Yesterday's sultry clouds had been blown away. On that Thursday the sun was a brilliant gold in the clear blue sky, only on the far western horizon was a shadow of cloud that foretold that this was no more than an interlude, an assurance that nothing lasts forever. That's what she must make herself remember: storms or sunshine, misery or joy, none of it lasted.

Chapter Thirteen

With uncharacteristic dignity Monica listened to the solemn words of the funeral service. To the familiar sound of the *Nunc Dimittis*, by Veronica's side she followed the coffin to the churchyard where the empty grave waited. It was her show of quiet courage that touched Veronica, seeming to sweep away the irritation she so often felt for her pretty and helpless mother and bring alive memories she wanted to cling to: memories of happy times through her childhood, the feeling of warmth and contentment on winter evenings when the curtains were drawn against the world and the fire burnt bright in the drawing room grate. She reached her hand to take hold of her mother's, expecting to feel the returning pressure of the slender, well-groomed fingers she knew so well. But there was no response. It was as if Monica was held apart from what was happening, as if when the coffin was lowered she was watching something that had no meaning. Veronica envied her. Her own mind was an agony of disbelief. They were lowering Dad into the ground . . . no, that was nonsense, Dad was free, Dad was with her still . . . that's what she must believe. But if he was with them and knew what Mum had done about the bakery, how could he be at peace? Please, please give him peace. I don't know how You can, not when he'll be so upset about what she wants to do. I'm not asking it just for *me*, honestly I'm not, although I can't bear to think that Blakeney's might belong to someone else – even Merrick. Merrick . . . well, if someone else had to run it, then surely better him than an outsider who wouldn't understand. Yet, how could he understand? Her thoughts moved on, somehow protecting her from the agony of the moment as Father Desmond sprinkled earth onto the coffin. '. . . dust to dust . . .' she heard. Memory carried her back to the classroom where she'd had to read aloud about the Diet of Worms and her childish fancy of what it meant. Remember how Dad had laughed when I asked him about a diet of worms, memory nudged again as she bit the corners of her suddenly trembling mouth. 'Though worms destroy my body, yet in the flesh shall I see God', more thoughts crowded in.

She realised that, the service over, Nicholas had come to stand at her side. She wanted to turn to him, she wanted to feel him take her hand. Instead he stood, hat in hand, motionless. She felt utterly alone. And Dad? If she was alone, how about *him*? Surely no one could be in Paradise unless they knew the ones they loved were happy. Could they?

Standing in a group away from the graveside, wanting to be there and yet not wanting to intrude, were men and women from the bakehouse. If Dad knows, he'll be pleased they're here. Yes, of course he knows, he must know. Just like he knows about what Mum has done and what it'll mean to them. Some of them had flowers in their hands, one or two had tied the stems and attached a card. He would have wanted them here, shoulder to shoulder with his family. Every one of them had been known to him, every one of them had been able to talk to him of their troubles and joys knowing he cared. Family . . . that's how he had looked on them . . . that's what Mum has never understood. She thinks they can be handed over to another employer along with the office furniture. Please, she cried silently, I don't know how, but please don't let it happen. If Merrick buys the business, how much power will he expect to wield? He once told me he wouldn't want to change the name. No, and I should think not! Blakeney's stands for every-thing that's good. Dad saw to that; yes, and so have I.

Father Desmond had closed his book. With the small group at the graveside she moved away and those from the bakehouse came nearer. Each of them looked into the deep hole in the ground as if they were saying a final farewell before they put down their flowers in a neat row nearby ready for the sexton to put in place when the earth was filled in.

The end of an era . . . the end of an era . . . Monica's words echoed and re-echoed.

Although none of his acquaintances in Deremouth had seen Herbert over the last year or more, he was remembered with affection and news of his death travelled fast. When Veronica arrived at the bakehouse the day after the funeral she found a pile of letters on her desk. There would be family friends and people from the village who would write to Ipsley House to her mother. But Deremouth traders, the proprietor of the Harbour Lights, even the man who came each week to clean the windows and the one who brought the daily delivery of milk and cream, expressed their sympathy to the daughter who had been so close to Herbert Blakeney.

Whose writing was she looking for as she scanned the envelopes? None of these were from Merrick. Taking her paper knife she opened the first and started to read, each brief note stirring its own memory of the part of her father's life she had shared. Most of them were in careful handwriting; only one was typed, and she put that to the bottom of the pile. It was a Deremouth postmark, but surely Merrick wouldn't have asked his secretary to type his letter to her!

When at last she opened it she was torn between relief and disappointment, relief that he hadn't done anything so impersonal and disappointment that there was no word from him. Of course, she made excuses to herself, he didn't know Dad, he often said how he wished he'd known him. But why should Mr Withers want her to telephone him? She had rather expected that, to save her mother the ordeal of visiting the office of Withers, Wright and Lambton, the solicitor would have taken a cab to Ipsley House to discuss the terms of the will.

Taking the receiver off the telephone on the wall, she turned the handle to alert the exchange.

'This is Deremouth 360,' she said. 'Will you get me a call to Deremouth 741 please.'

When she was told, 'They're on the line, Mrs Ellis,' she knew the telephone operator that morning must have been Elsie Sykes who had a reputation for knowing more of the local goings-on than the reporters on the *Deremouth News*.

'Thank you Miss Sykes.' A smile tugged at the corner of Veronica's mouth as she played the same game, sensing the operator's disappointment that, her identity known, she would feel unable to eavesdrop on the conversation.

'Mrs Ellis, thank you for calling me so soon,' Mr Withers said when he was called to the telephone. 'Very sad time for you, yes, indeed. You have my condolences.' She could almost see the balding solicitor who had looked after her father's affairs for as long as she could remember, his spectacles clipped to his nose, his head nodding to emphasise his words. 'I have spoken with your dear mother and she has agreed to see me this afternoon. I hope you are able to be present.'

'Has she asked for me?'

'Not in so many words. But the situation would be made easier if you could manage to be here too.' Knowing that the ageing solicitor didn't drive his own car, Veronica agreed to collect Monica and bring her to his office.

'I'm so glad you're coming with me,' Monica told her as they drew up outside the offices in Wellington Street. 'I've never agreed with your meddling in business things, you know that. But today I'm glad of it, at least you won't be as baffled by it all as I know I shall. He's a dear, kind man, but – oh dear, I find it overwhelming. *Me* having to bear the responsibilities that had always been dear Herbert's. Oh, I know I've learnt how to pay the household bills, but, oh dear, doing it for someone else isn't the same thing at all as knowing it's all mine. I just say thank God I've already set the wheels in motion to get rid of the bakery.'

Veronica's initial rush of sympathy for her mother evaporated.

Half an hour later she was cranking the engine ready to drive back to Ottercombe, her world changed.

'He signed his will five years go,' Monica sounded more mystified than angry. 'He gave me no hint. And you? Did he tell you what he had in mind?'

'No, Mum. I wish I could tell him how grateful I am. I won't fail him.'

'Nonsense! You know as well as I do that the firm isn't making the profit it did before Clampton's came here. Oh dear, why did I wait so long. If I'd taken the plunge a few weeks earlier, it would have been sold, gone. No good can come of this. I'll tell you what, Ronnie. Let's stop on the heath and have a word with that strange Matilda de Vere.'

Veronica's unladylike guffaw was her only answer.

'I mean it, Ronnie. She has a gift. You may laugh, but I *know*. Remember how I used to think you and dear Laurence were right for each other? She told me nothing would come of it. Now jeer if

231

you like. Oh yes and she's told me plenty more too. Let's ask her to guide us, tell us what's best. You know what it is that worries me: it's you and Nicholas. What sort of a man will play second fiddle to a bakehouse?'

'Rubbish,' Veronica forced a note of conviction into her brief retort, but she might as well not have bothered, for Monica ignored her.

'You'll live to regret it. He deserves better of you and you fill me with shame that you carry on like you do. When are you ever at home waiting for him? When do you put his wishes before your own? When do you ever even consider a wife's place? Never, never, never. It was one thing to treat me as though I was of no consequence – oh yes, you did, always rushing off with your father and giving no thought to my empty days. But that was when you were young and free. Now you have duties to your husband.'

'Nicholas doesn't need anyone else to fight his battle – if he has one. He is more than capable.'

'Indeed he is. He is a strong character, a good, upright character. I wish you'd start to grow up. Learn to take your role at the Abbey as the Master's wife, look after his establishment, be there when he needs you. What's happening to some of you modern young women is beyond understanding. It's never been the same since that dreadful, wicked war.'

'Never mind all that. On my way back to Deremouth I shall call at the estate agents' office and tell Mr Pyle I'm taking the bakery off the market. As for the rest of the things we heard this afternoon – you'll be all right, Mum. Everything else that was Dad's is yours, and you will be comfortably off. And you mustn't worry. For what I'm worth, I'm always here to help you.' She gave her mother a sudden smile. 'Take it all step by step, Mum, that's what we have to do. And as for Matilda de Vere and all her rubbishy hocus-pocus, I'm blessed if I'm going to talk our personal affairs over with her.'

'You're so strong,' Monica sniffed warningly, 'and you're not alone.'

'You're not alone either, Mum.'

'I wish you'd not be so unkind about him, Ronnie.' Monica answered, misunderstanding. 'Try and like him.'

Her words came as a shock. Nothing had been further from Veronica's mind than Hugo Holmes.

232

'That limp rag!'

'Just because he's a little artistic in his dress, you brush him aside. Stupid child, you are. Well, I'll tell you, if he hadn't been here for me I don't know how I would have lived through this last year and more. He's been my constant support.'

'And you lecture me on marriage!'

'Don't,' Monica let her tears fall, welcoming the relief of them, 'I've never been unkind to dear Herbert. Married to him for twenty-six years and always I've been there for him.'

' "Well done", is that what you want me to say? Then kiss your – your *paramour* on both cheeks and be grateful to him for taking over when Dad was too sick to fawn over you and flatter you.'

'You're unkind. You're not fair. All you've ever thought of is yourself.'

'A trait I must have inherited. Anyway, when Mr Wonderful finds Dad's entrusted the bakery to me, he may not be so keen.'

'How dare you!' All trace of the sorrowful, faithful widow was gone as she turned angrily on Veronica. 'It's me he wants, me, *me*, not the trappings I bring with me. He's a successful man, better off than we are I don't doubt. He loves me, I tell you, and I'm proud. If you won't talk to Matilda de Vere, then the loss is yours. You seem intent on doing things your own pig-headed way. But drop me off at the end of Picton Lane anyway.'

'You mean you're going to his cottage? Oh Mum, it's just because you're frightened and unhappy. Let me take you home. I'll stay a while if you like.'

'It's nothing of the sort,' Monica ignored the suggestion that she should go straight home, 'I want to be with him. It's what he wants too. I want to spend all my days with him. And I'm going to. There! Now, I've told you.'

Veronica looked at her mother in disbelief. A week ago her father had been alive, his never failing smile had greeted her each time she'd gone into the room where he was. Surely all this would pass, his memory would be interwoven into their lives, that's what her mother would want when the shock of these last few days faded.

'Marry him, you mean? I don't believe it! It's because you're miserable and he's there – but marriage—'

'I should think you'd be the last one to lecture anyone on marriage.' As Veronica brought the car to a standstill at the end of

Picton Lane, just for a second Monica hesitated then, in a plea for understanding, she rushed on, 'Because I'm nothing except Mum to you, you think I don't know about love. I'm a woman still, not just your mother. I'm not old—'

'Don't, Mum—'

'For me, having someone to love is the most important thing in life. I'm not like you, hard-bitten, believing a successful business is the passport to happiness. One day you'll wake up, Ronnie. Just make certain it's not too late.'

Before Veronica could reply, and with far less than her usual grace, Monica bundled herself out of the car and slammed the door shut. For a moment Veronica sat where she was, undecided whether to drive on to the Abbey or return to Deremouth. What if she went home, would her early arrival be received with sardonic surprise? Would it pass unnoticed? Would Nicholas show some sign of pleasure? Imagining the first, it was what she dreaded. As to the second, that would be the most probable. Or the third? She was frightened even to think of it. Yet think of it she did, as she turned the car and headed back towards town. That's how it used to be ... so what had changed things? Why couldn't he accept that carrying on with the business she knew and cared about needn't mean she loved him less? Surely she was a more interesting person than she would have been if she'd spent her days supervising a housekeeper who needed no supervision, having no life outside her home? If only he'd climb down from his high horse sometimes he might find their horizons widened by the things she did. Yet, since her return from London at the weekend and the bitter things they had said to each other before they knew about Herbert, he had treated her with the same distant courtesy he would have shown to a recently bereaved casual acquaintance.

She pulled her thoughts away from him and turned them in the direction of comfort. Dad trusted me, she told herself, he knew I would never fail Blakeney's. And neither will I. Haven't I proved that by bringing those orders from London? And soon I'll stretch my net further, much further. Merrick has confidence in me. Merrick ... he hasn't written. I was sure he would. But perhaps I'm taking too much for granted, perhaps all he wants is for me to learn to rely on his help so that I begin to trust him to run Blakeney's. Well, if that's his game he can whistle in the wind. It's up to me what happens now, no one can tell me, not Mum, not Nicholas – no and not Merrick either.

And still on that high note she arrived back at the bakehouse and imparted the news of her inheritance.

'I wanted you all to know right away,' she told them. 'You might have been getting anxious—'

'More than anxious, Miss Veronica,' Bert Jenkins spoke for them all, 'and I'll tell you for why. It was the day you went off to London, the day your mother came in here taking shelter from the storm, when my missus said she saw her coming out of Morton and Pyle's. It was Mr Pyle was seeing her out – and of course we all know it's him who deals with commercial properties. Maybe she was only testing the water, so to speak, but we reckoned there must be something; she wouldn't have gone to talk to old Mr Pyle for nothing.'

Only briefly did Veronica consider keeping the truth to herself But these people were loyal, they cared about Blakeney's and had a right to the truth. So she told them how worried she had been at her mother's idea that under a woman a business was bound to fail and, for that reason, her mother had taken the law into her own hands and put it on the market.

'But that's all over now. I've come to speak to you first, then I'm going straight to see Mr Pyle and tell him we aren't for sale.'

'Well done, Miss Veronica', 'We won't let you down', 'No one can run this place better than you', 'Blakeney's it is and Blakeney's it stays'. One after another they voiced their support. If only her father could hear them; perhaps he could, she hoped he could. Then, true to her word, she walked through the town to the estate agents.

Coming back into the yard, she found Merrick waiting for her.

'They told me you'd soon be back,' he greeted her. 'They said I could wait in your office, but I preferred not to with you out. Ronnie, I only got home this afternoon, until then I hadn't heard. I am so very sorry.'

She nodded, his sympathy bringing the sting of unshed tears.

'I had to go into town.' In her need to hang on to control she grasped at the first words that came to mind. 'But, Merrick, I'm glad you've come.'

'I wanted to see you rather than write.'

There was no logic in the comfort she found in his being with her. As she preceded him into the office, the memory flashed across her mind of that first letter she'd written to him, and the image she'd built in her mind of the sort of man who ran the factories where Clampton's 'cheap rubbish' was made.

Going to her usual chair behind her desk, she hesitated only a second before she indicated for him to sit in the place that had been her father's.

'No, wait,' he said. 'Before we go any further I want you to read this. It was on my desk when I arrived back today – from Morton and Pyle. It was written nearly a week ago. Why didn't you tell me, Ronnie? With appointments in London, what made you change your mind and do this? All we'd talked about – London, advertising, literature you intended to have printed to send to America—'

While he'd talked Veronica had read the letter Mr Pyle had sent him, realising that it must have been her mother's suggestion that he should be contacted before the business was put on the open market.

'I was out when you arrived. I was at Morton and Pyle's. Do you honestly think I'd do a thing like this? Is that why you came – thinking this was the opportunity you'd been waiting for? Well, you can say goodbye to any such fancies. Dad left the business to *me*, you hear me? Not to Mum so that she could sell it tomorrow, but to me. So I'm afraid you're wasting your time—' Her voice had risen higher, the tone becoming uncontrolled and raucous. She couldn't go on, she heard the ominous croak and, falling silent, held her jaw defiantly rigid. Seeing him waiting for her in the yard her feeling had been one of thankfulness. Only her father had known how much the business meant to her, her father and recently, she'd believed, Merrick. But he'd come in the hope that this was his opportunity, at last he'd been dealt the hand of cards he needed. If *he* didn't understand, then there was no one. She closed her eyes tight, how else could she hold back the tears. She'd held her misery at bay for days, now caught unprepared she could feel it welling inside her, a physical pain that ached in her chest and arms, that caught her breath.

Sitting very straight, her head bowed as if that would protect her innermost feelings, she didn't see him come around the desk to her side. The first she knew that he was near was the touch of his hand around her shoulders.

'You don't honestly think that of me,' he said quietly. No, she didn't believe it, yet she'd had to aim her wretchedness at someone and who better than him? Giving up the battle for control, her body shook with sobs. She cried for the father she'd loved and for the agony of watching him grow ever more apart from them; she cried that the rest of her life would be lived without him; she cried for aloof, polite Nicholas and the wonderful love she'd thought was theirs for ever; she cried for her mother's infatuation for Hugo Holmes and for how it seemed to cast a shadow even on memories she had thought untouchable. Did she say all these things as she sobbed? She heard her blubbering words, an outpouring of so much that had been held in check. It wasn't that she wanted to share her misery with him, yet had she been alone she would have fought down the rising well of unhappiness and wouldn't have found the strength-giving comfort that his presence gave her.

His hand was steady on her shoulder, his arm around her. Still sitting upright with her head bowed, her face was contorted as a child's. Never had she wanted her father more than she did in those moments. Hardly realising what she did, she turned towards Merrick standing close beside her, her arms going around his waist as she buried her head against him. Did she see him as a father figure? She didn't question, she only knew that he asked nothing of her, he was her friend. For so long she'd been frightened to face her desolation but now, like an unstoppable avalanche, her anguish was released. It was his fingers gently caressing the nape of her neck that brought home to her the reality of how she was behaving. Drawing away from him she scrubbed her eyes with the palms of her hands.

'. . . sorry. . . shouldn't . . .'

'Here,' he pressed the silk handkerchief he always wore in his breast pocket into her hand. 'You don't need to say anything, not to me.'

'Crying like that . . .' she snorted, '. . . ashamed . . . you hardly know me . . .

'I know loss and unhappiness. Don't be ashamed of crying.'

'You'll think me some sort of a weakling,' and another uncontrolled snort. 'Silly, but it was because you were here, you were being kind – that's what did it. Must look a frightful sight.' And that wasn't far from the truth. Her eyes were bloodshot, the lids swollen and red.

'No, my dear friend, you look like a girl who has lost the father she loved.'

But was that all she'd talked about as one misery after another had overwhelmed her? 'Don't know what I was saying – just blubbing like a baby – saying all sorts of things.' If she thought he was going to repeat her disjointed confidences, she was mistaken.

'No matter how hard we try, we all cry in the end.' His quiet reply helped her towards recovery; he'd lost the wife he loved. She even managed a semblance of a smile as she looked up at him, knowing she wasn't a pretty sight and knowing, too, that it was unimportant. 'Glad you were here,' she managed this time without any trembling hiccup.

'Now then, while you wash your face may I go along to the bakekouse and ask them for some milk so that you can make us a cup of tea? I want to hear about your trip.'

Perhaps it was fortunate there was no mirror in the make-shift kitchen where she filled the kettle and rinsed her face, rubbing it dry in a roller towel hanging on the back of the door. When he came back with a small jug of milk and two cakes on a plate, the kettle was already on and she was sitting at her desk with her order book ready to show him.

It was when he was leaving that she thought of Becky.

'I shall be at home this Saturday if Mrs Frewin would like to bring Becky over. And you, too, of course.'

'Becky will be pleased. But, no, perhaps it's silly of me, but I prefer not to come to the Abbey.'

She was puzzled by his reply, but more than anything she was relieved. It was only after he'd gone, as she forced herself to concentrate on her work for one last hour before driving home, that she questioned her reaction. Could it be that seeing him with Belinda Frewin would rub salt into the wound of her own estranged relationship with Nicholas?

That evening she told Nicholas the terms of her father's will.

'So the decisions for its future are yours now,' he said, his expression giving nothing away. 'I understood from your mother that it's on the market. What about your friend Clampton?'

'What about him? And if you think I intend to sell Blakeney's then you know even less about me than I thought.'

For a moment he looked at her silently, she felt he looked not so much *at* her as *into* her. Then he turned away and sat on the piano stool, opening the lid and resting his hands silently on the keys.

'Am I to understand that this fetish you have for the bakery is to continue throughout our marriage?'

'Not again!' She turned away, feeling trapped by the repetition of his criticism. 'We've been through it time and again. What's so different now from when we were first married? We were happy then, you didn't keep carping—' She broke off, realising that the afternoon's tears had left her vulnerable. She mustn't cry again, not now, not in front of Nicholas. Music was his retreat; he started to play Liszt's *Liebestraum*, Dream of Love. 'Nicholas,' she whispered, instinct drawing her to him, 'what's happened to us?'

Not answering, at least not answering in words, he looked at her as he played. His good-looking, angular face, was a mask, his eyes told her nothing.

'Say something,' she pleaded. 'If you don't love me, why don't you just say so.'

Mid-phrase he stood up, closing the piano lid and pulling her towards him.

'Love you? What do you mean by "love"? I want you as much as I have from the time I saw you playing tennis with your wonderful Chesterton. What's happened to us, you say. I'll tell you what's happened. What sort of a wife asks a doctor to ensure she can't conceive her husband's child? What sort of a wife sees running a tin-pot bakehouse as the most important thing in life? What sort of a wife lies so that she can spend nights with her lover? What sort of a wife, after all that, asks her husband why he doesn't love her like he did? But *did* he? That's the question, Veronica.'

'You're not being fair. I'm the same as I always was.'

'Perhaps you are. Perhaps all we ever had was sex. So let's play it your way. It seems that you're unlikely to conceive – and my God, what freedom that gives you! But let's share the freedom. What was it that made the beginning as wonderful as you say it was? It wasn't the coming together of two minds. We have one thing in common. I ought to be grateful to your doctor friend, I'm free to enjoy your body. Yes, that's what we had in common, a rich instinctive hunger for sex.'

239

'You make it sound horrid,' she mumbled.

'Horrid? Oh no, you can accuse me of many things, but never in failing you there.'

'It should be because of love—' She mustn't cry, she mustn't.

'Like it was with your friend Chesterton?'

'Damn Laurence,' she croaked, her fists hammering Nicholas's chest. 'Damn him, damn and blast the whole – whole – whole *bloody* trip. No, not that. Just going back to his place. It was because of us, because I was miserable that we'd quarrelled.'

'I don't want to hear.'

'Let it be good for us again, Nicholas. We can't go on like this.' She pressed close against him, thankful to recognise the familiar evidence of his arousal. 'Don't let's talk anymore,' she whispered, her mouth close to his. 'Tell me you still want me. Just that.' Perhaps she was being naive, but her body ached for his loving, for the glorious adventure, the miracle that burst on her anew each time.

Later, lying naked and wide-awake, she still clung to hope. The sensual craving of her body was satisfied, so why did she feel more shame than contentment? What had he said about the coming together of two minds? No, don't let yourself think about his cold words. But two souls? Had their souls played any part at all in the greedy clamour of their bodies, the uninhibited eroticism that had taken hold of them both? And when at last they could hold back no longer, in that final moment of release, had there been a union of spirit or no more than a feeling of physical well-being? She moved her hand down her nakedness almost as though she were touching a stranger.

Then, forcing her mind away from the last hour, she re-lived the day, a day that must surely be a turning point in her life. She pictured her mother's expression of disbelief as Mr Withers had read the will to them and they'd learnt the division of her father's bequests. Again she experienced the sensation of loss and anger as she watched Monica climb out of the car at the end of Picton Lane. Then that dreadful moment when her misery had seemed to drown her, when she'd heard her own sobbing. How strange it had been that as she'd turned to bury her face against Merrick, it had been as though her father was close. Is that what he was to her, a friend to guide her and protect her from the knocks, to give her the same unfailing support she'd always had from her father?

Still lying on top of the bed, she realised she was getting cold. Careful not to wake Nicholas, who'd already pulled the covers over himself, she wriggled between the sheets. Today she'd reached rock bottom; tomorrow would be better.

Belinda Frewin and Becky's Saturday afternoon visits to the Abbey became a habit as spring turned to summer, a habit that was the highlight of the child's week. It didn't enter her head to wonder whether Belinda looked forward to Saturdays as much as she did. Her father never stayed, he always drove them to Ottercombe and made the excuse that he had things to do; then after tea Veronica would take them home. It was Becky's only contact with other children, indeed it was her only contact with anyone outside her home, where Belinda combined the roles of teacher and carer. Getting to know the boys from the choir school was therapeutic, both mentally and physically. Sometimes she looked back to the days before the train crash that had so altered her life and felt it held the colour of an impossible dream. It was as if she had become a different person from the little girl who used to skip happily to Merfield House School each morning, her mother at her side. Lessons had been fun, she'd learnt to read and to add up. As for games and drill, as they'd called the outdoor activities of running races the length of the lawn or doing exercises, remembering it from this space of time every minute of it had been pure joy. Had it really been as she remembered? Had her mother really always been smiling and ready for fun? Or was it simply that that was how she thought of her because that's how she came to her some nights in her dreams? She never talked to any one about those dreams, not even to her father. She wasn't quite sure why she guarded them so carefully; he must have dreams about her too. The train crash had done more than take away her mother and hurt her leg so that for ages she couldn't even walk, but it had crushed something in him too. Lately he hadn't seemed so sad, but if she talked to him about her dreams it might upset him all over gain. And that frightened her. Suppose it made him cry . . . Even now the sound haunted her. It had been a night soon after Mrs Frewin had come to look after her. Something had woken her with a start, she hadn't known what. Outside the house there had been shouting. At any other time she would have recognised the sound of men who'd had too much ale,

241

but waking suddenly she was back in the railway carriage, all the horror alive in her mind. She'd wanted her father. Groping for her crutches she'd been too scared to consider how unused to them she was as she'd made her way along the carpeted corridor in the dark. Then she'd heard something that had been almost worse than what had driven her to him. From his room had come the muffled sound of sobbing, not like a child crying, not like a woman's quiet sniffling, but trembling sobs that came from the depth of his being. But men didn't cry! She mustn't let him know that she'd heard him. His unhappiness was a private thing. Propped on her crutches, in those seconds she'd come a big step towards a maturity ahead of her years: fear, unhappiness, even the way that in dreams she sometimes really saw her mother, those things belonged to her alone. She'd wanted to help her father, but with her new wisdom she'd known that this was something that belonged just to him; no one could share it with him, he wouldn't even want them to try.

'Did your father give you your penny?' Belinda asked as they let themselves through the gate to the Abbey grounds and the sound of Merrick's car grew faint.

'And an extra ha'penny too,' Becky dug in her pocket to bring out the two copper coins.

'Be careful how you spend it. And remember the rules, no eating sweets in the street.'

'We never do. The boys'd be in real trouble if Mr Ellis caught them. Seems awfully silly to me – but, Mrs Frewin, on the green isn't in the street.'

'Perhaps not, dear. But do be careful. No trying to keep up with the things those boys do. No tree climbing or rushing about. You know you'll only suffer for it.'

Becky said nothing. It seemed to her that 'no this' and 'no that' simply meant 'no chance of any fun'. Now that they'd got used to her being with them, she knew the boys looked forward to her coming. Already she could see that Johnny Downs was watching at the window. She waved and started to run, Belinda and her warnings forgotten. Her legs still looked wasted and feeble but kind Dr Bingley was on *her* side, she'd heard him tell Mrs Frewin that the best way for them to get strong was to learn not to depend on those horrid iron supports.

There were things on Belinda's mind too. Not often was

Nicholas Ellis at home to greet them and she knew it was silly of her to hope. It wasn't that she was interested in him as a man – although she would have had to be blind and insensitive not to have seen him as attractive. It was his kindness to her charge that so pleased her, Belinda told herself, remembering the afternoon when she had ventured the information that she was teaching her to play the piano. After listening to Becky's well-tutored performance of two exercise studies, he had commended her method of teaching, her insistence on correct fingering and precision of timing. Thinking of it as they crossed the grass to the cloisters and the door to the Master's Lodge, she could still feel the warmth his praise had brought to her cheeks.

Giving memory full rein, she recalled the previous Saturday when Becky had asked him to play to them. Belinda had marvelled at her audacity. If only she'd had the courage to suggest it herself, but if he'd refused she would have felt crushed. He'd not selected what he should play, but simply taken the music that was nearest to hand in the canterbury. Liszt's *Liebestraum* . . . she used to play it to Roderick! . . . but never like this. His was the touch of a master. Leaning back in her chair she'd closed her eyes and let the music carry her where it would. There had been no other sound in the room, she'd believed they'd all been held in the same spell. Yet as the last notes faded and she'd opened her eyes she'd been aware of an atmosphere that held no peace, no contentment. She'd looked from Nicholas to Veronica then back to Nicholas, suspecting that for them the music held some personal meaning and one that made her uncomfortably aware of discord.

'Perhaps you'll play for us now?' Veronica had turned to her.

'Perhaps one day. But not now, not after that. It was so heartrendingly beautiful.'

'Music means a lot to you,' Nicholas had said, a question yet spoken as a statement of undisputed fact.

'My brother was organist at our church. He was a lot older than me, even as a child I used to sit at his side and turn the pages of his music.'

'Lucky you didn't get the job of pumping the bellows,' Veronica had heard her own laugh as loud, forced, 'I used to do that for Dr Hardy before we got the one Nicholas plays.'

Belinda had smiled a sad smile. 'You would have been a much more strongly built child than I was, Mrs Ellis. Keith wouldn't

243

have asked that of me. Poor darling, he was killed just a month before Armistice.'

Veronica, the strongly built child grown into a tall woman, felt herself to be gauche and gawky compared with their petite and gentle guest who'd known so much sadness. Why was it she had this instinctive feeling of antagonism towards Belinda? Surely the poor woman had suffered enough, losing her husband and her home, taking a living-in job to keep her independence. But was it to keep her independence that she made herself so indispensable to the household in Vicary Terrace? Veronica left the question unanswered; after all, what business was it of hers?

'Are you in a rush to get away?' Nicholas, the polite host, enquired. 'I have to run the boys through tomorrow morning's anthem at five-thirty. After that I wondered, if you are interested that is, if you would care to hear something I'm working on?'

'Composing? Oh but I would love to,' Belinda's pretty face lit with pleasure.

'I haven't been over it with the choir yet but I have in mind a new setting for the Eucharist.'

Half expecting a rebuff, she took her courage in both hands and suggested, 'Would I be in the way if I came at half past five to hear the anthem too? Would an audience put them off?'

'I sincerely hope not, or it doesn't give much hope for tomorrow morning's service.' Nicholas's bony face broke into an unexpected smile. Then, turning to Veronica, 'We'll leave Becky with you. After choir practice she can join the boys in their common room if she wants to.'

Clearly she wanted to, her eagerness was no less obvious than Belinda's. Veronica knew she ought not to care. After all, when did she ever follow him to the Abbey to listen to him? These days the answer was 'Never'. In the beginning she used to, in the beginning he'd sensed her presence, wanted her there.

Choir practice was never less than half an hour on Saturday evening, usually more; after that, it seemed obvious that Belinda would be more than willing to hang on to every note as he lost himself in his favourite pastime.

'I don't have any games,' she told the child who was looking at her expectantly. 'But I tell you what we could do if you like, we could go and make some little cakes. You could take them home and share them with your father. Do you like baking?'

'Proper cakes? I've never done that. Wait till I tell Dad!'

So they went to the kitchen where Becky was wrapped in a too-large pinafore and she was given instruction in making fairy cakes. No corners were cut, she learnt to sieve the flour and to beat the butter and caster sugar until they were what she saw as 'a lovely gooey mess'. If she was to take her first efforts home, at least they would be made with the top quality ingredients insisted on by the daughter of Blakeney's. By the time the boys clattered along the cloisters past the window on their way back from practising, the end product had five more minutes in the oven. Becky was tugged in two directions, but the cakes won and it wasn't until she'd seen them put on the rack to cool, golden and glorious that, full of her own new importance she went to join them in their Saturday evening games. The younger ones didn't get a chance for table tennis, but there was a noisy game of tiddley-winks in progress in one corner, ludo and snap were in full swing.

'I've come to play, too,' she cried, full of confidence, as she opened the door on them, sure of her welcome. For the time being tall Edward Moffat was head chorister but his reign was almost over, although he was only thirteen Nicholas's perceptive ear knew that his voice would soon be lost. At the beginning of Michaelmas term he was being moved from the choir school and going into mainstream education and it was common knowledge that his replacement would be Johnny Downs So when Johnny suggested Becky might like to try her hand at table tennis there were no argumentative cries of 'It's our turn next'. The younger boys might look on enviously as their seniors stepped outside the rules but they accepted, after all *their* turn would come in a few years. And in any case, they all liked Becky and were happy to stand round retrieving ping-pong balls. In fact she acquitted herself remarkably well for a girl who had been so over-cosseted. She lost, of course, but not without winning enough points to find herself looking forward to carrying her tale home to her father. She'd come a long way in these last few months – and on that Saturday she had yet two more 'first times' to add to her list: making fairy cakes and playing table tennis.

'I do hope she won't suffer for having such an active day,' Belinda said to Merrick later that evening, 'She'd not been in bed two minutes when I peeped back at her and she was sound asleep.'

'I've not seen her as happy for years,' he answered. 'Isn't that the whole reason for taking her to the Abbey, so that she can play with other children? You know, Belinda, I think it's time we let her start attending school again.'

She was silent, lost for words, lost even for coherent thought. What was he telling her? That it was time she looked for another post? If Becky was fit enough for school, she wouldn't need a nursemaid to watch over her. But this had been her home for more than three years. No wonder her mouth felt suddenly dry and her heart thumped. Where could she find another post like this? It had seemed ideal, heaven-sent; so heaven-sent that she hadn't even attempted to hold her imagination in rein, trying to will her vision of the future to come true. Into her head came that expression about having 'the stuffing knocked out of one'. Until now it had been just so many words, but in that moment she knew the truth of it.

'I was talking about it to Mrs Ellis,' Merrick was saying. 'She recommends Perbeck House, that large stone house on the main road before the turning to Ottercombe. It's where she went herself. She says it's still run by a Miss Chadwick, the same as when she went there.'

If seconds before, the stuffing had been knocked out of her, his words put paid to that. She was filled with frustrated anger to think that he had looked to Veronica Ellis for advice. As if that woman hadn't enough in her life – a wonderful husband, a place in local society, a business just dropped into her lap. But, if her expression showed her feelings, he didn't notice anymore than he'd noticed her silence. His own thoughts were on a very different track. Veronica recommending her old school for his daughter, Veronica talking about her time there as though it were yesterday. How old was she? Twenty-four? Twenty-five or six? No more than ten years behind him, a married woman, an efficient business woman; yet to her he was a father figure. He valued her friendship. More than that, he realised, there were no lengths he wouldn't go to for that friendship. Friendship, that was all he asked, of course it was, he told himself. Dear God, why did You take Esme from me? I'm not made for the life I have to lead, no one to share, no one to care, no one to love. Think what Ronnie said that day when she cried so

246

. . . no, I mustn't think of it, I must forget. But if that swine makes her – no, of course he doesn't, the things she said that day were because she was overwrought.

It took no longer than seconds for all those thoughts to crowd into his mind, then visions of Ronnie returning to her Abbey home, visions of her with her husband – he pulled his mind back, getting up suddenly from his chair and going to the open window.

'Are you feeling all right?' Belinda was at his side in an instant. 'You looked strange.'

'Umph? Yes, I'm fine. Too good an evening to be cooped up inside. You didn't tell me what you thought about Becky starting at Perbeck House?'

'If Dr Bingley thinks she's ready then of course I'm delighted.'

How pretty she was, he thought. A sensitive woman, could it be relief that they'd brought Becky to this state of health that made her lovely violet eyes swim with unshed tears?

'Will you want me to stay until she is settled? Or is she ready for me to look for another post straight away?'

'Go? But, my dear, do you want to leave us? You've cared for Becky in sickness, won't you stay and care for her still? Perhaps that's selfish of me.'

Two tears over-spilled and rolled down her cheeks; eyes that shone with such happiness had no room for tears.

Chapter Fourteen

Merrick's visits to Blakeney's were casual and frequent. It was the way both he and Veronica felt comfortable.

'I'm negotiating for property in Chalcombe,' he told her one warm summer morning. 'I waste hours travelling to and from London. In the early days, when my only production sites were in the south east, London was the obvious place for a main central office. But that's no longer the case. The business can be held together as easily from any part of the kingdom, and where better than down here?'

Her pleasure started as a light in her eyes, touched the corners of her mouth before it turned into a radiant smile.

'You're really here to stay?'

He nodded.

'Did you hope I wasn't?' He asked it teasingly, there was nothing in his manner to hint at how much her reception of the news meant to him.

'You don't know just how glad I am,' she told him honestly. 'If I were as proud and sure of myself as I like to give the impression perhaps it wouldn't mean as much to me to know that you're here for me. There! What a confession! And to "Mr Clampton's Cakes" of all people!'

'It cuts both ways, Ronnie.' How easy it would be to say more, to ignore the fact that she had a husband and tell her that knowing her had changed his life. Neither of them had ever referred to the outpouring of her misery on that spring day after her father had died, and he doubted if, afterwards, she'd even remembered what she'd told him. Neither of them had mentioned her heartbroken confidences and his manner had given no hint that he knew how isolated she felt from Nicholas. But did that give him the right to feel as he did? An inner voice argued that marriage was no barrier to the importance of friendship. Somehow his hand found its own way towards hers and he felt no surprise when her fingers clung to his. When he spoke, his voice was even, calm. That was the joy of Merrick, he was always there for her yet he made no demands.

'After Esme was killed I lived through three years of – of – I can't describe how it was – a sort of isolation from society when I was driven by the need to work, to build Clampton's, to take over smaller firms.'

'What about Becky? She needed you.'

'Yes. Have you ever been afraid to love? I suppose that's how I was. Of course I loved her, everything I did must have been for her. Or was it? Was I building my empire to prove myself, was it no more than one in the eye for God Who'd done what He had to my life? Looking back, I suspect I was afraid to show too much affection to Becky in case she was taken from me too. I knew I could trust Belinda to take care of her, I could stand back like a benign provider and guard against being emotionally touched. Then I met you and somehow you found a way to melt the ice.'

Her fingers gripped even harder.

'I'm glad,' she told him. 'But Merrick, it's not been one-sided. Even when I first knew you, Dad was getting more confused all the time, slipping further away. Until then, he'd always been there for me. I believe now that even then I knew that's how it would be with you. Yet, that's silly isn't it. How could I have believed that? In the beginning we didn't see each other very often at all – I wanted to find reasons to dislike you. But I couldn't. I knew you were a friend I could trust. I wanted to tell Dad, to make him understand that he needn't be frightened I had no one.'

'It's your husband you should look to for support,' he heard himself say, some masochistic instinct making him want to hurt himself.

She caught her bottom lip between her teeth, thinking, undecided. Then, 'Over everything else, yes of course I would. But not about Blakeney's. He's a musician not a business man,' then, ending on a laugh she tried to make appear natural, 'He doesn't even care much for cakes.'

249

'Not care for Blakeney's cakes! And I'd imagined he must be a man of exemplary taste.'

Recognising the compliment, this time her laugh needed no forcing.

'By the way,' she changed the subject, 'if Belinda would like to take Becky over to the Abbey to watch, the boys play cricket on Wednesday afternoons. Nicholas suggested they might enjoy it. I shan't be there, of course, but it's somewhere different for them to go – a change from the beach. If they came on the afternoon bus, I could take them home again after tea. Nicholas says it's good for the boys to have Becky there. Some of them have left sisters at home and they must miss a girl's company. He probably thinks they ought to have a chance to encourage their chauvinist streak and show off in front of a girl,' and, although she laughed as she said it, he felt an unaccountable anger for the man who could prompt such thoughts. 'So pass the message won't you,' she said, moving on to the next subject with characteristic haste. 'Now Merrick, this is why I'm especially glad you've called in this morning. I wanted to show you these. I've had replies from the addresses you gave me in New England.' She passed him two letters, both of them placing sample orders. 'From little acorns great oak trees grow,' she said with laughing assurance and making no attempt to hide her pride in the new venture. He found himself sending up a silent plea that the sample orders would be but the beginning, that her pleasure and pride weren't misplaced.

So the weeks of summer went by. Wednesdays became as much a habit as Saturdays for Becky to be brought to the Abbey. Their return to Deremouth varied; sometimes Veronica drove them, putting them down at their door but not going into the house; sometimes Nicholas drove them, following the same practice; sometimes Merrick called for them, having told them to be sure to be ready and waiting when they heard the car draw up.

On the third Thursday in September Becky started school. At the Abbey cricket bats were put away, replaced by a football. Her mid-week visits were over but, enthralled with her new routine, she scarcely gave a thought to the summer Wednesday afternoons. The idea that Belinda should leave had never been referred to again, in fact increasingly her role became that of mistress of the

250

house. Each morning Merrick drove Becky to Perbeck House, sometimes it would be he who would meet her too but often she'd come out of school to find Belinda waiting at the gate and they'd come home together on the bus. With no one to care for, for hours of each day Belinda found herself a free agent. Others may have seen her as mistress of the house, but she was aware how far short of it she fell. It had become her home; she and Merrick liked and respected each other. In the early days she'd lived in the shadow of the loss of Roderick, but other aspirations had taken over. When had she come to accept that Merrick didn't see her as a replacement wife and mother? Indeed, she decided, he wasn't looking for anyone to fill that role.

Visiting the Abbey with Becky had started as nothing more than a duty, she'd not been drawn to Veronica Ellis and had resented the easy way Becky had taken to her. Then had come the evening she had gone with Nicholas to listen to the setting he was writing for Mass. It had been like stepping into a new and magic world . . . the atmosphere in the Abbey . . . the solemn music . . . his clear baritone softly singing the sacred words.

'It's so beautiful,' she'd whispered as he'd closed the lid of the organ, 'so beautiful that it – it almost hurts to listen.'

He'd not answered and for a moment she'd wished she'd done no more than tell him lightly how much she'd appreciated hearing his work. Then he'd nodded, looking very directly at her. 'I know,' he said softly, 'I hoped you'd feel it too.'

Wednesday afternoon cricket matches had held no interest for her, nor for him either. Becky had soon learnt to follow the game and to clap in the right places. What she liked best of all was if Belinda went off 'to turn the pages for Mr Ellis', that gave her a glorious feeling of freedom.

There was no 'For Sale' notice on Ipsley House for, except for the local people walking across the green to the few shops, there would have been no one to notice it. And Monica had made it clear to Mr Morton of Morton and Pyle that she had no wish for the neighbours to know her business. So he cast his net further afield, advising potential house-purchasers from as far afield as Torquay, Exeter, Newton Abbot and even, in one case, Plymouth, of the desirable residence that had come onto his books in the charming village of Ottercombe.

251

'Mum's had people to see the house today,' Veronica told Nicholas when she arrived home, having stopped on the way to see her mother. It was the last Thursday in September and over the summer months some sort of a truce had been built between mother and daughter. Hugo was a taboo subject: that way Veronica felt she had grounds to hope that the infatuation was dying, while Monica tried to believe he was being silently accepted.

'To see the house?' Nicholas looked up from what he was reading, pulling his thoughts into order and making a conscious effort to show an interest. 'Has she found a purchaser, does she think?' Sure that his mind was still on what he'd been reading and not on her, she wished she hadn't told him at all.

'I imagine she probably has. She said they liked everything, they were going straight back with the agent and she heard them tell Mr Morton that they wouldn't bother to look at anything else. Just damned stupid,' she growled. 'Why should she try and run away from memories? They used to be happy, Dad and her, I know they did.'

'Your mother has years of living ahead of her. Surely you can't expect her to spend them dwelling on the past, no matter how happy? Your trouble, Veronica, is that you refuse to try to see things from any point of view except your own.'

'Huh!' she jeered. 'Coming from you that's rich!' Like a rebellious child she pouted.

Folding the paper he put it on the occasional table by his chair, deep in thought as he looked at her. 'Perhaps she is showing more wisdom than the rest of us,' he commented.

She didn't even try to follow his meaning. Telling him about the people viewing her old home had been a plea for his understanding. His reaction left her feeling isolated. Ought she to care so much that the place that was so full of memories would soon be handed over to someone else? Surely after two and a half years of marriage, this ought to be where her interest was. Yet how could this ever feel like a real home, somewhere of her own? It was a beautiful building, but it belonged to the Abbey that had stood for centuries. Some of the furniture would fill an antique dealer with joy but none of it was their own, like the house, it passed from one Master to the next; Nicholas had brought nothing with him except his piano. Even the staff had come with the house, and the well-kept lawn, the well-planted flower beds, were tended by gardeners. No wonder she looked back to the days at Ipsley House when she used to paint the white lines on the tennis court or plant out the bulbs and wallflowers to be ready to welcome the spring. Here she was no more than a guest, part of Nicholas's personal effects. Had Mrs Hardy felt like that when she and Dr Hardy had lived here? She asked herself the question, but she avoided the answer, not willing to admit any of the fault was her own.

Nicholas returned to his newspaper supplement. For a second she was tempted to tear it out of his hands, to throw herself on him begging for his love and understanding. But the second passed.

'Time I went across to the Abbey,' he said standing up and laying the neatly folded supplement on top of the piano. 'The last rehearsal tonight before the Singers' performance. Inevitably it'll be a disaster.'

She was at his side in an instant, hearing a hint of weariness in his tone in place of the habitual coolness, believing what she wanted to believe – that he was remembering how the Singers' rehearsals had been the beginning of falling in love with her.

'They get nervous I expect,' she said, winding her arms around his neck and holding her face invitingly close to his. 'But it'll be good when the time comes, it always is.'

She saw the way he closed his eyes, she felt his hands firm on her buttocks as he pulled her against him. The movement was almost rough, and it was that roughness that excited her. He wasn't as indifferent to her as he tried to appear.

'Wish it wasn't Thursday, wish you weren't going out,' she whispered with more truth than guile. 'There are much better ways of spending the evening.'

'It's no use, Veronica,' he pushed her from him. 'There's so much more. We can't talk now. I have to go.'

'I'll tell Mrs Beckham to leave something cold for you to eat if you're late. But come back as soon as you can. Nicholas—' What was she trying to say? Whatever it was, he didn't wait to hear it. Picking up his conductor's score, he left her. After he'd gone she felt restless, the evening stretched ahead, long and empty. She glanced through the newspaper, not putting her mind to what she read. Then she picked up the Music Supplement he'd been reading. Reports of concerts in London and Manchester, notices of forthcoming performances, lists of Situations Vacant: first violinist for a national orchestra, second trombonist, teacher of oboe for a music school, nothing there could have been holding his interest. She idly flipped to the next page. But what was this? At the bottom of the second column was a notice in bold print, not only that but it had been circled in ink. Applications were invited for Organist and Master of the Choristers at his old college in Cambridge. Her mind carried her back to their honeymoon, she remembered going with him to the college chapel, meeting his one-time mentor, an elderly man whose name she had forgotten. Sitting in the choir stalls she had listened as they'd played, first the elderly man and then Nicholas; she'd listened and, even in those first days of marriage, felt she was forgotten as they'd talked. She'd sensed his affection for the man who had been so important to the shaping of his life and, of course, that must have been why he'd marked it, simply out of interest. Could it be more than that? His elderly idol had instructed organ students, presumably his replacement Master of the Choristers would do the same. The pivot of Nicholas's life was sacred music and the sacred music from that college chapel would be equal to any. Her imagination ran riot, with every second seeming to carry him further from her reach. But he had all the music he wanted here, she argued silently; the Abbey organ was one of the finest in the country, music lovers from far and wide came to hear it. No, of course he wouldn't want to leave here and return to Cambridge, he must have marked the paper simply out of interest because he would remember the retiring Master. Or was it his way of forcing her to give up Blakeney's?

She ate her solitary supper with neither interest nor enjoyment. The more she thought of that ink-marked notice, the more uncertain she grew. It was after ten o'clock when she heard the members of the Abbey Singers leaving, recognising in their subdued voices that the rehearsal had been all that Nicholas had feared. Even on a bad Thursday he usually sent them home earlier than this. She went to the window, drawing the curtains apart so that when he came out of the vestry door he would see she was watching for his return. But minutes passed. There could be only one explanation. Tense and tired after rehearsal he would

254

have turned, not to her, but to that instrument she'd come to hate. For the thousandth time, his brother-in-law's warning came to her – a more difficult mistress than any woman. It was a long time since she'd gone to him in the organ loft, but instinct led her, telling her that beneath the surface of his reserve he was as desperately unhappy about the void that had grown between them as she was herself Surely that was what he'd meant when he'd told her 'There's so much more. We have to talk.' And so they would. They would say what was in their hearts, they would find the elusive ingredient that somehow their relationship had lost.

She needed no light to walk across the grass to the door of the vestry, listening for the first sound of the organ. Nothing. Inside the vestry she stood quite still, listening, waiting. He must have finished playing and closed the organ, any second he'd come through from the body of the Abbey and find her here in the dark. Her heart was pounding but whether with excitement, anticipation or even fear she didn't ask herself Only when, after a full minute, she was still waiting alone, did she decide he must still be in the organ loft, probably writing quick neat notes into a manuscript book; she would go to him there. What was she hoping for? What was she expecting? Again, she didn't ask. All she knew was that pride must have no place, neither hers nor his. In the short years they'd been together they were still laying the foundations for the decades ahead of them. They had to accept each other; if not, the future was bleak. If what she really meant was that *he* had to learn to accept, she honestly didn't realise it. After all, she told herself for the umpteenth time, what she was now was the same as what she had been when he'd asked her to marry him.

There was no sense in the way she crept across the vestry, the way she soundlessly opened the heavy door then, in the near darkness, moved as silently as a shadow towards the main aisle. The first thing she noticed was that there was no light in the organ loft; the second, that the chancel was lit by the flickering flame of just one candle. Then she saw him, sitting in the priest's seat, his arms folded across his chest, his eyes closed as he rested his head against the wooden carving of the back of the chair. His face was an expressionless mask, she couldn't start to guess what thoughts were keeping him here. The distance between them was no more

255

than a few yards, but it was an abyss she couldn't cross. Hadn't she tried that same thing only this evening, hadn't she given him the opening he'd refused to see? It was something more even than that that stopped her cutting into his meditation. This evening he had stayed behind after rehearsal, not for the solace of music as he so often did when he was tired or tense, but for peace ... peace that passeth understanding, the familiar words jumped into her mind. Not that Nicholas was a devout man – at least he gave no appearance of being a devout man, she made herself add honestly; but who knows what goes on in a person's heart? Was he asking for help, asking for them to find the way back onto the path they'd lost? More likely he was listening with his mind to the sound of some chant or other he was writing! It was hardly likely he'd be thinking about *her*?

She'd come here looking for answers, and all she was finding were questions and uncertainties. The Abbey no longer drew them together, rather it thrust a wedge ever deeper between them. Better to go back to the house without his knowing she'd come here. Moving stealthily between the pews she made her way towards the vestry door to escape before he suspected her presence but, unfortunately, someone had omitted to hang a hassock on the back of the pew in front. In the dark she stumbled against it, knocking both hymn and prayer book from their ledge onto the floor.

'Veronica!' How could he have known it was her? Her escape was cut off, there was nothing for it but to retrace her groping steps to the aisle and then, guided by the light of that single candle, to the chancel where now he was standing.

'You said we must talk,' she heard herself answer, her voice calm, giving no hint of the pounding of her heart or the knotted pain in her groin. 'I wanted it to be *here*.' Half an hour ago she had believed that to be the truth but now she was conscious of the alien atmosphere, it made her feel an outsider to all that his world comprised. She told herself she was being imaginative and stupid. She was his wife, surely that meant she was the most important thing in his world. But even as she forced the thought into her mind, she knew it wasn't the truth. Perhaps it never had been. 'This was where we were married,' she ended lamely.

'Do you believe I don't think of that?' Turning on the electric light he snuffed the candle and came towards her. 'This is no place to talk, Veronica – not to say the things that have to be said.'

Like an obedient child she followed him to the vestry, stopping to hang the offending hassock and replace the service books she'd knocked down and which he stepped over as though they didn't exist. His action annoyed her, her anger at his arrogant disregard for anything that got in his way, for a moment overshadowing her desire to make things right between them.

From the vestry he ushered her into the autumn night before he switched off the Abbey lights and locked the door.

'Why didn't you put a coat on?' So he might have spoken to a thoughtless choirboy.

'Not cold,' she mumbled. 'Thought we'd be in there.'

'We have to talk.'

'You told me that. That's why I came.'

The one thing they both knew was that this wasn't working out the way they'd intended.

'You say you haven't changed, you're the same as the girl who took her vows there in the Abbey—'

'So I am. It's you who've altered. You used to pretend you loved me, now you treat me like a stranger, never properly talk, never share—' She shouldn't have said it, the words gave self-pity the opportunity it was looking for. She heard her own voice and was ashamed. Where was the fighter who could run a successful business? She sounded like a spoilt child, disgruntled at not getting her own way. Biting the corners of her mouth she glowered at him, whipping up the anger that had surfaced so naturally only a minute or so before.

'I believe you,' he was saying as if her last words hadn't been spoken. 'I don't blame *you* for the way things have gone between us. The fault was mine. I'm older than you, I'd known women before I met you. You know me well enough to accept that I hadn't lived to more than thirty like some celibate monk. But what you did to me was – was—' It was unheard of for him to be lost for the right word. 'You filled my every thought, I had to have you. I swear before God I believed what I felt was more than the overwhelming sexual need I had of you.'

'And it wasn't,' she answered, her voice flat. 'Is that what you're saying? And now that you've got used to rolling over and finding me warm and willing—'

'Don't, Veronica, don't talk like that.'

'Well, it's true isn't it? You can be as high and mighty as you like, but I still hold the trump card. Like you just said, you could never have been a celibate monk. Down here in darkest Devon no wonder you had to cast around for a wife to share your bed. If it was that or nothing – well, there was no choice.' She wanted to shock him, she wished she could have thought of something really coarse, something that would degrade the joy they had found as he'd brought her to her first sexual awakening.

He ignored what he thought of as a childish outburst. Perhaps he ignored it because it held a truth he didn't want to acknowledge.

'The honest truth is,' he told her in that calm, 'my word is law' voice she hated, 'we have nothing else in common. So it has to be enough. You wish I would be interested in your cake making. I'm not and I don't intend to pretend.'

'All right, I won't try and talk to you about it.' Then, clutching at pride and an easy point to score, 'Actually I don't care whether you're interested or not, you don't understand about business. I only try and tell you things because it would be mean to let you feel left out. I know really that as far as the business goes, you'll never learn to share the interest. But you even try and hold me away from the thing that really does matter to you – your music.'

'Hold you away? I've never even considered such a thing. Of course you are apart from what I do.'

'But I used not to be. Remember the evenings I used to come to the Abbey, the fun we used to have.'

'I remember you as a childlike Delilah, I remember the desire I had to make love to you. But music? Be honest, Veronica, what can the "fun evenings" as you called them have to do with music?'

'I thought they did,' her voice was low, he could imagine the accompanying pout, 'as far as I was concerned it was music.'

He sighed.

'There's a huge void between us, I ought to have had sense enough to see it. And I'm sorry. I fail you as much as you fail me.'

'Don't see that I do fail you. Just that you never talk to me.' Then, remembering the Music Supplement and the mark he'd made on the appointment notice, 'That college in Cambridge, your old college isn't it . . . I saw the mark you'd made in the paper you were reading this evening.' She said it hoping to steer the conversation into a channel she could handle. He'd tell her he was going to cut it out and send it to someone.

'Did you also notice the date of the paper?'

'No. Today? Yesterday? Why, is it too late to be any use?'

'You think it's a good idea? I'm surprised. I expected to meet with opposition. The paper is a fortnight old, I wrote my application immediately. Today I heard from them. I doubt if Professor Williamson's obituary in *The Times* meant anything to you although you did meet him when we were in Cambridge. His death was sudden, leaving no Senior Master. Hence the appointment is to be filled as soon as possible rather than waiting until the start of the next academic year when he was due to retire. These things have to go through the usual channels, so they will call me for interview, of course, but I get the impression my application was well received. If I'm appointed – and, as I say, I have every confidence – I shall try and arrange with your old friend Dr Hardy to stand in here until a replacement Master is found.'

'Go to live in Cambridge? Us?' Her resentment as he'd stepped over the hassock and fallen books was nothing to the rage that took hold of her, it ached in her arms, it made her throat tight so that she gasped for breath. 'You've no right to plan a change like that without so much as talking to me! All right, I'm only important to you in bed, you've made that clear. But being my husband doesn't give you the right to organise my life. I do have a life, you know. I'm not here to earn my keep being an on-hand – on-hand whore. That's all you want me for, you just said so. Why don't you arrange for the removers to take me along like they will your piano, just like any other possession? Is that what you expect? Then you can think again—'

'Behave yourself How can I talk to you when you act like a spoilt child?'

'Huh! Not a child, not spoilt – not even considered important enough—'

'Dear God!' His sigh only made her feel worse. 'But you're right, I should have told you right at the outset. It's a first class appointment, there will have been many experienced applicants. Today's letter gave me grounds to expect I have a good chance of being selected, that's why I said to you earlier that we had to talk.'

259

'Now we've talked,' and again that pout in her voice. 'I've talked too, but I doubt if you've listened. I don't see why you want to leave the Abbey. Is the music here so bad? And, if it is, whose fault is that? It's always had a splendid reputation, surely everyone can't be wrong. Or do you think you're the only one who knows anything?' He didn't answer. In the darkness the silence pressed in on her. Could this really be happening? A bat swooped out of nowhere, she heard rather than saw it go on its way towards the Abbey tower. Somehow the country sound she knew so well brought reality to the nightmare she was living.

'Tell me, Veronica – and I want the honest truth – are you happy in our marriage as it is? Is that why you want to persuade me to stay? Or is it because you intend to spend the rest of your days playing big business?'

Something in her snapped. She pounded his shoulders with her clenched fists, she kicked his shins.

'I'm not playing,' the croak in her voice was her undoing. In harsh light she might have hung on to her control, but out here under a moonless sky she felt herself cut off from everything but the need to fight, to cry, to let herself be dragged down by an over-whelming tide of despair. 'You never take seriously anything that I do. You never care about what matters to *me*. *Always you, you,* bloody you.' She knew she was behaving disgracefully, she knew it and was glad. Whatever dreams she had harboured for their future were gone. But if the dreams were gone, the future was still waiting for them.

In what seemed like a single action he brought his hand smartly across her check then pulled her into his arms, smothering her face against his shoulder.

'God forgive me, what have I done to you?'

'I wish we hadn't said any of it,' she sobbed, her voice muffled by the way he held her. 'I wish I'd stayed indoors. I wish – I don't know what I wish, don't know what I want.' Then when he didn't answer and the only sound was her gasping for breath as she tried to regain control. 'And you?' She pulled away from him, rubbing the palms of her hands against her wet cheeks, 'What is it you want, Nicholas? We've got forty or more years, is this how it's always going to be for us? What do you want?'

'I have to get away from here,' which was no answer. 'I can't do as you want.'

'Away from me? You mean you want to end being married?'
Divorce? But divorce was as unheard of in her world as flying to
the moon.

'From you?' He sounded surprised at the suggestion. 'No,
you're my wife. As you say, we have years ahead of us. But if our
marriage is to have any chance of seeing us through those years,
then just do as I say. I'm sure you've had experience enough to
find a man suitable to look after the bakery. If not, then do as your
mother intended and sell it. That's entirely your affair, you've
known my views right from the start.'

'You don't understand, you don't even try. How would you feel
if I said I wanted you to give up playing the organ?'

'Don't be ridiculous. If I get this appointment then as my wife
your place is to move to Cambridge with me. Whether you choose
to come is up to you.'

'I don't understand, Nicholas. Everyone has made such a fuss of
you here. What is it you're looking for? This is a good choir school
– and you've got the Abbey Singers – sometimes recitals—'

'Just let it go, Veronica. I'd already made up my mind I must go
even before this cropped up. That this appointment should have
come up when it did must surely be providential. Now let's go in.'
His arm around her shoulders he turned her towards the door into
the Master's Lodge. 'I don't think I want Mrs Beckham's sandwiches. I'll just have a nightcap.'

She nodded, the ghost of so many evenings when he'd 'just had
a nightcap' while she went on to bed and waited for him, seeming
to mock her. Even after bad days, arguments, silences of misunderstanding, in lovemaking they had always come together; but
what a fool she'd been to think that had ever been more to him
than sexual gratification.

She was in bed about five minutes before he came through from
his adjoining dressing room. Her back to him, her eyes tightly
closed – and how they stung, their lids reddened and swollen – he
was prepared to pretend her sleep was genuine.

Things moved faster than even Nicholas had expected. Before
October was out, the appointment was made and Dr Hardy, with
genuine care and loyalty for the Abbey, had agreed to take over on
a temporary basis.

'I envy you such an easy move,' Monica told Veronica. 'Just

261

look at the responsibility I have here, the cupboards that have to be emptied, the things we've let ourselves hoard for years. I've agreed to give possession by the tenth of November. I really do think you ought to give me some of your time helping to get rid of all this accumulation.' Until that day there had always been an element of doubt: perhaps the Hobsons would decide at the last minute they didn't want the house; even, although it seemed unlikely, perhaps she might decide she couldn't bear to part with it. Pointedly she'd avoided saying anything definite about where she intended to go, hinting at how she'd like to be near 'dear Ellen' again, bemoaning the fact that Veronica had failed her in not giving her a grandchild to keep her nearby. But now it was final. Contracts had been exchanged and a date for completion agreed.

'If only Nicholas was staying at the Abbey you could have come to us while you found somewhere, Mum. But we'll have to be out even before you.' No mention of Hugo or his cottage in Picton Lane. Her manner seemed to defy her mother to bring him into any suggestion of where she intended to stay.

Silently they looked at each other, memories crowding between them and as many accusations. If he'd been there in the flesh, they couldn't have been more aware of him.

'We shan't be married in Deremouth,' Monica said, as if the fact that she meant to marry him was already an accepted fact. 'I have too much respect for dear Herbert's memory. He was looked up to in the town—'

'But not by you. Is that what you're saying? You know what I think? I think you're frightened of the gossip, not for Dad's sake. No, for your own. Poor pretty widow, that's what you like to be seen as. Shame to destroy all that and let them see you as someone who left Dad at home with Alice while you buttered up to your precious Casanova.'

'That's hateful!' Time had been when such an accusation would have brought Monica to tears. But no longer. Standing straight she was ready for battle. 'Hugo has been my salvation. Not just for months, but for years he's given me the only happiness I've known.'

'Fancy that,' Veronica sneered. 'Now you won't have to get out of his bed and come back here to your miserable, lonely existence any longer.'

'That's a wicked thing to say. I was never unfaithful to my dear Herbert. You think I'm old, don't you, you stupid girl! Just because I'm your mother you think there's no place in my life for love. I dare say you take it for granted that you are loved. When I was your age, when Herbert was "himself", I used to take it for granted too. Perhaps I'm as wicked as you believe but, Ronnie, the very purpose of life is sharing it with someone who loves you. That's the rock, the foundation, the security . . . I wish I knew the right words.'

'Dad gave you all that.'

'Yes. He did. I took it all for granted – just like you do I expect – just like every woman in a happy marriage does. Then the foundation is knocked away. All right, I'm a silly, weak woman. But I can't live on memories. Anyway I love Hugo, it's not a one-sided thing. You can build an infatuation for someone, often that can be one-sided. But sharing, finding a relationship that grows and strengthens, oh Ronnie, why can't you try and see things from someone else's angle for a change? Since poor Herbert became changed, you don't know how frightened and lonely I'd have been if I hadn't had Hugo.'

'How providential he was on hand,' Veronica said sarcastically. In the past even a remark like that would have made Monica wring her hands and fight against tears. Now she looked coldly at the daughter she saw as insensitive and uncaring.

'You ask me where I'm going,' she said, choosing to ignore the remark. 'I'll tell you. Hugo is giving up the tenancy of the cottage, we are going to travel in Europe. I've never been anywhere, always here, always waiting for the few hours your father gave me of his busy life. You've never considered how dull – how insular – my life has been in this miserable little village. We're going to Florence, to Venice, to Paris.' She reached her hand towards Veronica. 'Won't you try and be happy for me? You'll be having a new start too. Nicholas will have a proper wife at last. My heart rejoices for you, yes, it truly does. At last you'll have to free your-self of the hold that wretched business has on you.'

'That's what I was going to tell you. He's going almost immediately. Dr Hardy is prepared to take over straight away, he and Mrs Hardy will shut their home and live at the Master's Lodge again until a replacement is engaged. They're wonderful, they've made it so easy for Nicholas.'

'Of course they've been wonderful, they care about the place, they always have.'

'I know that's what we all thought. But you've taught me not to assume we know any other person. Who knows what anyone really cares about?'

'You're being so mean-minded. I don't deserve it. When did I ever fail your father, or you either?'

If it was meant as a question, Veronica ignored it. 'The Hardys invited me to stay on there until I'm ready to go. But I shan't do that. I'd rather find rooms of some sort in town.'

'Oh, you silly child! Ready to go you say! Get your priorities in order or you'll live to regret it. What matters more, a good marriage and a new future starting together, or a lot of silly orders for Christmas cakes?'

'Put like that, the marriage. But Mum, nothing is as simple as you think. Nicholas will be in his perfect environment there. But me? Can you see me fitting into some academic society? I bet there's not a business brain amongst them. For the time being he is going without me.'

'No ... oh no ...' Monica breathed. She'd had her concerns over her daughter's marriage, but never had she imagined anything like this!

After Veronica had left, Monica fetched her writing paper and ink from the bureau and settled at the table to open her heart to her dear friend Ellen.

Coming out of a tall building in Clifford Terrace, Veronica bid farewell to Mr Morton's assistant and started to re-trace her steps to Merchant Street and Blakeney's. This was the third set of rooms she had seen, each one more miserable than the last. But did that matter so much? After all, she wasn't looking for a permanent home. The future held no ray of light, in fact it held no shape at all. She and Nicholas has stayed for just one night in Cambridge, long enough for her to see it as a beautiful city, steeped in antiquity and learning, a place removed from the hum and bustle of the business world. Soon she would have to face the challenge of turning herself into the sort of wife who would play an accompanying role in her husband's life, a woman without ambition except for his comfort and delight. Small hope of that, she scoffed silently. What sort of delight does he find in me, except for *that*? All that they had

264

in common, he called it. But since that night when he'd told her he was leaving the Abbey, what she had thought of as lovemaking had taken on the role of 'sex'. Rather than draw them together, it seemed to her to hold them apart; it was a physical function, one she came to dread. That's what's so awful, she mused, I find myself holding back even when my body screams at me to let go, to let it happen to me like it used to. But now I can't, now I know that I'm no more to him than a body. Does he realise? I doubt it. More likely for him it's the same as it always was, that's all he ever thought me, just a body, a warm, willing, feminine body. Oh yes, one he wanted, he told me that too. Probably used to fantasise about making love to me – no, not to *me*, just to my body. And I never knew; I believed, I trusted. Don't want even to think about it. Let him enjoy Cambridge and all his clever-dick friends, see if I care. He'll be back to fantasising, all alone like he was when I believed I was leading him on. I was so stupid! But he wanted me then, always in his mind, that's what he said. Perhaps after a while on his own in Cambridge it'll be like that again.

Deep in thought, she soon found herself in the yard of the bake-house.

'Visitor in your office, Miss Ronnie,' Bert Jenkins called as she came through the main door.

'Mr Clampton?'

'No. A surprise. That's what he said.' Bert grinned, clearly approving of the caller.

With a lighter step she hurried to her room. Merrick had been the most likely person. But if it wasn't him, then surely it must be Nicholas.

'I'm back,' she called unnecessarily, throwing open the door.

'I was away on a job, I didn't find Mum's letter waiting until I arrived back in town last night.' Laurence, elegant, beautiful, sure of himself, came towards her with both hands outstretched. For a second she was lost for words. They'd not contacted each other since she'd left so abruptly in the middle of the night in London.

'But what are you doing in Deremouth? Another job?'

'I told you. I had this letter. Ron, why couldn't you have told me what a mess your marriage was. Well, I knew it must be, you only married him because you thought I'd let you down. Why couldn't you have seen, Ron, I had to make a career. What sort of respect would you have had for me if I'd just stayed at home and worked in some tin-pot solicitor's office? None. Your marriage is on the rocks, Mum tells me. I'm not surprised. That's why you came to me in London, I ought to have realised it. Why else would you have let me love you like I did?'

'Stop it, Laurence.' His torrent of words seemed to be giving her no chance to think, let alone speak.

'Has he gone to Cambridge yet?'

'Next Monday. But Laurence, what Nicholas does has nothing to do with you and me. Well, nothing to do with you anyway.'

'Everything that has to do with you, has to do with me,' he told her solemnly. 'I say, fancy your old man leaving the business to you. Bet that made your mother sit up and think? But she's getting spliced to that fop Holmes, I hear. I say, Ron, what a lark, this place being yours. Listen, I've been doing a lot of thinking. Why don't you sell up and throw your lot in with mine? Eh, what do you say? It's what we ought to have done ages ago. But of course if we had, I doubt if this place would ever have come to you anyway. You've seen where I live, it's big enough for two. You're not a domesticated type – who knows you better than I do? – but you could get a job on the magazine, I could pull a few strings. We'd have a whale of a good time.' Then, with the laugh she'd always found so infectious, 'What's happened to your tongue, has the cat got it? Isn't that what Alice used to say?'

How could she ever have seen him as anything but a shallow, fun-loving boy? Even in London, until his swift and insensitive lovemaking had opened her eyes, they'd had what he described as 'a whale of a good time'. Now she saw him afresh and she envied him his casual acceptance of any good fortune life dropped into his lap. Well, she wasn't in that category! What if Blakeney's had belonged to her mother, would he have been sitting here today? She was ashamed of the thought . . . and yet . . . and yet.

'I'm not looking for a job, with or without your having to pull strings. On the contrary, I'm trying to bring myself to accept the fact I shall have to think of putting in a manager to look after the job I already have. As for what happened in London, it's not something I'm proud to remember.'

'Forget it then. We'll start afresh. You'd be happier with me than with Sobersides, we both know you would.'

She turned away from him, gazing unseeingly from the window.

'How do you define happiness? How do you ever truly find it?'

'Oh, come on, Ron, we found happiness a-plenty back when we were youngsters.'

Yes, she thought, but we're not youngsters any longer. Tree climbing, vying to catch the largest fish, racing along the Dartmoor lanes on bicycles carrying their picnics in their saddle-bags, how easy it was to believe you'd found happiness when you were no more than a child.

'Perhaps the truest happiness is the moment when you reach towards it. It's like climbing a steep hill, striving for the perfect moment when the view is there before you. Yet when you get to the top there can never be perfection; perhaps you've rubbed a blister on your heel, perhaps you've lost your handkerchief, perhaps—'

'Look what living with Sobersides has done to you.'

She tried to laugh. This was Laurence, the Laurence at one time she'd believed she'd loved and wanted to spend her life with.

'Go back to London, Laurence, and be grateful I've sent you away.'

'But Ron, think about what I said. If your marriage was half what it ought to be, then you wouldn't have hopped into my bed so willingly. Flog this place and let's start again, do what we ought to have done right from the start.' She looked him squarely in the eyes and said nothing. After a minute he reached for the hat he'd thrown onto the stand. 'Seems I'm wasting my time and my talent.' Then, with a smile that came nearer to touching her heart than anything he'd said so far, 'Not every girl gets an opportunity like it, I hope you know what a plum prize you're refusing.'

After he'd gone she found it impossible to concentrate on the work that was waiting for her. She must make a decision about the rooms she would rent. After all, did it matter so much that none of them were better than drab? Putting on her hat, a tawny-brown velvet beret, and touching her lips with colour she surveyed herself in the glass. Did he come because you inherited the business or did he mean the things he said? She asked the solemn-faced girl in the looking glass. The thing is, we none of us really know what another person feels. Even Mum, even after all the things she tried to make me understand, I'm still just eaten up with anger at what she's doing. Yet, if I'd been kinder to her, put on a show of making a fuss like she seems to need . . . The sentence went unfinished. What was the use of 'if'? What I have to do is walk past each of those three houses where I've looked at rooms, I have to see if any of them 'call out' to me. Just listen to me! I sound like that stupid Matilda de Vere Mum thinks is so clever.

None of them 'called', none of them so much as 'whispered' as she strode purposefully by. It was as she came towards the top end of Merchant Street that Merrick came round the corner towards her.

'They said you were in the town,' he told her. 'Ronnie, I've been thinking. Have you found rooms – temporary rooms, I mean, until you're ready to join your husband?'

'I've seen some. I suppose it doesn't really matter that they're drab, after all I'm not looking for more than somewhere to sleep and hang my clothes.'

'I have more than enough room for that.' Then, before she had time to speak, 'The house is large, I wouldn't intrude on you. I'd been thinking about suggesting it, but perhaps I was frightened you'd turn the offer down. Then Becky suggested it. She's fond of you, you know.'

Veronica beamed her pleasure. 'Come and live with you. Why, Merrick, if you could put up with me I'd like that.' She imagined their easy companionship, she pictured them together in the evenings always with things to talk about. She imagined – no, whatever it was she imagined she gave it no chance to come to the front of her mind. 'If Becky likes me, that's because I've never made a great fuss of her. I hated being fussed when I was a child.' It was a relief to talk about Becky.

She wasn't sure what she hoped Nicholas's reaction would be when she told him she was moving into Vicary Terrace with the Clamptons.

'It seems a good idea,' he said. 'The Clampton man you have such regard for may know of someone who can look after the bakery, since you seem determined not to get rid of it.' And that appeared to be as far as his interest went.

It was her mother's reaction that surprised – surprised and angered – her.

'The very idea!' Monica said when she heard. 'Think how it will look. How the tongues will wag that you let poor Nicholas take up his new life ahead of you while you move in with Mr Clampton. Sometimes I despair of you, Veronica, have you no sense of decorum? It's just the sort of scandalous behaviour the gossips love.'

'Then good luck to them,' Veronica said scornfully. 'If they've nothing better to do than mind other people's business, then I pity them.'

But there was no pity in her voice.

Chapter Fifteen

It was Veronica's idea that she and Nicholas should spend the days of Christmas on their own, away from both Deremouth and Cambridge. Privately she acknowledged that she was running away from the changes the year had brought. Of course she could have joined him in his new quarters, and she knew that's what she ought to have wanted. 'This must be the first time for years,' she wrote to him, 'that you have no festival music at Christmas. With the colleges closed and my orders filled, we shall both be free for a few days. Let's go right away. I could come by train to, say, London and then we could drive off to – where? Anywhere our fancy takes us.'

His reply came by return of post. What made her assume that because the university had gone down there would be no services at the chapel? However, he appreciated this would be a difficult Christmas for various reasons. The sooner it was behind them, the better. He had been invited to spend the day with the Dean and 'I have no doubt the invitation could be extended to include you, should you so wish.' She could almost hear him speaking the words, his voice void of emotion. Not a word that he wanted her with him. And why should he? She didn't share his music, she didn't share his sober, academic turn of mind. All they had in common was – no, don't think about it. His voice echoed in her memory, humiliating her. Aware that Merrick was watching her as she read, she forced her face into a smile.

'It seems I was wrong. There will be Christmas services in the chapel so he won't be free. He's been invited to spend the day with a colleague and suggests I can go too if I'm there.'

270

'Is that what you want?' The words were spoken even as they were thought, and as quickly covered by his next sentence. 'But of course it's not just what *you* want, he must be looking forward to introducing you into his circle. And it's time you got acquainted with your new home, Ronnie.'

Their eyes met across the breakfast table where they were looking at their mail. It was rare for Veronica to welcome Belinda with them, missing nothing; but in that brief moment as she read a silent message that said so much more than the friendly, polite words she was thankful for the presence of the other two at the table.

'Who's taking me to school this morning?' Innocent of anything more important than her thickly spread toast, and still full of her own importance at the novelty of having to be at school by nine o'clock, any undercurrents went over Becky's head. Her life was altered, no more 'Be careful' with this or 'Promise you won't try to' do that. That dreadful 'Clamper' she used to wear to support 'your poor weak leg' was like a fading nightmare even though she still looked as though she were supported by two broomsticks. In her mind – and she wasn't quite sure why she felt this way – she associated her new freedoms with Veronica. More recently there had been no Saturday afternoon visits to the Abbey, that was her one disappointment. But with so much more happening in her suddenly busy days, she had no time for regrets.

'I'll take you in,' Merrick answered her. 'I'm meeting wholesalers in Bristol at mid-day, so I'm afraid it'll mean the bus for the return journey, Belinda.'

'I can bring you home if you like, Becky,' Veronica offered.

'Oh good,' Becky beamed her approval. 'That's much better than waiting for the bumpy old bus.'

Looking from one to the other, Belinda felt ousted from her place as 'near-mistress of the home'.

'How useful it is to be able to drive a motor car,' she sighed. 'It's my greatest regret that I've had no opportunity to learn.'

'Not a lot of point if you have no motor car to drive,' Veronica pointed out, irritated by delicately pretty Belinda's hint and the way she fixed her wide eyes on Merrick. This morning, though, he seemed not to notice. 'I must give Nicholas my answer about Christmas,' she went on, having disposed of Belinda's pointless

271

suggestion. 'He's worked every Christmas we've been together, the boys from the school never go home until after the morning service. But other years have been different.' She dreaded this one, her father gone, her mother presumably 'swanning off' somewhere in Europe like some teenager falling in love for the first time.

Veronica tried not to remember their parting. She hated to think of the emotion that had gripped her as she'd called at Ipsley House, knowing it would the last time she'd see her mother there. She'd even wondered whether it would be the last time she'd see her anywhere, for she'd arranged to leave Ottercombe the following morning. Bertha had been left in charge of seeing the furniture on its way to Exeter for auction before she joined her sister in Eastbourne. If Herbert hadn't remembered her in his will, Veronica believed she would have started her retirement empty-handed for Monica had been living in a dream world.

'Aren't you going to kiss me goodbye? Aren't you going to tell me you care that I've found a second chance of happiness?' No matter how hard Veronica tried to forget, her mother's words stayed with her. So did her reply and the gut-wrenching misery that had seemed to encompass so much more than what she saw as Monica's betrayal.

'I seem to remember even Judas managed a kiss.' They must both have been aware of the sneer.

'You're so unkind. Sometimes I can't believe you're my own daughter.'

'Amazing, isn't it? But then, I'm Dad's daughter too.'

'Go away and stop taunting me. What a way for us to part . . . my own daughter. You're making me cry and I don't deserve it. I suppose if I stayed shut in this place for the rest of my life, alone and in widow's weeds, you'd be happy. Well, I can't and I won't. Think what you like. I don't care. I don't care what anyone thinks. I've found a man who loves me, loves me *my* way. Not one who pets me and spoils me when he has time on his hands. I've never known such − such − contentment, peace. So now you know. Hugo isn't second best. And, yes, if you're interested, I have been to bed with him. It was the most wonderful thing that's ever happened to me. For the first time in my life I feel like a complete person. Me, you hear me, me, me, *me*.'

Standing in the middle of the drawing room, a framed sepia photograph of Herbert on the table behind her, she had thumped her chest as she repeated the word.

'You make me feel I never started to know you.'

'And that's the truth,' Monica had sniffed into her dainty handkerchief. 'No one knew me, I didn't even know myself. But I do now. I'm alive for the first time. My life is more than half over and yet I'm only starting to live.'

'You won't be wanting this in your brave new world.' Brushing past her, Veronica had picked up the photograph of her father. Her action had been slow and deliberate, she had willed her mother to snatch it from her. Even at that eleventh hour something might have been saved between them. But Monica had stood aside and watched.

'He would want you to have it,' was all she'd said.

Hurt and disappointed, angry and disgusted, Veronica had left. Despite the wet October day, Monica had opened the window and managed to have the last word. 'Instead of looking for rooms, just do your duty to your husband and go with him to Cambridge. You're storing up trouble.'

'Huh!' Hardly an answer, but it had spoken volumes.

That had been more than a month ago. Each morning since then, as Veronica checked the post at Blakeney's, secretly she had hoped to see the familiar handwriting, but there had been nothing.

'If you decided to stay here, nothing would please us more,' Merrick was saying, having no idea where her thoughts had travelled in the brief silence.

'Yes, oh yes, please say you'll do that, Mrs Ellis,' Becky had said through a mouthful of toast.

'Mind your manners,' Belinda had reminded her, 'never speak while you're eating.'

Becky bolted her half-chewed mouthful. 'Please, Mrs Ellis. If you're here you can help us do a tree. Tell her, Dad, tell her we want her to stay home for Christmas.'

'I think she knows it without our telling her, Becky,' he said, casting discretion to the wind.

'If you've finished your toast, go and wash your face and hands and get your things on.' It wasn't like Belinda to sound so snappy. Father and daughter looked at her in surprise, only Veronica believed she understood her reasons.

273

Veronica wrote telling Nicholas that, as he would be working over Christmas and had accepted an invitation to visit friends, she suggested she would wait until afterwards to come to Cambridge. She didn't mention any particular day, putting the ball into his court and secretly willing him to spin it back in her direction with some plan that would set them on the road that somehow they had to find.

Fortunately for her, trade had improved, her new outlets in London were proving worth their weight in gold for, apart from the orders she filled for them, she was able to let it be known to customers nearer home that Blakeney's supplied the best retailers in the country. Dreams cost nothing and she even let herself imagine a Royal Coat of Arms over the main entry of the bakery. Already they were into December, Christmas orders were being prepared. She engaged an extra skilled confectioner; rich fruit cakes, well-steeped in brandy, were iced. Some represented snow scenes, others depicted the nativity, then there were those with smooth icing bearing a sprig of holly and an expertly piped Christmas greeting. Only when they were finally ready did the newly appointed packer take over to wrap them in protective greaseproof paper then seal them in the appropriately decorated tin. December had always been a busy time in the bakehouse, but never as busy as that year. By the middle of the month the rush was over. Fruit cakes of the same recipe were still going into the ovens, but the pressure was off and those which were baked as late as this would probably be held back to be piped with New Year's greetings, or even kept un-iced in readiness for weddings or christenings.

It was a different story at Clampton's. Reading the recipe used for their Christmas cakes, Veronica was ashamed of her one-time ignorant scorn. Knowing Merrick had given her a new under-standing. At Blakeney's the fruit was soaked overnight in brandy before it went into the mixture; at Clampton's the nearest a cake came to brandy was a spoonful of essence. It was essence that gave the flavour to the marzipan too, for it certainly had no contact with ground almonds. But when the finished cakes came to the table at teatime on Christmas Day, she suspected it would be Clampton's that caused more excitement. Many a careful house-wife had saved her few pence each week in a Christmas Club for just such a seasonal treat.

She said something of the sort to Merrick. They were in his study late on a Sunday afternoon, that time of day that is neither afternoon nor evening. As daylight had faded neither of them had switched on the light, instead he'd thrown another log on the open fire and they'd drawn their chairs closer. Earlier, Becky had persuaded Belinda out for a walk but, if she'd hoped by that she would have avoided her piano lesson, she was disappointed. From the drawing room came the plodding sound as the child counted her way through the bars. The tempo was right but it would take more than correct tempo and fingering to turn Becky into a musician. From the distance of the study, though, there was something reassuringly comfortable about the sound of her efforts.

'And another thing,' Veronica added, her mind on Clampton's festive offerings, 'I wouldn't mind betting that every crumb of yours will be eaten – a treat to the last. I'm not so sure about ours. A Blakeney's rich Christmas cake probably costs as much as a lot of people spend on the whole day's over-eating. And people who can spend that sort of money must take it all so much for granted. Sad, really, for Jenkins and the others, they put heart and soul into what they do.'

'And what they do is appreciated, Ronnie. If it weren't, you wouldn't get people coming back year after year. What shall we have on our table here? Blakeney's or Clampton's?'

She opened her mouth to answer – as if there could be any comparison! – then, in the light of the flickering flames, she saw the twinkle in his eye.

'We'll have both.' She chuckled. 'Then we'll blindfold each other and guess which we're eating.' Had she said something wrong? His expression changed and even though he hadn't moved, she felt he had drawn away from her. 'Merrick . . .?'

'Ronnie—' But whatever he had meant to say – or whatever had almost escaped him – didn't get said.

In an instant she moved across the space between them then, in a natural, unconscious movement she forced his legs apart and dropped to her knees in front of him. Did he lean back in his chair to keep a distance between them? Why wouldn't he open his eyes and look at her?

'Did I say something? Can't you tell me?' Across the hall Becky had started on a series of scales, from outside came the clip-clop of horses as a pair of riders started home from a low-tide gallop at the water's edge. 'Merrick?' Still he didn't open his eyes, but his hands raised as if they had a will of their own, reaching out to hold her head and draw her closer. Willingly she leant against him, she had no power to stop herself.

'I ought to be surprised, I ought to fight against it,' she whispered. 'I've never felt so right, so at peace with myself.'

Drawing back just far enough to look up at him, she saw now that his eyes were open. In the firelight she read their message.

'You're married to another man. Tell me you love him and I swear I'll be your friend, just your friend, and we'll never speak of this again. But tell me the truth, Ronnie. I've fought against it almost from the day I met you. I promised myself I'd never let you guess.'

'If I really were just a friend, if I were just someone staying here until I could leave the business and join' she couldn't say Nicholas's name, 'join her husband, then I wouldn't have known. But it's not like that. The weeks I've lived here have been so *right* – well, no, not wholly right. I've never been so *myself* with anyone. When I was younger I used to think Dad and I had proper and complete companionship. But, I was a child. I believed I'd found that same understanding with you – well, I know I have. But I'm not a child now.'

Kneeling as tall as she could she wound her arms around his neck. For a moment they looked at each other silently, fighting the inevitable. Like people being dragged down into quicksand they had no chance. His mouth covered hers, her fingers caressed the back of his head. In the drawing room scales gave way to Becky's favourite party piece, 'Love Letters' it was called, an easy tune in the key of G where she showed off and played with crossed hands.

Those brief moments had room for nothing but each other. Then reality and sanity forced themselves between them.

'I ought to wish we'd never got to know each other, really know each other,' she said, turning away from him and gazing at the fire as if the flickering flames hypnotised her. 'When you were just Mr Clampton's Cakes I could despise you without knowing you. Now what have we done?'

'We've found friendship, my darling Ronnie. You remember I told you once how I'd been frightened of letting myself love –

276

afraid of the hurt it could bring. But it doesn't matter how determined we are, emotion is our master. Love, hate, yes and jealousy too, they rule our lives. You didn't answer my question. Or perhaps I didn't really ask it – fear, again? Do you love your husband?'

'Don't ask me to say it, don't ask me to put it into words. I vowed I would love him for the rest of my life. I believed it was true. Being young and inexperienced is no excuse, I know plenty of girls of my age who married, had children, built a life. So why couldn't I? I thought I wasn't ready for a family because I had a duty to Blakeney's, but I know now that that was only part of it. One day I'll be ready, that's what I told myself. And truly I believed it. When I married, do you know what I did?' Of course he didn't know, but she found herself telling him about her visit to the Family Planning Clinic, confiding in him the thing that she had never been able to talk about to Nicholas. As she talked, temptation nudged her. She heard the echo of Nicholas's voice taunting her with the freedom Dr Bingley had given her. Merrick's thoughts must have been on the same lines.

'No, Ronnie. I love you too well. Yes, I want you, only God knows how much I want you; but not like that, knowing that what we do is wrong—'

'How could it be wrong?' But she didn't expect an answer. Her words were no more than a cry from the heart. Once more he drew her against him. When she spoke again, her words took him completely by surprise. 'Do you still want to buy Blakeney's? I'd never let it go to anyone else, but if you took it I wouldn't feel I'd failed Dad's trust.'

Her meaning was clear. One unguarded moment had made the future for them impossible. His hold on her tightened.

'I can feel your heart,' she whispered. Then, still clinging to him, 'I know what I have to do. We both know. First I shall go back to Dr Bingley. Then I shall move to Cambridge. I'll have children, I'll build a life – that's what Mum said I should have done right from the start. Not that she knew about the Clinic. Build a life ... if I'd done that in the beginning I'd never have known there could be anything more.' Then, her movement sudden as she knelt tall, looking him straight in the eyes. 'But now I do know. I wish I didn't. I wish I thought that was all there ever could be. And something else I wish, Merrick.'

'About us?'

'No, not this time. About Mum. She said she felt she'd come alive and I didn't even want to understand. I suppose that was because I always loved Dad more than I did her; that may be wrong, to love one parent as obsessively as I did him. She must have always known that she came a poor second. Perhaps it was partly my fault she turned to Hugo Holmes. Anyway, the reason doesn't matter. The thing is, when she begged me to understand I didn't even try. Now I know something of what she felt. And I wish I had a chance to tell her. But she doesn't contact me and I don't know where she is.'

'Give her time.' This was Merrick, her friend, trying to reassure her, the Merrick she'd let herself come to rely on and look on as an integral part of her life. 'If you and I did what we know we can't and rushed off to make a new beginning together, it might take you a little while before you were ready to reach out to her.'

'What am I going to do without you?' she murmured, holding her mouth rigid, frightened to look at him. 'I don't know how I can bear it. I feel so *low*, such a cheat. It's honestly not Nicholas's fault that I think of the future as just a duty, an obligation. He's always treated me well, I don't blame him for growing away from me. You lost your Esme, yet you were close to her, if she'd been here with you you would never have seen me as anything more than "that pigheaded woman who runs Blakeney's".'

His laugh surprised her, it even surprised him. A sign perhaps that, just as so many people said to him after the accident, time is a great healer.

At the sound of footsteps crossing the hall she moved away, so that when Becky and Belinda came to look for them she was kneeling on the hearthrug, her hands held towards the blaze.

During the evening, despite Belinda's reservations about card games on the Sabbath, they passed the time playing whist, Merrick and Becky against Veronica and Belinda. Of the four of them the only one wholeheartedly to enjoy the game was Becky; but at least Merrick and Veronica put on a good show, thankful to hide from the hornet's nest of emotion that fireside hour had created. Later, when only the three adults were left, she wondered whether his suggestion of some music was a need to keep the image of Nicholas firmly between them.

It was Belinda who played the piano, her ability coming as a surprise to Veronica. Petite and delicate in appearance, yet her rendering of Chopin's *Revolutionary Etudes* was note perfect and fired with passion. Not for the first time she saw the young widow with new eyes. But, at last, the evening was over and she could escape to the solitude of her own room. Now, though, there was nowhere to hide from her thoughts.

Purposely she turned her mind to Nicholas, to the girl she'd been when she'd so willingly and completely believed herself in love with him. So she had been, she told herself – so she had been, as far as the immature person she'd been had been capable. Remember how he brought the miracle of love alive for me – miracle of love, I call it, but was it ever that to him? Or was it the one thing that was good between us, sex? I ought to say thank God for *that*. Imagine being married to a man you hated making love with. I must go back to him, I've always known that I must. But now, after this evening . . . it was at that point her thoughts raced ahead of her unspoken words and she gave herself up to the luxury of re-living those moments, of hearing what surely deep in her heart she'd already known. No, think of Nicholas, imagine how it'll be when he and I are together, together in bed. That's the time when we come closest, call it sex or call it love. Would I feel like this if I'd never known what making love could be like? But I do know. In the silent darkness of her room she lay very straight, her eyes tight closed, her hands warm on her body as she tried with every fibre of her being to bring Nicholas close. Yet, only minutes later as she bit hard on the bed covers to hold back her cry as, just for a second before cold reality brought her back to earth, she reached the goal she'd yearned, the imagine of Nicholas faded, it was Merrick she reached out to. Please God, help me be strong, help Nicholas and me find what we've lost. Yet how can I, now that I know there's something so much more? Please help me, help us both, help all three of us.

The night was long and lonely, the future challenged her with cold duty. But duty would have its compensations. Tomorrow she'd make an appointment to see Dr Bingley, so that when she went back to Nicholas she could tell him she wanted them to have a proper marriage, she was ready to have children. Merrick would take care of Blakeney's . . . she turned her pillow that was wet with tears.

Next morning it was Becky who collected the post as it landed through the letter box.

'All for you, Dad, except this one. It's your cousin, Mrs Frewin. I know who it's from because she always uses a typewriter. She never used to, did she?'

'She's only recently had lessons in how to type. I wonder if it might be a good idea if I learnt too. There is always work for a woman who can use a typewriter.'

'Silly,' Becky laughed. 'What sort of work would you do here on a typewriter?'

So the conversation dropped. And Belinda put her unopened envelope under her plate to read later in her room. Reading at the breakfast table might be allowed for Merrick, she conceded, but for anyone else it should be strictly taboo; and it was important that Becky grew up with automatic good manners. As for Veronica Ellis, she seemed to think she was a law unto herself! The look she cast across the table in Veronica's direction spoke volumes, something that no one seemed to notice. For weeks she'd felt herself to be of no consequence in the house. Was it simply since Merrick had planted their guest on them, or was it more deep-rooted? Was she looking for somewhere to lay the blame for her frustration and hopelessness? Life wasn't fair. Oh, but she'd known that for years, right from when it had given her a glimpse of happiness with Roderick then replaced it with the strain and anxiety of caring for him until it took him from her and left her alone. As for Veronica Ellis, she had everything and always had had. Married to Nicholas and yet she put that stupid business before the joy of making a home, of sharing his career, of giving him children. Turning the knife in the wound of her own empty existence Belinda imagined the chances Veronica had scorned, before her thoughts turned to her own hours spent at the Abbey and of the injustice of her position. As soon as breakfast was over, she escaped to her room with her letter even though she had no reason to rush for, within minutes, the flurry of departure would be over and she would be faced with a day on her own. Overseeing the running of a household that progressed smoothly with or without her seemed only to add to her sense of futility.

Minutes later, with most un-Belindalike haste she ran down the stairs just as Merrick was taking his hat and cane from the stand and Becky struggling into her fur-trimmed overcoat. She'd already watched from her window and seen that Veronica was safely out of the house, for she had no wish to discuss her plans in front of *her*. 'Before you go, can you spare a moment,' she said as she came. 'That letter I had this morning from my cousin. Poor Helen, she's feeling so wretched. Influenza, that's what the doctor says but she says she feels so ill it must be something more. I hate to think of her alone, struggling to look after herself when she can hardly drag herself from her bed. With Mrs Ellis here for company for Becky, could you spare me for a few days?'

'But, my dear, of course. We'll take care of each other won't we, Becky? You must feel free to stay as long as she needs you.'

'So sad to be alone,' Belinda's blue eyes were full of compassion. 'She's like me, she has no one.'

'She has you, my dear, and there's no one better able to care for a patient.'

'Promise me you'll be a good girl while I'm away.' Dutiful to the last, Belinda turned to Becky, 'Each day you'll practise the piano for a full half hour.'

Becky nodded. Somehow a nod didn't seem to her to carry the same obligation as a spoken pledge. Belinda didn't notice, her mind had already leapt ahead. She wanted them gone, she wanted to pack her bag and hurry to the station in time for the ten past ten London train. When Merrick pressed two sovereign pieces into her hand she managed to smile with the gratitude of one in her position, but already in spirit she was free of the house.

Knocking and entering in one movement, Veronica came into Merrick's office. It was soon after eleven on that same morning and, despite her intention to put everything personal out of her mind, she had found it impossible to concentrate on her work.

'That'll do for the moment, Miss Dobson. Before you start typing up what I've given you perhaps you could find a cup of coffee for us. You'd like coffee, Ronnie?'

'That's kind. Good morning, Miss Dobson. I'm sorry, disrupting your routine, it's just that something cropped up I wanted to talk over with Mr Clampton.'

'You come and take my chair, Mrs Ellis. The kettle'll be singing already, I'll be along with the coffee in a trice.' And off she bustled, her curiosity at what had cropped up given an extra fillip by something she'd sensed in their manner. None of her business, she told herself, but she'd worked for Mr Clampton ever since he'd opened the factory in Deremouth and she hoped young Mrs Ellis wasn't playing with his affections. Didn't they say that a lonely man was easy prey? Now then, she'd best send for a cake or two to go with their coffee.

'Merrick, I couldn't concentrate, couldn't seem to settle down to work. You know what I said yesterday, about my selling out to you. Is that what you want?'

'I can't have what I want. But if you mean, am I in the market to take Blakeney's, you know I am.'

'And you wouldn't change it, wouldn't alter Blakeney's in any way? Oh, I shouldn't even ask. I know you wouldn't.'

'Neither in name nor quality, that I swear.'

'I've made my mind up. That's why I want to do it quickly – before I have time to look from different angles, before I even have time to face what it is I've decided. We both know that's how it has to be. But, Merrick, I have another favour to ask of you. I'm going to Cambridge right away. Yesterday didn't make any difference to how we feel, but it did make it impossible to go on as we were.'

He came round the desk and took both her hands in his.

'Even as friends—' he started, but she cut him short.

'No! Last night – the night I mean, not just the evening – didn't that tell us?'

He drew her into his arms. 'There's never a night you're not the last person in my thoughts,' he whispered, pulling off her hat and throwing it onto the desk, then running his fingers through her short hair. 'But last night, knowing it was the same for you—'

'It was so hard not to come to you. Just a wall between us.'

282

'In my heart there was nothing to separate us, nothing, nothing,' he whispered.

Pulling back far enough to look at him, willing him to meet her gaze, she nodded. 'It was like that for me, too. You must see, I can't stay on like some casual visitor. I expect people would say it's wrong to tell you, but I don't care. Today I'm going away, but I can't go without telling you. That's really what I've come for.'

Miss Dobson was approaching with a tactful rattle of cups and, just as they had yesterday before the study fire, so again they drew apart. Her interruption gave them some sort of normality to cling to and, grasping it, Veronica poured the coffee. Purposely she placed the cups one on each side of the desk, then sat down in the chair Miss Dobson had vacated. Then, picking up where she'd left off, she went on, 'What I have to say ... I've never had a dearer friend than you – not Laurence who I adored when we were young, not Nicholas, not even Dad. It's as if we're two pieces of a jigsaw, made perfectly for each other. But two pieces of a jigsaw need a background to make the picture complete. And that background is the whole of our days, the whole of our nights, all that we are. I want you to love me, not just with your mind but with your body. Last night was dreadful, I tried to believe it was Nicholas I wanted, but it was you, just you.'

'And me. Imagination is cruel comfort. Promise me one thing, my darling love, promise me that if it doesn't work out for you, no matter when, you'll come back to me.'

'Suppose you find someone—' she started, trying to save them from emotions that would make their parting even harder.

'Don't joke,' he cut in. 'Promise me.'

'I promise,' she told him solemnly. 'But Merrick, I have to make it work. That's what marriage is about.' Then, turning with something like relief to an easier topic, 'I shall write to my solicitor about Blakeney's.'

'And to your accountant. Dear friends though we are, this must be on a proper business footing. And, in the meantime, while we're waiting for the legal side I promise you, you can leave Blakeney's safely in my hands.'

'I knew you'd say that.' The seconds were ticking past, already it was more than half past eleven. 'I shall catch the ten past twelve train to London. Tell Becky I'm sorry about Christmas.' She put on her hat and gathered up her bag and gloves. 'Don't say goodbye, my dear, dear Merrick,' and without a backward glance she was gone. As she passed Miss Dobson's open door, the busy secretary looked up from her typewriter to wish her good morning, but she disappeared across the foyer as if the furies of hell were on her heels.

Hiding behind the *Daily Telegraph* she journeyed towards London. How many times she read the same paragraph she had no idea. There was a strange comfort in the memory of her scene with Merrick, it was as if the warmth of his friendship wrapped itself around her on that cold December day. A cab from Paddington took her to Kings Cross Station, then came nearly an hour's wait for the next train to Cambridge. Daylight had already gone by the time she started the last leg of her journey, the windows of the compartment were running in condensation and, when she wiped a patch with her glove, the view was of nothing but dark, flat land, as dark and as flat as her spirit. The city was behind her, only now did she start to imagine Nicholas's surprise, his pleasure and relief, that at last she was doing what he had always wanted. Don't think of Merrick, don't think of Merrick, don't think of Merrick, sang the wheels as they dashed over the sleepers. Except for her there was only one woman in the Ladies Only compartment, a woman who must have had a tiring day shopping in London to judge from the many packages and from the fact that she gently snored for most of the journey. As the train slowed down on the approach to Cambridge Veronica checked her appearance in the speckled mirror on the opposite wall, squared her shoulders and made herself ready for the next stage.

Once on the platform, for a moment she felt lost and suddenly uncertain. That's when the memory of Monica sprang into her mind. Would she be pleased about today's turn of events? Go to Cambridge and learn to be a wife, wasn't that what she had said? And the business, at last it was to be sold. So why, of all the memories of her mother, should the one at the forefront of her mind be those haunting words 'For the first time in my life I feel like a whole person, me, me, *me*.' And that's how it would be for me too, Veronica tried not to listen to the give and take in her mind. No, there was only one way to go, and *this* was it. To snatch at happiness at the expense of broken promises, of failing a husband who in all honesty had done no wrong, that would be impossible. Getting into a station cab she gave the address of Nicholas's quarters. Only minutes now ... suppose he was out ... imagine when she told him the decision she'd made. Oh, not about Merrick. Not only for Nicholas's sake would she say nothing about Merrick, but because she couldn't bear to talk about it; what they had was too precious, too personal, too achingly painful.

'This is the college, ma'am. Reckon you'd best ask at the Porter's Lodge where to find the rooms you're looking for.'

So to the next stage. No light shone from the windows above the door pointed out to her, but that could mean the living room was on the other side of the building. With her chin high and more determination in her step than there was in her fast-beating heart, she approached journey's end. Make it work ... help to make it easy ... for me, for Merrick ... what must he be feeling tonight? Please let him know nothing will ever change for me ... but it *must change*, that's what's so hopeless. Round and round went her thoughts as she found herself on Nicholas's doorstep. With unnecessary force she knocked, listening as the sound seemed to echo in the silence. She'd hear his step, in seconds now he'd be with her. Like a trapped animal she looked round at the unfamiliar and alien surroundings. Nothing broke the silence of the house. That he wouldn't be at home was something she hadn't even considered. It was hours since she'd eaten, perhaps she ought to try and find a restaurant or hotel, then come back later.

Turning from the door she looked around her at the place that was to become her home. She shivered, not from cold so much as from a feeling of isolation from her surroundings. When the students were here it would be different, she told herself, but now although shafts of light escaped from some of the curtained windows the place was still as the tomb. It was then that she noticed, on the far side of the grass, what must have been the chapel. She'd been here before, she ought to have remembered where it was. Clearly she remembered the interior, just as she recalled sitting at a distance watching and listening to the organ, aware of Nicholas's pleasure in being where he was. Her most vivid impression was the feeling of release as they'd driven away from the lovely city that seemed to have such a hold on him.

She crossed the grass in the direction of the stained glass window but, before she reached her goal the light went out. He was coming. This is where they would meet, out here in the dark she would take him by surprise. Help me . . . make him pleased I've come, well of course he'll be pleased . . . let him make it easy for me . . .

'Just two steps,' she heard his voice. 'Wait while I lock the door and I'll take your arm.' He had a visitor, someone who'd come to hear the organ. She drew back, glad that emerging from the lighted interior he wouldn't see anyone was here. To greet him suddenly and in front of a stranger would be impossible, she must wait until he was home – with or without his visitor – and at least give him the opportunity to come face to face with her at the door and on their own. Silently she backed further away, unsure whether he would cross the grass or walk all the way round on the path. Her eyes were used enough to the darkness to know that the second person was short – hardly a choirboy though, for he'd not have suggested taking a choirboy's arm! Perhaps a boy's mother, or even a female organ student. The figures disappeared and in a minute she heard the sound of his front door closing. Count to a hundred slowly, then go and knock again. By the time she got to ninety, lights were on upstairs and down too. That must mean the sitting room was upstairs. Ninety-nine, a hundred . . . here goes! She squared her shoulders and for the second time approached the front door that would soon become a familiar part of her home.

She heard him hurrying to answer her knock, his familiar step crowding her head with memories. What wasn't familiar was his expression of speechless disbelief when he saw her.

'I've done what you said. I'm selling the business. Nicholas, it'll be all right won't it, we'll make it wo—' The word died on her lips as she looked beyond him and saw the figure on the stairs.

'You'd better come inside,' Nicholas ushered her past him and closed the door. 'Why in God's name couldn't you have told me you were coming? But perhaps it's better this way.'

'What's *she* doing here?' Somehow the three of them were in the room to the right of the front door, presumably his study she supposed, seeing the pile of neat manuscripts on the desk and a typewriter on the side table. A typewriter. If she'd ever taken enough interest to look at the postmark she would have wondered why Belinda never mentioned the coincidence of her cousin living in Cambridge!

'She's here because I want her here,' Nicholas said in that quiet, remote tone she'd come to dread, a voice that defied any hint of emotion.

'Is your poor cousin going to need long-term care, I wonder?' Veronica had always hated sarcasm, yet now it was in the scorn she turned on Belinda.

'Don't pretend you'd care,' Belinda rasped with a spirit Veronica had never considered she possessed. 'No wonder he turned to me. What you think about me isn't important. Now that you've come, I suppose it's all over.' She rammed her fist into her mouth, perhaps to hold back her words. But from the way her shoulders shook as she turned her back, it was clear she couldn't hold back the tears. The evening had been wonderful, the days ahead had promised to be all she'd dreamed. That morning when she'd opened his letter and read that he had rented a terraced cottage in town she'd believed heaven had fallen into her lap. But no! As if Veronica hadn't got enough with the business she was so wrapped up in, with Merrick hanging on her every word, with Becky looking on her as some sort of saviour. Now she swept back to claim Nicholas as if he were there to pick up and put down at a whim.

'Don't,' he said, this time to her. Veronica heard the one word as unemotional; Belinda heard it as gentle. As his arm came around her shoulder she turned to him, hiding her face against him. 'Veronica, you know we have no basis to build a marriage on. Are you trying to tell me that what we shared could ever be enough?'

Veronica felt like a prisoner released of her shackles. She wanted to shout for joy.

'You mean you don't want me?' Her question and her expression were on different planes, but there was no way she could keep her face from smiling.

'Apparently, it's mutual,' came his answer. 'Our marriage was a mistake. You were consoling yourself for Chesterton's rejection, I was hit by some sort of temporary madness. We have nothing else in common, nothing.'

'But *we* have, Nicholas and I,' Belinda cut in. 'His music holds us together, but it's more than that. Go back to your bakehouse, work yourself into a lather of excitement about the orders you're getting from abroad. Just leave us alone.' Such an outburst from the prim and docile widow took Veronica by surprise.

She started to laugh. 'It's like a charade!' she said. 'Suddenly the final word comes clear. And this is clear too. Nicholas, do you have a telephone in the house? If not, where can I find one?'

She stayed that night in a hotel, having asked the night porter to see she was called by half past six and to arrange for a cab to collect her at seven. Tomorrow she was going home.

The past reached forward to nudge at the present, the present seemed rooted in the past. It was the evening of Good Friday 1939. The Abbey was crowded, there was a soft buzz of whispered voices as they waited. Notices had been posted throughout the district but music lovers had travelled from further afield. In the past decade the Ellis Easter Oratorio had found a place amongst the best-loved English church music but, on this occasion, the performance was special for more reasons than that. For not only was Nicholas Ellis visiting Ottercombe to conduct, but the work had been written during his brief sojourn at the Abbey, making local people – and especially those inaugural members of the Abbey Singers – feel a personal right of possession.

Of all those congregated, there were few who realised the importance of the evening to those who sat in the front where the pews on either side of the main aisle bore 'Reserved' notices.

'Was he nervous?' Monica whispered to her daughter. Still pretty, still smart, and clearly still happy, the years had been kind to her.

'I only looked in at the choir school for a moment to see him, but he seemed fine. But I talked to Nicholas and he was pleased with him at this afternoon's rehearsal.'

'Are any of his children musical, did he say? I wonder what he makes of *your* little boy singing the solo.' Clearly it was a feather in the family cap.

'Don't let Jeremy hear you call him little, Mum. He's twelve.'
A long silence, each following her own thoughts. It was more than
twelve years ago when, only days after being granted her Decree
Absolute, Veronica and Merrick had been married at Deremouth
Registry Office. She suppose it must have caused plenty of local
gossip, for divorce was rare, and to present herself at the Registry
Office on the very day forecast for the delivery of their child must
have turned her into little short of a scarlet woman. How happy
she'd been – and still was. Her hand crept instinctively towards
Merrick. He must have known for he touched it with his, their
glance brief.
'We all think we know how to map out our lives.' Unaware of
the silent interchange, Monica went back to the whispered conversation, her blue eyes seeming to plead for an understanding
which at one time Veronica would have found impossible. 'You
and Nicholas – divorced and yet there's no animosity, or there
doesn't seem to be.'
Veronica smiled. 'Should there be? Our mistake was in marrying not in divorcing. Yet, it wasn't altogether a mistake, I expect it
was part of the pattern. I'm glad things worked out for Belinda
and him,' she said, glancing across the aisle to the corresponding
pew. 'They have so much in common. She's quite a serious
musician, you know.'
'Oh but Ronnie, think of how you used to enjoy playing.'
Veronica smiled. The void between her love of music and
Nicholas's had no power to hurt. 'The only thing we have in
common . . .' Nicholas's voice echoed down the years. And she
was woman enough, honest enough and perhaps vain enough too,
to glance across the aisle towards Belinda and her three children
and be glad to imagine what Nicholas's thoughts must have been
when he'd come face to face with the woman who'd once been his
wife. Always pretty in a pale, delicate way, fourteen years and
three children on, Belinda's figure was thin, her shoulders slightly
hunched.
'I never thought we'd all be here like this,' Monica said. 'Do
you think my darling Herbert can see us?'
'Yes, Mum, I'm sure he can.'
The choir was filing towards the chancel. Then to a clamour of
applause came Nicholas, as handsome and distinguished as he had
been seventeen years before when he had conducted Fauré's

Requiem from that same rostrum. Glancing beyond him across the aisle she watched Belinda and their children, the way four pairs of hands clapped, four faces were turned to him in pride. But it was more than pride she saw in Belinda's gaze, it was more akin to worship.

As he raised his baton the silence was almost tangible, then came the slow, beautiful opening bars. To hear it again in this place, to watch him and recall the hours he'd spent within these walls, to remember her own youth and shallow understanding, was like seeing and hearing something from a different life. It had no power to hurt her, it brought neither joy nor sorrow, only a sense of the rightness of where life had brought her. Again her hand moved an inch, this time to be taken firmly in Merrick's.

Listening to Jeremy's pure treble voice she was as proud as any mother might have been, but what she felt was more than pride, it was humility and gratitude. Into her mind came something she'd always believed about Merrick and her: they were like two perfectly fitting pieces of a jigsaw puzzle. But hadn't she always known that a puzzle has to be complete? A smile touched the corners of her mouth.

The listening congregation may well have been following every glorious note, perhaps it was only Veronica who gave her mind the freedom to take her where it would. There in the Abbey she had known as long as she could remember, she gave a silent Thank You for the blessings of her life. She and Merrick were interlocked like pieces of a wooden puzzle with the grain perfectly matching. But they weren't alone, the background of the picture was complete. Beyond him was Becky in her mid-twenties and married, mother of a three-year-old daughter. On her other side, Monica, no longer young, but clearly happy with 'that fop' who, since the hatchet had been buried, Veronica had made an effort to accept on the rare occasions they came to Devon. And her father, no picture would be complete without him; years couldn't dim the memory of him, a spirit she kept alive. Her imagination took another leap. Laurence? The last she'd heard of him he'd been transferred to the Paris office of the magazine; still single, but somehow she couldn't imagine Laurence with a wife. Then Belinda and Nicholas, they and their family firmly settled at Cambridge. Clampton's Cakes, eaten in households up and down the country; Blakeney's, still hand-mixed, still the same fine quality even though the bakehouse was grander these days, and with a market amongst the wealthy élite on both sides of the Atlantic. People and things she loved, all of them had their place in the background of her puzzle, every piece was dependent on those around it.